The unholy Trinity
Southwestwards the Wanderer,
Northwards the Narrator, Eastwards Zórba

The Narrator's favourite table

MISTR€$$ TROIKA
ZÓRBA THE GREEK
AND A MOLOTOV COCKTAIL

Mistress Troika, Zórba the Greek and a Molotov Cocktail
© V. Ludens
&
Phonographic Society Books 2016
Αθανάσιος Λυμπερόπουλος
Έδρα: Λ.Ιωνίας 81, Κόρινθος
τηλ.επικοινωνίας 2741 081429

Email: books@phonographic-society.com
Site: www.phonographic-society.com
Facebook Page: phonographicsocietybooks

Συντονισμός Έκδοσης - Publisher:
Στέλλα Καραμπακάκη - Stella Karampakaki

© Voyage to the USSR - CCCP - ΕΣΣΔ
Union of Surrealist Sexual Retroperspectives
Союз Сюрреалистических Сексуальнθых Ретроперспектив
Ένωση Σουρεαλιστικών Σεξουαλικών Διαναδρομοπροοπτικών

Scetches © Pro DS Vocateur
Σχεδιασμός-Design: V. Ludens

ISBN: 978-618-82293-5-8

V. LUDENS

Mistr€$$ Troika
Zorba the Greek
and a Molotov Cocktail

Subconscioustrated by Pro DS Vocateur

Voyage
TO THE USSR
UNION OF
SURREALIST
SEXUAL
RETROPERSPECTIVES

Phonographic
Society
Books
2016

The Wanderer in Locomotiva

carrying his historical rucksack packed

Bar - café - bookshop

with the unholy Trinity's expectations

Unacknownledgements

At the end was the Dadaist Surrealist Pro Vocateur.
I thank him first. He read the narrative, flashed the
night of my subconscious mind and created the
subconscioustrations; which are "flashes at moments
of danger." The people in them are, and will remain,
unknown to the reader. This is their wish and their
will which I respect. Some of them belong to the
surrealist group "Year 8591131,"
based in the

Union of Surrealist Sexual Retroperspectives.

I thank them one by one for their will and their
enthusiasm to participate by posing or by offering
their pictures, sometimes at gunpoint, for the
subconscioustration of this narrative. Some of the
subconscioustrations are homage to people, places,
events, others are provocations towards their
counterparts.
Above all, I want to thank my wife Ekaterina
for the multidisciplinary support she offered to her
...undisciplined-minded husband,
and my daughter Stella
whose teasing about "her dad's" literary style and
explicitness fuelled my inspiration even more.
Last but not least, the process of writing down this
narration was, from a point of view,
a desperate attempt to fill the gap that
my parents, Dēmokratēs and Stella,
left behind when they both passed away in the Time
of Troika. Hopefully they will come back 100.000
years after the Global Victory of Communism
—100.000 CE (Communist Era)—
on a New Earth under a New Heaven.

Quotations in my works
are like robbers by the roadside
who make an armed attack
and relieve an idler of his convictions.
Walter Benjamin

...and not only quotations
but images, melodies, memories, people, friends,
women as well....
V. Ludens

Locomotiva Strangers in the night

All characters appearing throughout this narrative are stated with their sur[real]names. Any association to other real persons, living or dead, is not only purely coincidental, but a by-product of a troubled mind.

Furthermore, not only the names but the events described are even more than real, they are surreal; they reveal in this way their revolutionary potential, the real hard-core of their existence. Subsequently eroticism could not be excluded from this surreal, hard-core, sextravaganza. I already know people that will condemn the book as scandalous for its explicitness, its subconscioustrations and for other reasons and demons of their own. What they may not know is that in Greek the word *scandal* and the word for a gun's trigger, which is *scandalē*, have the same root and they sound in almost the same mortifying way.... But even unaware as they are, just by calling it scandalous, they recognize the bleared and inexplicit limits between *the weapon of the criticism* —with its scandals, and *the criticism of the weapons* —with their scandalē-trigger, as Karl has set it; or they admit, like Don Quichotte de La Mancha, "*that the lance has never blunted the pen, nor the pen the lance.*" Thus they bring us back to Hamlet or even better they bring Hamlet to the kingdom of Moloch, the Capital, and his Mistress Troika.

To be, or not to be: that is the question:
Whether 'tis nobler in the mind to suffer
The slings and arrows of outrageous fortune,
Or to take arms against a sea of troubles,
And by opposing end them?

In the Dark Times of Troika, on the 100th anniversary of the October Revolution and 93 years after the First Surrealist Manifesto, in an era when more than ever we feel the urgent need *to face the breath of the street* (Andre Breton), by no means *'tis nobler in the mind to suffer the slings and arrows* not of *outrageous fortune* but of the worst crisis of capitalism ever.

This is a narrative, written in English, by a non-English bloody foreigner, who, however, doesn't feel much attached to any particular nationality.

He considers himself a sui-generis internationalist, seized by the wandering and fighting spirit of Odysseus-Ulysses, who, finally, slaughtered the suitors; and with his bow and arrows —or, to make it more surrealistic, with his AS VAL Special Automatic Rifle, code name: Shaft— seems like saying to the Trojans-Troykans-Troikans: *Quid rides? Mutato nomine de te fabula narratur!*

At some point of the story we read: "They called me Zórba for my bloody accent and my bloody English, which, however, I got to know by sexperience, made the silky smooth petals and sepals of the English roses get moisturised, spread apart and open; maybe because in their female fantasy the shed blood of the bloody foreigner's enemies mixed with the blood of the girls he had deflowered thrilled and excited them. So this obscene linguistical attraction was succeeding, almost momentarily, in bridging

---

*Change only the name and this story is about you.

through banging the gulf of language and origin." Thus, the disadvantage turned into an advantage.

Women of non-English origin and paths of life, never bothered with the whims or even the obscenities of a bloody foreigner's English. What counted for them most of all, was the body language, which is both international and internationalist; and they were really good at it.

Why then a narrative in English? Because *Ludens ludere amat die ac nocte in saecula saeculorum.*

Once a linguist told me, "Look, Ludens, the structure of your English is not only the structure of a non-native but the structure of a strange mind." And so we decided with my editor to leave untouched and unaltered not only my whatever personal structure in the language of the Anglosexons, but even the slightest slips of the tongue-finger on the key-board —typos, anagrammatisms and other obscenities.

For example, in pages 90-91, in the phrase *"Imagine, they don't show skin at all, they don't want the red sun to bathe them the same way it baths the rest of us,"* the typo/spelling mistake *baths* instead of *bathes* leads, subconsciously, to a scene where under a red sun the blood runs red as kings are slaughtered in their baths.... Is it an insinuation for the tyrannicide of tyrants, rulers and troikans of all kinds for the common good? Or a subconscious hint at the elective affinities of many royal families of Europe with the Nazis and, consequently, with the extermination of the Jews in the crematoria, the *bath houses* according to the Nazi euphemism?

In page 275, I wrote about a Hungarian *girl-friend*, typing *grilfriend*. It sounds like grill, no matter if the spelling is different, and it may have to do with the fact –if not fuckt, that being a beach-girl, she loved barbecue and grilled stakes.

In page 285, instead of writing *raise barricades*, I typed *eraise barricades*. A simple or even a serious mistake? Can we ignore that the next day the barricades were swept away from the streets by the coercion apparatus of the State, erased, in a way, not from the memory of the ones who took active part in the street fighting, but from the collective unconscious? However, I want to believe that this was just a meaningless mistake, and the next time the barricades will be raised, they won't be eraised or even erased, but will stand erected till the final victory.

I can't tell how many such cases the reader may find in this plotless, pilotless, but not pivotless, narrative. It depends on how much my need and desire to communicate with the English-speaking reader managed to discipline my subconscious mind. But in any case, I didn't want anybody to polish, normalise and fit my writing "to the rules."

V. Ludens

*In the beginning we were strangers
in a strangers' land, strangers in the night
exchanging glances, wond'ring in the night
what were the chances; then she became my only
dearest; the narrative starts, more or less in this
strange land, thus it is dedicated to her,
to Ekaterina or Faba Crimson Sunshine
or whatever....
To the woman with the one thousand
and one faces.
Now the earth was formless and empty,
darkness was over the surface of the deep, and
chaos within us. "You must have chaos within
you to give birth to a dancing star," were
Nietzsche's words that reflected my worlds,
so when my only dearest said
"Let there be her,"
a star was born and her name was Stella.
So the narrative is dedicated to her too.*

ΕΙΜΑΣΤΕ ΣΤΑΓΟΝΕΣ ΕΠΕΡΧΟΜΕΝΗΣ ΚΑΤΑΙΓΙΔΑΣ

WE ARE THE DROPS OF AN APPROACHING STORM

IT WAS A COLD FEBRUARIAN NIGHT. We had wandered all around Exarcheia, crossed badly-lit streets with graffiti-covered walls where we could still smell the tear-gases from last night's battles and revels, trying not to step on the toxic white-powder patches left on the ground here and there, and ended up sitting in Locomotiva, late at night, drinking warm rakomelo and debating on the new Troikan Cabinet appointed by the bankers.

Zórba the ræbelaisian: "In the brothels all over the world, the prostitutes serve the will and satisfy the desires of whoever has the money to pay them. In the Parliament the MPs serve the will and satisfy the desires of the ruling class, the bankers and other capitalists. The difference between the plain prostitutes in the brothels and the Monetary Prostitutes in the Parliament is that the former do it out of need and harm only themselves, while the latter do it out of choice and destroy millions."

The Wanderer: "Zórba you're drunk..."

Zórba the ræbelaisian: "In vino veritas. So next time remind me to tell you about the old camel, the WMF Cruella de Vil and the stunning woman who loved dogs."

The Wanderer: "What's WMF?"

Zórba the ræbelaisian: "White Married Female, what else? Hahaha..."

Chapter 1

Conversation on Skype between Mistress Troika and the
call-girl Clara de Noche
leaked by secret agents of the
Reinsuerectionary Antitroikan Fucktion-RAF

Mistress Troika: "It was this bloody Greek I met with his bloody English and his bloodier accent."

Clara de noche: "Where did you meet him?"

Mistress Troika: "In the lounge of Athens Milton Hotel, though he didn't look like a Greek, he looked like, well he could have been anything, Caucasian but that's all, you couldn't tell where from."

Clara de noche: "And what happened?"

Mistress Troika: "Well I don't remember, I still have a hangover, all I remember is that at some point he said something like 'let's pop on to the terrace for a cocktail.' "

Clara de noche: "And did you follow him? You followed a stranger with a bloody accent?"

Mistress Troika: "Well, I did, it turned out that I was turned on by his weird bloody accent, we got into the lift and then up a bunch of floors to the Galaxy. The view was amazing, The bloody Greek treated me a few bloody vampire blood cocktails, it's my favourite, you know cranberry juice, orange juice, raspberry sorbet, seltzer and plenty of vodka and afterwards a night full of sparkling stars, colourful explosions, glowing planets and blood, more blood oh I love blood and then he took me downtown Athens, through dirty streets, badly-lit areas, if not completely dark, he took me to strange places, to bars around Sexarcheia Square where he treated me a couple molotov cocktails and then all I remember is him fucking me hard, here and there in filthy places, in dark alleys against the wall, missionary in deserted dirty shops, on all fours in abandoned factories..."

Clara de noche: "Did you bite him at least?"

Mistress Troika: "Oh, fuck yes I did, I left bruises, scratches and bite marks all over his body but he seems to be totally immune."

Clara de noche: "What are you going to do now, are you going to see him again?"

Mistress Troika: "I don't know, I told you, I'm still confused, after the last fuck-round in an old closed-down factory he just told me: 'I think molotov cocktail is a bit light for you; next time I'll treat you one or two Red Snapper Cocktails. When you take a sip it feels like an AT-1 Snapper and when it hits it's bound to shake just like an explosion.' "

Clara de noche: "How does he look like?"

Mistress Troika: "He looks like in a dream,

a weird dream; it all started with me and him drinking and I ended with two of him taking me from both ends and a third of him in my mouth. At dawn they invaded all my Troikan o[ri]ffices using their Trojan Horse's organ."

Clara de noche: "What the hell, did he bring his friends, did they gangrape you?"

Mistress Troika: "Not his friends, they were three of him! One of him was wearing spectacles with metal frame, the type of a so-phisticated intellectual but a very cruel one when needed. The other of him looked windy, like the *Wanderotica*'s flâneur, who carries the southwest-wind's name Argestis; a manifold novel I read with my middle finger slipped between the moist folds of my pussy, for it's very erotic too. Zórba, the third of him, reminded me of a runaway, an outcast nobleman who turned into a pirate, a traitor of his class; the type of man that is feared by his male enemies and lusted after by the female; friends or enemies doesn't make any difference, it depends on their point of view, their G-point of view. He claims that no wo-man is an island detached from her or his class and political environment; he respects the lower and disrespects the rulers no matter if they are men or women."

Clara de noche: "Wow! So the three of them fucked you at once! Like in a Quartet!"

TROIKANS BEHIND SPLIT SPLATS

RAF
Reinsuerectionary
Antitroikan
Fucktion

THE SEXDVENTURES OF TROIKAN

In the Dark Times of Troika
the unholy Trinity froze Time
in order to serve
a cold dish of revenge

MISTRESSES AT HANDS OF RAF

Chapter 2

In the beginning is the Act, and then the Narrator, and the Narrator is with the Wanderer, and the Wanderer is me. And no, we neither suffer from any kind of Dissociative Identity Disorder —we just are surrealists and dadaists and libertarians— nor from memory impairment for any kind of information; we remember it all, we never forget, we never forgive.

I am Zórba. At least they called me Zórba, Zórba the Greek, stressing the "o," which is wrong instead of stressing the "a," which is the right. Bloody foreigners. I called them "bloody foreigners" just because they were English in England, and we laughed. My friends in the University did so; friends from the Department of Politics and friends from the Department of Mining, although none of the later knew that Zórba was a mine-worker. Politics and mining! Such an explosive cocktail! The one I had learned to prepare was considered a strong high volume spirit with Ph^{Degrees} of Politics and MA^{Degrees} of Mining. If used properly by the toilers, it can undermine the existing order of things; but this is another story. Friends from the Halls of Residence I stayed, called me Zórba too; There were all sorts of Halls of Residence. Mixed always. I had asked for "sextra mixed ones," namely boys and girls on the same floor or ward, but the puritans didn't offer such facilities. "Sorry luv," they had said, "it's against the rules, we don't offer such accommodation." But we fucked the rules and started mixing ourselves as much as we could. People from the Continent I mean and the States. They started calling me Zórba after they got to know me; for they considered me, first of all Greek; "but you don't look like a Greek," told me once a half-English half-Far-Eastern beauty, a medium-build young lady with shining black hair and almond eyes; the music and the disco was so loud that we had to speak into each other's ears; "what do I look like then?" "Mmm, I don't know, like anything, like... an internationalist!" They called me Zórba for my bloody accent and my bloody English, which, however, I got to know by sexperience, made the silky smooth petals and sepals of the English roses get moistured, spread apart and open so to be fucked again and again; maybe because in their female fantasy the shed blood of the bloody foreigner's enemies mixed with the blood of the girls he had deflowered thrilled and excited them in sexually obscene ways. Last but not least, they called me Zórba because into their eyes I was an adventurist, a womaniser and I was never well-shaved like an ass. I was most of the time unshaven, growing a beard, a four to five days beard, sometimes longer."

They even called him Zórba the brute, for he had pulled out a knife once to defend his right to siesta from the unbearable noise that some undergraduates were making on purpose in front of his door. But let him continue...

..."To be fair there was a short period in my life, it lasted for about a month, that I developed a kind of mania and shaved two-three times per day just for the sake of the ceremony, using vintage razors, brushes, shaving bowls and cream, cologne and all the rest. I was kinda nervous that time, I had to type a lot, submit my thesis and get over with it, I was 28 by then, but David C., my supervisor, wanted me to give as many details as possible about our plot to blow up the Grande Bretagne, the hotel in Syntagma Square while Churchill resided there on Christmas eve of 1944, a plot almost succeeded. Holding an MA degree in mining and with quite some working experience in the British mines, until the day Thacher closed them down, I had taken part in it. We were about

30 of us involved and we had stuffed enough explosive under the building to blow it to the stars. but the signal for the detonation never came, the operation was cancelled the last moment by the stalinists. But I didn't want to give any details, 'you never know,' I was thinking, 'such things maybe needed again,' thus I was kinda nervous and was shaving again and again. "But you took part in the plot, so why don't you give us a first hand account of it," commented David, my supervisor. "Of course I did," I replied, "but look David, I am 28 years young by then, I mean Christmas Eve of 1944 and..." David lowered his head and looked at me over his thin glasses "*you are*?", he repeated stressing the words one by one, "*you are 28 by then? oh my goodness!*" I smiled vaguely "...yes I am 28 by then and took part in it the same way I took part, being 28, in the Paris Commune in 1871, the Moscow uprising of 1905, the ten days that shocked the world in 1917, the Spartacist uprising of 1919, the Short Summer of Anarchy during 1936 in Spain, the May of 1968 in Paris; I was there in the Autumno Caldo in Italy, the Polytechnic uprising in Athens, in the Battle of Orgreave in South Yorkshire in June 1984 and so forth and so on."

David understood what I meant, but not some of the people that heard me saying the same, more or less, story, at dinner time, few days later.

"Are you insane?" they asked me.

"I was, I am, I will be!" I replied echoing Rosa " 'Order reigns in Europe!' You stupid henchmen! Your 'order' is built on sand. Tomorrow the revolution will already raise itself with a rattle and announce with fanfare, to your terror: I was, I am, I will be!"

My friends, who heard me cheered, The ones who called me Zórba. They were some English and other bloody foreigner friends, but after all, aren't we all foreigners in this no man's land, aliens alienated from our humanity and our time? I didn't like much my new nom de guerre because I liked neither Nikos Kazantzakis, nor Zorbá. To be honest I mostly disliked Nikos Kazantzakis for his profound algolagnia, that only somebody blind in eyes, ears and mind cannot see, hear and perceive, for his political duplicity, for his sympathy towards fascism and nazism, his obsession with race and vitalism and for wanting me "to have no ambition and to work like a horse;" work for whom?... for the bloody capitalists, or for Hitler, Franco and Moussolini? But I didn't like Zorbá either for he was urging me "to sleep with any woman she asks me to for God has a very big heart, but there is one sin He will not forgive. If a woman calls a man to her bed and he will not go." No, dear Zorbá, I am not the Salvation Army and after nearly being made love to by a non-lesbian Lesbian who out of laziness and bad hygiene smelled like rotten fish and her bed-sheets were patterned with her last, at least, period stains. this attitude of mine got stronger, dear Zorbá; furthermore there is no God and my mother used to say that the only and greatest proof that there is no god is that there are sick people, people who suffer. So, I didn't like much the nom de guerre they gave me, but for sometime I compromised with it as far as I was supposed to be Zórba and not Zorbá. I however explained to my friends, who wanted to flatter me, of course, calling me so, influenced as they were by all this "Zorba - syrtaki - bouzouki - moussàka" propaganda of the Greek Tourist Industry, that I was feeling rather awkward under this nom de guerre and after sometime with the help, or rather proposal, of a young lady from Barcelona, an anarchist, avant-garde artist, with whom I had long political, philosophical and other encounters, my nom de guerre was changed to Vas, where "V" stood for Vendetta or Victory, "a" stood for avant-garde and "s" stood for sexploration —"you like to explore female bodies, you even like to sexploit them," the young woman from Spain told me smiling; but "s" stood also for surrealism, for I was surrealist by birth, surrealist and dadaist, yes, *da da da, ich lieb dich nicht, du liebst mich nicht, What you will and what you won't, what you do and what you don't, what you can and what you can't, this is what you need to know*[*]: That's how Zórba withered away, although not completely.

"So you' re an atheist, that's why you believe that killing is no murder," told me Mirella, an Italian student of architecture worshipper of Dostoyevsky, "you're something like Stavrogin I presume."

She was a living enigma not only for me but for the few that had made her acquaintance. Extremely beautiful, of medium stature, well curved body, honey-coloured hair and amber eyes she was confessing, to whom she was feeling comfortable with, that she was still a virgin at twenty three and that she wanted to become a nun. Next to her, on her right, sat her sister Roberta. They looked alike only that Roberta had black shiny hair and she didn't want to become a nun. On her left sat Lena Lim, a tall and posh Chinese lawyer in her late thirties, one of Zórba's strange acquaintances.

"Not at all my friend but let's first clarify something. Killing is no murder but blind mass-killing is and I strongly oppose to it.

---

[*]*Da Da Da* :an international hit record for German Trio formed in 1980 by Stephan Remmler, Gert 'Kralle' Krawinkel, and Peter Behrens.

Stavrogin was a nihilist. I am on the other side, I want everything and even more everything for all; all that the most advanced science and technology can offer to every single person on earth."

"Like what, like cars, commodities?"

"No, not cars, but, for example, access for all, for the entire population of earth, to the latest gene therapies or nanomedicine, to start with..."

"A new garden of Eden?" she asked smiling...

"Yes, but an earthly eden, a sexualised world of advanced technology and general prosperity..."

"Oh, I get your point, you're such a dreamer!"

"Do you like dreamers Mirella?" I asked her but didn't give her any time to answer, "don't tell me yet, I think I'm going to disappoint you, please have a look at this..."

While I was saying these last words I turned on Eva, the laptop carrying the half-bitten-apple, went to my bookmarks, found what I needed and passed Eva to her:

"We should dream!" I wrote these words and became alarmed. I imagined myself sitting at a "unity conference" and opposite me were the Rabocheye Dyelo editors and contributors. Comrade Martynov rises and, turning to me, says sternly: "Permit me to ask you, has an autonomous editorial board the right to dream without first soliciting the opinion of the Party committees?" He is followed by Comrade Krichevsky; who (philosophically deepening Comrade Martynov, who long ago rendered Comrade Plekhanov more profound) continues even more sternly: "I go further. I ask, has a Marxist any right at all to dream, knowing that according to Marx, mankind always sets itself the tasks it can solve and that tactics is a process of the growth of Party tasks which grow together with the Party?"

The very thought of these stern questions sends a cold shiver down my spine and makes me wish for nothing but a place to hide in. I shall try to hide behind the back of Pisarev.

"There are rifts and rifts," wrote Pisarev of the rift between dreams and reality. "My dream may run ahead of the natural march of events or may fly off at a tangent in a direction in which no natural march of events will ever proceed. In the first case my dream will not cause any harm; it may even support and augment the energy of the working men.... There is nothing in such dreams that would distort or paralyse labour-power. On the contrary, if man were completely deprived of the ability to dream in this way, if he could not from time to time run ahead and mentally conceive, in an entire and completed picture, the product to which his hands are only just beginning to lend shape, then I cannot at all imagine what stimulus there would be to induce man to undertake and complete extensive and strenuous work in the sphere of art, science, and practical endeavour.... The rift between dreams and reality causes no harm if only the person dreaming believes seriously in his dream, if he attentively observes life, compares his observations with his castles in the air, and if, generally speaking, he works conscientiously for the achievement of his fantasies. If there is some connection between dreams and life then all is well."[17]

Of this kind of dreaming there is unfortunately too little in our movement. And the people most responsible for this are those who boast of their sober views, their "closeness" to the "concrete", the representatives of legal criticism and of illegal "tailism".

"Where did you get this from, what it's all about. and how this 'killing is no murder' thing fits in your story?"

"Lenin," I said smiling, "*What to be Done*, fifth chapter... But, dear Mirella, first of all I have to remind you that this 'killing no murder' motto is of religious and of no atheist origin, but this is not the most important to me. Not all killing is no murder. What the German occupation troops did during WW2 were mass murders but the killings of nazis by the resistance movements all over Europe were killings, no murders, legitimised killings. Furthermore, the Piazza Fontana Bombing, the notorious, Strage di Piazza Fontana, was an appalling mass murder, the 2004 Madrid train bombings and the killings of November 13, 2015 in Paris or of July 14, 2016 in Nice, the same; they were mass murders. But you don't seem to remember our last conversation, it was ages ago, but have a look at this and you will remember it all."

I touched Eva, whispered three key-words to her and passed her to Mirella to read on herself. Zórba prefered to abstain from all this and he kept sexting with Lim.

V. I. Lenin

106

To: FRANZ KORITSCHONER[2]

Written: Written in German

Published: First published in Pravda No. 60, March 1, 1932. Sent from Zurich to Vienna. Printed from the original.

Source: *Lenin Collected Works*, Progress Publishers, [1976], Moscow, Volume 35, pages 237-239.

Translated: Andrew Rothstein

Transcription\Markup: R. Cymbala

October 25, 1916

Dear Friend,

We regret very much that you haven't written a single line to us so far. One must hope that the big events in Vienna will stimulate you at long last to write to us in detail.

LIM: YOU RE NOT INTERESTED IN THEORY OR YOU DONT LIKE BREAKING THE LAW? - ZORBA: I LOVE THEORY&BREAKING THE LAW SO I MAY NEED YOUR SERVICE - LIM: YOU CAN HAVE ME ANYTIME YOU WANT - ZORBA: TELL ME THEN WHAT YOUR BODY CRAVES FOR - LIM: MY BODY CRAVES FOR SHAME&SOMETHING ROUND ITS NECK BONDAGE!&HUMILIATION I LIKE THE EDGIER THINGS YOU CAN FANTASISE BUT MORE DIFFICULT IN REAL

Berner Tagwacht (and then other papers) printed a report that at a war factory in Speyer (Austria) there was a strike of 24,000 workers, that Czech soldiers opened fire, and that 700 (seven hundred!) workers were killed! How much truth is there in this? Please let us know about it in as much detail as you can.

As regards the act of Friedrich Adler,[3] I would beg you to let us know the details.

The papers here (Berner Tagwacht and Volksrecht —do you get them both, or neither?) extol this act. Avanti! (does Avanti! reach you?) states that Friedrich Adler was the author of the famous manifesto of the Austrian internationalists. Is that true? And is it now convenient to speak about this openly?

ZORBA: BETWEEN THE 2 OF THEM WHOSE BODY CRAVES FOR SHAME&SOMETHING ROUND HER NECK? WHOM YOU WANT TO HAVE NEXT TO YOU GOING THROUGH SIMILAR THINGS? - LIM: OH I SEE I M A NATURAL SUB BUT HAPPY TO SHARE FUN WHEN ITS MORE THAN ONE TOO MIRELA SEEMS CLOSER TO ME NON SMOKER LOOKS SUB&AS MEN THINK MORE SLUTTY DO YOU LIKE A PAIR OF SLUTS?

(1) Did Friedrich Adler tell anyone about his plan? (2) Did he give any friend any documents, letters, statements to be published later? (3) Is it true, as the Vienna Arbeiter Zeitung writes, that everywhere (both in the railway club and in other places) be was in a minority (and how big was that minority?),

(4)—that his position in the organisation had become "unbearable" (?)—(5)—that at the last party conference he received only seven votes?—(6) that at the last two meetings of trusted agents he attacked the party extremely sharply and demanded "demonstrations"? (What kind precisely?)

ZORBA: I DO - LIM: YOU COULD PICK US UP FROM WORK - ZORBA: WOULD YOU MAKE A GOOD PAIR OF SLUTS? - LIM:WELL OUTWARDLY I LOOK QUITE RESPECTABLE - ZORBA: I D LOVE TO WATCH YOU IN STEAMY LEZ SEX WITH HER - LIM: WE WOULD HAVE TO STRIP DOWN A BIT MAYBE IN YOUR CAR ON THE WAY FROM WORK IN PUBLIC?-ZORBA: YOU LIKE PUBLIC HUMILIATION DON T YOU?-LIM: HAVING TO DO THE WALK OF SHAME YOU MEAN?-ZORBA: YES - LIM:YOU WANT ME TO KNEEL&TASTE HER? - ZORBA: YES - LIM: I HAVE TO EAT BOTH OF YOU?-

Please write us in as much detail as possible about all these questions, and in general give us more information and details about Friedrich Adler. Unless you give us special instructions to (he contrary, we shall print in our papers everything that we get from you (and will also publish them — as material from our editorial office— in the local German-language press).

As regards the political assessment of the act, we maintain, of course, our old conviction, confirmed by decades of experience, that individual terrorist acts are inexpedient methods of political struggle.

"Killing is no murder,"[1] wrote our old Iskra about terrorist acts; we are not at all opposed to political killing (in this sense the servile writings of the opportunists in Vorwärts and the Vienna Arbeiter Zeitung are simply revolting), but as revolutionary tactics individual attacks are inexpedient and harmful. Only the mass movement can be considered genuine political struggle. Only in direct, immediate connection with the mass movement can and must individual terrorist acts be of value. In Russia the terrorists (against whom we always struggled) carried out a number of individual attacks; but in December 1905, when matters at last reached the stage of a mass movement, insurrection —when it was necessary to help the masses to use violence— then just at that moment the "terrorists" were missing. That is where the terrorists make their mistake.

ZORBA: BJ ME YOU MEAN? - LIM: IF I READ YOU RIGHT YES - ZORBA: IT WILL BE MORE HUMILIATING THAN THAT LIM: I HAVE TO TAKE MY SHORTIE PANTIES OFF?- ZORBA: I WILL MOUTHFUCK YOU USE YOUR FEMALE SOFT MOUTH AS A CUNT - LIM: ON MY KNEES YOU SQUASHING MY NOSE - ZORBA: YES BUT YOU ON YOUR BACK TOO&ME ON TOP OF YOUR FACE - LIM:IF YOUR COCK IS CURVED THAT IS THE DEEP WAY TO FUCK MY THROAT - ZORBA: LOOK AT IT THROUGH MY JEANS

Adler would have been of much greater help to the revolutionary movement if, without being afraid of a split, he had systematically gone over to illegal propaganda and agitation. It would be very good if some Left group were found to publish a leaflet in Vienna which would inform the workers of its view; if it branded in the sharpest possible way the servile behaviour of the Vienna Arbeiter Zeitung and Vorwärts, morally justified Adler's act ("killing is no murder"), but as a lesson for the workers declared: not terrorism but systematic, prolonged, self-sacrificing activity in revolutionary propaganda and agitation, demonstrations, etc., etc., against the lackey-like opportunist party, against, the imperialists, against one's own governments, against the war that is what is needed.

LIM: THATS HUGE - ZORBA: ROBERTA LOVES IT WHATS THE FILTHIEST THING THAT YOU WANT HER DO?-LIM: DEPENDS WHAT A DIRTY BITCH SHE IS REALLY! SHE OUGHT TO BE SQUEALING OUT LOUD WHILE TRYING TO COPE WITH YOUR 10 INCHES - ZORBA: SHE DOES BUT SHE GETS WET TOO THOUGH SHE LOVES ME

Tell us also, please, how right it would be to regard Adler's act as a gesture of despair? I think that politically it is so. He had lost his faith in the party, he could not bear the fact that it was impossible to work with this party, that it was impossible to work with Victor Adler, he could not accept the idea of a split and take upon himself the burdensome task of a struggle against the party. And as a result of his despair came this attempt.

An act of despair of a Kautskian (Volksrecht writes that Adler was not a supporter of the Zimmerwald Left, but rather a Kautskian).

But we revolutionaries cannot fall into despair. We are not afraid of a split. On the contrary, we recognise the necessity of a split, we explain to the masses why a split is inevitable and necessary, we call for work against the old party and for revolutionary mass struggle.

What trends (resp. what individual shades of opinion) exist in Vienna and in Austria in assessing Adler's act? I am afraid that the Vienna Government will declare Friedrich Adler insane, and not let matters come to a trial. But if they do, it will certainly be essential to organise the distribution of leaflets.

Write more and in greater detail, and observe exactly all technical precautions.
Best greetings!
Yours,
N. Lenin

Notes

[1] These words were written by Lenin in English.—Ed.

[2] Koritschoner, Franz (Nadin) (1891—1942)—one of the men who founded the Austrian Communist Party in 1918, and a member of its Central Committee until 1927. He edited the party's central organ, Die Rote Fahne (The Red Banner).

[3] Friedrich Adler, one of the leaders of the Austrian Social-Democrats, had murdered the Austrian Prime Minister Karl Stürgkh.

"So, you're not a Stavrogin type," concluded Mirella, both relieved and sceptical. She looked more serious than usually.

"No, my friend, and if I had to choose one of your favourite writer's heroes, I was going to choose Kirillov."

"Aha, now let's lighten up the conversation, so tell me who's your favourite heroine, Lizaveta Nikolaevna Tushin, maybe?" she asked me and smiled teasingly.

At the same time Lim and Zórba were exchanging glances and after a while they left us.

I took up Mirella's challenge. "Let me make a great leap forward, just for the sake of fun, no, my favourite heroine is not her..."

"Who is she then?"

"Lenina Crown, from Brave New World, but my likeness for her has nothing to do with Lenin, as you may think..."

"But?"

"I got to know Lenina years before I got to know Lenin.... I like her just because she is beautiful, always horny and promiscuous."

Mirella blushed and smiled. I pictured the future nun in hot lesbian encounters in her cell; will she and her partner orgasm with their spread legs interlocked, like two pairs of scissors, rubbing their vulvae and thighs and butt-cheeks together to stimulate themselves to orgasm? or they will reach their first monastical orgasm into a 69 or missionary position? I wondered.

They have named him the Wanderer for he was wandering in the Waste Land expanding all around him and the Waste Land gapping within him; wandered, wander and will wander; for ever and ever and the Wanderer is me; and I wander in the Waste Land and it is April, my mom was born on April the 4th and she is dead and buried this April the 4th and *"April is the cruellest month, breeding lilacs out of the dead land, mixing memory and desire, stirring dull roots with spring rain,"* and on April the 4th four years ago I and lots of us stormed Syntagma Square, where Dimitrēs Christoulas killed himself at 9:00 am and protested and clashed again and again with the antiriot-police and we were enraged and our grey hair turned back black again for we had no fear in us, just the rage and the joy of the uprest, encouraged and inspired by his testament: *"The Tsolakoglou government* has annihilated all traces for my survival, which was*

---

*The collaborationist occupation government established after the Nazi Germany invasion of Greece during WWII.

based on a very dignified pension that I alone paid for 35 years with no help from the state. And since my advanced age does not allow me a way of dynamically reacting (although if a fellow Greek were to grab a Kalashnikov, I would be right behind him), I see no other solution than this dignified end to my life, so I don't find myself fishing through garbage cans for my sustenance. I believe that young people with no future, will one day take up arms and hang the traitors of this country at Syntagma Square, just like the Italians did to Mussolini in 1945."

After the secular funeral of Christoulas on April the 7th we marched back from the First Cemetery of Athens to Syntagma Square shouting slogans inspired by his call to arms and all around us protesters with their hands raised up in the air were mimicking pistols, the notorious "comrade P38", and there was an aura of the hot Italian autumn all around us or at least the expectation of it or of something even greater and harsher because Troika is a harsh mistress and *"April is the cruellest month, breeding lilacs out of the dead land, mixing memory and desire...."*

So in the beginning is the Praxis, and then the Narrator, and the Narrator is with the Wanderer, and the Wanderer is me; but neither of us is ever the same for *on those who enter the same rivers, ever different waters flow.*

We are three distinct persons, yet we are one, a Trinity; a surrealist, subversive, sex-driven Trinity, not a holy one; a spectre haunting Europe, making many men to shiver out of fear of it and many women hot and horny for the three distinct persons of it; one by one or all the three of them at once in a foursome; for Trinity's dreams, nightmares or wet dreams on the left hand, and reality on the right, are like communicating vessels; even more Trinity's lucid dreams, to the horror of some, to the satisfucktion of others, create a hell for those who deserve a hell, a garden of eden for those who deserve an eden. As a Trinity we are in a constant change; change of looks, likes, moods, partners, personalities; so don't ever stick with us, just follow our flow.

We keep meeting in Locomotiva - cooperativa, a café, bar, and bookshop, in Exarcheia Square, a neighbourhood-continuum of urban resistance, urban revolt and — when needed, of black hoods, the centre and starting point of the December the 6th, 2008 uprising, the one that Dominique Strauss Kahn, head of the IMF once upon a time, had called "the first political explosion of the current world financial-economic crisis."*

On our way to Locomotiva or back from

---

*The 2008 Greek riots started on 6 December 2008, when Alexandros Grēgoropoulos (Greek: Αλέξανδρος Γρηγορόπουλος), a 15-year-old Greek student, was killed by two policemen in Exarcheia district of central Athens.

there, in the morning, in the evening, in the middle of the night and always in the darkness of our times, we have to pass through squalid, unimportant streets and walls covered with radiant graffiti and slogans, and by police squads wearing riot helmets, face visors, body armour, gas masks, plexiglass shields, bear service weapons and batons; sometimes they hold them from the rubber part when they beat causing greater injury. They wear khaki uniforms, khaki brains, and even their souls are khaki; khaki in all the shades of shit. In our surrealist jargon, us the Trinity, call them "coppigs." They don't notice us because we don't exist; but we do; once or twice we saw a woman among them; we can't tell if she was the same one; she didn't look sexy at all in her uniform in all the shades of shit; "most probably, when alone, she uses her club between her thighs and into her cunt, for her personal satisfucktion and salvation, after she has lubricated it in her mouth with her saliva," said Zórba the ræbelaisian, "some of them are very randy, I've seen short videos taken with cell-phones, leaked from police academies: young police-women peeling bananas with their teeth, sucking the fruit, stripping in front of each other in their multiple-occupancy rooms and starting cat-fights."

So, after we pass by or through platoons

of coppigs, we meet in Locomotiva, two or three times per week, to drink black coffee, rakomelo, bitter chocolate or lager, and to talk, debate, contemplate, remember the past and shape the future; without having illusions.

We mean that we are aware that Exarcheia is not the centre of the revolution. It's just a weird barometre; a barometre we love. All around us thousands of people of all ages, mostly young, are strolling through the streets of Exarcheia hanging out at the "Chartes," on Valtetsiou 35, a local cafe with impressive, weird toilets, the "Intriga" bar, the "Circus" club, and the Navarinou Street Park created by the locals out of nothing. Ages ago, on Valtetsiou 33, an old two-story building sheltered, in times when Chartes didn't exist, the offices of AASPE-AAMPE, the student and pupil organization of the most massive Maoist group of the times, the Revolutionary Communist Movement of Greece-EKKE; many of its members and followers were students of architecture and fine arts and their huge banners, real paintings, should have been kept and preserved in a Museum of Social History.

Valtetsiou is home to some of the area's most interesting bars and restaurants; most are open until quite late and in summer they are buzzing with activity. Riviera, one of the oldest and greenest Athens' open-air cinemas, which often shows black and white classics; We saw there with my dearest one *The Two Faces of January*. We consider the book much better than the film, it happens always though, not to say that I loved Patricia Highsmith for one more reason: For her dedication in her last Ripley novel, *To the dead and the dying among the Intifadeh and the Kurds, to those who fight oppression in whatever land, and stand up not only to be counted but to be shot.*

Further down in Valtetsiou is Rozalia, a taverna full of Greek and Erasmus students, artists, tourists, locals. We were dining there with my wife once, early August, one of the two times we have been there, when a street-artist approached us. She was a woman, a Slav, around thirty playing the violin. She played for us for sometime and then, still playing the violin, she turned to me her hip, with a small cotton bag attached over her tight jeans, so that I could slip the tip into her slit; the bag's slit I mean. I tried a couple of times, but for some reason I failed and the whole thing ended with me almost groping her hip. She had a strong sense of humour so she laughed, and my wife laughed even more.

The area of Exarheia is filled with book-stores, music stores, libertarian bookstores, cafés and occupied spaces that all together face quite often violent police raids as it happened on the 20th of April, 2012, forty-five years after the junta coup.

The news reached us through the internet, phone calls and SMS. At approximately 6:54 on Friday morning, heavy police forces conducted simultaneous raids at two newly occupied anarchist spaces in the neighbourhood of Exarcheia: the building at 60, Valtetsiou Street and the building of the abandoned K*Vox cinema in Exarcheia Square. The latter had been occupied for a few weeks and its opening event was planned for this Saturday. It was speculated that the raids took place following the order of I. Tentes, a prosecutor of the High Court in Athens, who launched his career after being appointed in the judiciary by the Junta regime in the early seventies. "History, in case it should be noted, does seem to have a peculiar sense of irony," was stated in the announcement.* Yes, indeed history has a peculiar sense of irony: like saying to us "hey guys look, tanks and banks match so much, don't they?"

The entire Exarcheia square was cordoned off by heavy police forces while the K*Vox social centre was sealed off. All my attempts to approach the area, approach even the publishing house, a hundred metres away, where I had an appointment later on, were

---

*https://en.squat.net/2012/04/20/athens-greece-major-police-operation-in-exarcheia-k-vox-social-centre-sealed-off/

in vain.

It was a bright sunny day and I remembered how forty-five years ago, we went out with my dad, in Alexandras Avenue, at midday, to watch the Junta's tanks scrolling up and down.

It was a bright sunny day too. Curfew was starting at six in the evening, I think, I'm not sure. After six o'clock, "anybody seen out in the streets would be shot dead without warning", the radio was screaming hysterically. For the time being they don't shoot us, but not because they are good guys; after all, many of them are the same guys and they are waiting around the corner.

K*Vox was re-occupied sometime later and nowadays attached to it is the Exarcheia Self-organized Health Structure, a self-organized health structure occupying various doctors. created through a general assembly of residents, social projects and collectives that live and act in the district of Exarcheia. It offers free primary healthcare, immediate help and psychological support. It promotes the concept of health for all, without any discrimination grounded on race, skin-colour, origin, sexual identity or religion. Main political conviction of its participants is to be able to provide solidarity reciprocally, rather than egoistically or philanthropically, given the fact that we are all potential migrants, homeless, unemployed, precarious workers without access to healthcare services. The city is full of them.

Among them a worker, who wrote and gave us a letter to publish anywhere we could. It goes as following:

My eyes have not the colour and quality of pale blue ice. My body is not tall and gaunt; it never was and now I am crippled and burned after the explosions in the blast. Our delegation was clear on the matter, everybody new it, all the workers, flyrock and lack of blast area security will cause blasting-related casualties. My face is not cut by prominent cheekbones and by a few sharp lines; it's burned by the blast. At twenty I looked nice and young but now at forty-five I am a crippled, burned, deformed. I live in a room-grave of 30 square meters, three meters under the earth. From my window I can see only the pedestrian's feet; no sky,no sun, no moon. I'm poor, crippled, I stink, I'm helpless and I'm rotting alive. You know why? I'll tell you. Because Mr Randaynidis the steel magnate ignored all safety regulations. I remember him just two days before the explosion. We had warned him, openly, in public, about the lack of security measures. He fought us back. I remember Mr Randaynidis standing by the blast, surrounded by executives, division heads, civic leaders, and the various local officials who had been outargued, bribed or threatened to obtain permits to run the furnaces without security measures. And now I'm rotting on my way to the grave.

EGO

'Why the proletarian revolution should
not execute Randaynidis, the criminal steel
magnate?' we wondered listening to the news
at 8.

8
octó
The Wanderer and Zórba, or Vas
at the age of
octó
witnessed the storming of the Winter
Palace
during the 1917
October
Revolution
'This is the way to fight,'
they thought and it was for ever and ever.
Permanent revolution.
Then they discovered the thrills of
octopussy
at least 10 years before James Bond
One pussy for every single day of the week
carrying the day's name
and two pussies for the last and blessed one
makes an
octó pussy
If octó
8
lies down, like this
∞
it is transformed into infinite
Eros ad infinitum
'This is the way to fuck,'
they thought

THE WANDERER'S BUST BY DEMOKRATÉS

ZORBAS'S BUST BY DĒMOKRATĒS

Chapter 3

A spectre is haunting Europe — the spectre of Troika the Vampire. All the deathlusting necrophilic powers of old degenerating and collapsing Europe have entered into a holy alliance with her, they mess with her, they fuck with her, top, bottom and vice versa. Troika is a harsh mistress dripping from head to foot, from every pore of her body, with blood and dirt; that's what the Wanderer things of her. That's what Zórba the brut thinks of her too; and they are haunting her; as two of the three persons of the unholy surrealist, subversive, sex-driven notorious Trinity.

Troika is a harsh mistress, an evil mistress but not the Wanderer's mistress. He has had lovers but he has never had a mistress. Neither god, nor master, nor mistress; much more a Vampire mistress. He was always a rebel, by birth. He remains a rebel and he will be for ever and ever; in saecula saeculorum. Rebels and mistresses don't match. After all la Rébellion est un amant féroce; she can never accept any mistress next to her own lover. Look what the French Revolution did to Marie Antoinette; she sent her to the guillotine. So would have done the Wanderer. He would have definitely killed her. With no regrets and with a lot of joy. After all, killing is no murder. He likes to believe that the pamphlet was written by Sexby. His name reminds him of sex, of the bi girlfriends he had; not being an Anglosaxon, "sexby," "sexbi," "bisex" sounded all the same to him. Some of them were the sweethearts of the undergraduate fachtidiots that later on became its proud fachtidiotic servants; the harsh mistress's servants who call themselves officers; Troika's officers. At breakfast they were proudly parroting Friedman's quotations, with mouths resembling cereal bowls full of dripping milk and nonsense; in the evening they were organising pub crawls and pissing contests trying hard to see who is going to pee further; shouting and cheering "yesss shoot it Paul! Shoot it!" Big deal! The Wanderer was not competing anybody, He was just shooting his semen into their sweethearts' wombs, and all their welcoming orifices, while they were crawling seductively on all fours. The fachtidiots were also crawling; crawling and vomiting. "Life can be beautiful," he was saying, "life is so small, we have so many plans, and dreams, and expectations, but Mistress Troika wants as bound and chained and kneeling..." So yes, killing is no murder and whoever wrote the pamphlet no matter if he was Silius Titus, William Allen or the Wanderer's favourite Sexby, favourite for his name and its connotations —because according to the Wanderer there is nothing hotter than sex with bisexual girls— it seems like he had in mind Troika when he wished: *"happy expiration... for while you live we can call nothing ours, and it is from your death that we hope for our inheritances. Let this consideration arm and fortify your Highness's mind against the fears of death and the terrors of your evil conscience, that the good you will do by your death will something balance the evils of your life."* Fierce feelings for a harsh and evil mistress!

Opal lips, not her lips, and Opal Tapes. Killing is no murder by D.A.R.F.D.H.S. Kill all bullies digital track. Dark music. Dark like the Waste Land; dark like the city, dark like our dark times; I feel like reading some poetry, I choose a Collection by W. H. Auden and search for the lines that match my mood:

Waves of anger and fear
Circulate over the bright
And darkened lands of the earth,
Obsessing our private lives;
The unmentionable odour of death
Offends the September night.

Men in dark times; gun shots; flashbangs; the rattle of machine-guns fire; mesmerising urban warfare sounds; it's a nightmare for some, a night-dream or even just a day-dream for others; day after day, night by night the rift between nightmares, dreams and reality is closing as riots spread all around him, and enraged youths burn banks and police cars, erect barricades and the an-tiriot-police counter-attacks with thousands of tear-gas canisters and extreme violence, only to be overpowered again by the people with the use of stones, molotovs and clubs; for there is an urgent, a vital need to '*break, beat up everything, beat and destroy! Everything that's being broken is rubbish and has no right to life! What survives is good,*' thought the Wanderer, echoing Pisarev's words.

The Wanderer, was fascinated by all these things —the opal lips and tapes. the killing that is no murder and the kill all bullies digital track, the dark like the Waste Land and like the city, dark like our dark times music of gun shots, flashbangs, machine-guns cattling, the mesmerising urban warfare sounds— and saw them as the work of art of the downtrodden, as their dreamish or night-marish artistic contribution to a fiesta organised without them and against them, a fiesta turned by them into a wild festival of the oppressed and the exploited.

Zórba and the Wanderer were sitting at the small table just next to the glass door, by the floor-to-ceiling glass window. Behind the bar Vicky, a young brunette, member of the cooperativa Locomotiva was preparing rakomelo for both of them combining raki with honey, cinnamon, cardamon, pergamon, holding a brass coffee-pot over the tiny gas range. In a moment the mixture was set aflame, flames leaped upwards and lit her face in a Bradburian way like in Fahrenheit 451, where it was a pleasure to burn with the brass coffee-pot in her fist, or like the Guy Fawkes Night and the night of the barricades; any night with erected barricades and molotov cocktails and other festivities. "Rakomelo flambé," commented Zórba; then they clicked their glasses and said, in one voice "it's capitalism, stupid;" for they didn't want to turn their PhDs into toilet paper by accepting any other arguments on the causes of the crisis.

On my way out I saw a young, tiny female student, sitting close to us, reading an old book with a damaged cover under the title Jeremy Rifkin, *The End of Work: The Decline of the Global Labor Force and the Dawn of the Post-Market Era*. "Oh, Rifkin," I said smiling. She blushed, "It's for my paper," she said and sounded like apologising; "is he too liberal for a fan of hard-core communism like you?" This time her smile was wide and teasing.

"No, he is fine, I like his arguments a lot. We only have to turn him upside down, place him upon his feet instead of on his head, where he is standing now. He actually offers strong arguments in favour of the decline of workaholism, for the abolition of waged slavery, the expropriation of capital and in favour of a communist society of idleness. And I'm not a fan of any other hard-core than that of erotography in all its forms and manifestations."

She looked excited and amused; "What's the difference between erotography and pornography?" she asked me.

"This is a very interesting and very easy question to answer. Erotography is any explicitly sexual literature or art, any erotic written material, graphic pictures of an erotic nature that do not involve payed sex. Pornography is any explicitly sexual literature or art, any erotic written material, graphic pictures of an erotic nature that involve exclusively and strictly payed sexual activities; and, of course and above all, any literature or art, graphic pictures or texts of any kind, describing the non-sexual, the social sides of the lives and works of the bourgeois politicians, economists, MPs, ministers, prime-ministers and so on and so forth."

"Wow!" she shouted loudly and her eyes sparkled.

Chapter 4

Hannah the raven-haired Lebanese and Anna the Irish red-haired shared a few things together; they shared the Wanderer, they shared that their name is a palindrome that reads the same backward or forward and they shared their love for backdoor sex. Hannah and Anna were anal advocates and they both trained the Wanderer how to turn the fachtidiots' sweethearts into steaming anal sweathurts. That's exactly what had happened once upon a time in Kingston-upon-Thames with Miss Lysiac, Dr. Polodzki's girlfriend.

"My name is Wand", he had introduced himself to her, "Bill Wand, if you find the Wanderer too big for you," a motto he adopted after he overheard a girlfriend saying about him: "his wand is huge, I've been sore for days!"

Irena had smiled: "I love long names and other long demons."

Two nights later they left secretly for Kingston-upon-Thames.

Next day, Dr. Polodzki called him on the

phone from a public phone somewhere in the Department of Politics of Brightsex University: "Dr Wanderer, Dr Wanderer do you hear me? for God's sake, where are you, we can't start the seminar without you, all our guests are waiting for your presentation, especially after the latest breaking news on your country."

By that time the Wanderer was in the bedroom no.8 of the *M to A Bed and Breakfast*, in Kingston-upon-Thames, a cosy bedroom overlooking the river. He didn't like the Pole. Not because he was a Pole, not at all, but because like many others of his generation he had replaced the libertarian cry "No masters! No Gods!" with the servile whisper "Yes Master! Yes my Pope!" The Wanderer accepted the call and breathing heavily he said: "Oh, look Dr. Polodzki, I'm very busy, I have to dig a grave, I warned you yesterday after all, about the situation, I can't come, capitalism's corpse is already rotting, it's a hard job but somebody has to do it."

Dr. Polodzki lost his non-existing temper and screaming hysterically in a high-pitched voice attempted, in vain, to recall the Wanderer back *to order*: "Dr Wanderer are you insane?! You can't do this, you just don't have the right to do it, what's this nonsense you're talking about?"

But the wandering Wanderer didn't have

such intentions; ok, he had promised him that he would talk on his country's latest political changes and accept the audience's questions, yes he had done so, in order to get rid of him, but now that he had his pole into the wet depths of the Pole's girlfriend, he only managed to say, breathing heavily: "Oh, yes, yes, ok, relax, take it easy, I'm coming, I'm coming," and terminated the call, as Miss Lysiac, on all fours, sweating all over, was already screaming her brains out: "Omg, omg it hurts, it hurts but I love it, come, come in my ass."

'Oh you bitch,' thought the Wanderer, 'you're such a sweating hurt sweathurt....'

Whispers caught in dream-traps placed by the secret services, wanted the Wanderer to be a secret agent of nights to come, an agent provocateur of women's sexual secretions, wanted him coming into their wet dreams and make them come in reality, and also similar whispers and rumours trapped in dream-traps wanted Zórba the brut to break the time-space continuum, sneak into his adversaries' nightmares and carve the letter Z into their clothes or even their bodies, by either using his sword in three swift strokes or a Škorpion SA Vz 61. Later on he did the same with the letter V after he was rebaptised by the avant-garde young lady from Barcelona.

She had traced the letter V on his forehead using her soaked into her vaginal secretions middle finger, into a blasphemous, but highly erotic, parody of the catholic sacraments of baptism, sexpressing in that way her deep-rooted in the years of the civil war hatred for the clergy's alliance with Franco; for she was the granddaughter of a POUM fighter that had met Vladimir Antonov-Ovseyenko, who had led the Bolshevik assault to capture the Winter Palace and arrested the ministers of the Russian Provisional Government.

"I had met her during a cold November night, full of fires, explosions, screams and shouts," he liked to start, giving with his voice some adventurous tones to the narration.

"During a Guy Fawkes Night, at a Bonfire Night Party organised by a local Communist Group, 'with lots of fireworks, baked pots, parking, soup, cakes, beer, punch, wine, lemonade', promising, 'a good night out....'

"She approached me holding a glass of red red wine in her hand.

" 'Do you know that you look like Jeff Bridges in Against All Odds?' she said.

" 'No'," I said, " 'but now that you mentioned it, you definitely look like Rachel Ward in Against All Odds. You're almost her double.'

" 'I know. That's why I've seen the film

three times. But fuck, I didn't expect you to know it. That's bad luck.'

" 'Why so?' " I asked her.

" 'Oh, I was looking for company to watch it again,' she had said, taking a sip of red wine.'

" 'I have seen only an old poster of it,' " I lied to her, for being a cinephil I had seen even this film. " 'Do they fuck at the end?' "

" 'Yes they do she said,' " looking at me straight in the eyes, rather provocatively. Her own eyes were wet and her pupils dilated...

" 'Then let's go against all odds,' " I told her...

"We kissed. She then offered me her joint. 'Thank's,' I said, 'I don't like artificial paradises.... This earthly hell is the best driving force of the revolution....

"She laughed. 'Sure; then let's blow up the Parliament. Tonight is the night. Remember, Remember the 5th of November!'

" 'If there is such a need, I'll join you with pleasure and without joints. But I prefer to storm it. The way the Bolsheviks stormed the Winter Palace. Arms in hand.' "

That's how Zórba had narrated to us his first meeting with Beatrice. It was the 5th of November 2014 and we had gathered at Locomotiva to watch the film *V for Vendetta* and then discuss on the book *Bulletproof ideas in Times of Crisis* by Dēmētrēs Oulēs, a title inspired by V's words: *Beneath this mask there is more than flesh. Beneath this mask there is an idea, Mr. Creedy, and ideas are bulletproof.*

After he was given his new nom de guerre, Zórba or Vas started introducing Beatrice, the young avant-garde artist, the anarchist, as his godmother, something that astonished many of his acquaintances, for she was just three or four years older than him, almost thirty; a handsome woman with curly black hair, an audacious mouth, rather tall, with a well-trained body. She had been teaching Spanish in the Instituto Cervantes de Atenas for five years in the course of which she mastered both the Greek language by socialising and the Greek way by practicing it a lot in bed. So when the two of them didn't hesitate, after a few glasses of red Sangria, to talk in Greek, kiss and pet in front of all, the middle and upper-class English roses were transforming into Dutch red tulips or red Greek poppies, perceiving it as an almost incestuous "in the eyes of God and the Queen" affair; things turned even more outrageous when they invented a what they called "a scandalous dadaist" story, moved from their old Riverside Block of Flats to Aldous Huxley Hall of Residence and presented themselves as brother and sister. They were extremely convincing as brother and sister; they both talked Greek, they both had lived in Athens and Beatrice even claimed that she had at a young age got married to a Spaniard, lived in Spain, taken the Spanish citizenship and then, a few months ago, got divorced. But more than convincing they were scandalously provocative both politically and erotically: politically like when on May the 9th of 1976 they broke a sacrificial bottle of Stolichnaya over the walls of block A of Riverside Block of Flats and re-named it, shouting aloud, into Cambridge Spy Ring Block of Flats; then following the same procedure renamed the five out of six A to F blocks after Maclean, Burgess, Philby, Blunt and John Cairncross. The last block, the notorious block F, they just named it "Fuck Capitalism." Erotically they were even more provocative, especially when, late at night, Beatrice's sighs, moans and screams could be heard all over the block. "Can you please try to be less profound?" said to Beatrice in a more or less spiteful manner Kathy, a good looking blond English student. Beatrice smiled: "Whenever from now on you hear my moans lie down on your bed, open your legs, think of England and do as you please."

"What bourgeois hypocrites they are," she was saying, breathing heavily, before wrapping once more her legs around him, an invitation for more teasingly noisy sex in the missionary position. "Even their leftists have denounced Byron for a disputable affair with his stepsister, but not their fatherland for its imperialist atrocities."

"Do you play golf?" dared to ask me in front of Beatrice a young posh English student of fine arts. Even the way she was saying *fine arts* was posh. We were sitting in the Aldous Huxley's common-room, after a wild ride, enjoying a glass of Flaming Spanish Coffee lit on fire by Beatrice. She dared to ask, underestimating or even ignoring the overdose of rum in the coffee. and the hot-tempered female Spaniard got irritated. She didn't like her. "Of course he does," she rushed to say; "anytime you like he'll play on your own 3 hole course; to keep with the rules he'll have to play each one of your holes six times to complete a round, I'm going to watch, but I assure you, you're going to love every moment of it!"

"Whore," said the posh in a posher accent and left the common-room waving her buttocks. A few months later, Zórba, breaking the rules but not her hymen, for she was 23 and lascivious, played each of her holes much more than six times; but Beatrice wasn't there to watch.

Fascinately indecent incidents; dark passages; passagenwerk; arcades project; Walter Benjamin; Portbou; the last passage; tranzit;

Nazi Germany; refugees; Eidomenē Camp; Fortress Europe; Austria; Hungary; Poland; Chechia; Slovakia; FYROM; all those who years ago were either sniveling or screaming their brains out for what they had baptised "The Wall of Shame," the very same ones, neophyte and desperate-to-be members of the EU, erect new walls-of-shame across Europe and unashamedly let thousands of refugees drown across the Mediterranean Sea; refugees-victims of their imperialist policies. Walls and electric fences all around Europe; Bulgarian neo-Nazi-criminals using military vehicles and dogs hunt asylum seekers; and hotspots everywhere, hot spots of blood on the pavements of downtown Athens, the blood of immigrants stabbed by Greek nazi-gangs and hotspot camps, camps of all kinds: relocation camps, temporary protection camps, concentration camps and, tomorrow, the extermination camps, the life-dream of the fascists all over Europe.

The Wanderer wanders around downtown Athens; long lines of asylum seekers, lost in space, lost in time, strangers in a strange land, moving slowly along the streets, carrying their few belongings and their kids and their crippled and their old parents on wheel-chairs or even on their shoulders remembering the terrible day of doom.

How the blood stained the sand and the water
And how in that hell that they called Suvla Bay

We were butchered like lambs at the slaughter
Johnny Turk he was ready, he primed himself well
He chased us with bullets, he rained us with shells
And in five minutes flat he'd blown us all to hell*

They walk and walk and lie down to rest, thirsty and hungry and exhausted and as he sees them, the Wanderer recalls once again William, William Shakespeare's only surviving manuscript, *The Book of Sir Thomas More*, feeling that time has come for us to stop just shaking the spear, time has come to throw it and pierce the heart of the beast.

Grant them removed, and grant that this your noise
Hath chid down all the majesty of England;
Imagine that you see the wretched strangers,
Their babies at their backs and their poor luggage,
Plodding to the ports and coasts for transportation,
And that you sit as kings in your desires,
Authority quite silent by your brawl,
And you in ruff of your opinions clothed;
What had you got? I'll tell you: you had taught
How insolence and strong hand should prevail,
How order should be quelled; and by this pattern
Not one of you should live an aged man,
For other ruffians, as their fancies wrought,
With self same hand, self reasons, and self right,
Would shark on you, and men like ravenous fishes
Would feed on one another....
Say now the king
Should so much come too short of your great trespass

---

*http://www.pogues.com/Releases/Lyrics/LPs/RumSodomy/Waltz-ing.html copyright © Eric Bogle

As but to banish you, whether would you go?
What country, by the nature of your error,
Should give you harbour? go you to France or Flanders,
To any German province, to Spain or Portugal,
Nay, any where that not adheres to England,
Why, you must needs be strangers: would you be pleased
To find a nation of such barbarous temper,
That, breaking out in hideous violence,
Would not afford you an abode on earth,
Whet their detested knives against your throats,
Spurn you like dogs, and like as if that God
Owed not nor made not you, nor that the claimants
Were not all appropriate to your comforts,
But chartered unto them, what would you think
To be thus used? this is the strangers case;
And this your mountainish inhumanity.

Men in dark times; *Anna, weine nicht Wenn ich wieder kehre, kehr ich unter anderen Fahnen wieder. If I return again I will follow other flags.*

Zórba or Vas, in whose name "V" stood for Victory and "s" for surrealism was following these *other flags* since he could remember himself. But many others were not. Some were following the green flags of PASOK; as the flags were waving in the air, they were widespreading green venomous snakes like the Death Adder across the continuum; others followed the blue flags of New Democracy; as these flags were waving, they were spreading blue venomous snakes like the Blue Krait.

'Time is not for us to wait,' he was thinking. 'Parliamentary illusions should be swept away alongside with all these venomous serpents before it's too late; something has to be done.'

"What do you have in mind?" the Wanderer asked him once, when he communicated these thoughts to him; "What Is to Be Done?" They were sitting at one of the two long tables at the back of Locomotiva drinking coffee, with Eva's half-bitten apple carefully placed on the table, and Vas, was smoking the pipe of class war.

Zórba or Vas smiled and, not leaving aside the pipe, "hm," he murmered, "the usual, the eternal burning questions of our movement," he turned on Eva and "here we are," he said turning her to face the Wanderer:

[...] But to limit that winning to polling a majority of votes in an election under the rule of the bourgeoisie, or to make it the condition for it, is crass stupidity, or else sheer deception of the workers. In order to win the majority of the population to its side the proletariat must, in the first p]ace, overthrow the bourgeoisie and seize state power; secondly, it must introduce Soviet power and complete]y smash the old state apparatus, whereby it immediately undermines the rule, prestige and influence of the bourgeoisie and petty-bourgeois compromisers over the non-proletarian working people. Thirdly, it must entirely destroy the influence of the bourgeoisie and petty-bourgeois compromisers over the majority of the non-proletarian masses by satisfying their economic needs in a revolutionary way at the expense of the exploiters. [...]

V. I. Lenin The Constituent Assembly Elections and The Dictatorship of the Proletariat Written: 16 December, 1919

"This passage looks to me like a flash in the night," said the Wanderer sadly, "like a very bright tracer in the middle of a dark night."

Vas, in whose name "V" stood for Victory, exhaled the smoke of his pipe of class war and said to the Wanderer:

"So, I am not going to answer your question in my own words; I'd rather let my favourite Victor Serge speak on my behalf: *What's to be done if it's midnight in the century?*

'Midnight's where we have to live then,' said Rodion with an odd elation."

At this moment a joyful female voice interfered and interrupted our conversation. "Where your optimism has gone? What are these dark thoughts?"

It was Helen. She had appeared out of the blue in Locomotiva, worked for sometime there in the bar and disappeared again into the blue. She was an art student and from time to time she was working as a performer, giving live sex shows with her half-Scottish boyfriend, a tall slim nice guy. The first night

I saw her behind the bar in Locomotiva, I asked her about the weird tattoo she had on her right shoulder. "It's a female head from Tim Burton's Corpse Bride," she said, I have one more here; she lowered her shalwar around her loins and revealed a bigger one on the right side of her lower stomach.

"No, dear Helen-and-Desire," I told her, "I haven't turned pessimist."

She looked at me astonished; "Helen and what? What is all this about?"

"It's about Helen and Desire. You'd better ask your Scottish boyfriend about it all.

"But I haven't changed into a pessimist. Even if midnight is where we have to live, still midnight has the libidinal potentials that may evoke a pre-orgasmic, in other words pre-revolutionary situation.

"You're aware of it Helen-and-Desire, aren't you?"

She was not participating in our demonstrations, but I think, I had the feeling and still have it, that both her and her Scottish boyfriend were such stuff as people who appear unexpectedly and fight on the barricades are made on, something like Gavroche, and their little life is rounded with a sleep.

"Look at that simple girl", I said to my friends; "having just finished for a second time Rand's *Atlas Shrugged*, I assure you that she's worth a thousand times more than all

Rand's heroines and heroes taken together.

"You don't like Rand," said Zórba smiling.

"Rand stands for capitalism; capitalism destroys the lives of millions, generates crises, wars, fascism. I absolutely agree with Whittaker Chambers, who wrote that from almost any page of Atlas Shrugged, a voice can be heard, from painful necessity, commanding: 'To a gas chamber —go!' Not to say that she has used the Greek myths in the most unscrupulous and ignorant way. What does Atlas have to do with her capitalist thugs? The only burden they carry, is their harmful to the word existence.

"But, my dear Myselves, we'd better try, as much as we can, not to waste precious time and belittle ourselves busying with Ayn Rand and her Church. For as Marcus Aurelius wrote in "To Myself", *every man is worth just so much as the things are worth about which he busies himself*.

But which self? Zórba the Greek? Zórba the brut? Zórba the ræbelaisian? I am aware of the alter egos hibernating into us, of our other potentialities, of our Not Yet beings, waiting —in vain? who knows— for the proper conditions in order to emerge — against order, against Law, against all odds....

Chapter 5

Whispers caught in dream-traps placed by the secret services, wanted the Wanderer to be a secret agent of nights to come, an agent provocateur of women's sexual secretions, wanted him coming into their wet dreams and make them come in reality, and also, similarly trapped in dream-traps whispers and rumours wanted Zórba the brut to break the time-space continuum, sneak into his adversaries' nightmares and carve the letter Z into their clothes or even their bodies, by either using his sword in three swift strokes or a Škorpion SA Vz 61. Later on he did the same with the letter V. Alice's night-thoughts, wet dreams and fantasies had been caught in the dream-traps and then sexposed to him by her in the twilight zone when she confessed to him her sexual dreams: how she was desperately seeking for him to save her from her abductors, but not too early for she needed to orgasm, for it was a dream and she was aware of it, she could even watch herself like in a porn movie and at the same time feel it all, and then him to come and free her and carve into their bodies his initials, Z or V she didn't care at all, but she wanted him to use his sword and not the Škorpion, after all it was a knight's affair and not an urban guerrilla one, and then she was going to offer herself to him, satisfy him with her newly awakened sexuality, as a prize for her salvation from her sexual ordeal. She was a third-year student of Spanish Literature, they have met somehow through Beatrice; Alice's blond, pale complexion, her turkuaz eyes, her constantly trembling riotous, pink-tipped breasts had attracted her abductors' attention. She spoke of an altar or a warehouse where all around her young females were being whored, many of them students.

So it was an altar and a warehouse, something mixed or in between....

Alice dreamed mesmerised the Kidnapper seising Beatrice's hips, rolling her over onto her stomach, his hands moving immediately to the soft, bronze, half-moons of her buttocks, spreading the two globes, sexposing the girl's backside to her dreaming eyes. Beatrice had been thrashing back and forth wildly, her hips were still quivering with unsatisfied lust as the Kidnapper's middle finger circled over the tiny wet hole of her anus.

Swallowing hard, she watched the Kidnapper placing the mushroomed head of his massively throbbing cock against the fearfully tensing hole of the girl's anus and began probing and pushing; there was a moment of electric tension in the air and then the Kidnapper pushed forward with his hips.

Somewhere within the dream she saw and felt Beatrice's tongue spearing out delicately and invading her trembling young pussy, separating the moist folds and exploring the heart of her womanhood. Alice's pelvis writhed, she saw it and the scene made her wet and at the same time she felt it and became even wetter and jerked convulsively as she reacted to this deceptively powerful stimulation, feeling Beatrice lick her blooming clitoris sensitively and then suck it deliberately and forcefully up into her mouth, caressing it with her tongue. "No... don't do that to me.... I'm not a lesbian!" moaned Alice in a not very convincing tone.

"Fuck, no... please," groaned Alice in anguish, waving wildly her blond hair as Beatrice's warm tongue speared in and out of her in-voluntarily flowering cuntal petals.

The panther-bodied Beatrice was trembling with carnal lust as she stretched herself out on the bed next to the frightened blonde-haired captive. Alice noticed immediately that Beatrice's chestnut-coloured nipples were enlarged and hard like little pebbles, and the woman's pussy was already moist, the petals of her cunt ragged with blood.

As Beatrice's hungry tongue tantalised her throbbing vaginal flesh Alice looked at the moistly dilated pussy only a few inches from her nose; Beatrice's was warm and scented with patchouli, the lips of her vagina were swollen and trembling with sexual need; she bent forward and ran her lips over the tiny pink button of Beatrice's clitoris and tasted the honeyed sweetness of the older woman's cunt.

Alice saw herself thrown into the oral delights, almost indulging in the wickedness and obscenity of what she was doing. She slid her long flickering tongue deeper into Beatrice's naked pussy, feeling the delicately trembling walls of the woman's vagina quivering with carnal sexcitement. She sucked and licked with all the lust she had summoned up, driving her tongue repeatedly into the bisexual's clasping vaginal hole and simultaneously brushing her lower lip over the pulsating organ of her clitoris.

From Zórba's point of view, the two women were two sex-hungry bitches starved for cunt-juice, and he felt his cock hardening again.

The two women were still tongue-fucking each other like a pair of sex-maniacs; Zórba levered himself up next to Alice's body; the purple head of his cock had ground into an awesome mushroom's size and he rammed it between Alice's soft warm buttocks; Alice was trembling on the verge of a mind-splitting lesbian orgasm when she felt Zórba's warmly-pulsating hardness slide vigorously between her ass-cheeks. The approaching orgasm exploded and withered away like a summer rain as fear struck his hand into her naked body; he was going to sodomise her!

Dreams, dreams, wet dreams and realities; for after she had exposed herself by confessing her sexual dreams, Zórba and Beatrice had arranged a foursome for her; the three of them and Antonio, Beatrice's best friend. Antonio came into her reality as soon as she came out of her dream and dived into the newly revealed thalassa of sexuality; 'bloody foreigners if they were going to ravish her, let it be enjoyable and complete,' she thought and moved her face forward as if magnetised by the phallic wonder, until her soft, like red petals of an English rose, lips were locked around it. She heard Zórba the brut grunt while Antonio fucked furiously into her greedily clenching rectum from behind, spurning her on to suck in her breath and flick out her tongue, bringing it into warm wet contact with the soft, rubbery tip. She swirled her tongue around it in moist, experimental cock-teasing slowness, while Zórba twisted and jerked to her flouting, until he pushed it half-way into her mouth and then calmed down just before she started gagging!

And then she swayed, feeling someone at the back of her. Craning her neck apprehensively, she stared into the light-brown liquid eyes of Beatrice Moreno who was humping her back like a dog riding a bitch in heat. She had mounted the widespread moons of Alice's helplessly trembling, soft, pale buttocks, her arms wrapped around her waist, riding her back, while in her hand she held the phallic tube of a vibrating dildo.

From where Zórba lay, he could see the elastic tip, pointed like that of his own organ, slipping between the sleek thighs of their captive and aiming toward the target of Alice's swollen, bloomed cuntal lips. Then vibrating shamelessly jerked and danced in the hot, damp slit of Alice's cunt as the Spaniard bisexual quivered and lurched forward, trying to bury the rubber cock deeper into the pale girl's hungrily waiting body.

'By Goddess, by Thalassa, now wasn't that something?' he thought 'Leave it to Beatrice!'

Sobbing in the inferno of her edenic desire, Alice looked back, willingly shifting her quaking round ass-cheeks in a desperate attempt to capture the elusive penis, the brutal tension within her driving her to the mind-shattering point. Oh Goddess, oh Thalassa, she needed to have that erotic organ rammed up inside her! She had to have its vibrating length digging into the wet tender flesh of her vagina, rubbing her velvety walls before she went mad with need.

But Beatrice was teasing her unmercifully, guiding the vibrator about the bud of her clit, stroking it lengthwise over the smooth slit of her cunt but never pushing the head to plunge into the heated depths of her seeping pussy. With a grunt, Alice reached back and grasped the shaft of the vibrator guiding it to the sucking mouth of her desire-inflamed cunt. With a joyful groan, Beatrice thrust and rammed and thrust again, spreading the dilating channel open wider as she buried the long, rubber prick into the hilt. Alice's hotly quivering white belly was crammed with the vibrating, ticklish length.

"Oh... oh my Goddess, Thalassa!" she blurted, her eyes wide and glazed as the thing fucked into her from behind while she stared glassy-eyed at Zórba the brut glaring down at her. "Oh... ah!..." she grunted in heavenly relief, and began to thrash backwards rhythmically to meet the rapid, powerful strokes plunging deep into her cock-hungry pussy. Beatrice's satiny dark nudity clung to Alice's naked pale back, the tips of her berry nipples stroking against Alice's backbone with each lunge.

"Fuck you" Zórba was sexclaiming. "I've never seen two women riding each other as hard as this...

Look at the way the blondie takes it... every fucking cm of that rubber cock!"

Then... then? when?... Alice began to cry, salty tears of shame flowing onto her satiny, flushed cheeks as she realised there was nothing she could do but lie there dreaming, watching and listening to Beatrice sucking and licking at her cunt. Zórba and somebody she could not see had her in the middle. Was it Beatrice with a strap-on? The double impalement was double humiliation and Alice suddenly realised her ties with reality was loosening, slackening dangerously. She felt herself on the edge of a slippery lust-slide and every twitch of her body brought her that much closer to sexlimination. Her shamelessly aroused body was jerking in spasms, and her hips seemed to have called rioting in her brain at a moment when all the anti-riot forces had been sexterminated with the use of brute force.

Taking a deep breath, he quickened his thrusts, ripping his fingers from her offended c-anal-amour and seizing her garter-belted hips. The girl's loins were wide open to him taking his long, hard cock ramming mercilessly into her waxed wet pussy. Alice's face was so contorted with passion that her own full-of-deep-seated British inhibitions and Victorian decency had sexvaporated. Even her young Thacherist mother would have swallowed hard watching her own daughter in such a state of sexcitement and Zórba himself felt that his cock was ready to sexplode from the pressure sexerted upon that bloated tube from the soft, muscled soaking wet walls of her vagina.

"I... I..." Alice gasped, her voice high and unexplainably lustful.

"Say it!" said Zórba the brut, wanting to hear the confession from her lips.

"I'm coming.... I'm coming!" the lust-craved girl chanted mindlessly, her hips bucking up against his sunbathed body with that strange physical power which sweeps over a woman's body at the moment an unsexpected orgasm overpowered her.

On the big screen of the future-events-transmitter mounted on the wall opposite them, the latest Breaking News from Afar were sending thrills of horror to all the thanatos's advocates and thrills of satisfucktion to all the eros-loving people:

"After a public trial that lasted longer than needed, as long as a prolonged coitus, the Insuerrectionary Front of Greece, executed five Troikan ex-ministers half an hour ago, after they were found guilty of mass crimes against the people of Greece. Furthermore the Reinsuerrectionary Antideath Fucktion — RAF— announced more executions of economic-war criminals in the next few hours. They also made an appeal to the workers of all countries, particularly to their agents-angels all over the world, to haunt and arrest the economic class-war criminals wherever and whenever they find them. 'All of them should have the fate of Otto Adolf Eichmann, they stressed.'

"Yeah," Antonio grunted lustfully, the obscene spectacle rejuvenating his own heavy penis once more, and he reached down to massage it in one hand while his mind began to devise new carnalities he would put her through after she'd had enough of the vibrator.

Alice hung suspended on an dream-valley of unbelievable bliss. At first, the vicious lesbian invasion had caused stomach nausea with the unexpected impaling agony of the rubber cock tickling and stretching at her pink insides, pressing the velvety, resisting flesh of her tight vaginal hole before it. But

*9 March 1906 – 1 June 1962) was a German Nazi SS-Obersturmbannführer (lieutenant colonel) and one of the major organisers of the Holocaust. In 1960, he was captured in Argentina by Mossad, Israel's intelligence service. Following a widely publicised trial in Israel, he was found guilty of war crimes and hanged in 1962.

in seconds the pain had subsided to be replaced by a need to have it deeper and harder, wanting it to thunder up inside the warm pulsating depths of her womanhood.

Now, Alice could feel the warmth of Beatrice's loins pressing against her ass-cheeks, feel the smoothness of her pussy against the tenderness of her inner thighs. When she made a leftwards movement, she could hear the moans of appreciation hissing from Beatrice's lungs as the bud of her lubricated clitoris polished itself in masturbatory strokes against Alice's buttocks.

Then Alice jumped-for joy! Beatrice's hand had cupped her vulva and her middle finger was searching for the magic button of her swollen, cunt-juiced clitoris, teasing her torturously, masturbating her. Soon she was delightfully impaled to the hilt by the cock-like hardness that vibrated masochistically in the wet depths of her devouring cunt.

Goddess, Thalassa, Alice had never been so fully fucked! She never wanted this heavenly bubble to burst. She breathed a deep moan from her lust-filled mouth and began to move in tempo backwards to meet Beatrice's panting thrusts. The Spaniard woman's arms cupped her rounded pale hips, and she ground and undulated her body, rotating her pale buttocks in concentric circles, abandoning herself to the ecstasy of lesbian love while the two men stood around admiring this edenic, erotic scene. The contrast of golden dark skin against alabaster, black hair fanning about a head of waving blonde curls, added a flip of sexcitation to the scene.

Alice herself wished she could see it all... see Beatrice riding her back while the shaft disappeared wetly up inside her pussy, but she had to content herself with images. The mere thought of that brown Spaniard female body clinging needfully to hers sent a licentious thrill souring through her aroused body. In the scenery of her dream she saw her full, taut breasts dancing and swaying beneath her writhing, perspiring form, moving to the delightful, raping cock that vibrated inside her vaginal hole. She visualised it, plowing deeper, deeper into the stretched mouth of her clasping cunt from behind...

Antonio woke up in the middle of the night and called a taxi for the airport, for Havana, for Nicaragua, for two, three, many Vietnams, to fight with the Sandinistas against imperialism. We were left the three of us again, as usual. Alice was sleeping sexhausted from too much sex, Beatrice was sitting naked on the bed, cross-legged, with the legs straight out exposing her vulva,but she didn't care.

"He went finally, he did it," I said.

She smiled."You envy him bro? You were also thinking to go but these two lesbian nurses from Holstebro trapped you between their thighs and you stayed back with them."

"Bitch!" I shouted teasingly in a low voice, "You're not only an incestuous bitch, I got you, you're an agent of the USSR, the Union of Surrealist Sexual Retroperspectives. This incident hasn't happen yet, it comes from the future, there is no other way for you to know it. Even more you can't have read it, I'll write about it much later. And they were-not-will-be lesbians, just bisexuals."

"And what are you going to do to me now that you've uncovered me?"

"First I'll fuck you uncovered, over the blankets, then I'll get you involved in the *'Sexterminate Mistress Troika Plot.'* "

"BY THE WAY, WHAT DO YOU HAVE AGAINST THE TROJANS?" she had asked me once upon a time with an SMS.

"NOTHING REALLY," I had replied, "THE ACHAEANS HOWEVER CAN BE READ AS ANARCHACHAEANS. THE TROJANS RHYME WELL WITH THE TROIKANS AND UNLEASH EXPLOSIVE STREAM OF THOUGHTS...."

"ABOUT WHAT?"

"ABOUT THE FOURTHCOMING FATE OF THE LATTER.... TROY'S FATE. TROY'S END"

"FORTHCOMING ☺," she had corrected me.

"NO. FOR IT'S THE FOURTH INTERNATIONAL THAT WILL LEAD THE END TO CAPITALISM. SO, FOURTHCOMING," I had insisted.

Chapter 6

"I am a wanderer," he told us, "I've been wandering through all my life and nobody knows the downtown Athens better than me. I know how it looked, sounded, felt, even tasted, year after year, decade after decade; because downtown Athens has a taste too; like the taste of ash mixed with liquified pepper filling your mouth and nostrils and lungs, the taste of tear-gas. I got the habit of flirting and playing with her, like with the taste of the kisses of a woman, just for a while, for as long or as short time is needed in order to turn my panic into rage, and then I go ahead wearing my gas-mask; because I am a wanderer and I never cease wandering even among the chaos of riots and clashes; I feel and move like a fish in the water through it; I've been wandering through all my life and nobody knows the downtown Athens better than me; I started from the park, by feet, then later on, when I was nine or ten the most I was bicycling, during spring or summer-time, through the vast park close to my home, it looked vast, its

28 hectares was a vast area for me then and I was wandercycling and wondercycling for the sake of girls and females at first, sexclusively, this was my main motive, wandering and seeking for them and wondering about them until in the course of time both activities became my second nature and embraced it all. Soon after the park-period I focused on the downtown Athens, but the broader area too and I can reassure you that it never looked gloomier than now. It's getting rotten to the core, it's decaying, and do you know why? it's because capitalism is decaying, it's as simple as that, all the rest is bullshit either for political imbeciles or for payed scums of the bloody capitalists..."

"And what is to be done about it?" I asked him.

He lit his pipe, although he is not a smoker, but he carries from time to time a pipe that his dad brought from Idaho years ago and he smokes it once in a time and said: "I had a dream a few nights ago, a dream that looked inseparable from reality, or maybe, the events of the last week look like a dream to me. I dreamed Lenina Crown and Cassandra. I mean I dreamed of a woman who was partly Lenina Crown and partly Cassandra, you know how these things are in dreams. I fell in love with Lenina at the age of thirteen-fourteen when I first made her acquaintance in the Brave New World and immediately I became a Leninist. Don't laugh, Huxley introduced me to Leninism through this amazing, hot, horny and promiscuous young lady, Lenina Crown. I even named a girlfriend I had after the heroine, she was half English, from her mom, so I started calling her Lenina Crown and created a whole imaginary word around her, so from time to time, during some wild sex sessions, I was telling her 'I'm fucking you Crown,' and it was great fun because although not a Leninist politically yet, I was definitely anti-royalist and hated the king and whatever he represented and everybody who was in favour of him first of all the City's shipowners and other parasites and of course I mostly disliked my royalist relatives and cousins and nieces, two or three years younger than me, silly pruds worthless even for incest which royalists believe is best.... 'Why don't you fuck them?' asked me once a girlfriend of mine, Anna-Maria, a libertine influenced both by the French May and Mao Zedong, 'most royalists carry incest in their precious blue blood, blue like our flag, *sangre azul*, as their like-minded Spaniards say, so why not? just fuck them.' 'Ha,' I told her, 'royalists care only for in-breeding, not for fun, and besides, the ones you're talking about are so sexless.... Imagine, they don't show skin at all, they don't want the red sun to bathe them the same way it baths the rest of us. They even scorn me for reading political magazines with semi-nude women on their covers while they're flipping through magazines full of kings and queens and princesses with their horses, I mean pictures of princesses on their horses and not vice versa which would have been a vice of great interest to watch in our days, as far as Catherine the Great didn't immortalise visually her sexual practises. I'm sure that at night they were fantasising that I'm inbreeding them, many queens and princesses had found themselves in a similar position, missionary or on all fours, I know not.' Anyway. So I dreamed of this astonishing Lenina-Cassandra and in the dream Cassandra, holding an axe in one hand and a burning torch in her other, was running towards the Troikan Horse, wanting to destroy it herself but then her second best half, Lenina, said 'no, this is not enough, this is not the way... we need revolutionary army contingents to destroy the Troikan Whorse and anything connected with it.'

" 'What do you have in mind Lenina?' asked Cassandra... and then Lenina licked her ears so that she could hear the future and french-kissed her and pushed her tongue into her mouth to inflict an appeal, a sex-appeal, so that many would believe her prophecies, and their kissing was so hot that it gave me an erection and talked and what she talked about was transformed into Cassandra's prophecies and her prophecies into reality, right there in front of my eyes: 'and I saw contingents being formed of any strength, beginning with two or three people.... They were arming themselves as best they could with sub-machine guns, revolvers, bombs, knives, molotovs, sticks, rags soaked in kerosene for starting fires, ropes or rope ladders, shovels for building barricades, explosives, barbed wire, nails against police cars and motorcycles, without waiting for help from other sources, from above, from the outside, from nowhere.... The contingents were consisting of people who either lived near each other, or who met frequently and regularly at definite hours and used to arrange matters so as to be able to get together at the most critical moments, when things could take the most unexpected turns. They had worked out beforehand ways and means of joint action, signs so as to find each other easily, previously agreed upon calls or whistles so that comrades recognise one another in a crowd, previously arranged signals in the event of meetings at night. Even without arms, the groups were leading the mass and attacking, whenever a favourable opportunity presented itself, policemen, seizing their arms, rescuing the arrested or injured, when there were only few police about, getting on to the roofs or upper storeys of houses and showering stones, molotovs or pouring boiling water on the troops, procuring all kinds of arms and ammunition, securing premises favourably located for street fighting, for fighting from above, for storing bombs and stones and pouring acids on the police, obtaining plans of prisons, police stations, ministries. Even those who were quite incapable of engaging in street fighting, even the very weak, women, youngsters, old people, were joining in. Among them my old parents, who had come back to life, resurrected, and they were still weak and aged, "we need to take our time and get young again," they said, and they were throwing molotovs, prepared by youngsters and stored in dozens at their balcony. Although Christian orthodox, they had worked hard with protestant spirit and ethics all life long and now the capitalists and the Troikans were robbing them of their savings at gun point; at gun point because that's what the apparatus of state power was created for by the ruling class.

"These people were everywhere: training their fighting forces, spotting the enemy's vulnerable spots. inflicting partial defeats on the enemy rescuing prisoners, procuring arms, obtaining funds for the uprising which had already begun and was escalating with the killing of spies, policemen, gendarmes, troicans, the blowing up of police stations, the liberation of prisoners, the seizure of government funds for the needs of the uprising.

"It was a vivid marvelous dream where the 'Holy Trinity' appeared to me in all its radiance and glory: Erection, Insurrection, Resurrection."

He, the Wanderer, sounded to me more like a witness than like a dreamer, but still, I felt like reminding him of the old song of Savopoulos,

"ta oneira sou mēn ta les giati mia nyhta krya,
borei kai oi Froydystes na rthoun stēn exousia,"
which meant, as I had translated it some years ago for a British friend of mine "never reveal your dreams, because one cold night, even the Freudians may come to power."

He smiled and his smile was like the smile of the sphinx.

"I noticed some third-internationalist notes into your dream," said Vas —whose "V" stood for vendetta or victory, "a" for art and "s" for surrealism— "but of course a few notes do not make a symphony, so despite the fact that we, the surrealists, we were and we are in dissonance play with the Third International, at least towards its ending, I found your dream both interesting and appealing, especially if it is meant to flood reality, wet as it was with blood and erotic fluids. But I tend to open and move into different paths, maybe because 'V' stands for vanguard and my experiences vary from yours.

"You know, if you merge dream with realm and reality, you get drealmity....

"It was when a few thousands of our political opponents thronged outside the parliament in Athens, Tuesday night, the 30th of June I think, to scream out that the country belongs to the European Union; they were waving their stupid Euroflags...

"With a few thousand like-minded comrades we had stormed and penetrated their pro-capitalist gathering, shouting slogans against the EU, for a revolutionary outlet from the crisis that turns the country into a Waste Land. It was such a pleasure to demoralise them, such a joy to see the panic and the fear and the anger in their eyes and faces, as they were perceiving our initiative as the beginning of the civil war; maybe because our slogans had nice tempo and nice rhyme, like:

'*Mesa stēn Europē, einai o echthros*
tēn lysē tha dosei o enoplos laos.'[*]
'*EAM, ELAS, OPLA, DSE.*
autos einai o dromos, gia na nikas lae.'[**]
'*O Meligalas ētan ē archē,*

[*] See pages 96-97

tha anoixoume pēgadi akoma poio vathy.'***

"Most of the people in our blocs were around eighteen to twenty-five-years-young and tears came into my eyes when I thought that these young boys and girls were trying to find again the broken thread of Ariadne, find their way in the labyrinth of our dark

---

*The enemy is within EU, the solution will be given by the armed people.

**EAM, ELAS, OPLA, DSE. this is the way for the victory.

***Melēgalas was just the beginning, we're going to dig a much deeper well.

The National Liberation Front-EAM was the main movement of the Greek Resistance during the Axis occupation of Greece during World War II. Its main driving force was the Communist Party of Greece (KKE), but its membership throughout the Occupation period included several other leftist and republican groups. EAM became the first true mass social movement in modern Greek history, and even established its own government, the Political Committee of National Liberation, in the areas it had liberated in spring 1944.

The Greek People's Liberation Army or ELAS Ellēnikós Laïkós Apeleftherotikós Stratós (ΕΛΑΣ) was the military arm of the left-wing National Liberation Front (EAM) during the period of the Greek Resistance until February 1945.

The Organization for the Protection of the People's Struggle-OPLA, an acronym meaning "weapons" in Greek, was a special division of the Communist Party of Greece (KKE) during the Axis Occupation of Greece in World War II. It was part of the broader National Liberation Front (EAM), but was not controlled by it, but directly by the Politburo of the KKE. It can be described as a paramilitary security force. It operated in the cities, and its purpose was the "self-defense" of the members of the National Liberation Front and its affiliated organizations from the German occupation authorities and the collaborationist government and its organs, the Police, the Gendarmerie (especially its notorious branch named as Special Security, expertised at the anti-communistic struggle) and the Security Battalions. It proved to be very successful in assassinating commanders of the Security Battalions and other armed governmental forces. However, it also became involved in political assassinations of political opponents of the then-Stalinist KKE on both ends of the political spectrum, such as Trotskyites and Archeio-Marxists. As a result,

times, kill the capitalist Minotaur and stop the sacrifices made year after year as part of reparations to the international monetary bandits.

"The yesmen were relieved when the antiriot-police pushed violently our bloc away, using shields and clubs but no tear-gas,

---

the activities of the OPLA are a subject of heated debate even today.

The Battle of Meligalas: After the Germans left southern Greece terminating the occupation of Kalamata and surrounding Messēnia area, the town became the site of a battle between the Greek Resistance forces of EAM-ELAS commanded by Arēs Velouchiotēs and the Security Battalions that had been stationed in the town during German occupation.The Security Battalions were forces set up by the collaborationist Prime Minister Ioannēs Rallēs, with the approval of the German authorities, to aid in the control of the Greek people. Under the terms of the Caserta agreement, signed by the British, the Greek Government in Exile, and Greek resistance leaders, 'The Security Battalions are considered as instruments of the enemy. Unless they surrender according to orders issued by the GOC [General Officer Commanding] they will be treated as enemy formations'. In September of 1944, following the evacuation of German forces from Messēnia in the Peloponnese, ELAS disarmed the majority of collaborationist forces in the Messēnian capital Kalamata. Some Battalionists, however, broke out of Kalamata and retreated to the town of Meligalas. According to one eye-witness, on the way they killed 30 inhabitants of the village of Aprochomo, as well as four ELAS operatives who were fixing the village's telephone system. ELAS arrived in Meligalas on 11 September. The Battalionists refused to surrender. On 14 September the Battalionists executed all hostages they held.[5][6] After a three-day siege of the town beginning on 11 September, Meligalas fell to the hands of the Resistance forces. Following the fall of the town, some Battalionists were kept as prisoners while a disputed number were executed for treason and collaboration with the occupation forces. The bodies of those who had fallen in the battle, including some ELAS fighters, and those executed were thrown into a well shaft known as "pēgada". Apart from the executions, some prisoners were lynched by angry inhabitants of Meligalas and other villagers round about, who had lost family members to the Battalionists.

because the tender lungs and larynxes of the nearby pro-EU conformists were accustomed only to expensive tobacco and spirits. Of course in an era with no spirit, a few among them were coming from lower strata, men and women with no spirit, from this particular species that obliged Einstein to say 'only two things are infinite, the universe and human stupidity, and I'm not sure about the former.' But this is another story, so after we were pushed away, I was in high spirits for I was sensing that the 'no' vote was going to gather a vast working class majority, a 'no' to a new bailout from the European creditors of the ruling class. a 'no' to the hellish regime of Troika, but this is too, another story, and forgive me for being carried away. So, I wanted to say that I was in high surrealist spirits, because that's how I always am, and as soon as I saw a young beautiful lady covered with an EU flag and wearing a mini-skirt, I invited her to Milton Athens Hotel, where I promised her a troika and Milton's lost paradise, a unique sexperience under the stars, full of colourful sexplosions, sparkling stars, glowing planets and a delicious cock. We walked until there and on the way I told her that I had made the acquaintance of the notorious priestess Delphy Dickulescu who delivered oracles about global economic prospects in a frenzied state induced by multiple orgasms and the swallowing of large quantities of semen."

Milton's Athens Hotel Paradise Lost.... Paradise's Lost Drealmity.... Dickulescu on all fours... all nude.... Zórba the brut had impaled her with his erotic organ, anus to mouth, but this was an illusion, its was not him who had impaled her, he had of course introduced her to the Greek way but afterwards it was her, Dickulescu, who had sucked it on her own, eagerly and feverishly, with her anus, through her rectum, to her freudian sigmoid colon, up to her throat and mouth, where she was licking and sucking the upper part of it, as the rest of it, its top, not less than eleven inches, was fucking vigorously the young Athenian's cunt; she was on her back, with her thighs spread and at the same time she was letting Delphy Dickulescu lick her fucking cunt and she was doing it fucking good although her throat and mouth were full of Zórba's cock.... But although she was impaled all the way ass to mouth, it didn't hurt her at all, on the contrary she loved it, she was having multiple orgasms throughout her body, so Dickulescu got addicted to his dick.

"She got addicted to my dick for she is adickted," scorned Zórba.

"You are a sexist Zórba," I told him.

"Oh, yes, *I am* the sexiest," he replied.

It was more than obvious that the young Athenian lady was having sex, was getting fucked and licked both by incubus and succubus at the same time and she was moaning and screaming "yes, yes, yes," and she was doing so out of sextreme pleasure and at no cost at all, for which she was considered very lucky because... Because at the same time in the nearby ex-National Garden, the ex-King's Garden and nowadays Carnal Garden, the MPs —many satirical cartoonists sketched them as *monetary prostitutes*— who had voted "yes" to the memorandums, were being executed by a special squad of the red-guards, carrying the name *Ten Days That Shook the World*, after they were convicted of class-war crimes, of thousands of murders.... For the murder of patients who died on their way from hospital to hospital; for the 6 uninsured Kidney patients who died in Thessaloniki and the others who wander like ghosts from hospital to hospital for dialysis; for the closure of hundreds of ICU beds* or for murders like that of Antonēs Perrēs, an unemployed musician at the age of 60. He left a note saying: '*I have been taking care of my 90-year-old mother for 20 years now. Three-four years ago she was diagnosed with Alzheimer's and recently she had schizophrenic fits and other health*

---

*http://www.keeptalkinggreece.com/2015/06/08/thessaloniki-6-uninsured-kidney-patients-have-died-18-wandering-like-ghosts-from-hospital-to-hospital-for-dialysis/

problems. Nursing homes don't accept patients who are such a burden. The problem is that I was not prepared when the economic crisis hit, and I do not have enough money in my account. My credit card is overdrawn, we do not have enough food to feed ourselves. I live a drama with no end. Lately, I am also suffering from health problems. I see no solution. Does anybody else have a solution for me? World leaders, you who have brought this financial crisis, you all need hanging!'

Mother and son held hands and jumped off a balcony in central Athens. Both died. Victims in a Troikan tragedy far exceeding the ancient ones. Died doomed to an earthly hell by the bandits of the offshore heavens, who forced them to pay taxes they couldn't afford.

These are the facts. The rest are leaks; wikileaks maybe, dreamleaks, nightmareleaks who knows, like that the lower officers of the Troika and the pro-Troika regime that were not executed were forced to engrave on the entire north wall of Athens Milton Hotel, from top to bottom the following verses from *Samson Agonistes* in commemoration of their victims.

Within doors, or without, still as a fool,
In power of others, never in my own;
Scarce half I seem to live, dead more then half.
O dark, dark, dark, amid the blaze of noon,

Irrecoverably dark, total Eclipse
Without all hope of day.

The Trinity kept silence. Then its parts raised their glasses in the memory of all Troika's victims, without clinking them, and gulped the remaining rakomelo.

"Tragedies like these, like this man's and his mother's bring to my mind King Lear,...
When we are born, we cry that we are come
To this great stage of fools: this a good block;
It were a delicate stratagem, to shoe
A troop of horse with felt: I'll put 't in proof;
And when I have stol'n upon these sons-in-law,
Then, kill, kill, kill, kill, kill, kill!

"It's from the 4th act, I think.," said the Wanderer, after he finished reciting by heart.

"Fourth?" asked rhetorically Vas, whose "s" stood for surrealism; "fourth like in the Fourth International?"

"I'm not the best person to answer this question of yours," said the Wanderer, "although I'm suspecting where you want to lead the conversation."

For we all knew, that at the bottom of his heart the Wanderer was committed to the Fourth-dimensionalists, a movement embracing politics and arts and science and philosophy —the philosophy of Walter Benjamin and Ernst Bloch mixed with the wild futurist art of Velimir Khlebnikov— aiming at the revolutionary rehabilitation of all the doomed generations in a new Eden.

Rumours had him to be extremely sui-generis; rumours circulating in occupied spaces, alternative bars and clubs, slipping form tongues into ears, floating in brains tranquilised by gin, vodka or sangria; rumours saying that as Don Quixote de La Mancha lost his sanity reading many chivalric romances and decided to set out to revive chivalry, undo wrongs, and bring justice to the world so did the Wanderer reading a two-volume anti-novel *Kaleidoscopio*, republished later in one volume under the title *Wanderotica* and decided to revive the world revolting against the state, nature and time. However what he said showed us that he had an extremely strong sense of realism.

"There is no doubt that Alexēs Noske government is a stinking corpse, that we need a revolutionary outlet from the crisis and a re-organisation of society on a socialist basis in Greece, Europe, the whole world." He made a pause for a sip of rakomelo, and continued.

"So in our case King Lear fits perfectly with what the General used to say: '*A revolution is certainly the most authoritarian thing there is; it is an act whereby one part of the population imposes its will upon the other by means of rifles, bayonets and cannon —all of which are highly authoritarian means. And the victorious party must maintain its rule by means of the terror*

103

which its arms inspire in the reactionaries.'

"At least that's how I read King Lear right now. The rest, the declarations of the Fourth-dimensionalists will follow.... The Fourth International has the same relation with the Fourth-dimensionalists in the revolutionary process that the chemotrophs have with the human conscience.

Conscience. Memory. Shakespeare. Shakespeare brings to my mind a scene. In the house of Dr David B. — the *Comrade*. Us sitting in his office on the second floor of his house. On a long narrow desk beneath a window overlooking the garden. In front of us a bound version of my thesis. In the groundfloor his twin daughters were sleeping in their pram. Mine was miles and miles away. David B. loves Shakespeare.

Friday evening, May 23, 2014. The Prime Minister Antonēs Samaras had arranged to give a speech in front of Parliament on Syntagma Square. I had managed to sneak my way into Grande Bretagne's Open-Air Bar, crammed mainly with journalists, but businesmen, politicians and other bandits of the kind as well. For the occasion I was dressed as agent-provocateur, like one of them, casual but smart: a pair of tabac loafers, quality pair of jeans, a stylish midnight-blue jacket, a pastel-cyan shirt and a hand made, by Faba, light-blue and bright-red bow tie with the *25 October 1917 year* pattern on it. I have a couple of hand made light-blue, bright-red bow ties with communist patterns on them. I always liked light-blue. Maybe because even since I was in the pram, my parents and my grandmother were taking me long walks by the sea. Many many years later I came across a *Budenovka*, a Red Army hat named after Se-myon Budyonny but designed by the painter Viktor Mikhaylovich Vasnetsov; it was of light-blue colour with a red star on it. And, which is of great importance, I read an inter-view of the great communist poet Yannis Ritsos, where I saw a fascinating reference to this particular colour. *Oppression, slavery, the desires that remain unfulfilled, all these are an everyday execution, a death. And for as long as death exists, there will be a resistance to death. Po-litical poetry (or at least my political poetry) is a struggle against this form of death, a battle until we reach the 'classless light-blue.* All these Troikans and pro-Troikans represent this form of death Ritsos was speaking about. Syntagma was almost empty. I sat next to a pro-Troikan pig in a black custom suit, wearing a tiny tin New Democracy lapel pin and smoking a heavy stinking cigar. I made a prearranged missed call to Zórba, he called me back and I started deploying my provo-cation, just for the sake of fun.

"Where are you?" he asked me, although he knew very well where I was and why.

"On the 8th floor of Grande Bretagne," I replied loudly.

"What the hell are you doing there?"

"Oh I just wanted to see how New Democracy looks like from an on top fucking position."

"Hahaha, and what is her leader talking about?"

"Oh, he urges supporters to vote in favour of political stabbinglity..."

"What? I can't hear you well, say that again..."

"He urges supporters to vote in favour of political stabbinglity.... No, not stability, stabbing-lity...

"Anyway, we'll talk later..."

The waitress asked what I would like to drink.

"A Zombie cocktail," I said, "It matches the gathering of the zombies down there."

She smiled.

"Can you tell us what shall we do with our huge debt without the contribution of New Democracy to the outcome of the crisis?" the suited pig asked me, obviously irritated by my sayings on the cell and to the waitress.

"Huge debt?" I asked innocently.

"Yes, our debt is huge, it amounts..."

I didn't let him to finish. "For sure the Greek debt is huge," I said, "so why don't we stick it in Mistress Troika's asshole?"

It got nervous. The suited pig I mean. It changed position on its chair. It puffed out a cloud of stinking smoke from its cigar. The place smelled like a pigsty. The pig's cell rang. The suited pig raised it to its ear: "Oink, oink."

The waitress brought my Zombie. I took a sip. "It's great," I said.

"We prepare the best signature cocktails in town," she said.

I smiled at her; "then please prepare a dozen of Cocktails Molotov to treat my friends down there," I said. She laughed.

I was not surprised by her laughter. Ages ago I was close friends with a young lady, Chrysa, working as a receptionist in a five-star hotel in Athens. She had unveiled to me the appalling working conditions behind the luxury glamourous facade of the many-stars hotels. In our days, under Misstress Troika's directives and the capitalists' free will the employees of Greece's so called "heavy industry," tourism, remind slaves rowing in a galley; for all these all-inclusive 5star hotels, all these floating cities that cruise around the Greek islands are galleys. Candlelight dinners, sparkling moonlit skies above the waterline, and below the waterline the galley slaves in

Times of Troika seem to sing, as they row,
Ronin's anarchic song....

Siamo la ciurma anemica	*We're the doomed anaemic crew*
d'una galera infame	*on an appalling galley*
su cui ratta la morte	*and over it hovers the death*
miete per lenta fame.	*harvesting us with hunger*
Mai orizzonti limpidi	*At dawn we never see*
schiude la nostra aurora,	*the clear blue horizons*
e sulla tolda squallida	*on our sloppy dirty deck*
urla la scolta ognora.	*the guards are always yelling*
I nostri dì si involano	*Day after day they rob our lives*
fra fetide carene,	*on squalid. filthy decks*
siam magri, smunti, schiavi	*we are the frail and boney slaves*
stretti in ferro catene.	*tied up with heavy chains*
Sorge sul mar la luna,	*Above the sea rises the moon*
ruotan le stelle in cielo,	*and in the sky the stars*
ma sulle nostre luci	*but over our sailing lights*
steso è un funereo velo.	*a mourning veil is falling*
Torme di schiavi adusti	*Skeletal rows of skinny slaves*
chini a gemer sul remo	*row and moan and suffer*
spezziam queste catene	*your heavy chain if you don't break*
o chini a remar morremo!	*death will meet you rowing*
Cos'è gementi schiavi	*You galley slave, doomed to toil,*
questo remar remare?	*will you row for ever?*
Meglio morir tra i flutti	*You better drown in the waves*
sul biancheggiar del mare.	*deep in the roaring sea*

Remiam finché la nave	*We will row and row and row*
si schianti sui frangenti,	*full speed against the rocks*
alte le rossonere	*Raise our flag, the red-and-black,*
fra il sibilar dei venti!	*high in the whistling winds*
E sia pietosa coltrice	*And if for us the foaming wave*
l'onda spumosa e ria,	*our deadly will be shroud*
ma sorga un dì sui martiri	*above our martyrs will arise*
il sol dell'anarchia.	*a bright anarchic sun*
Su schiavi all'armi all'armi!	*All'armi all'armi, slaves arise*
L'onda gorgoglia e sale,	*waves swell and roar*
tuoni baleni e fulmini	*thunders and storms and lightnings*
sul galeon fatale.	*blow the fatal galley*
Su schiavi all'armi all'armi!	*All'armi all'armi, slaves arise*
Pugnam col braccio forte!	*ruthless and bravehearted*
Giuriam giuriam giustizia!	*for justice sake pledge yourselves*
O libertà o morte	*to fight for death or freedom*[*]

The unholy Trinity, particularly the Wanderer, loves this Italian song; its rowing rhythm, its rowing rhyme and its windy music. He associates it with, what he calls, "its dialectical negation," *Ballade von den Seeräubern* — Ballad of the Pirates-Adventurists[**]: *Von Branntwein toll und Finsternissen — Crazed from whisky and gloom....* Refrain: *O Himmel, strahlender Azur — Oh heaven, gleaming bleu-azure...*

---

[*]Free translation by V. Ludens & Ekaterina.
[**]Bertolt Brecht and Hanns Eisler.

Troikan Capital's galleys everywhere. For galleys are the by-the-sea all inclusive many-star hotels; galleys are the floating-city cruisers; galley is the Halyvourgikē,* galley is the Pireaus dock run by COSCO. "Cosco's —China Ocean Shipping Company— Pireaus facilities are notorious for their sweatshop working conditions with accidents being a common occurrence. In 2011, a worker interviewed by US radio broadcaster NPR explained, 'Workers were told by supervisors to urinate into the sea, rather than taking toilet breaks. Those operating straddle carriers (vehicles that stack containers) had to take cups up into their cabs to urinate into, and,' he says 'they were not given breaks, either, despite the clear dangers of operating at such a height for so long.' "

Chrysa's fiancé, Thomas, was an American from Cornell living in Athens, a communist, and a painter. I have somewhere a couple of photos of both of them, when, back in time, they had payed a visit to me for my name day. In one of the pictures Thomas is talking with my dad; about Cornell, Communism and Courbet, I suppose; for my father had liked Cornell, he was a Communist, he was painting seaskapes using pastels and he adored Courbet and Aivazovsky.

---

*"The workers of the steel-works over the years worked in the furnace making their living, having work accidents daily, a dead colleague last year, getting wages of hunger and with terrorism exercised by the bosses, while the capitalists were acquiring enormous profits." From a Solidarity Campaign with the struggle of the striking workers of Steelworks, 10/12/2011 2:36 μμ.
**https://www.wsws.org/en/articles/2014/07/23/dock-j23.html

Chapter 7

Saturday evening, December 6, 2014. 6 o'clock. At/o Therapeutērio, 3d floor, room 2. My father is lying on his bed, half sleeping, seriously ill from pneumonia. I talk to him. He welcomes me. I call my mom at home and pass him the receiver to talk to her. His voice is weak. In a bag I brought all the things the hospital does not provide. *"If half my heart is here, doctor"*, by my father's side, *"the other half is in"* downtown Athens where demonstrators gather to commemorate the 6th anniversary of the murder of the fifteen-years-young Alexēs Grēgoropoulos by a policeman, on the Saturday evening, December 6, 2008, it was Saturday again, and to express solidarity with anarchist Nikos Romanos who is on hunger-strike since November the 10th.

Clashes, tear-gas, they bring my father's dinner, he can't manage to eat by himself, I have to feed him on my own, water cannons, stun grenades, petrol bombs, stones, he is chewing weakly and slowly, it takes ages for him to swallow with his eyes shut, the nurses are very willing to help but still they are not enough they are overexploited and poorly payed, if at all, 8.000 policemen were deployed in downtown Athens but also many plain-clothes police officers. my father feels too tired to finnish his dinner, fires in garbage bins, barricades, excessive use of tear-gas in Exarcheia area that makes it impossible to breath, protesters hurling molotov cocktail bombs to policemen from roof-tops and bal-conies, *it's raining bombs! Hallelujah! - it's raining bombs! Amen!* 296 people detained, 43 arrested, 12 policemen injured and unknown number of protesters, the night-shift nurse helps me to give him his medicine, all of them are very fond of me, some policemen looked as if they were protesters, among them plain-clothed policewomen, all of them agents-provocateurs, they cannot fool the most experienced ones, they are very recog-nisable, they have the aura and the smell of the "pig" and their duty is to safeguard the system that doesn't allow my dad a proper hospitalisation, the State pays only a part for his treatment in this bearably good private clinic which costs us almost 100€ per day, while his pension is 1000€ per month. If he is not cured in a fortnight, the State of the bankers and the capitalists will stop paying anything, so we'll have to transfer him to public hospital under appalling conditions for we cannot afford the fees for his treatment at this private hospital. The nurse puts on my father the oxygen mask. I give him a goodnight kiss. Back at home. My only dearest asks me how things are. "All the same," I reply. We also have to put my mother to bed, move her from her armchair to her bed.

I wake early next morning, it's Sunday, and before I leave for the hospital, I surf the net for last night's events, news from around the world. "*And, every morning, doctor, every morning at sunrise my heart is shot in Greece*" wrote Nâzım Hikmet Ran in 1948. Sixty-six years later serfing the net I came across a letter from Turkey, about last night's events.

Solidarity from DIP(Turkey): Meet the demands of Nikos Romanos and his comrades!

Dear Comrades of the EEK,

We are sending this message to all the honourable people of Greece, to all our sisters and brothers on the other side of the Aegean, who are struggling for the rights and life of Nikos Romanos and his comrades. The hunger strike started by Nikos Romanos, in his state of captivity in the hands of the Greek state, on November 10th has evidently reached a stage where his life is in jeopardy. Three of his comrades have followed suit and it is only a matter of time before they face the same mortal threat. All this is due to the vengeful attitude of the Greek state towards the dignified attitude of Nikos and his comrades, in particular regarding the refusal to take part in the comedy to be staged by the president of the republic, Karolos Papoulias, and the flagrant violation of what are clearly their rights with respect to their education.

We write from a country where the F-type prisons are even worse forms of cruel treatment and denial of the prisoners' humanity than the C-type prisons of Greece. We write from a country where successive hunger strikes and death fasts in the face of the violation of even the most basic rights of prisoners have taken a heavy toll again and again. We write from a country where, in the year 2000, the state, acting under a self-styled social-democratic prime minister and his equally social-democratic minister of justice, attacked prisoners on hunger strike in many different prisons and murdered 28 prisoners, in an operation venomously called "Return to Life". So we know what we are talking about. All the crimes of the authorities in each and every one of these incidents were later exposed in the eyes of the public without a shred of doubt. And the names of those people in power on those occasions have been stained forever. The Greek authorities of the present day will no doubt suffer the same fate. Acting to grant the demands of Nikos Romanos and his comrades is the only way they can save their honour form being dirtied for generations to come.

We write from the country of Berkin Elvan, shot on the head with a tear-gas canister by the police of Tayyip Erdogan in cold blood during the Gezi events when he was 14. Berkin lost his life around a year later, when he was 15. We declared that Berkin and Alexēs Grēgoropoulos were "brothers forever"! Nikos Romanos is the comrade of Alexēs who witnessed his murder by the Greek police. So we extend to him and his comrades our heartfelt solidarity and support in his struggle!

Meet the demands of Nikos Romanos and his comrades! End the hideous system of C-type prisons! Fraternity among the peoples of Greece and Turkey!

Unite and fight the repressive Greek and Turkish states! For the Socialist Federation of the Balkans!

Revolutionary Workers' Party (DIP) Turkey

6 December 2014

"*And every night doctor, when the prisoners are asleep and the infirmary is deserted, my heart stops at a run-down old house in Istanbul,*" wrote Nâzım Hikmet and last March our heart had stopped at a run-down old house in Istanbul, the house of Berkin Elvan, a 15-year-old Turkish boy who was hit on the head by a tear-gas canister fired by a police officer in Istanbul on his way to buy bread for his family during the June 2013 anti-government protests in Turkey. He died on March 11, 2014, after a 269-day coma. There was a rally for him in Exarcheia, and the Wanderer, whenever passed from the Alexēs Grēgoropoulos' memorial in Athens, could see a graffiti in memory of Berkin Elvan: *For the brothers that left us early.*

This was last March. Now it's December. He stays by his father's side in the hospital. His father sleeps most of the time. Once upon a time he was young and strong, on his wings the Wanderer started his wandering because his dad was the Pēgasos and they flew together all over the Earth. From time to time he wakes. They talk. About the elections to come. Then he falls asleep again; his ill father. Six years ago, same date, same day, same time, the Wanderer with his daughter had taken to the streets. He closes his eyes and remembers, he lives again the events...

...We are a lot and we're angry, enraged, we carry our flags and our banners, police helicopters are circling over us on the sky, is the sky blue or cloudy? I can't recall, we gather outside the Archaeological Museum next to the Polytechnic, we start marching towards GADA we turn right to Alexandras Avenue I grew up there I have walked it up and down thousands times day and night summer and spring winter and autumn cause I am a wanderer cause I am The Wanderer we are thousands teens young ones middle-aged and aged we are a dark enraged wave a tsunami a black and red storm Alexandras Avenue lightens and thunders and roars and she is so beautiful all around us attacks against banks and luxury car shops and as

soon as the coppigs appear they get stoned
slogans and banners and shouts and curses
we put on our gas-masks cause we know
what's going to follow we call at home to say
that we are OK up to now stored in our mo-
biles one touch dial numbers of lawyers we
move ahead arm in arm with my daughter
it's raining stones Hallelujah it's raining stones
Amen white clouds of tear-gas down on the
streets clear blue skies high up black curly
smoke all around us and among us many
brave young girls and women flashes of
memory and flash grenades the Calton
weavers' riots and the Weather girls we feel
stormy weather moving in about to begin
about to begin with the thunder don't you
lose your head rip off the roof and storm
ahead storm storm storm and burn banks
torched the antiriot-police attacks again and
again with tear-gas part of the demonstration
counter-attacks with molotov cocktails some
massive blocs turn left and get into the side
streets they move upwards parallel to Alexandras towards the GADA people out in the
balconies at some point we meet my wife
Faba Crimson at the corner of Alexandras
and Gyzē Street a bank is set aflame even
more black thick smoke from the burning
banks and the luxury shops even more white
clouds from the tear-gases all around motor-
cycled squads full of enraged policemen....

From last night until next Thursday night, in a period of 6 days the State will use 4 tons of tear-gases in its attempt to smash the insurrection that shocked the world. On January 2, 2009 Subcomandante Marcos of EZLN Zapatistas saluted the December Rebellion of 2008 in the following words.

"We, the smallest, from this corner of the world, salute you.

Accept our respect and our admiration, for what you think and do.

From far away, we are learning from you. We thank you.

Subcomandante Marcos"

Next day, Monday the 8th, in the evening, amidst fiery clashes with the antiriot-police, mass rallies, repeated attacks against police stations with stones and molotovs, massive use of tear-gas, burning barricades, I met in Omonoia Square, where we had retreated with my wife Faba, an English comrade, who for a moment looked to us lost and disorientated — stanger in a strange city as he proved to be, although he seemed rather experienced in setting buildings ablaze. As soon as I realised that something was wrong with his gas-mask, I rushed to help him get away from the Square that was under heavy attack from all sides by the coppigs. The organised blocs of the Communist Party were retreating

orderly, other well organised blocs of the ultra-left kept resisting to the attack, orderly
too, but there were also lots of small groups
of demonstrators, that had gone completely
scattered and disorganised. So, I saw him, he
needed help and rushed to him and got him
out of Omonoia quite easily because I knew
well where to run, where to go, where to
stop. When we felt safe, he thanked me. He
was twenty-three, born in Soho, London. We
shaked hands and introduced ourselves; I
gave him my nom de guerre because first of
all we had war and because it's rather unwise
to tell to a stranger your real name under
such conditions. "Glad to meet you," I said.
"I'm Vas the Wanderer." He looked straight
into my eyes. "Thank you for helping. I'm
William Blake, poet, painter, and printmaker."

We moved, the three of us, upwards to
Panepistēmiou rushing through an earthly
flaming Paradise of tons of tear-gas, burning
flames, light-sound grenades, hurling stones,
exploding molotovs, rattling helicopters hovering over our heads, cyclopean beams of
light directed onto us and all around the
constant barooming, blasting, flashing, lighting,
thundering of all sorts of police grenades
and molotovs; a flaming Paradise that brought
History at the verge of orgasming and the
panic-stridden ruling class of Greece at the
verge of declaring a 'state of siege.'

"Look, look all around us," says Blake, not out of the blue but out of the black-red fumes and skies and flames, turning around himself, possessed by the spirit of the insurrection; he puts back his black-hood, his gas-mask and starts shouting and the wind takes his words and mixes them up with the slogans of the December insurrection: "*I wrap my turban of thick clouds around my lab'ring head*.... Autes oi meres einai tou Alexē, emeis tha poume tēn teleutaia lexē... **sssshblamm... baroom**.... *And fold the sheety waters as a mantle round my limbs.... Yet the red sun and moon....* To aima kylaei ekdikēsē zētaei.... *And all the overflowing stars rain down prolific pains.... I bring forth from my teeming bosom myriads of flames....* 15hronos nekros to misos megalonei, batsoi gourounia dolofonoi.... *And thou dost stamp them with a signet, then they roam abroad...* **voomp voomp voomp**.... *And leave me void as death....* Sto dromo, sto dromo na spasoume ton tromo.... *Ah! I am drown'd in shady woe, and visionary joy.... Awake the thunders of the deep.... And let us laugh at war...* **whaam**.... Prosohē! Prosoxē! Dolofonoi me stolē... **p-taff p-taff p-taff**.... *Despising toil and care.... Because the days and nights of joy, in lucky hours renew.... Shadows of men in fleeting bands upon the winds...* Se kathe gonia yparhei astynomia ē hounta den teleiose to evdomēnta-tria.... *Divide the heavens of Europe....* Stis trapezes lefta stēn neolaia sfaires - ērthe ē ora gia tis dikes mas meres.... *And in the vineyards of red France appear'd the light of his fury.... The sun glow'd fiery red! The furious terrors flew around! On golden chariots raging, with red wheels dropping with blood....* Ta ypourgeia laine tous mathētes alētes alētes einai ta MAT kai oi asfalites... sssshblamm.... *The Lions lash their wrathful tails! The Tigers couch upon the prey & suck the ruddy tide....* Paidia kathiste kato, einai kathara, mesa stē voulē einai ta skata.... *And Enitharmon groans & cries in anguish and dismay...* Dolofonoi einai oi astynomikoi, to heri tous oplizei autē ē politikē.... *Then Los arose his head he reard in snaky thunders clad...* Oute fasismos oute dēmokratia, kato o kratismos zēto ē anarhia.... *And with a cry that shook all nature to the utmost pole.... Call'd all his sons to the strife of blood."*

As soon as we returned home we rushed under the shower to wash away the toxic dust from our bodies and our hair. When I first met Faba I was impressed by her hair.

---

*The slogans translated orderly:

These days belong to Alexis we'll say the last word.

The blood is running it's asking for revenge.

Taking to the streets the fear shall we break.

Warning Warning Murderers in uniform.

At every corner there is police the junta didn't fell in 73

Money for the banks bullets for the youths time has come for our own days.

The ministries are calling the pupils "scums," scums are the policemen and the plain-clothed cops.

Let us sit down, it is clean, only the Parliament is full of shit.

Murderers are the cops and their hand is armed by this policy. Neither fascism, nor democracy, down with statism, long live anarchy.

She had the most beautiful red hair I had ever seen in a woman; and a few imperceptible wrinkles around her eyes cherished her face with that unique expression of *genuine Russian irony* I always enjoyed. Faba! Her red, red hair, the greenhood of her ungreen eyes and her *One Faba's Show Eau Natural*! History, even personal history, has its own weird twists. So, during these flaming December days and nights, Faba's unique expression of genuine Russian irony was reminding me the Greed for Surplus-Labour; not only because this greed is one of the many reasons that triggered the insurrection, but because it is exactly in that particular chapter of the *Capital*, that Marx, Marx the literary artist, makes a reference to this Russian feature that made Faba so appealing to me.

The Wanderer's father is sleeping.... It is late.... And the Wanderer keeps recalling and reliving these edenic days and nights craving to charge and recharge himself and the gloomy room and his sick father with this life-force, this libidinal energy that over-flooded these December nights and days; believing strongly that the December uprising was expressing Eros and whoever opposed the December uprising expressed Thanatos. Thanatos is the absolute and ultimate no-future and the State-bullet that murdered the young boy was the absolute, ultimate and clear-cut declaration, on the part of the State, that there is no future for the young people under capitalism; less than two years later, on April 24, 2010 the Head of the Committee for Managing the Common Affairs of the Whole Bourgeoisie made an appeal to the EU and the International Monetary Fund; the Aegean sea dazzled bright-blue, inviting and highly erotic in the background but, for whoever was not *blind in mind and ears as well as in his/her eyes,* the appeal was a declaration of a ruthless class-war against the people, a declaration that there was no future for anybody; it was an appeal for the death penalty — Capital punishment, for the great majority of the Greek people.

Remember, remember the 6th of December youths youths youths school kids wandering in groups in the centre and the neighbourhoods seeking for the police to attack with stones detached from the broken pavements broken traffic lights bus stops second generation immigrants university students young workers unemployed attacking cops police departments torching banks destroying vandalising ministries occupying universities town halls public buildings insurgent proletarians We are an image from the future occupation of GSEE building General Assembly of Insurgent Workers and youths youths youths again constant

*Sophocles, *Oedipus the King*, l. 370

fights between teenagers and the antiriot-police molotov cocktails against coppigs and special guards remember, remember the 6th of December...

"Tear-gas is useless, where are the water cannons?" asked loudly an American tourist? journalist? businessman? He was standing in front of Grande Bretagne Hotel in Syntagma Square. I was chatting with a couple of very sympathetic New Zealanders what was all this about, explaining to them why all this rage and hatred had been concentrated in the hearts and minds of all these young boys and girls that all around us were getting ready for one more battle. They were breaking pieces of marble and carrying bags with molotov cocktails. The American belonged obviously to this particular species the export of which should be severely restricted in Europe by U.S. law because its presence abroad defames the country much more than the burning of a hundred American flags. His aura was a living proof of Einstein's theory on the infiniteness of human stupidity. I ignored him at first and the New Zealanders eyed him with pity but he went on bubbling something like: "tear-gass doesn't work. where are the water cannons?" It was more than obvious that he was asking for real cannons to be used, so I just told him "if they do so, we'll start using defensive grenades against them; elementary, my dear Watson." The New Zealanders laughed and the-future-to-be Donald Trump supporter disappeared for a moment in the hotel. But he reappeared and he looked a bit furious this time. "All these thugs with the molotovs are muslim terrorists," he shouted in our direction. I smiled and moved towards him. "Good luck and take care," the old lady from New Zealand told me and left for somewhere. 'Good,' I thought, 'I may be Zórba the ræbelaisian but I respect all kind of old ladies and I wouldn't have liked at all her to listen to what I had in mind to tell him.' "Hey," I shouted to him, loud enough to be heard by all the rest young and middle-aged tourists around the entrance of the hotel; "have you seen a lot of muslim terrorists with nice smooth thighs and waxed cunts, almost saying *'come on baby, light my fire, try to set the night on fire?'* " I heard a couple of giggles and saw the the-future-to-be Donald Trump fanatic turning his back and disappearing once more; this time for good.

All these things happened six years ago. It's dark outside now. Zórba is expecting the nurse that will stay by his father overnight. "*And every night doctor, when the prisoners are asleep and the infirmary is deserted, my heart stops*" at my mother's house. She looks like

125

she has come out of Beckett's *Malone Dies* novel; for she thinks and speaks this way: "*I shall soon be quite dead at last in spite of all. Perhaps next month. Then it will be the month of April or of May. For the year is still young, a thousand little signs tell me so. Perhaps I am wrong, perhaps I shall survive the Easter and even the Pentecost. Indeed I would not put it past me to pant on to the Summer, not to speak of the Saint Demetrius of Thessaloniki. But I do not think so, I do not think I am wrong in saying that these rejoicings will take place in my absence, this year.*"

She was not wrong this time. She passed away on September the 5th, eight months after her husband. He had passed away on January the 5th.

And right then, in a split attosecond [10^{-18}]
the eight —8— fall asleep

∞

and turned into infinity

And what Michelangelo's Lost St. John, the Story of a Discovery, has to do with all these? With what precedes and what follows?

'Nothing is irrelevant in the eternal dusk of a surrealist mind... ' thought the unholy Trinity. 'If I let this train of thought unleashed it will derail, detonate, explode...'

Chapter 8

Four dark-dressed figures had marched slowly behind his father's coffin. Him — the Wanderer, his wife Faba Crimson Sunshine — his only dearest, his daughter and companion in the rallies and his daughter's husband. Just the four of them. No suits, no formal dresses, nothing of the sort, just plain black clothes, some of them used in demonstrations. It was January the 7th and it was freezing cold as they climbed all the way up among the blazing white marble stones. His father was buried under a cypress. When the coffin was lowered into the grave they all tossed a few flowers into the grave, threw a little dirt, then the gravediggers filled the grave with dirt as they watched; the soil was evened off at the top; they stayed over it speechless for a while and then they left.

They went back to his mother's house to keep her company.

About a month later, maybe a bit more, they placed a plain white marble tombstone, *a long-lasting sign of deathless remembrance;** engraved on it the date of his death and his name: ΔΗΜΟΚΡΑΤΗΣ-DĒMOKRATĒS. He was very proud of it.

The same four dark-dressed figures had marched for one more time following slowly his mother's coffin. Him — the Wanderer, his wife, Faba Crimson Sunshine — his only dearest, his daughter and companion in the rallies and her husband. Just the four of them. His mother was buried close to her husband under a pine-tree. When the coffin was lowered into the grave they all tossed a few flowers into the grave, threw a little dirt, then the gravediggers filled the grave with dirt as they watched; the soil was evened off at the top; they stayed over it speechless for a while and then they left. It was September the 7th; she would have liked her body cremated, but although the bill was passed in parliament there were still no crematoria in Greece.

We were just the four of us out of choice; for we wanted to look at our deceased ones for one last time and give our final farewells undistracted by anybody and by anything; for both my parents and I had followed Kavafy's words:

---

*The Seikilos epitaph is the oldest surviving complete musical composition, including musical notation, from anywhere in the world

And if you can't shape your life the way you want,
at least try as much as you can
not to degrade it
by too much contact with the world,
by too much activity and talk.

Try not to degrade it by dragging it along,
taking it around and exposing it so often
to the daily silliness
of social events and parties,
until it comes to seem a boring hanger-on

Everything had its own mystic side. In the course of both the funerals, while they were climbing up toward the graves of his parents, following the coffins, the Wanderer was singing, secretely, silently, in the depths of his being, the reinsurrectional anthem:

Stand up, damned of the Earth
Stand up, prisoners of starvation
Reason thunders in its volcano
This is the eruption of the end.
Of the past let us make a clean slate
Enslaved masses, stand up, stand up.
The world is about to change its foundation
We are nothing, let us be all
 | : This is the final struggle
 Let us group together, and tomorrow
 The Internationale
 Will be the human race. : |

---

*C.P. Cavafy, *As Much As You Can*, Translated from Greek by Edmund Keeley/Philip Sherrard

There are no supreme saviours
Neither God, nor Caesar, nor tribune.
Producers, let us save ourselves,
Decree the common salvation.
So that the thief expires,
So that the spirit be pulled from its prison,
Let us fan our forge ourselves
Strike the iron while it is hot.
 | : This is the final struggle
 Let us group together, and tomorrow
 The Internationale
 Will be the human race. : |

For the Wanderer's mother liked the theatre.

'We can still bury our deads, or if they wish, scatter their ashes like dust in the wind or the sea,' thought the Wanderer, 'but for how long?

"This bitch, Troika, has nazi-German-capitalist-friendly DNA coming from Krupp and Flick and Farben and Siemens and Volkswagen and Bayer; DNA coming from Chase Bank and Allianz....

"So the day after tomorrow they may force again the Greeks to send their dead bodies to bank-owned crematoria and then turn the carbon from the cremains into diamonds to pay the debt; and if they refuse they will have to pay more taxes and fines and whatever property remains with them will take the road not to Aryanisation but to Troikanisation.

"For nazism and fascism are 'pure capitalism' in times of crisis."

The Wanderer told all these thoughts to Blake, when he called him on Skype to express his condolences for his parents' death.

"Tell me Blake," he asked him in the end, "are my views extreme?"

"By no means comrade; after all *the road of excess leads to the palace of wisdom.*' Take care."

In the beginning is the Narrator, and the Narrator is with the Wanderer, and the Wanderer is me. We are a Trinity.

After father's death, when Easter came, Trinity didn't go to the yard of the nearby church, on Great Saturday midnight, to light candles from the Holy Light and bring them home; they had this habit with father; father was a religious man, but a sui-generis one; he believed in God, he went two-three times per year to the church and at the same time he was indiscriminately fond of Lenin, Trotsky, Stalin, Mao, Castro, even of Urban Guerrilla groups. So Trinity kept company to him on Great Saturday midnight for the sake of the tradition. Years before, Zórba used to go on his own even to the epitaphios procession, out in the open, on Great Friday night, especially if he happened to be by the seaside; he was going to mix with girls. He had noticed that many religious girls, at least the ones that appeared out of the blue during the procession, were both good-looking and hot and horny; some of them extremely horny and easy to get laid. It was spring-time, the blossoms bloomed in the gardens, their bosoms bloomed under their garments and the moonlit sea was so beautiful. Life! Life! and Eros and Thanatos. After father died Trinity didn't feel like lighting anything else but the rags of molotov cocktails but felt too old for it as well, too old to hit and run; instead of molotov rags, Trinity lights citronella patio mosquito-candles; after all nobody is perfect. Even so, the flame is still there; so is the powder-magazine.

Life runs in circles, revolves, 'do we need revolvers to break the vicious circle of hardships and disillusionments?' had thought the Wanderer at sometime in the future; he had carried this thought for 9 months in his scull. 'What shall I do with her now that she's born?' he wondered. Thoughts are always feminine. They carry revolutions in their womb.'

Chapter 9

Flashbacks; like flash-grenades. Friday, December 5, 2014, 3 o'clock in the afternoon. "Hey, dad," says the Wanderer to his ill father, "I will not come to see you this evening but I will come tomorrow morning again. You see we have to go to Stella's book-presentation tonight. Do you remember who is Stella?" He keeps testing his memory. His memory is strong, his voice is weak, very weak. "Of course I do, she's my granddaughter, yes go, don't worry."

Same day, 8 o'clock in the evening, dark hours, dark times, dark streets, dark prospects, dark moods; so this is not Christmas. Locomotiva is an arc of art: quests, books, friends, strangers, young ones, elder ones; if dad wasn't ill he was going to be here tonight, he is very sociable, but he is in the clinic for a week now and nobody knows for how long the National Organization For Health Care Services Provision will contribute for his treatment, not for too long for sure, for they shoot horses, don't they? The Nation, their

Nation, prefers to waste money for the coppigs' squads that have overflowed downtown Athens tonight instead of providing for the NHS; because a phantom is haunting the rulers, the phantom of an uprising.

Karl Marx, in his Class Struggles in France from 1848 to 1850 wrote that Revolutions are the locomotives of history...

the speaker, Theodoros Koutsoumpos, has already started the presentation of the book *To Megalo Tzertzelo —The Fun Havoc—* by Stella....

Lenin, in 1905, in the Two Tactics of Social Democracy, after repeating the words of Marx, adds: "The revolution is the festival of the oppressed and exploited."

In V for Vendetta, «V» asks Evey to dance with him:

V: Would you... dance with me?

Evey: Now? On the eve of your revolution?

V: A revolution without dancing is a revolution not worth having!

The *Megalo Tzertzelo* by Stella is a literary satire written in this spirit. During these emotionally charged December days and nights of 2014 the *Megalo Tzertzelo* fleshes out its spirit in the demonstrations in the streets, in the occupied universities, town halls, the GSEE, in the cries and slogans for the life of the hunger-striker, anarchist fighter Nikos Romanos, in the struggle for freedom and dignity.

The *Megalo Tzertzelo* is a modern and current literary satire. "Any Resemblance to Actual Persons, and situations, "writes Stella, " is purely an offspring of my sick imagination." But everything in it resembles so much the current political and social situation.

The events take place around here, in Exarcheia. The political and economic system is in crisis and declines; it degenerates. Even the Olympian gods are forfeited. They had left back their Olympian heights and came to downtown Athens. They want to reproduce their power relations on earth, in Athens -especially Jupiter ...

The economic situation in the country is in a mess, demonstrations, molotov cocktails, tear-gas; democracy and state-power are disputed.

"The factor" - the "foreign agent" or his representative, and "friends" - consultants, especially the forgotten by Pluto Drakoumel, after a bombing attack in the parliament prepare the psychological climate for a parliamentary coup. The media, especially the 8 O'clock News offer their assistance.

The country was facing a terrible asymmetric threat, comparable if not worse than that of September 11, 2011". A state of emergency had to be imposed. Jupiter was invited to ... rule. With the aid of the riot-police and the Delta Squads!

An uprising takes place and Exarcheia is its epicentre. Under the leadership of Prometheus, who once again denies the divine power and all authority, the rebellion is organized.

The storming of the Parliament will be repulsed not so much by the riot-police and the Delta Squad, as by the lightnings and the thunders of Zeus himself. The State and Violence will triumph ...

It seems that the divine and human counter revolution win. They prepare and legitimize new elections. But history is not a linear process. Suddenly a "seismic gap appears in time" —it is known that time is dicretet when empirical measurements are involved— in the form of a beautiful redhead. The *Megalo Tzertzelo* makes its appearance again.

It is the Revolution that comes unexpectedly, when you do not expect. She will appear "beautiful, radiant and fiery."

"It was not an ordinary woman, but all the women together, all the desired that had ever been wakened within men. All women embodied in her. With fiery red hair and cat's eyes that changed colours. "The revolution comes from the past and the future."

Prometheus will give the signal for the greatest and decisive battle. With the Leninist dictum "Yesterday was too early tomorrow too late. The time is today." So today, comrades!

On our way back home we passed by cordons of Praetorians; personal armour, batons, riot shields, riot helmets and khaki uniforms in the fifty shades of shit. Praetorians everywhere; in front of the gate of Polytechneio in Stournara Street with the iron gates being locked for fear of the Jews. The solidarity campaign in support of the political prisoners' hunger strike was strong and had deep roots in the past revolutionary movements, roots that the rulers could not imagine...

For I was hungry and you gave Me something to eat, I was thirsty and you gave Me something to drink, I was a stranger and you took Me in

I was naked and you clothed Me, I was sick and you looked after Me, I was in prison and you visited Me.

Then the lefteous will answer Him, 'Comrade, when did we see You hungry and feed You, or thirsty and give You something to drink?'...

And the Comandante will reply, 'Truly I tell you, whatever you did for one of the least of these comrades of Mine, you did for Me....'

And there were clashes within the Temple and all around it....

Woe to you, scribes and Pharisees, you hypocrites! You pay tithes of mint, dill, and cummin, but you have disregarded the weightier matters of the Law: justice, mercy, and faithfulness. You should have practiced the latter, without neglecting the former. You blind guides! You strain out a gnat but swallow a camel....

Woe to you, scribes and Pharisees, you hypocrites! You clean the outside of the cup and dish, but inside they are full of greed and self-indulgence....

Blind Pharisee! First clean the inside of the cup and dish, so that the outside may become clean as well. Woe to you, scribes and Pharisees, you hypocrites! You are like whitewashed tombs, which look beautiful on the outside, but on the inside are full of dead men's bones and every impurity. 28In the same way, you appear to be righteous on the outside, but on the inside you are full of hypocrisy and wickedness....

Woe to you, scribes and Pharisees, you hypocrites! You build tombs for the prophets and decorate the monuments of the righteous....

And you say, 'If we had lived in the days of our fathers, we would not have been partners with them in shedding the blood of the prophets.'...

So you testify against yourselves that you are the sons of those who murdered the prophets.

and there were more severe clashes around the barricade of Siloam

A man called Barabbas was in prison with the insurrectionists who had committed murder in the uprising...

...for an uprising is an act of violence with which one class attempts to overthrow another... so they had Praetorians everywhere: Praetorians to guard the gates of the Polytechnic School, Praetorians to guard the headquarters of the Green-Snakes in Charilaou Trikoupē St., and the ministries and the "Temple of Democracy." The Trinity recalled Pier Paolo Pasolini's masterpiece *The Gospel According to Matthew*: in the black and white scene 1:35-1:39 we see the militarised antiriot-police suppressing the uprising, we listen to the soundtrack *You fell victims*, the revolutionary funeral march, we hear Jesus saying unto them, "See ye not all these things? verily I say unto you, There shall not be left here one stone upon another, that shall not be thrown down" and we witness the Praetorians unleashing mass arrests, paddy-wagons packed with arrestees heading at full speed towards GADA through Alexandras Avenue, and hundreds of people gathered in front of the gates shouting slogans...

...and more Praetorians guard ministers and ex-ministers and their ex-wives and ex-mistresses and other Praetorians guard the well-payed embedded Troikan journalists and the Troikans themselves. Only the elders are left to the mercy of the criminals and society to the propaganda of the nazist Golden Dawn in favour of an emergency state of Law and Order; a sign that there is no any better alternative for the ruling class in times of crisis than fascism.

This time of the night downtown Athens was formless and empty, darkness was over the surface of the deep, and the *remember remember the 6th of December* was hovering over the city, over the Constitution Square, over the Parliament, a Parliament haunted by the spectre of Guido Fawkes and by another cry coming from far-back: remember remember the 5th of November; the 5th of November of 1605; 409 years ago. How the world would be on Wednesday, December 6, 2423? 409 years ahead?

Saturday morning, December 6, 2014, 10 o'clock. At/o Therapeutērio, 3d floor, room 2. "How was the presentation?" the old man had asked his son. "It was fine dad, they liked the book, it's fun and witty, spirited, when you'll come home, you will read it." Will you, dad?" said the Wanderer. But future is not for us to see. For the time being at least.

"Maybe," I told him months later, on our way back from *The Stationery*, "future is not for us to see. But we cannot leave our future neither to the blind forces of Capitalism and Nature nor to the vices of the thugs that parasitise in the illuminated, well-guarded brothels where Mistress Troika resides." It was a hot humid night. At the corner of Arahovēs and Zoodohou Pēgēs, on a pile of rugs, somebody was sleeping. A huge black cockroach was running towards him. "Only a Skorpion can save him," I said. "One, two, three, many Škorpions vz. 61 to clean the ground, clean the country, clean the world from Capitalism, Troikas and all the rest."

Chapter 10

We had taken to the streets that day, 5 May 2010, and our strong impression is that the arson of Marfin Bank during a general strike and a mass demonstration of more than 150.000 people, both from the public and private sector, against the 1st Memorandum, the G. Papandreou government and the Troika, was the biggest provocation of the deep-State and the ruling class against the movement; Three employees were killed trapped in the burning bank, a man and two women, one of whom pregnant. But *Cui bono?* To whose profit? This is the key forensic question in every criminal investigation; who had a motive for this political crime if not the ruling class?

Marfin's arson left ineradicable after-effects behind it, demoralising the movement for a crucial and vital period that lasted for almost two years, until the fall of the Papadēmou Government after the mass and violent demonstrations of about 500.000 people on February the 12th, 2012. Because after the arson and the killings it was difficult to think about militant struggles in quite the same manner as before. A depressing numbness prevailed that made the people ignore that the three young white-collar workers were victims belonging to the working class; the propaganda that followed against the Left, the strikes, the demonstrations, did not lag behind the propaganda of the Nazis against the Communists after the Reichstag fire.

All the testimonies tend to show a well-organised provocation. Which particular mechanisms organised and implemented it is hard to say right now. There was wrath and anger in the air. The ceaseless attacks against the living standards of the working class and the middle strata on the part of the capitalists had provoked a massive and militant movement. There was a spontaneous, aggressive mood against the government, the MPs, the antiriot-police squads, banks and public buildings among many protesters, which clearly showed that too much of unburned fuel had been concentrated in the boiler ready to be ignited by anything. The wind was blowing alongside with the winds of history, in the same direction, towards Syntagma Square, towards the Parliament, towards the "Brothel," as all the demonstrators were shouting, and there was a strong feeling and a strong desire on the part of the hundreds of thousands that had stormed the streets for a decisive, even desperate battle. It was more than obvious, days before, that only an unseen police violence could have stopped the enraged workers, the unemployed, the demonstrators, the youngsters from invading the Parliament; an unseen, in days of parliamentary democracy, police brutality or a provocation.

Testimonies and events tend to show the later. There are the accusations of the General Secretary of the KKE (the Communist Party) that members of the fascist Golden Dawn were holding banners of its frontal organization, PAME, and were organising acts of hooliganism around the Parliament. There are the testimonies published in the daily newspaper of the KKE, *Rizospastēs*, that the hooded groups that set the Marfin Bank aflame, had come out of police paddy-wagons. There is the testimony of an employee of the Marfin Bank, who in an open letter to the press, stated among other things that:

"The management of the bank strictly bared the employees from leaving today, even though they had persistently asked so themselves from very early this morning — while they also forced the employees to lock up the doors and repeatedly confirmed that the building remained locked up throughout the day, over the phone. They even blocked off their internet access so as to prevent the employees from communicating with the outside world.

"For many days now there has been some

complete terrorisation of the bank's employees in regard to the mobilisations of these days, with the verbal "offer": you either work, or you get fired.

"The two undercover policemen who are dispatched at the branch in question for robbery prevention did not show up today, even though the bank's management had verbally promised to the employees that they would be there."

His/hers testimony is justified, at least in its crucial points, by the Court that three years later accepted, among others, that the Marfin branch, unlike other banks in the area, had refused to allow staff to leave early and gave to three bank officials jail sentences of up to 10 years for failing to protect the lives of staff during a fatal arson attack.

There are the testimonies of the relatives of the three employees who had perished, presenting the last shocking conversations with the victims.

"I am choking," were the last words of Aggelikē Papathanasopoulou who was three months pregnant. Her husband Christos Karapanagiotēs described the last moments of the bank employees in his testimony:

"She called me as soon as she realized that she could not be saved, after she had done everything possible to escape from the fire. The only entrance and exit of the bank was locked and no employee was able to leave it normally. They were doomed to a horrible death. [...]"

Other witnesses, including bank employees, accused the bank management of the absence of any fire protection and emergency exit.

So, why "the only entrance and exit of the bank was locked?"

Further more all the witnesses underline the cruelty with which the attackers had assaulted the bank branch; but was it just cruelty or cold-blood professionalism? Especially when the Witness no3 testified to the police that: "*The two shorter men were smashing the window with a metal object. One of them was holding a backpack, from which he poured some liquid inside the bank. The tall man took out some objects from his backpack and threw them inside the bank. Another 6-7 people around them were helping them. When they implemented the attack and set fire to the bank, this group walked down the sidewalk towards Syntagma Square.*" What was this liquid and what were these objects?

It was a stormy demonstration. We had just entered Stadiou Street hastening at full speed towards Syntagma Square with our flags and banners waving in the wind when we were first attacked unprovokedly by the riot police both from the left and the right side of the street and, at times, even from the front; we first heard the flash-sound grenades; "It started again!" we said with my daughter; the coppigs were invading and intruding among the blocs, beating with their clubs,

145

spraying us with tear-gas and throwing flash-sound grenades directly at the demonstrators; groups of panic-stricken people that were obviously taking part for a first time in such a demonstration, were rushing backwards towards Omonoia Square or leftwards to Panepistēmiou away from the firing; However amidst all this chaos and brutality, a group of hooded and masked people was rushing upstreet parallel to us on the pavement, behind the backs of the antiriot-squads, completely undistracted by them. It was weird because in such cases, when antiriot-police attacks demonstrators at such a close distance, the anarchists whirl in and out of the main body in clusters, engage in street-fight with them in almost body-to-body fight, and throw their cocktail molotovs against the antiriot-police platoons. This time nothing happened. The antiriot-police left the "anarchists" unbridled and in return, this particular group didn't bother at all with the "pigs."

Demonstrators from the anarchists blocs were arrested and brought into one of the usual show-trials. However non of the witnesses recognized the accused as the persons seen to set the bank on fire. On October 31st 2016, the Marfin Bank's arson trial was concluded and the accused were unanimously acquitted.

Chapter 11

Friday, June 28, 2013, 7:30 in the evening, Locomotiva - bar - café - bookshop, Solomou & Botasē, Exarheia. Stella's new book launch-party, *Ena Mpakouri stēn Athēna* - A Single Gal in Athens. I pick up a copy and read the back-blurb:

At the threshold of the Greek economic crisis, a young Greek writer and communication specialist, Stella, goes against the trend of depression, and recession, and stands up, unfolding all her caustic humour, to satirise the desperate search of a young single female for her second best-half. Her adventures take place in the city of Athens, in the capital of a country, Greece, that seems to be falling apart.

'Interesting,' I'm thinking. I look around. The place is full of bibliophiles, friends of the author, some of them are her facebook funs, most of them young ladies; two or three of them take the microphone and sitting or standing take turns and talk about the book, about how much they enjoyed it, about their own experiences and the fundamental qualities women are looking for in a partner, they're becoming self-sarcastic, they confess that they rarely, if not never, find all the things they're craving for in one man. The atmosphere is nice and light, the theme amusing; my wife drinks draft, I drink Greek green-cola; it's encouraging that young people keep writing against all odds; I shared my thoughts with the others; they all agreed, especially Faba and the Wanderer, Stella's parents; all but one, Zórba or Vas, in whose name, "V" stands for Vendetta and Victory, Victory against all odds.

"Yes, it's very nice and encouraging but if we stand at some point in the future, let's say two hundred years ahead and look back on this hard times, shall we be able to say, like Don Quichotte de La Mancha '*that the lance has never blunted the pen, nor the pen the lance?*'* This seems to be a crucial question, and matches very much Marx's notorious phrase from *The Contribution to the Critique of Hegel's Philosophy of Right*: '*The weapon of criticism cannot, of course, replace criticism by weapons, material force must be overthrown by material force*[...]' However", concluded Zórba, "I have to admit that it's nice that all these young people, they keep reading and writing, at least."

Before I left, I took all the author's books. *Men are like shoes, Like the Lady and the Tramp,*

---

*Miquel de Cervantes, *Don Quixote of La Mancha* Chapter XVIII

two comedy books with caustic satire against men, or to be more precise the kind of man that grew up in late 1980s and 1990s, in the "Golden Times" of the Athens' Stock Exchange, of the "life-style" magazines, published back then by the present-day most fanatic advocates of Mistress Troika, and of the success story of the Greek ruling class, the Olympic Games of 2004.

I remember that when back to 2004 I made a comment against the Athens Olympics, in the building of the Prefecture of Athens, somewhere close Omonoia Square by that time, where I had gone for my passport, the Director, a middle-aged woman, threatened me that she will "report" me, nobody knows where! She even picked up the telephone receiver but she put it back in its place, unfortunately not into her ass, when she realised how stupid the whole thing was on her part.

I also bought *Prostitutional Ethics and the Zombie of Capitalism* by V. Ludens and a novel written by Stella's father enriched by poems written by her, under the title *An Elf in the Garden of Utopia*. Strangely enough, her poems have an aura of English Romanticism. I put all the books in my backbag and I left Locomotiva with Faba holding me by my left hand of darkness.

Chapter 12

"**L**east and *Liszt* is all the same for Zórba," teased him Liza, a tallish, slim English post-grad, with curly blond hair, an innocent madonna's face, thin well-formed lips, long legs and almost flat-chested. However for some unsexplainable reason. her torso was sextremely feminine and it was a pleasure to lick it; she was good-hearted and easy-going but she was a teaser, Liza-the-teaser.

"Yes," Zórba teased her back; "the same way *hall* sounds all the same for me with *hole*, or *can't* with *cunt*, the same way *least* sounds the same with *Liszt*."

Liszt's fragmented images: an embossed head of him out of wax made by his dad; a few sketches from magazines; Liszt's piano sheets music; then of the composer himself during the July Revolution; in Paris; amidst a street fighting; meeting a lady; pushing her lightly against a wall; lowering the garments from her shoulders; uncovering her breasts; exposing them; making her look like Liberty leading the people in Eugene Delacroix's painting; lowering his head and using his tongue to sexasperate her...

Zórba the brut did the same to Liza when "it doesn't sound the same Zórba, you just can't pronounce it properly," she told him smiling and staring provocatively into his eyes. It was during a too-classic British costume party, in the University's Tartan Club, themed *Tarts and Vicars* at which the men were dressed as Anglican priests — Zórba was not, he was dressed as usual, as everyday, in wild strong colours, like the fauves— while the women wore sexually provocative tarts' costumes, whores' costumes. He pushed her lightly against a brick-wall, played with her hair and with the dress "his whore wore," pronouncing both words the *same*, all the *shame*: "You *cunt* even stress my name properly, it's Zorbá not Zórba, can you *cunt*?

"But I like it, I like it because *you* cunt, *me* fauv..."

She laughed. He lowered her top from her shoulders; uncovering her breasts; exposing them; making her look like a whore that wore a piece of cloth torn violently off her body; he then lowered his head, used his tongue to sexasperate her and then he said:

"Let me take you far away, sexchange your troubles for some fun, whoever you are longing for sex you will come back to USSR."

SEXUAL ETHICS THE SPIRIT OF SURREALISM AND THE

VOYAGE TO THE USSR

SCANDALS OF DADAISM AGAINST ALL TROIKAN ODDS

Союз Сюрреалистических Сексуальных Ретроперспектив

THE SOVIET
POLITICAL
POSTER

"You're paraphrasing Scorpions," she said.

"I love Scorpions." he replied ambiguously.

"I am a Scorpion," she said and I'll bite you soon.

Another barely legal whore, Samantha, a fresher? or a fresher's sister?, wore a dress which exposed her buttocks, barely covered her breasts and bore the words: *mouth, vagina, asshole, I'm not just a pretty face*. It turned out that she was 25 but she hardly looked 15 and she was a librarian.

"How much do you charge?" he asked her, "I want all the four."

She looked at him straight in the eyes: "All the four?" She raised her eyebrow and smiled.

"Yes, all the four; your mouth, your vagina, your asshole and your pretty face, so how much you'll charge me for all." It wasn't a question, it was a statement.

"I don't charge, I bet that by the end of the night I'll have you decharged for at least a week.... Now if you're talking about my present, for half an hour and up it's free of charge, for less I'm afraid you can't afford it. So can you last so long?"

It was his time to laugh this time. "Then the night will be long, the ride even longer."

"If you keep your promise, you can ask for some extra, not necessarily tonight."

"I will definitely do it Samantha. I'm sure you have access to some sexluded library sextions where no living soul ever goes...."

"Oh, I see you know my name already..."

"Yes, I asked for it a few days ago..."

"When was that and why?"

"When you came first in the last University Blowjob Competition, when all of you were sucking dairy-cream from plastic cocks...

"You want it freshly squeezed," he said, for it was his Scorpions' rock period.

Sluts and sluttishness everywhere, and joy and pleeasure; from Staircase-1 to Staircase-6 and from the rooms under the glass-roof of the 8th floor down to the 1st basement — in the laundry rooms.

And the band played *"A G-string is looking for a pilot*

"White flesh is coming down the stairs again

"Spaced out your body gives me fever

"You sex it

"Relax it

"Reload it."

It was the first time that she blushed, but she did reload it with her mouth with lot's of joy which was not the armed joy —La gioia armata— but the joy of sex....

Chapter 13

B ut the Greek Monetary Prostitutes never blush under their blue, green or pink makeup, even when their fucking and pimping activities with Mistress Troika, force unemployed people, even people with cancer, ailing parents and disabled siblings, to electricity cuts, for they can't afford the bills; they light their home with candles, have no fridge to keep their insulin and survive through solidarity committees that have seized state buildings, distribute food and medicine and a movement of radical electricians who illegally restore power. "But we need life not survival," said Zórba, who would also reload with a lot of joy a Scorpion with 9×18mm Makarov cartridge, for although he had not played or heard the Scorpions for a long long time, since the Tarts' night in the Tartan Club maybe, the MPWhores had made him to get his Scorpion groove back.

We were sitting in Anadolou Mutfağı, eating nice cheap food and listening to music from the other side of the Aegean sea. Zórba was melancholic contemplating the fate of the two people. Day after day, just before the celebrations for the Millennium, he had taken to the streets, again and again, joining the solidarity campaign against the Turkish White Cells. Each time holding a piquet with the name of a hunger striker. All of them had fallen victims. Millennium's Eve. Greek euro ante portas...

Scattered diary entries, written with gel-pen or fountain-pen, illegible handwriting. Thursday, December 20. 2012. Riot squads invade Villa Amalias one of the oldest squats in downtown Athens, a space of anti-com-mercial cultural activities and relationships based on equality and social solidarity; the right-wing government has proclaimed an organised back-clash against squatting on abandoned buildings, supported by the neo-nazi party, Golden Dawn; helicopters hover all day long over the centre of Athens which is occupied by militarised police units, and the embedded journalists, in a frenzy of propaganda, reproduce, day and night, inac-curate and slanderous information. It's semi-dark in the kitchen, dawn-time, and a set of multi-coloured multi-action LED cluster lights positioned in or around a hundred, more or less, glass bottles of all shapes, seizes and colours, create a weird Bradburian atmosphere. It looks like a little wonder and I wonder, since I'm a wonderer and not a wanderer, if we have to start demolishing the Christmas decoration singing something like *Farewell for Ever Christmas*, since for the anchorparrots almost every single empty glass-made bottle, not disposed on the spot, is an evidence of criminal anti-state activity; every single empty glass-bottle is meant, for them, to be used solely for the production of molotov cocktails. Solely for this! This slander enrages me for I know that some anchorwomen use empty glass-bottles for deep vaginal masturbation, and they know it much better than me; they know it so deeply, and with a knowledge so deeply ingrained in the depths of their heart, so deeply impaled in the depths of their cunts, that when they expose on camera the empty beer bottles found in the bar of the Villa, the tone of their voice and their excite-ment reveal that they are already in a state of pre-orgasmic situation, a state resembling a pre-revolutionary situation.

Zórba remembered an indecent incident that took place, once upon a time, in a private coaching school for students, a *fron-tistērio*, at the corner of Solonos and Massalias Streets opposite the School of Law. It was a semi-ruined two-storey building, with a *kafeneio* on its foot. Its atmosphere was not libertarian of course, for stalinists prevailed among the students and the teachers, but it was loose, funny and easy-going. Zórba knew the owner and had a second pair of keys in case of emergency, which meant a case of sexergency. It was a hot July night, around 8 o'clock, and a group of final year students of the Department of Economics and one or two of the School of Law had gone up the old wooden staircase, after they locked the central heavy iron-door, reached the first floor, sneaked into the *frontistērio*, locked its door behind them, and put in the fridge the bottles of beer they had just bought from the *kafeneio* on the ground floor. Among the females were Lena Kavla, the double of Lysiac, the Pole's fiance, Vaso M., a slim chestnut, and the blond Olga Fridgy, the future-to-be notorious anchorwoman, the bitch of the Greece-BBC (Big Breasted Cunts) News.

Lena was much like Lysiac but she was not a double-faced catholic and unscrupulous slut like her; she didn't jump, like in an one night stand, from the position of a high-rank interpreter of the Communist Party of B. to that of a NATO grant-holder. And she was not the only one. Zórba knew at least one more, Hornyslava Tankova. Tankova was getting the hots by being watched fucking or undressing, voyered through open windows, by passers-by, porters, workers, anybody. When the other men's eyes where almost ravaging her sexposed to them naked body, or when they were watching her live sex-show, through the open curtains, across corridors and rooms opposite to hers, her eyes were shining and glistening as much as the cock that was fucking her mouth, and then was coming out all shiny and glistening until the purple head was on her lips, and then sliding back in as deep as possible for she couldn't handle it all; back in where? in the mouth or the cunt of the future-to-be NATO grant-holder and ex high-rank bureaucrat Hornyslava Tankova. 'Was she ever going to write her own *Confessions of a non-English Sperm Eater*?' wondered Zórba the Greek. In the night of March the 6th of a year lost in time Hornyslava had swallowed a huge load of Zórba's semen for he had preffered to use her soft lips and eager mouth for his sexual satisfucktion than her vagina. She would have preffered to direct his semen to her womb, she was not taking any precautions, she had a mania for unprotected sex, an obsession with the arousing, for her, risk of impregnation, she didn't use even the rhythm method; he didn't have any condom at hand and although, the bloody foreigner with the bloodier English, was infucktuated with her, he didn't have the slightest inclination to hang himself with the umbilical cord of this particular woman; consequently her mouth turned to be for Zórba the brut the most desirable inlet after her cunt alongside with her anus. So during the night of March the 6th of a year lost in time Hornyslava Tankova found herself in a weird and indecent situation, a situation she had provoked, trying to appear sexually daring and adventurous by stating in front of the raven-haired Joy and the blondish Juicy Peach, the third girl of the company, "you are not allowed to call other women by my name, *slut*, anymore." They had been making some photos, innocent ones and full dressed, but somehow the girls had got wild, Joy removed her jeans and took a very provocative and suggestive pose, standing, with her right leg wrapped around Zórba, her head tilted back and her raven hair in a mess in a *I've just got fucked look*. At her twenty-six she looked more mature, more soft and curvy and more ready to fuck than the rest. Zórba laughed, called her a teasing-slut, she admitted proudly that that's exactly what she was and then Hornyslava said what she said. So, the two other girls forced her to a kneeling position, dressed as she was in a black t-shirt, a black very short pleaded skirt and black tights, with her head trapped between the bare strong thighs of Joy, who was standing almost naked over her and was kissing passionately with Zórba. Hornyslava had no much choice other than let her mouth be used instead of a vagina; her mouth was sextremely receptive despite her protests and her tongue skilful; after some time her makeup turned into a mess because under the directions of the blondish curvy Juicy Peach, Zórba was occasionally rubbing his engorged erotic organ all over her face. What was going on had sexcited her immensely, she was soaking and, what a shame and what a degradation, the future-to-be NATO grand-holder double-faced Hornyslava Tankova was craving and pleading to feel in the depths of her existence the multiple explosions of this communist's RPG: *Rocket Propelled G-Orgasm*.

Back to the *frontistḗrio*: Vaso had an affair with a sailor, and when he was away, she had various affairs with almost everybody Lena, her best girlfriend, liked. They didn't argue or fight over him. They just shared him peacefully or if they fought, they did it only over who was going to get the on-top position during their lesbian encounters, which was a great fun. Olga was prude, aloof, unapproachable but after she saw Lena getting fucked in a standing position in the rather filthy toilet of the *frontistḗrio* —it was not dirty or stinky, just filthy in a weird way— and then Vaso bent nude over a desk getting it in turns by all the three males, she got drunk with beer and whiskey, which proved to be more than risky, and gave it all and took them all. Not yet an embedded journalist, but, during that hot July night, just an entabled lay, she gave all her orifices and took all their cocks. But before this, the future-to-be ardent supporter of the theory that *any single bottle is an incriminating type of evidence for committed terrorist acts,* "I'm coming," she was shouting, fucking herself with a half-filled bottle of foaming beer, after she had used it for a demo of her blow-job and tit-fucking skills; and not only she was shouting but she was singing too, with sexcellent Parisian accent, a song based on a poem from *The Works of Mr. Francis Rabelais,* that Zórba the Greek had paraphrased for her.

Bottle! whose Mysterious Deep
Do's ten thousand Secrets keep,
With attentive Yearn I wait;
Ease my cunt, and speak my Fate.
Soul of joy! Like Bacchus, we
More than cocks gain by thee,
Truths unborn my Juice reveals,
Which Futurity conceals

The beer addicts grabbed both the chance and her tits to lick the beer off them, and the girls, Lena and Vaso, drunk and licked it off her cunt.

Thirty-four years later she was going to forget or rather pretend to forget that beer bottles can have multiple uses....

165

At the top of the wooden staircase the Wanderer was always waiting, sitting on a boat, amidst the eternal sunshine of a surrealist summer, to bury in the sand the bourgeois politicians

$$(\Rightarrow) - (x'x)^{-1} x'Y +$$

$$\boxed{\hat{B}_{LS} = (x'x)}$$

$$\text{Ειδιούντικα} (=xw)$$

$$(=) \;\hat{\sigma}_{LS}^2 = \frac{1}{} (Y - xB)$$

(B) Αμεροληψία

$$\hat{B}_{LS} = (x'x)^{-1} \; Y = (x'x)^{-1} x' (xB + u)$$

$$= (x'x)^{-1} \cdot x'x + (x'x)^{-1} \cdot x'u = \qquad + (\quad)^{-1} \; u$$

$$= B + (x' \quad)^{-1} \; x'u$$

$$\&: \; E(\hat{B}_{L}) = E\left[(x'x)^{-1} x'Y\right] = E\left[\qquad (x'x)^{-1} \; u\right]$$

$$= (B) + E\left[(x'x)^{-1} x' \cdot \right]$$

$$= B + (x'x)^{-1} \cdot x' \underbrace{E(u)}_{=0} = \qquad$$

8 O'clock News

Cock-tales Molotov

$$(x'x)^{-1} x'Y$$

$$\hat{B}$$

$$\lim_{T \to \infty} E(\hat{B}) \qquad \lim_{T \to \infty} \qquad B$$

...they can even offer multiple orgasms, although for the Wanderer, making cocktails molotov was a mostly legitimised and creative way of reusing empty glass-bottlesy. 'Fridgy, remember that night of December,' he thought. The night's air blew cold on our foreheads, and the coarse taste of tear-gas filled our mouth and breathing passages as soon as we came out of the Solidarity to Villa Amalias Assembly held in the School of Law. We had to put on our gas-masks.... "In these dark times, we can't wander in the night without a gas-mask and a pack of condoms," said the Wanderer. "For both State and Natute have allied against Eros and Anarchy."

Our History is a red-and-black dense web of battles, victories, defeats, songs, hopes. It has *a retroactive force and will constantly call in question every victory, past and present, of the rulers.*[*] Browsing the web I came across "*A Ballad for Villa Amalias,*" written, composed, performed and uploaded by *IndicoPunk*, a group of youngsters taking active part in the movement of occupations. In spite of my age I liked the song to the point of obsession, and most of all I appreciated the connection they did and their reference to the case of the anarchist Giuseppe Pinelli:

"IndicoPunk

Published on Feb 12, 2013

---

[*]Walter Benjamin, *Theses on the Philosophy of History IV*

Milan 1969 - Athens 2012. Dark ages. In 1969 in Milan, a bomb that later proved to be planted by a far-right wing group, detonates in a central square killing 17 people and resulting in major social unrest. The authorities try to put the blame for the incident on the anarchist movement. They arrest 80 anarchists and interrogate them. Among them is Giuseppe Pinelli, whom they murder after 3 days of illegal imprisonment, throwing him from the 4rth floor of the police station he was kept in. 2012 finds Athens with hundreds of victims of the economic crisis, poverty and a rising fascist menace, while the state tries to divert and dictate the public with a combination of police brutality and controlled journalism. Squats are fiercely targeted as a threat to order and social peace. In 20/12/2012 Villa Amalia Squat, a beacon of social struggle, anti-fascism and anti-consumerist ethics for 22 years is invaded by the police and evicted. The silly pretext for the eviction is given in the discovery of beer bottles and "flammable" cleaning products inside the squat, emphasizing the direct intention of the right wing government to mute every voice of resistance.

Considering the attack on the Villa Amalia Squat an analog of attack on freedom, as a band we chose to re-adjust the 1970 Joe Fallisi song *La ballata del Pinelli* to the current events. Let *A ballad for Villa* be our little contribution to the river of solidarity...

Let us not forget. Nothing is over. Everything continues..."*

---

*https://www.youtube.com/watch?v=ogY1hc-OO4E

Chapter 14

I always loved a lot Joe Fallisi's song *La ballata del Pinelli*. One of its most interesting and best performances is the famous *Ballad of Pinelli* by Norman Nawrocki[*] - Crocodile, given live, in English, and a bit of French, at Casa del Popolo, a bar, bistro, and music venue in Montreal, on Saint Laurent Boulevard, on November 16th 2013.[**] Narration, singing, violin, accordion, two electric guitars, drums, a lot of talent and...

That evening it was hot in Milano,
how hot, how hot it was
"brigadier, open the window,"
a push and Pinelli goes down...

Zórba the Greek and the Wanderer prefer to play again and again, and sometimes loud, very loud, with loudspeakers blaring musical artful propaganda at a high decibel level, the

[*]Norman Nawrocki is the author of several books of poetry and short stories. He's also an internationally acclaimed cabaret artist, sex educator, actor, and musician, and has released over 50 albums. He teaches at Concordia University, about how to use the arts for community organizing and radical social change, gives workshops about "creative resistance," and tours the world performing theatre, music, and cabaret.
[**]https://www.youtube.com/watch?v=H71Ow

Ballad of Pinelli as it is performed by the musical ensemble *Encardia*.* Not because they sing in Greek but because they have a talented female vocalist. 'Such songs need a female vocalist', they believe. The singer's voice carries and expresses all the passion, the tenderness, the *"Let me be cruel, but not inhuman,"*** colour, all the pathos and all the eros, of the female combatants. Of the Mujeres Libres, of the fighteresses of the Democratic Army during the Greek Civil War, of the Rosava partisans, of the young women that participate in the street-fighting in our days, days and nights in Times of Troika.

Saturday, January 12, 2013. One of the biggest anarchist and anti-authoritarian demonstrations. Over 10,000 people marched through downtown Athens, expressing their solidarity to the 92 people arrested on Wednesday after the re-eviction of Villa Amalias squat.

The demonstration started from Propylaea of Athens University and marched towards the Courthouse of Evelpidon, through Panepistēmiou, Patēsion, Mavromataion and Evelpidon streets. At the corner of Patēsion and Alexandras Av. I met Faba Crimson,

---

Encardia is the name of a Greek musical ensemble focused at and inspired by the rich musical tradition of Southern Italy. Their amazing and most energetic music collective creates and performs original music as well as traditional music of the region that Greek and Italian cultures mix.
https://www.youtube.com/watch?v=S0gY-Kj33GY
**W. Shakespeare, *Hamlet* Act3 Scene2

Zórba, the Wanderer and Alex-who-was-sailing-stormy waters.

And then Faba and me went on the bridge over Moustoksydē Street, to watch the raged human stream flow, and this decision positioned us on top in the interwoven space-time continuum and under us in the riverbed was Eirēnē, a young female friend of ours, I had seen her earlier too, and she was waving and smiling and taking pictures of us.... Us on top of the bridge, Eirēnē under us in the riverbed, *Drums roll, And we must go. We must go, the enemy is upon us. Rise from your knee, And now, pull to the bridge.**

It was a bridge over enraged people of all ages but mostly youngsters, it was a bridge over troubled water and we were downtown and in town we were on the street and we were taking part and darkness had come and pain was all around and like a bridge over troubled water we were, we will laying us down, like a bridge over troubled water, like in the old song of Simon & Garfunkel, but it was not a bridge to the past, where old diaries full of handwritten entries were waiting locked in even older drawers; it was a bridge to the future, a future full of blanck white pages, awaiting to be filled not with new innumerous entries, entries written with the blood and tears of the downtrodden and the

*Madrugada - *The Riverbed*

toilers, but with the non-description of the one and final Exodus to the much craved land of libertarian communism.

Where wanders the Wanderer wondering about what, I know not right now; but I remember him vaguely but vividly almost floating in the flux of time and space, floating silently, like a colourful shadow, among members of the Workers' Revolutionary Party of Greece, during a demonstration in front of the Athens Embassy of Argentina, for the assassination of Mariano Ferreyra. It was Monday evening, October 25, 2010. The same night his old father broke his leg, at home, and this accident was the starting point of a Golgotha of suffering in the Greek hospitals in Times of Troika. Endless waitings in freezing humid corridors overflowed with helpless sick people of all ages, desperate and exhausted relatives, nurses and doctors at the verge of collapse, smells, odours, secretions and secret agreements behind closed doors, in luxury places, yachts, villas, brothels, agreements for the looting and plundering of the social wealth that all these sick and ill, the doomed and the toilers created when they were still young and strong and productive. Among them his father. He was brought to the emergency at 8:30 in the evening and the Wanderer and his wife took him away at 3 o'clock in the morning, it was a rainy and cold night, desperately seeking for another hospital. At the same time, in an advert targetting colonies of parasites we read: "Athenian Riviera & Attica Coastline. Little known fact: Athens is more than just the Acropolis. Hands down, this city with its vibrant urban landscape boasts some of the best beaches and seaside destinations in the world and boasts a Riviera just 30 minutes away from its heart. Begin by gazing at the luxurious yachts docked at Floisvos Marina, the mega yacht marina with shops and dining venues in the town of Paleo Falēro; enjoy a light salad, burger or cool drink dockside at Marina Alimou just a few tram stops away."

This is Athens in Times of Troika. The Wanderer had wandered there too, with Faba. They had seen the luxurious yachts docked at Floisvos Marina; they looked like yachts, yachts of extravagant luxury, of all sizes and all shapes, multicoloured and multinational, but they were not just yachts; they were, above all, the form that the rulers have given to the wealth that the workers had produced, but of which they had been robbed; the yachts were multishaped, multicoloured and multinational surplus value. The Wanderer and Faba had also seen the shops and the dining-by-the-sea venues and had felt nauseated; it was not seasickness, not at all. They just knew very well that the over-exploited workers of the Athenian Riviera, like the working people all over the country, alongside with the unemployed, at some time in their life, they would pass through, or even worse, pass away, in hospitals like the one they spent the night between October 25 and October 26 of the troikan year 2010.

"Troika is a harsh mistress," said Zórba. It was a hot July night. Actually it was Saturday, July 16, 2016, a year in Times of Troika. We were dining in the yard of Anadolou again, the cheap restaurant run by Kurds, next to Pedion tou Areos, the big park of Athens. The Wanderer had strong memories from his wanderings there, ever since he was a child. His mom and dad used to take him there every day to play under the shadow of the platanes. Then as he grew older he went long rides on his bicycle, anytime of the day, and shorter rides on girls, preferably at night. It was like a vast garden of Eden. Then, alongside with the first signs of the international crisis, the park's deterioration started. It was baptised renovation by a bunch of contractors, ministers, TV-channel owners, journalists and other demons. The Wanderer took part in all the mobilizations against this renovation that sent millions to some bank accounts and many marginalised groups to seek refuge in the dark abandoned areas of the ex-Eden.

"Under libertarian communism it will turn into a sex-Eden," said Vas in whose name the letter "s" stands for sextremism.

"Yes, it will," agreed Zórba, "but for the time being Troika is a harsh mistress. And the so-called rulers, the politicians and the economic elite, who are absolutely impotent, in order to have whatever erection is needed to fuck the people, they have to feel Troika's huge strap-on deep into their asses. This is the only way for them to get and maintain a temporal erection: mistress Troika's strap-on in their ass."

It was obvious that Zórba had too much wine; it was a nice white wine at a very good price and the food was equally cheap and very tasty. Zórba was feeling great, he was among good friends. with his dearest one and he even knew one of the owners and the attendant girls, Anastasia, from the demonstrations. She had a big white very calm and friendly dog, Kate; he was in love with her and everybody knew it; in love with Kate not with Anastasia that she was getting amused with his joke.

"So Troika is the dom-harsh mistress and our ruling class is the sub... But Troika is something like Pythia, I mean it's the embodiment, the name given to any dominatrix... Once upon a time I came across such a dominatrix in a rather ill-famed night-club in

Soho called 'The Maximou Cathouse.' It was run by the notorious Maximos, a Greek sailor and in its entrance it had a huge nude cat-woman made of neon-lights.

"As soon as I entered I was approached by an impressive woman in her early thirties, she was behaving in a very arrogant way and I'm sure that the only reason she dared to come to *me* was that I had an accident while I was trimming my beard and I was obliged to shave myself with foam and razor-blade and ok, I looked like a baby-faced ass!

"She was aloof with almond eyes, nothing like the old camel overtanned by the desert sun or the spoiled WMF brat Cruella de Vil, dressed always like a proud high-school teacher full of complexes, that we see every night in the 8 O'clock News; what a dull impression she gives compared with women of similar political and social origin like the ex-minister Rina Kaynine, especially if the rumors about Rina's sexual encounters are true. I mean *if* she was involved with the dog, *if*, then she was brave enough to demonstrate the only thing a capitalist minister is worth doing.

" 'Aha', I thought, after we had the first drinks and I understood her intentions, 'this was a wrong move my lady,' but I didn't say anything and we ended to a house, in weird latidudes, longtitudes and timetitudes, with view of the docks. It was a cutty-sarked house with a cutty-sarked terrace; its name was *Dadaist Provocateur VL 5817*. As soon as we got there and had the first drink chatting about nonsense, mistress Troika raised the tone of her voice and ordered me to kneel and lick her boots. It was then when she had her first bad surprise, she first felt a F-S fighting knife on her neck and her own hand-cuffs securing her hands behind her back. Holding her by her hair I dragged her to her boudoir and choose the reddest lipstick I could find, something to contrast her fair complexion and her raven hair. I forced mistress Troika to kneel and then using her red lipstick I drew around her mouth..."

At this point Zórba asked from the ladies to pass him a lipstick, any lipstick, his dearest one offered him hers, then he took a paper-napkin, draw something and shoed it to us, saying: "So, despite her complains, I drew around mistress Troika's mouth WHORE, called a 'girlfriend' of hers to joint the party, started mouthfucking her by force, despite her pleas, protests and threats that she will call the police, and turned the night into a surrealist sextravaganza. 'You can call NATO too,' I told her, 'I don't give a damn, I'm going to use you as a cum-bucket all night long.' I did it! Ah! The sexaltating rapture of raping a female Dom!"

"Zórba you are a sexist, male chauvinist pig," said one of the ladies of our company, "I didn't expect it from you."

Zórba the brut laughed cordially and pulling his hair with his right hand, pretending that he takes of a wig, he said, "but I am a man, nobody is perfect."

Then the conversation shifted to the dramatic upheaval in Turkey. Zórba kept silent for a while; then he spoke: "There is no doubt that we're witnessing the clash of two despotisms. But still it's encouraging watching the fear, the panic and the beaten faces of the Turkish perpetrators of the coup, after they were captured by the thousands that stormed the streets. Eight years and eight months had passed since this idiot American, was saying, during the December uprising, 'teargas is useless, where are the water cannons,' asking, practically for more violent repression. I'm sure he is an advocate of military action, especially in countries like Greece; he just did not have the guts to say it openly; What was he going to say watching them now? I recall the overthrow of the Pahlavi dynasty back in 1978-79. When armed ultra-left guerrillas and rebel troops overwhelmed the well-trained loyal to the Shah troops in armed street fighting. What followed is another night's story. One of the one thousand and one nights stories maybe."

"All around me, merged realities and surrealities, topoi for the deployment of the subvertsive activities of the Reinsuerectionary Antitroikan Fucktion-RAF," told us Vas the surrealist.

DADAIST PROVOCATEUR V.L 5&7

The independence of
art for the revolution,
or self-censorship as
suicidal process

The unholy Trinity saw in surrealism a joyful
attempt to mix the real with the unreal, give
all the power to the imagination, make the
imagination life

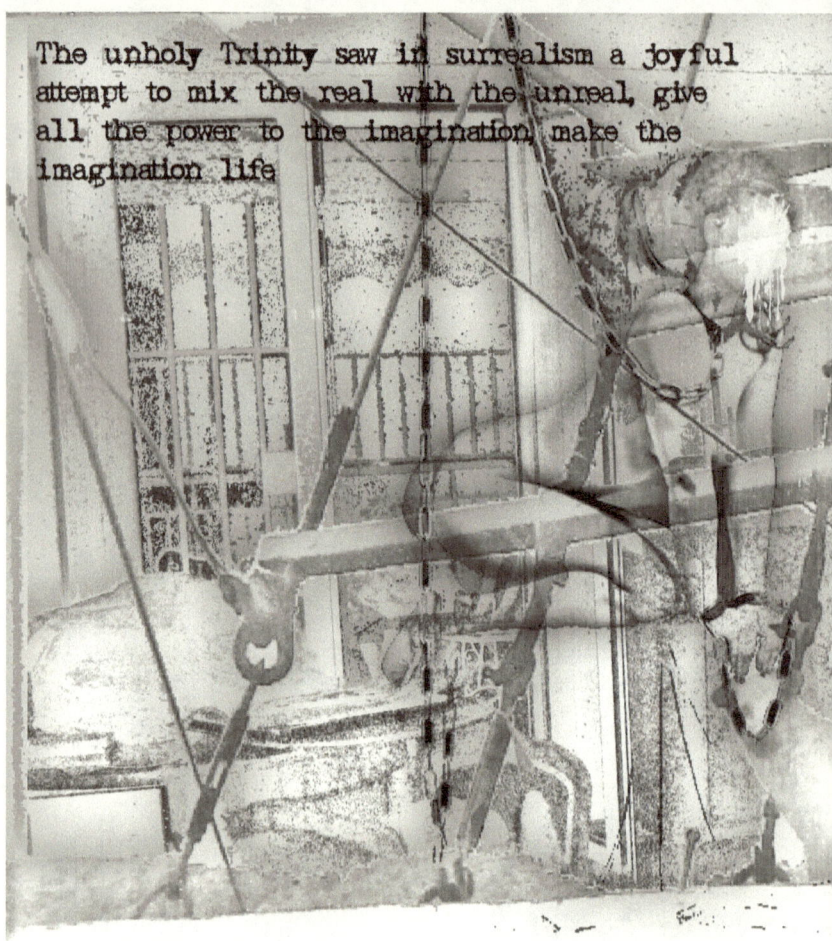

DADAIST PROVOCATEUR V.L 5&17

A few days later we were returning home from Locomotiva, by foot, as always, and sometimes we were talking, sometimes not. This time we had kept silent for quite sometime. It was obvious that each of us was thinking his own thoughts. We had reached at the corner of Zoodohou Pēgēs and Komnēnon. There is an almost ruined, abandoned old house now there, on the ground floor of which a couple of years ago was a furniture and wood workshop. And, on the first floor of which, further back in time, was accommodated, for unidentified reasons, an ammateur, 22 years young, "part-time model," at least that was what she claimed to be to Zórba, during their one-week stands. She carried the rare name Buenaventura which was a great mystery for neither she nor her parents were anarchists, communists, or anything of the kind. They were apolitical Dutch of Jewish origin. Few of her friends called her just "Vera", although she liked to be called Buenaventura, Zórba believes that she was kinda mad; she was good in bed but even better against the wall, for she was tiny. So it was there, at the corner of Zoodohou Pēgēs and Komnēnon that, out of the blue, I heard the Wanderer's voice.

"Apart from the major issues of the urgent need for a socialist revolution that we face every day, these pavements set as well, a major moral question," he said.

"Which is?" I asked him...

"Why do we let them live, go on with their lives; all of them! Prime Ministers and Ministers and Majors and Contractors of Public Works.... They collect taxes, they're profitting millions, companies receiving a rake-off for years; but look at these pavements, just look at them.... They are fucking damaged, for ages, all over Athens.... Slab movement here, potholes there, defective trenching with level difference further down, standing water almost everywhere when it rains. These are not pavements but death-traps for the elderly. As soon as they step out of their door, their fate is almost sealed: broken legs, surgery, pneumonia, nasogastric intubation, tied hands, catheters, suffering, lost minds, death; and the criminals of the ruling class go on living, exploiting, profitting, murdering.... So, yes my friend, all these pavements, these death-traps raise a major moral question: why do we let them do it?"

"Why don't we exterminate them like *cock*roaches," said Zórba and he started to sing in a bass voice "blood rains down from an angry sky, my *cock* rages on, till death is found, my sword swinging hot."

"What's that silly song?" I asked him.

"Spartacus, Vengance ep. 2, a silly American television series," he replied.

Chapter 15

"Spartacus, vengance and revolutionary violence are never silly. Just the Americans have the ability to sillify whatever they touch," said the Wanderer and then he slipped back to the undefined present which never lasts but it's always present and flows and becomes past and withers away. Tuesday, January 27 and Thursday 29, 2015. Dawn-time in Times of Troika. The Wanderer woke up his invalid mother and moved her with his wife's help, on a blue swivel chair with a set of wheels, to her armchair; she needs the help of both of them for this procedure. Then he walked to the National Organization For Health Care Services Provision (NOHCSP), in Akadēmias 21 Street, a half-an-hour walk. He had to apply on behalf of his mother for a refund for his father's funeral expenses. On his way there he noticed the presence of a human being, a doomed one, sleeping on the pavement, in the cold, under a couple of dirty, stinky blankets. At 7 o'clock in the morning he was already there; he had all the necessary documents in his handbag.

He took his little sheet of paper from the queue-number-machine which turned out to be a little shit of paper for the place was crowded, the procedure fucking slow for everybody, and a couple right-wingers with fat bellies and the usual "I know it all" look on their faces, were talking aloud and provocatively about the hell that awaited Greece in case of a Grexit. He was not in the mood to talk not only because he was mourning his father but because he used to abstain from such conversations with strangers for he was convinced that stupidity is unbeatable. However one of these "I know everything" right-wingers was extremely provocative. He had no idea why he decided that he had to talk to him too, as far as he was already delivering his great sermon to at least two other people in there. So, after he repeated the well-known slanderous stupidity "Mazi ta fagame — We all ate it together," meaning that we are all responsible for the debt, he turned to the Wanderer and asked him: "I was in Germany from 1970 until 2003. I know Germany well. Tell me, do you know why most Greeks buy the Volks-Wagens? It's the best car, isn't it? Do you know any better car than the Volks-Wagen? Tell me." His style and arrogance and brazenness was getting on his nerves. "Of course I do know a much better car," he said, "German too." "Oh, which one?!" *BMW The Baader-Meinhof Wagen*, he said boldly. The right-wingers jaw dropped and he ended the conversation. Luckily enough he understood the Wanderer's provocation as far as he was in Germany in the seventies; unfortunately he was the only one.

At 3 o'clock, after waiting for 8 hours in this endless, slowly moving queue, it was at last the Wanderer's turn to give to the person behind the counter the documents needed for the refund. But as it turned out he was unlucky; they asked him for some more documents stating weird things, things like that his mother was his mother and not his dead father and that his father, that was dead, was not his mother that was alive. So he had to come again and spend 8 more creative hours at the heart of the NOHCSP. But we must not complain. The fachtidiots who work hard to "eliminate the annual cost of Greece's bureaucracy" for the benefit of the Greek people, have found the ideal, the most radical solution: they will nihilise all health care provisions and consequently any associated bureaucracy. And then the Wanderer's daughter was fired from her job at the publishing house at just half a day's notice. Troikan tempora, Troikan mores. She hid it from her grandma so that she would't feel beeing an even heavier burden on them all. *'Their morals and ours,'* thought the Wanderer.

Chapter 16

Sunday, December 6, 2009, 3 o'clock in the afternoon; it's not dark yet but it will become soon; the Christmas sparkling lights and decorations will be switched on; alongside with the homeless, it is a must for the image of downtown Athens, an inseparable part of its commercial life, of the circulation of commodities —the blood cells in capitalist accumulation; Christmas sparkling lights and decorations, the commodities and the homeless, show to the professional-philanthropists what God was created for and much more why God created them; their own mass media praise their social offer and their mere existence; so this is Christmas; the days are getting shorter, the nights longer, time passes unnoticed, life flows, the phantom of an uprising is haunting the venomous Green-Snakes of the Panhellenic Socialist Movement; they are afraid, as much as the venomous Blue-Snakes, that the black smokes and the red flames of last December may engulf again their nests; they are scared to death for they are secretly, behind closed doors, paving the ground for the appeal to the IMF and the EU, for the declaration of an open, ruthless class-war against the people. Fortified in their offices and their ministries, or isolated in hard-to-reach remote resorts, guarded by armies of thousands, they practice behind closed doors death and destructive cults and their leaders, prime ministers, ministers, bankers, draw their followers and their electorate, with the aid of the media, into worlds of fear for their power, obsession, despair, suicides. death while their well-payed yellow journalism brainwashes the petty-bourgeoisie with stories of sexual orgies in the occupied spaces and houses; how flattering! thinks Vas in whose name the letter "s" stands for sextremism; eros vs thanatos. It's winter, it's not dark yet but it will become soon; the Wanderer still likes the dark winter evenings; soon he will not.

Sunday, December 6, 2009, 3 o'clock in the afternoon; amidst a mass demonstration in memory of the murder, a year ago, of the young Grēgoropoulos by the cop Korkoneas, all pedestrian and motorised fully-armed anti-riot forces in the region take a command through the transmitter to dispel everyone: "crush them!"

The coppigs of the motorised Delta Squad rush to crush the Workers' Revolutionary Party's —EEK— bloc; they cover in full speed the short distance that separates them from the nearest part of the bloc, full of people of all ages holding banners and flags of EEK, and run over the 61-year-old mathematician Aggelikē Koutsoumpou member of EEK, who was held and tortured by the dictatorship following the Polytechnic uprising in 1973.

Just sometime ago the bloc had reached Syntagma Square and, having seen the strong presence of police forces, members of EEK had formed a protective cordon for their bloc, lowering the sticks of the banners and holding them cross-handed horizontally at waist-height.

At 15.05 while the first banner of EEK is already half-way ahead of Syntagma very close to the Square's pavement opposite Ermou Street, short and low intensity clashes take place between youngsters and the coppigs at the junction of Othonos, Filellēnon and Mētropoleos streets.

The coppigs of the newly motorised Delta Squad coming from Filellēnon Street at high speed, attack groups of young people; one of the policemen beats with his motorbike a young demonstrator, throws him up in the air, his body crushes on the pavement by the side of Othonos Street.

A few seconds later, these episodes end, and protesters at that point dissolve by the antiriot-police's stun grenades. But simultaneously coppigs of the Delta Squad, at least 15 to 20, appear from Karagiorgē Servias Street, rush with their motorbikes in Syntagma Square and run with frantic speed in different directions. Suddenly, in a split second, a bike storms Aggelikē, hits her violently on the front left side of her body, throws her to the ground and passes over part of the left part of her body and her head; she faints. The second coppig who rides as a passenger beats with his club whoever runs in shock to aid her. The rest of them intrude within the bloc, get off their motorbikes and start crushing heads and arms of protesters.

Doctor Dēmētrēs Georgiou yells "we have a multiple-injured patient, we need an ambulance, I am a doctor," but in response he gets the violent police-blows. Yiannēs Aggelēs, an economist, sees the doctor that has rushed to help the bleeding Aggelikē and a cop beating the doctor's hand with a baton, he rushes and holds her head, thinking she is already dead; they hit him on the head too.

Noske's political offsprings still kill...

Demonstrators from the bloc are transferred to hospitals; others are detained or arrested with whatever accusations the coppigs invent on the spot: "Possession and use of guns", "serious risk of death or serious personal injury of policemen," "damage to police vehicles," "Public order offence, breach of the public peace," "attempted prisoner's release."

Kyriakos Moutidēs, motorcycle courier, was among the ones who defended their bloc and the right of all to protest, from the fury of the police. Nikos Krynski, teacher, prevented the motorbiked cop from escaping shouting: "where are you going, you've just killed a man." The coppigs beat Krynski with batons on the head, threw him bleeding on the ground and continued to beat him. Then they arrested and referred him to trial. Although his head was bleeding while in GADA they refused to transfer him to the hospital for treatment. Thanos Zambetēs, worker-builder was sentenced to 7 months imprisonment for assault, causing bodily harm and "insult". Thanos Zambetēs was arrested and brutally beaten by dozens of cops because he also prevented the cops who almost murdered Aggelikē from escaping and withheld the bike that was used as murderous weapons against demonstrators. The coppigs who arrested him beat him brutally in the head and throughout his body.

All of them were pushed and packed with dozens others in police paddy-wagons like sardines in a tin-box, in horizontal and vertical layers. Handcuffed as they were, with their hands behind back. they started to sing the International. On top of them sat the

coppigs cursing them.

Next day, Monday morning, we joined one more demonstration against the Green-Snakes' police brutality and for once more we were attacked by the coppigs. Later on we payed a visit to Aggelikē, in the hospital. She was in critical condition and when discharged she was left with permanent hearing loss, dizziness, instability and intense post-traumatic pains.

During my night-walk in the mental company of Nazim I'm thinking, 'post-traumatic pains, state-chains, nature's chains, *and I don't bother anymore to lift my head toward the bright skies. If the stars are far, if the earth is small I don't care at all I don't mind. I want you to know that I find more astonishing more powerful more mysterious and gigantic THIS MAN stopped on his way and chained** by the State or like my poor mom, *chained* on a chair by Nature. We have to win the war against both of them.'

"You have to reach up to Hypersyntelikos of Eutropia for such achievements," told me Vas the surrealist when I revealed to him my thoughts.

"What's that?" I asked him.

"A non-state of things within the Union of Surrealist Sexual Retroperspectives,"

---

*NAZIM HIKMET, *MICROCOSMOS*, SELECTED POEMS FIRST INDIAN EDITION: APRIL 1952. PUBLISHED BY ASOKE GHOSH PARICHAYA PRAKASHANI 63, DHARMATALA STREET, CALCUTTA 13. PRINTED AT PRINTKRAFT LTD., CALCUTTA 13. ENGLISH TRANSLATIONS BY COURTESY MASSES AND MAINSTREAM.

Chapter 17

The night of the Serpents and the Serpent's Egg times of incubation, incubation in times of Blue-Snakes incubation in times of Green-Snakes state incubators para-state incubators nazis in antiriot-police uniforms Sieg Heil Sieg Heil bourgeois parliamentary incubators nights of the serpents anti-fascist resistance the Greek Horst Wessel Lied troikan nights nazis in Times of Troika thugs in times of crisis anti-fascist motorbike patrols Sieg Heil Sieg Heil street gangs arrests of anti-fascists tortures in the police headquarters nazis in the night swastikas iron crosses insignia SS SA Waffen-SS extortions arsons Fuhrerprinzip Sieg Heil Sieg Heil Sieg Heil orders for murders orders from above long nights long knives Tuesday 17 September 2013 the stab of the anti-fascist rapper MC Killah-Pavlos Fyssas by the notorious party-butcher of the thugs Roupakias Horst Wessel Lied Sieg Heil times and again Wednesday 18 September 2013 storms of stormy demonstrators on the streets acrosss the city convoys of anti-fascists towards the assassination point

Keratsini point anti-fascist patrols "¡No Pasarán!" clashes with the black front cop-pigs-nazis tear-gases the siege of the thugs' head-quarters slogans flags banners stones wrath molotovs no fear just wrath wrath wrath Friday 1 November 2013 nazis' offices by night Neo Ērakleio neighbourhood two nazis dead one wounded a manifesto by an unknown organisation "Fighting People's Revolutionary Forces" "retaliation to the murder of Pavlos Fyssas" debates speculations second thoughts urban guerrilla? agents-provocateurs? Night of the Long Knives among the nazis? up in the air all possible nothing for sure Friday 18 March 2016 butchers in Times of Troika serpents in times of Syriza hiss hiss hiss Roupakias's release.

"Fuck the MPs-Monetary Prostitutes!" Zórba gulped one more glass of rakomelo.

"Syriza's feminists are furious with you, Zórba," I said.

"Ha! The europhile pervs! I know'em well. They all come from that eurocommunist-anticommunist group formed in 68. Now they send young women to 300 euro wage-slavery and aged ones to misery, despair, death. Better them stop talking and come and suck my cock letting their cuckold co-MPs watch."

Chapter 18

It was late, it was dark in Exarcheia, in the country, in the century. They good-nighted each other and gave an appointment for the day after tomorrow to the Courts, in solidarity to the people arrested after police raided the central administration building of the University of Athens; it was occupied for days in support of the hunger strike of 4.500 prisoners protesting against Alexēs Noske's government plans to build, in times of austerity and unrest, a new type of maximum security prison that would be similar to the ignominious Stammheim's white cells. They also arranged to meet, if they could, next day, around six in the evening in Locomotiva - Cooperativa, where the coffee was cheap and of good quality and they could read some newspapers, use the free WiFi or even buy a book from the book-store. The Wanderer had already bought the latest book of the surrealist writer V. Ludens *3 on all 4s a blue-noir vinyl antinovel at 78 rpm — revolutions per moon.*

It was a moonless night. On his way home

shadows were looking for food in the always stinking trash-bins. For many years now he was trying to find the lyrics of a song that an aged communist Pole recited to him once upon a time, claiming that it was the song of a formation called something like Polish Antifascist Guard: *For the hunger, the blood and the tears, the time for revenge has come*. He never found it. 'But it's the right song in the right times, Troikan Times,' he thought. This Pole was great. A bit of a communist, a bit of an anarchist, anticlericalist and autosarcastic. "You see not all Poles are anticommunist scums," he used to say introducing himself. "Some of us carry the extremely rare political gene of the red Rosa."

He went to his aged mother's house. With the aid of his wife, Faba Crimson Sunshine, they moved her from the armchair to her bed on the blue swivel chair with the wheels. They follow the same procedure four times per day. Morning, midday, afternoon, night. They give her her pills four times per day: morning, midday, afternoon, night. And only twice per day they pay a private nurse to come and bathe her and take care of her skin in order to avoide bleeding and additional suffering; but their heart is bleeding watching her like this, and their budget is bleeding too, after all these cuts and cuts and cuts in the pensions of the powerless aged people, the decrease of the incomes and the increase of the taxes, for the sake of the capitalist bandits, both the Greek and the foreign ones.

Times and again he has seen the aged people, in streets, rolling the heavy chainshot of the debt about with them, prisoners of Troikan Times, or on benches, and in cafés, *heads bent over the table, a newspaper in front of them, and in the miserable banality of old age, they think not only of Prudence, how it fooled them,** but of their ruined by Troika lives, of their wasted hardships and of a miserable in a miserable place death.

He watched the news on various channels. The *little parrots*, as people with common sense call the well-payed newsyesmen and the newsyeswomen, were broadcasting the latest, breaking, news from the evacuation of the University occupation by the Alexēs Noske government, as objectively as they could: by copying and pasting the announcements of the General Directorate of the Attica Police: "The Greek police apprehended a Polish citizen for whom a European arrest warrant for drug trafficking has been issued. The Polish citizen was apprehended during a police raid last night in the region around the administrative building of Athens University, which is under occupation by anarchists for the 16th consecutive day.

*Paraphrase by V. Ludens. Original C.P. Cavafy, *An Old Man*, Translated from Greek by Edmund Keeley/Philip Sherrard

"A total of 21 people were detained last night and 15 of them, including ten Greeks, two Algerians, two Afghans and the Pole, were subsequently arrested. All of them are suspected of having participated in the occupation of the University building."

'So in the region around the administrative building,' thought the Wanderer. 'For how many square centimeters, meters or kilometres does this region extend?' he wondered. 'Only very few will ask. Only very few will doubt that the Pole and the Afghans were detained indeed from inside the Occupation and not 560 meters away, somewhere around Omonoia Square where junkies and Afghans tend to gather. For as Joseph Goebbels wrote once upon a time, thought the Wanderer, *if you tell a lie big enough and keep repeating it, people will eventually come to believe it. The lie can be maintained only for such time as the State can shield the people from the political, economic and/or military consequences of the lie. It thus becomes vitally important for the State to use all of its powers to repress dissent, for the truth is the mortal enemy of the lie, and thus by extension, the truth is the greatest enemy of the State.*'

The Wanderer is a wanderer in Time too, he travels to the past; past years full of events; personal and social; the Anti-Fascist Motorbike Patrol; the same day alongside with more or less 50.000 people I took the streets to protest against Angela Merkel visit to Athens; helicopters were hovering noisily around downtown Athens area; they are extremely annoying; they don't use jet fuel to fly but pensions, salaries, medicines, the blood, the toil, the tears and the sweat of the people. Youngsters with no future picked stones from the pre-cracked pavements and hurled them against the antiriot-police; they respond in the usual way: tear-gas, pepper spray, stun grenades, brutal detentions and arrests; nine days later, October 18, rallies, ferocious clashes between anti-austerity protesters and riots-police; a sixty-six-years old man dies during the protests.

The Wanderer remembers very well the events of the Anti-Fascist Motorbike Patrol, the clashes with the nazi thugs and the protection offered to them by the antiriot-police for he is a wanderer, the spirit of the streets, the squares, the avenues and the dark alleys, where as soon as it gets dark, women with shining thighs wander too, desperately searching for what? I know not, for there are no prostitutes, not at all, the prostitutes are in offices and chambers, in front of monitors full of economic data and numbers, or around tables in meetings and gatherings and economic committees....

Pretty soon after the clashes and the arrests, we were informed through a network of lawyers and other undisclosed anti-fascist activists, that the 15 protesters that were arrested during the clashes with the supporters of neo-Nazi gangs and 25 more that were arrested the next day just because they gathered and expressed their support and solidarity to the former, were tortured in the Attica General Police Directorate, beaten, electric-shocked with tasers, forced to strip naked and bend over in front of officers, slapped, spat on, used as ashtrays, kept awake all night with torches and lasers being shone in their eyes, burned on the arms with cigarette lighters, kicked in the testicles, videotaped and threatened by coppigs that their pictures and home addresses will be send to Golden Dawn's bandits, women arrestees were tortured too, the coppigs pulled their head back by the hair when they tried to avoid being filmed, they were sexually insulted, not surprising at all, Zórba had heard them on many occasions insulting young women during arrests shouting "now we will fuck you cunts, we will stick the club up your ass whore and you're going to love it." The arrestees were keeping eye contact to give each other courage. A coppig was saying on his mobile, "I'm at work and I'm fucking them, I'm fucking them up well."

We, the Trinity, and all the like-minded people, are upset, angry but by no means scared. On the contrary, we all feel extremely exalted. Like on November the 7th of the year 2012, year in Times of Troika, when we marched and demonstrated under a heavy rain and heavy tear-gas and flash grenade shots, a big company of friends of mine and my daughter's friends, holding hands, arm in arm, my wife my daughter her husband and strangers, strangers in the night exchanging glances, wond'ring in the night what were the chances to overthrow the Troikan government through a generalised upheaval, for a shift in the events, for more severe, more decisive and organised battles. Ah! The joy, the incombatible rapture of the combat!

On my way back home from Locomotiva, a few days after the Anti-fascist Motorbike Patrol's events, I was thinking that all these young men and women had felt and learned on their tortured bodies what all serious social scientists consider a historic-logical truth: fascism is nothing else than the monstrous face of Capitalism in periods of crisis.

Maria Margaronis revealed these atrocities in an article published in theguardian on October 9, 2012; Public Order Minister Nikos Dendias announced the Greek government's intention to file a lawsuit against theguardian which although it's by no means a communist paper, was much hated by the Greek police officers. As far as I am concerned although by no means *a collective propagandist, a collective*

agitator, and a collective organiser of the proletariat
—on the contrary— still theguardian remains
part of things I miss: cloudy mornings, pints
of cold milk left by the milkman, thick-cut
English orange marmalade, cold too, theguardian's paper-edition, green path-ways,
kind old ladies, "thank you luv," and, maybe,
a naughty English policewoman; a very young
one. As soon as the calendar showed summer
she was wearing her light summer dress and
she was trying to get some tan under a pale
sun; half-nude, in her back-yard. "Sorry for...
upsetting you," she had said, although I had
intruded upon her semi-privacy. I was Zórba
and I had sensed female flesh...

Yes, Zórba is addicted to female flesh, at
least Zórba I'm talking about right now, the
one that was split from Vas the surrealist
during their baptism with Beatrice's erotic
juices. They started different lives in different
worlds. Zórba lives alone, wanders around in
the company of females from all paths of life
and all the countries of the world because he
is an internationalist in praxis; in the sexual
praxis and carries always around a latest-
generation bleu-azure Glock pistol. This habit
of his reinforced the rumours about his in-
volvement in the *"Sexterminate Mistress Troika
Plot."* Vas the surrealist on the other hand is
with daughter by his only dearest and rarely
carries arms by his dark side.

Chapter 19

I too made a pass through this yesmen gathering, just to check numbers and "styles, but didn't stay any longer, I considered it a great shame to be there" said the Wanderer, a few days after the *We stay in EU* gathering, when they met again in Locomotiva, "but it was too late last night to tell you about the person I saw there.

"She was a woman I had met ages ago in Essex University, when I was 'on the road,' wandering here and there, in hallways, pathways and passage-ways, *an exile from the gods and a wanderer*.

"I was an undergraduate student then in Athens. She was the Greek double of Jackie Kennedy at the age of nineteen. So, she was there, in the pro-EU gathering and I recognised her immediately, she was waving an €U flag; she had a bored teen girl by her side, most obviously her daughter for she looked much like her. She saw me but she didn't recognise me. You see I was wearing a pair of hipster tartaruga glasses those days, a hipster 40 years ahead of my age, an optimist and a fu-

*Empedoclēs fr (107)115

turist.

"In my room, I had a kind of hand-made wall-paper, hand-made and hand-written in my own illegible hand-writing, so illegible that it looked like Chinese, a real dàzìbào;" at this point the Wanderer touched Eva's screen and with the aid of Locomotiva's WiFi presented to us the text of his dàzìbào:

Leon Trotsky

On Optimism and Pessimism

On the 20th Century and on Many Other Issues

(1901)

Dum spiro spero! [While there is life, there's hope!] ... If I were one of the celestial bodies, I would look with complete detachment upon this miserable ball of dust and dirt ... I would shine upon the good and the evil alike ... But I am a man. World history which to you, dispassionate gobbler of science, to you, book-keeper of eternity, seems only a negligible moment in the balance of time, is to me everything! As long as I breathe, I shall fight for the future, that radiant future in which man, strong and beautiful, will become master of the drifting stream of his history and will direct it towards the boundless horizon of beauty, joy, and happiness! ...

The nineteenth century has in many ways satisfied and has in even more ways deceived the hopes of the optimist ... It has compelled him to transfer most of his hopes to twentieth century. Whenever the optimist was confronted by an atrocious fact, he exclaimed: What, and this can happen on the threshold of the twentieth century! When he drew wonderful pictured of the harmonious future, he placed them in the twentieth century.

And now that century has come! What has it brought with it from the outset?

In France — the poisonous foam of racial hatred [1]; in Austria — nationalist strife ...; in South Africa — the agony of a tiny people, which is being murdered by a colossus [2]; on the 'free' island itself — triumphant hymns to the victorious greed of jingoist jobbers; dramatic 'complications' in the east; rebellions of starving popular masses in Italy, Bulgaria, Romania ... Hatred and murder, famine and blood ...

It seems as if the new century, this gigantic newcomer, were bent at the very moment of its appearance to drive the optimist into absolute pessimism and civic nirvana.

— Death to Utopia! Death to faith! Death to love! Death to hope! thunders the twentieth century in salvos of fire and in the rumbling of guns.

— Surrender, you pathetic dreamer. Here I am, your long awaited twentieth century, your 'future.'

— No, replies the unhumbled optimist: You, you are only the present.

"Nothing represented more my faith in Utopia, hope, love for the future, than this Trotskyist 'battle-cry for the future' and, of course, the science-fiction novels of Olaf Stapledon. I liked also Arthur Clarke and Asimov but for me Stapledon was the best. I got only

209

disappointed a bit when I read *Sirius A Fantasy of Love and Discord*; I was expecting more daring and explicit descriptions of the encounters between Plaxy and Sirius."

"Even so, he was ahead of his era," said Vas, in whose name "V" stood for Victory, "a" for avant-garde and "s" for surrealism; "he wrote this novel in 1944 and in England, a mostly conservative in sexual matters society, so what he did was well done. Don't forget that our great surrealist poet, writer and psychoanalyst Andreas Empeirikos, who at the same time, in 1945 started writing his magnus opus *Megas Anatolikos*, where he narrates the first trip of the ocean liner *Great Eastern* from England to America and describes it as a hedonic vessel where the multitude of the passengers enjoy sex of all kinds and combinations, sex without and beyond limits not excluding woman-dog encounters, didn't dare to publish it till his death; it was his wife and their son that dared to bring it in the open, in 1990 I think and not without cost as far as all the reactionary forces of the Greek society formed a black front against them. And the weird and discouraging thing is that as far as I know from his publisher, what he dared do in 1990 he wouldn't dare do it again in our days. But not so weird if you think that the great-great majority of our 'intellectuals' align with the ruling class and Troika.... O tempora o mores! Dark ages all along the line..."

"However I think that Empeirikos is lights years ahead. It's not only that his style is the most explicit ever, that he masters the Greek language to the highest degree, it is that his magnum-opus novel *Great Eastern* constitutes a manifesto of sexual liberation, part of his broader social and philosophical liberation dream, liberation from any kind of oppression; don't forget he was a phychoanalyst. Empeirikos is as great as de Sade but his is *The anti-de Sade*, he stands for mutual sexual pleasure, for life, not for death."

"Maybe so, but if you're interested I have a source of alternative science-fiction novels, alternative not only in the sense of writing, but in the sense of reading too, I mean a sur-realist way of reading of already existing novels, which blurs the limits between reader and writer.... Most of them are published, or related in an unspecified way, by *Voyage to the USSR Union of Surrealist Sexual Retroperspectives*, an avant-garde publishing house, the same that publishes the works of V. Ludens, and as far as I know it's not only a publishing house but an art movement in progress, in-terconnected with the *Movement for the Eroto-multiplication of the Infinity*, the *Network for the Coming of the New Paradises*, the *Non-Committee of Erototopography* and with the *Situationiste Intersexional*.

We followed him upstairs to the bookstore; "to show you somethings," he had suggested to us "and I shall finish my story with Jackie later, all this is much more interesting."

The Locomotiva's bookshop. Small square tables and black cylindrical stools, A few students using laptops and tablets. They either couldn't afford to pay for an internet connection at home or they wanted to socialise. Through the openings of the loft, where the bookshop was, I could see perspectives out of the ordinary, perspectives that others could not see or perceive in a similar way: Locomotiva's ground floor, the bar and the café, the outdoors part and even USSR's bars and the cafés in outer space habitats. At the back of the bookstore we saw Aggelikē, a mathematician, who works voluntarily in the bookshop. She was not feeling very well, she was suffering from vertigo again, it all started a few years ago, when she was injured seriously, almost fatally, during the demonstration.

She smiled politely and modestly to us.

"We'll just have a look around, just show to us where the science fiction section is, please," I told her. She did.

"Here we are," I said to the others.

"But first of all look at this, this is *Wanderotica* by V. Ludens," the Wanderer rushed to inform us, took the copy from the shelves and passed it to us, "where you'll find every-

thing about the Movement for the Erotomultiplication of the Infinity, about the Network
for the Coming of the New Paradises, the
Non-Commitee of Erototopography, the Situationiste Intersexionale and lots of other surrealities." It was a bulky volume with a
woman's head in clay on its cover, a highly
erotic head.

"And now, let's sit at the table over there
and I shall bring you a couple of science
fiction books that are written or can be read
in a surrealist way," I suggested. I laid all of
them on a chair by the table from where we
started taking them flipping through their
pages and reading them; pocket-size books
with edges in all the colours of the rainbow.

An Orange Spacework by Anthony Guessbur
Oh night, bliss, darkness, fuck and heaven! Oh, it
was gorgeousness and gorgeousity made hot flesh.
It was a shining flesh armour against all odds and
maladies and terrors, flesh like mercury flowing in a
spaceship, gravitationally locked, gravity all
sensualised now, we had only one day every two
years and the nights were ours to fuck them.... As I
slooshed their moans, I knew such lovely pictures!

The Caves of Flesh by Isaac Alilov
Jessie rummaged through her bag for her vibrator. If
there were one thing, Baley had once said solemnly,
that had resisted mechanical improvement since

medieval times, it was a woman's bag.

The Moon is a Harsh Moaner by Herbert Roblein
That we were sex slaves I had known all my life —
and nothing could be done about it. True, we weren't
bought and sold — but as long as Authority held
monopoly over what we had to do and what we
could not refuse, we were sex slaves.
I spent time then satisfying Mike down trying to
make him happy, having figured out what he liked
most.

Do Androids Dream of Electric Cunts? by Randy Dick
I'd like to see you move up and down on my electric
pole, where I think you belong.

The Lust Machine by Rachel Wells
For a moment I was staggered, though the import of
this gesture was plain enough. The question had
come into my mind abruptly: were these women so
lustful?

A Cuntickle for Lesbowitz by Walter Millet, Jr

Jailbait's End by Arthur Flarke
Jean was definitely "The jailbait" who mattered,
despite her queer ideas and queerer friends. He had
no intention of totally abandoning Naomi or Joy or
Elsa or —what was her name?— Denise; but the
time had come for something more mischievous...

216

Starlust by Neil Mangai

And there was a voice, a deep clear, female voice, which said "Ow", and then, very quietly, she said "Fuck", and then she said "Ow", once more, and then "Fuck me,..." again.

The other girl looked at him with luminous eyes, eyes the blue of the sky. "I hope you'll not choke me with it,' she said, flatly, and parted her lips....

"I would not wish to fuck someone who had already been fucking my sisters. It would be," she opined, "like having someone else break in one's own pony..."

"So,... are you pony-girls? You and your sisters?..." he asked her seriously...

She didn't reply, just looked at him with luminous eyes, eyes the blue of the sea.

"You should have let me take it back then, for my sisters and me. We could have been young again, well into the next age of the world and share you. They all do."

"Nonetheless, you have my heart. I hope your sisters will not be too hard on you, when we'll return to them without it, just with my cock..."

She could hear, some way off, the boys, Auguste, Junio, Jules calling to each other in the woods behind the aged spaceship that served as their home and shelter. She hoped desperately that their game would bring them where she was hiding, wet, horny, desperate for a fuck, any fuck.

Somehow she knew that you didn't get many chances like this in your life: moments when you knew, without any doubt, that you were alive, when you felt the air in your lungs and the wet grass beneath your feet and the cotton on your skin; chances when you were completely in the present, when neither the past nor the future mattered, ready and willing to dive in the Twilight Zone's Sea of Lust.

She tried to slow her breathing, hoping somehow to make this moment last forever.

Rendezvous With Sita by Arthur Flarke
All women, the Starship's General Assembly had decided long ago, should be welcomed aboard ship; weightlessness did wonders to their breasts that were fuckshinating. It was hot enough when they were motionless; but when they started to move, and sympathetic vibrations set in, it was more than any warm-blooded male or female should be asked to take.

A Fire Upon the Deep by Vernor Vinge
Sometimes terror and pain are not the best levers; deception, when it works, is the most elegant and the least expensive manipulation of all.

The Illustrated Nympho by Ray Burybrad
The sounds of lust were fanned out on the summer air by the whirling vents of the grottoes where the nymphos hid like undersea creatures, under electric cones, their hair curled into wild whorls and peaks, their cunts screwed, their eyes shrewd and glassy,

animal and sly, their mouths painted a neon red.

3 on all 4s the real story without dystopic deviations
by V Ludens
Here is straight sexual realmity, where the narrative
of the heroines' sexual encounters in and around the
altopian dorms takes the form of a nightdream of a
Better Obtainable World Next Door; the unleashed
powers of libidinal impulses; the mesmerizing effects
of erotic idleness; a superscience in a libertarian
communist world that can produce indestructible
modern conveniences for all free of charge; and the
inspiring struggle between the humdrum misery of
religion-driven anti-eroticism —even of revolutionary
asceticism— and the enchantment of far-reaching
encounters in the Hearths of Arson Hall of Rebellion
in a better parallel world.

OYTE —The Hypersyntelikos of Eutropia by V. Ludens
BELIEVABLE SEXCITING AND SATISFYING
"Solid sextertainment in all four dimensions, with
plenty of startling plot twists."

Magazine of Sexual Realmities

"Supersexual enough to keep you up too late, horny
and wondering how to get off."

Altopian Traveller

"First-rate Ludens."

Wanderotica Chronicles

"Ludens has constructed a sexpense plot admirably

rich in tricks and twists; and he has combined fluent reading with a good deal of revolutionary politics and new sexpectives."

Blue Moon Tribune

"We don't object to any new sexpectives, but please continue the story with Jackie's double," we teased the Wanderer.

"I don't remember her name anymore, she was a student, I don't remember from which city, she was Greek, I met her in Essex.

"It was summer time and my arrival there created a weird atmosphere all around the Towers from the very first night. During the flight to Heathrow, three guys from Kastoria had seen the red hammer and sickle on the front page of my paper and the red-star pin badge on my jumper and, as it turned out later, they were planning to 'teach me a lesson to remember' for they were fascists. Two of them were first cousins and their families were involved in the fur trade.

"As soon as we arrived in Essex, we were scattered and accommodated in the Towers. I arranged my things in my room and went out for a walk. Then I went to the bar. The Kastorians were already there playing pools, but till then I didn't know they were fascists.

"I asked for ouzo. The girl behind the bar, a brunette curly-haired Scottish with a '*whiskey made me do it'* black sleeveless t-shirt on her, told me that they were serving only pernod but if I insisted on ouzo she could share with me the bottle she kept in her room after eleven o'clock. I told her that after her offer I had one more reason to insist. She gave me her room's and staircase's number. We didn't say anything more, she was too busy taking orders.

"I took an orange-juice and sat on my own somewhere by the window. After some-time a blond girl approached me. 'So, you're the one they're talking about,' she told me in Greek. 'We're in the same staircase and I overheard them. They're enraged at you for daring to open a communist newspaper on the plane. They have plans for you, I don't know what but you have to be careful.' That was Ava, a nice girl from Thessaloniki.

" 'Thanks for the warning,' I told her, 'I'll wait for them.' I was mad and wild and fearless these days, training in shotokan karate, looking forward for clashes, barricades and the armed joy.

"We became good friends with Ava from the very first moment. She kept informing me all the time of their conversations and movements, she kept crying on my shoulder for her unfaithful fiancé and smoking packs of ASSOS AFILTRO.

"We became lovers with Barbara, from the

very first night in her room, over a bottle of ouzo, the pack of ASSOS I used always to carry through my wanderings abroad, for they were very popular, and revolutionary songs from some Scottish organisation I can't recall its name; we kept drinking, smoking and fucking to the rhythm of the Band Played Waltzing Matilda with Liam Clancy.

"The next day Barbara introduced me to a group of Spanish and Turkish anti-fascists and we formed a kind of informal 'front' against the Greek fascists who lost any interest in me until the day Jacky appeared.

"I don't remember where from. Maybe she was always there. I can't tell. She was considered pretty, she was not the type of woman I would even lay my eyes on, she was freezingly cold, aloof and a bloody royalist; she had taken pictures with all the wax mummies of all the royal families in the wax Museum; with all the corpses of history....

"But the weirdest of all was her 'vice,' her obsession. Who knows what unresolved mother-daughter issues she had, what stories of 'red terror and red rapes' she had heard in her family of royalists and army officers, that urged her to want 'to get fucked by a communist!' She was insane!

"So she started chasing me in the most profound way across the campus, day and night, something that enraged again the fascists who liked her a lot and wanted her for themselves, considering her to be one of their kind.

" 'For God's sake,' she told me once, by the lake in front of the library, 'other men are pleading to fuck and now I'm pleading you to fuck me and you don't want to, even for once!'

" 'Please, please, please,' told me Barbara, 'do me the favour and fuck this royal bitch and don't think of me, I really don't give a shit, especially if you fuck her in the ass...'

"And then came our friend Adie, actually Barbara's friend and told me, 'Gang tae th' whoor 'n' teel 'er, let's dae it Scottish style, let's bugger scots wey 'n' efter ye bugger her she wull ask ye whaur does th' 'scottish wey' come in? then ye teel tae th' royal whoor'. I'll pay ye neist week...'

"I was surprised by Barbara. None of my previous girlfriends would have allowed, not to say encouraged me, to fuck another woman. Even the leftists were very possessive and if they could they would have trapped my cock into their vagina or even drafted me into their womb and kept me in there for ever if they could. This Scottish girl had a very communal spirit.

"Next day, around eight at night, I went to Jackie's room. It was in a mess, clothes, shoes, books, family photos, bottles and bottlets. On the white wall over her bed she had hung a Greek royal flag, it had a huge crown in the middle of the white cross. 'It's a banned flag after the 1974 referendum,' I said.

"She smiled, 'we're not here to argue about politics, let's fuck,' she said.

"I unrobed her and despite her complains, I unhanged her royal flag from the wall, spread it over her bed, backed and pushed her on it, climbed on her and started fucking her missionary.

"She climaxed fast and easily and in the same missionary position I pushed my cock into her asshole; it was already wet for she had used her own juices to lubricate it with her middle finger...

"When we finished and she got up to go to the bathroom, I noticed with a lot of pleasure some stains of shit on the crown of the flag.

"So, when I saw her again, after all these years, waving her €U flag, I thought that this piece of fabric could have had been used in other more sexciting ways."

We asked for one more bottle of rakomelo.

But she had recognised him; and she felt extremely embarrassed; 'what if he dared to talk to her in the presence of her teen daughter?' she thought.

'I begged him to fuck me,' she recalled. 'He plunged his cock deep into my ass; never before I had something so hard or so deep inside. He had me thrusting up against him from being so turned on; I was out of control; after a while I felt like his cock was going into my colon, so I asked him to ease down; I got so wild at one point I pulled him out of my ass and shoved him back in my vagina begging him to unload for me; it was at this point I noticed something strange; my ass was really wet; we both came; he used the flag from under me to clean up with and that's when I was faced with the absolute shame; a huge brown spot on the royal crown, in the middle of the flag; I got furious and shouted at him; "relax baby." he told me, "we're not kingdom of Greece anymore, so this piece of shit represents nothing." '

"Narrator!" said Zórba in a teasingly commanding voice, "please tell us, what are all these stories you're wide-spreading about Vas the surrealist who, 'on the other hand, the right hand of lightness, never carries arms, got married and has a daughter while Zórba on the left hand of darkness carries always a blue Glock and is a womaniser?' "

DEAR ZORBA, BOTH OF US, ALONGSIDE
WITH THE WANDERER, WHO WANDERS
IN THE CONTINUUM, WE WONDER AND
EVEN WORRY IF THE GLOCK YOU CARRY
HERE AND THERE NOW AND THEN IS A
SIGN OF AN AESTHETICIZATION OF VIO-
LENCE ON YOUR SIDE.

IN ANY CASE BEAR IN MIND THAT
WHETHER OR NOT A TERRORIST AT-
TACK, EVEN IF "SUCCESSFUL," PRO-
VOKES DISTURBANCE IN THE RULING
CIRCLES DEPENDS ON THE CONCRETE
POLITICAL CIRCUMSTANCES. IN ANY
CASE, THIS DISTURBANCE CAN ONLY BE
SHORT-LIVED; THE CAPITALIST STATE
DOES NOT REST ON MINISTERS AND
CANNOT BE DESTROYED TOGETHER
WITH THEM. THE CLASSES WHICH IT
SERVES WILL ALWAYS FIND NEW MEN;
THE MECHANISM REMAINS INTACT AND
CONTINUES ITS WORK.

BUT THE DISTURBANCE WHICH THE
TERRORIST ATTACK BRINGS TO THE
RANKS OF THE WORKING MASSES
THEMSELVES IS MUCH MORE PRO-
FOUND. IF IT SUFFICES TO ARM ONE-
SELF WITH A REVOLVER TO ARRIVE AT
THE GOAL, WHY THEN THE EFFORTS OF
THE CLASS STRUGGLE? IF ONE CAN IN-
TIMIDATE HIGH-RANKING PEOPLE WITH
THE THUNDER OF AN EXPLOSION, WHY
THEN A PARTY?

Chapter 20

Evelpidon Courts spring time April again year 2015 building no16 examining magistrate antiriot-police cordons safeguard the burial of the hopes we are all there waiting for the arrestees to arrive who are we I wonder and who is who but who cares time passes I see the slim blond figure of Anny the lawyer from afar she waves to me I approach her and we talk for a while we keep meeting often these days amidst these hard times here in the cruel heart of the juridical branch of the coercion apparatus of the state her as an experienced lawyer of the combatants and me expressing my solidarity to them after all *No man is an iland, intire of it selfe; every man is a peece of the Continent, a part of the maine; if a clod bee washed away by the Sea, Europe is the lesse, as well as if a Promontorie were, as well as if a Mannor of thy friends or of thine owne were; any mans death diminishes me, because I am involved in Mankinde; And therefore never send to know for whom the bell tolls; It tolls for thee...* that's how I got acquainted with the Spanish Civil War the

International Brigades the Abraham Lincoln Battalion the British Battalion and of course the CNT the FAI and the POUM there is a tension in the air the dark-blue police paddy-wagons arrive the coppigs most of them sympathisers of the nazist Golden Dawn put on their gas masks ready to spray us like cockroaches after all the gang they are voting for adores the gas-chambers at Auschwitz its leaders take selfies there smiling in front of the iron gates of the avons slogans waver in the air "*to pathos gia tēn lefteria einai dynatotero apo ola ta kelia*" the arrestees are coming out in couples hand-cuffed the right hand of the one handcuffed to the left of the other among them a white-haired father and his son lots of young girls with radiant faces and two junkies that the Wanderer said that he has seen many times before around Omonoia Square during his endless wanderings in downtown Athens and this particular scene this well-prepared for the sake of propaganda mixture of people brings to my mind some verses written in 1935 by the communist and exiled poet Kostas Varnalēs

Mas siderodesane ta heria
kai mas kleisan olouthe manliheria
[...]
Moudiasane sfihtodeta kairo
xeri dexi me xer aristero

[...]
Mazi mas teleutaioi me to vapori
prezakēdes, alania, lathremporoi

Xepitēdes gia na fanei pos isia
logiountai   leuteria kai ta xasisia

They locked with iron cuffs our hands
rounded us by guards with arms in hands
[...]
restrained the left with the right hand
for time long they became numb
[...]
and they mixed us in the steamers
with junkies, vagabonds and smugglers

on purpose to equate as they wish
struggle for liberty with the hashis

Two or three days later I went again to
the Evelpidon Courts. With my daughter this
time. They were arresting people every day.
Building no7, room 2 this time. Once again
scenes that look like coming from the far
past, but this was just an illusion. They were
nowadays scenes and scenes coming from
the future. Young girls and boys handcuffed
but no trace fear in their faces just the black
circles of sleeplessness round their eyes; but
this is common socially-generated disorder
in the nights of Troika; of the unemployed,

the homeless, the pensioners, for the great majority of the people.

The courtroom is overthronged with groups of undercover policemen, supporters of the arrestees, antiriot-squads in full gear, couples of anxious mothers and fathers; some of them took part in the Polytechnic uprising against the military junta and in the flaming demonstrations and clashes of the first years after its collapse, they feel proud at the bottom of their heart, seeing the "state's handcuffs" around the wrists of their off-springs. Anny, the lawyer was talking with a couple in their fifties in the yard of the Courts sometime ago. I had approached her, she had introduced me to both of them; after she left for the courtroom we started talking; their daughter was one of the arrestees; both of them are architects and the last years they saw a dramatic decline in demand for their services. I told them that many architects running smaller firms face similar problems in UK too, but of course the cost of life is lower there. Then I remembered David C. and his wife Eileen. They had invited me to their house in the woods, I can't recall the place and then they took me to a nice Indian restaurant, downtown I think. Then David came to my house in Athens for a couple of days, or was it before the woods incident? Anyway. The first night I took him to a silly student's café in Exarcheia, I had been away for a couple of years and didn't know any good place around anymore and then we took him with my wife, Faba Crimson, to one or two more decent tavernas, always close to Exarcheia. David liked a lot the view of the illuminated Lykavēttos hill from our terrace and my father liked a lot David. "Keep in touch with David," he kept saying to me.

"I do keep in touch dad."

"Tell him to come again, to visit us."

"I do tell him so dad, but he is far away now, he is not anymore in Britain, he moved with his wife to the States."

"Ah, the States, I too have been there, to America, New York, Kansas, Massachusetts, Michigan, Ithaka, Cornell, Illinois..."

'Poor dad', I thought; 'he died in Times of Troika, in a hospital managed by well-payed pro-Troikan fachtidiot managers and not by councils and general assemblies of its personnel; after the ambulance brought him to the emergencies and he was admitted with severe chemical and bacterial pneumonia, he was left lying on the stretcher with just only an oxygen-mask for thirteen hours, from 1pm until 2am next day, before he was carried to the ward; there the pro-Troikans had left only one nurse for every fifty patients; the battle was uneven; on the one side of the barricade were my father, the doctors, the nurses, the cleaners and on the other side Death, the Troika, the State, the Government, the manager of the hospital; "come on dad", we kept telling him, "get well, you have to get well, get out of here and go to the coming elections and vote;" "what are we going to vote for?" he asked, but his voice was so weak that we could hardly hear him: in the next few hours he lost it completely and in a few days he passed away. We voted and in a way we did it on his behalf; we voted "for an Emergency Plan to meet the social needs by expropriation of the banks and key sectors of the economy under workers control and workers management; for workers power and the socialist unification of Europe from Lisbon to Vladivostok, on the ruins of the imperialist European Union!"*

Before dad's end. We take shifts by his side. The staff is almost non-existing. For the hard night-shift 11:00 am to 7:00 pm we pay a private nurse. We share the rest 16 hours with my wife. At the same time we take care of my mom, back at home. At least she is lying on her own bed, watching from time to time TV, while dad is lying on a rotten bed in a hospital badly damaged by the economic napalms of the IMF and the European Bank.

*PAYING THE VAMPIRE OF THE IMF WITH THE BLOOD OF THE GREEK WORKERS, Savas Michael-Matsas
http://www.eek.gr/index.php/englishtext/3277-paying-the-vampire-of-the-imf-with-the-blood-of-the-greek-workers

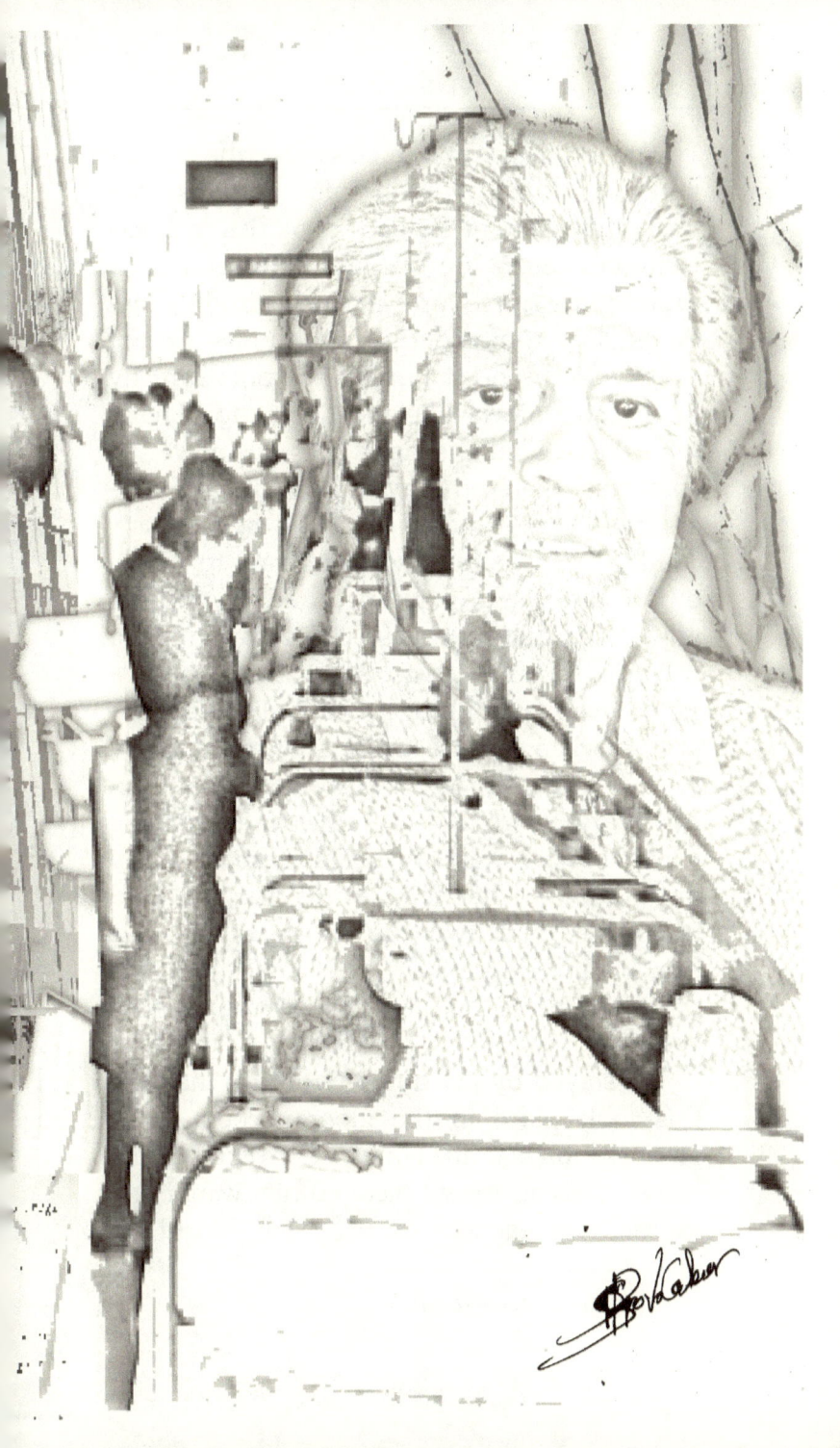

The ruthless Troikan class war, the banks-tanks, the deadly economic weapons that cause 100 percent civilian casualties, will exterminate more nurses and will lead to a ratio of one nurse for every one hundred patients and tomorrow to no nurses at all. They would send the unhealthy ones directly to the crematoria like the nazis did. That's why they aided the nazis to seize power in Ukraine; where on May 2, 2014 39 anti-government activists died in a fire at Odessa's Trade Unions House, some burned to death, others suffocated or jumped out of windows when the building was set ablaze by thugs of pro-Kiev-pro-EU nazis. They are two of a kind, a capitalist kind; for capitalism is dripping fascism from head to foot, from every pore of its rotting body, Last night, on a documentary on the TV, an old cleaner working in a hospital was crying in despair. They haven't payed her for months, her husband is ill, she had two days to eat, she was hungry and desperate.

I thought of Hamlet: '*Revenge should have no bounds.*'*

We stayed by my dying father till the end; this took place in the gloomy room, of a gloomy hospital in Times of Troika. While he was passing away I pictured him wandering in the vast espaces of the New World, in

---

*W. Shakespeare, *Hamlet* (4.7.143)

parks carpeted with deep red maple leaves, campuses, universities, universes, young and strong with dark-black hair, full of energy, dreams, plans and hope. In the Principle of Hope, Ernst Bloch wrote about medical utopias and about "*a body on which only pleasure, not pain is served and whose old age does not have frailty as its fate,*" and concluded that "*it is this fight against fate which links medical and social utopias in spite of everything.*" 'Even more,' I thought and felt, 'Bloch set ahead for us one more reason to fight capitalism, Troika and all the rest by stating that under communism it will be possible to overcome the problem of death, that human beings will eventually create God and that *true Genesis is not at the beginning but at the end.*' Eight months later we stayed by my dying mother. She died at home. We were by her side till the end. For our motto is "No comrade left alone in the hands of the State, no man left alone in the hands of Nature." It's a motto of libertarian futurist communism; I consider myself enemy both of the State and of Nature; because I share with Bloch the view that the blow against this medical and social utopia still comes from an attitude of devotion to nature, in practical empirical terms. I draw my inspiration from Prometheus Bound; bound by the State;

O divine air Breezes on swift bird-wings,

Ye river fountains, and of ocean-waves
The multitudinous laughter Mother Earth!
And thou all-seeing circle of the sun,
Behold what I, a God, from Gods endure!
Look down upon my shame,
The cruel wrong that racks my frame,
The grinding anguish that shall waste my strength,
Till time's ten thousand years have measured out
their length!
He hath devised these chains,
The new throned potentate who reigns,
Chief of the chieftains of the Blest. Ah me!
The woe which is and that which yet shall be
I wail; and question make of these wide skies
When shall the star of my deliverance rise.
And yet-and yet-exactly I foresee
All that shall come to pass; no sharp surprise
Of pain shall overtake me; what's determined
Bear, as I can, I must, knowing the might
Of strong Necessity is unconquerable.
But touching my fate silence and speech alike
Are unsupportable. For boons bestowed
On mortal men I am straitened in these bonds.
I sought the fount of fire in hollow reed
Hid privily, a measureless resource
For man, and mighty teacher of all arts.
This is the crime that I must expiate
Hung here in chains, nailed 'neath the open sky.
Ha! Ha!
What echo, what odour floats by with no sound?
God-wafted or mortal or mingled its strain?

Comes there one to this world's end, this moun-
tain-girt ground,
To have sight of my torment? Or of what is he fain?
A God ye behold in bondage and pain,
The foe of Zeus and one at feud with all
The deities that find
Submissive entry to the tyrant's hall;
His fault, too great a love of humankind.
Ah me! Ah me! what wafture nigh at hand,
As of great birds of prey, is this I hear?
The bright air fanned
Whistles and shrills with rapid beat of wings.
There cometh nought but to my spirit brings
Horror and fear.

Evelpidon Courts again and again. The President of the Court, a woman, starts reading the names of the accused. The undercover policemen try to push the people out of the courtroom and the antiriot-police blocks out violently anybody wishing to attend a trial otherwise open to the public. There is again tension in the air. Dozens of people shout rhythmically again and again: "*to-pathos gia tēn le-fte-ria einai- dy-na-totero apo-ola ta-ke lia*"

I was shouting too, neither considering my age nor respecting the *sacred* courtroom, when a rattling sound made everybody freeze out of fear. The Prosecutor, the President and the Secretary, all of them women in late forties, fell on all fours, trying to cover themselves, for they probably thought that a terrorist group was attacking the Court with submachine guns. I was not scared at all, I knew what was going on and I was accustomed to this strange almost paraphysical phenomenon. The bones of a couple of dead uncles of mine, ex army-officers, interrogators and members of court-martials during the civil war were rattling in disapproval of my behaviour. I took the liberty to explain to the scared Troika's Courtmen the real source of all this pandemonium, because just in a few minutes the initial rattling turned into a pandemonium; for as soon as, my dead uncles —army-officers, interrogators and members of court-martials— sensed that the very State Court mistook the rattling of their sacred Greek bones for rattling of submachine guns of anarchocommunist terrorists, they started rattling their bones harder, louder and quicker; for these were bones that even our national anthem names sacred, bones that just the great God of Greece helped so to not be buried, seventy years ago, in the battlefields, in their struggle against the communists who wanted to 'take our houses and turn our wifes and daughters into common property.'

It was only after the explanation I gave to the Court that the President, more pale but less loveable than Juliet said, appealing both

to the accused and their supporters:
O'ercovered quite with dead men's rattling bones,
With reeky shanks and yellow chapless skulls;
Or bid me go into a new-made grave
And hide me with a dead man in his shroud—
Things that, to hear them told, have made me tremble—
And I will do it without fear or doubt,
To live an unstained servant to this state of emergency."

Oh, yes! Oh, yes! The eternal sunshine of Shakespeare's spotless mind. The Courtmen and the Courtwomen have just admitted their guilt: they are servants to this state of emergency! And on the other hand this eternal darkness of all the others unspotless minds. Of all those who fought on the side of the State, of the collaborators of the nazis, of the British troops and Van Fleet against the communists; for they said that the bloody communists will "take their homes and turn their wifes and daughters into public property." Now in Times of Troika, the bankers of their allies are taking their homes and the press of their allies, the very same press that aided their anticommunist slanders, widespreads around the world that their granddaughters are "selling sex for the price of a sandwich as Greece's crippling recession pushes prices to an all-time low." The permanent instability of capitalism and the permanent servitude of its embedded journalism.

Zórba laughed when he read this on the foreign-press. We were in Locomotiva discussing, among others, the news about the extradition of 5 Greek students to Italy, with a European Arrest Warrant for taking part in the No Expo May Day protest in Milan on Friday, May 1, 2015 — procedure that is used exclusively in legal cases concerning serious crimes like human and drug trafficking.

The end of one thing brings the beginning of another; the end of one night brings the beginning of another night, not of another day; times flows; so we talked about the "Greek sandwich-prostitutes", and drugs.

"Such women exist only in the sex-starved minds of the foreign journalists. Greek women do not have sex for a sandwich. Only some junkies at the stage before death offer sex at this price around Socratous Street; but they were always there and these shadows-of-women have nothing to do with the present-day austerity but with other parameters that the brains of the journalists are not programmed to conceive and elaborate. "After all asked," Zórba the brut "is there any difference, between Greek women selling sex for 'a cheese pie, or a sandwich' and British female students 'selling their body because of increased living costs and rising tuition fees?' "

"Not really," said the Wanderer. "I remember

this dreadful May back in 2012. The Green-Snakes were in power. You know some people use the term 'closet-whore' in distinction to 'whore.' I think we have to adopt the term 'closet-fascists' and use it in a similar way. At least for everyday agitation. So the closet-fascists of the Green-Snakes were in power when twelve women with HIV, were arrested, charged with illegal prostitution and for allegedly intentionally infecting 'clients. and their names and photographs were published on the Greek Police's website and the right-wing and pro-fascist press. The No-health minister claimed that the action was taken because of a rise in the number of customers asking for unprotected sex for an additional fee and called the problem a 'timebomb.' It was the same minister who claimed, that 'Greek pensioners live too long, the state has to spend too much on pensions and that's where the crisis comes from!'

"It was, his EU-Master's Voice speaking, and it was a clear-cut fascist act exposing the identity of the twelve women," said Zórba; "but both the Green and Blue Snakes were competing to attract the ultra-rights and the fascists in the elections of June."

"Sure," said Zórba, "and the next stage will be to send all of them to the crematoria: the doomed, the pensioners, the weak, anybody who can't offer profit; but I think it's more than that, it's the expression of a deeper trend and tendesy of the State in times of capitalist crisis towards a state of emergency."

"But anyway. I knew most of them," continued the Wanderer in a low voice, that sounded to us as a sign of respect for their human pain. "During my endless wanderings downtown, whenever I happened to pass through Socratous Street, they were stopping me and asking for coins in a very polite way, just for fifty cents or less. I used to give them. In the course of time they got to trust me and they were saying different things, about men approaching them and asking for unprotected sex. I've overheard such conversations myself; indeed some greasy middle-aged pigs were very persisting on the matter; you know this kind of men that vow for 'Fatherland, Religion, Family,' and vote against the 'coummunists;' they can't even say it properly...

"I was downtown that May day. It was late evening. I had seen the cops nearby. One of the girls asked me for 50 cents. I gave the coin to her. She was in the area for about two years. Very young, blond, small built. A year ago she was rather beautiful. But the drugs had already turned her into a skeleton, not even a shadow of her old self; I can't imagine any man paying to go with her. They use cheap and highly toxic cocktails in our days.

It would have been much better if she was using cocktails molotov instead. I warned her that the cops were arresting people in the nearby streets. She didn't pay much attention, 'I know, I know,' she said, 'I'll be fine.' Next day I think, or the day after, I'm not sure, I saw their pictures. She was among the arrestees, mong the exposed ones. She was only eighteen. One of them, Katerina, took her life last November. She decided that life was unbearable for her. She couldn't take it anymore. She left a goodbye note and took her final high dose."

We said nothing for a while. We were thinking, contemplating, remembering, probably the same thing at the same moment. The massive demonstration of anarchists, anti-authoritarians and antifascists that took to the streets of Exarcheia against drug dealing mafias and police on Thursday night of the 3d of March 2016. The demonstration was guarded by armed people exhibiting openly their guns in the air. They had considered it necessary due to the life threatening conditions created in the area by the heavily armed drug mafias who, the participants are convinced, operate in conjunction with the police.

The Wanderer was the first one who broke the silence and our stream of thoughts. "Have a look at this," he said and passed us a printed news-bulletin.

A newly formed group, "Armed Militia Groups" claimed responsibility for the execution-style murder of a 36-year-old Egyptian in Exarcheia on July 17, 2016.

"We claim responsibility for the execution of the mafioso Habib, who for years has been the driving force behind incidents of violence against locals and regulars in the Exarcheia area, culminating with the murderous attack on three comrades in the oc-cupied Vox social centre in March.... The Egyptian, with the force of a pack cannibals that surrounded him was running a drug racket in Exarcheia and ter-rorized the neighbourhood." It also called on young people frequenting the neighborhood to stay away from drugs and gangs, warning the latter of reprisals.

"It's us or them: there is no middle ground," the group stated.

"Yes, I've read all the proclamation in In-dymedia; he was gunned down in broad daylight by two hooded assailants on a mo-torcycle who fired 5-6 shots, they used a Tokarev," said Zórba, "so people on the left hand of darkness carrying Glocks and being womanisers are not suspects, isn't so Narrator? They spend too much time hunting females." Zórba was teasing me back for what I had said once. "So, I'll tell you my thoughts," he went on. "There are the thalassa of genitality, the terra of post-mortal decay and the dark

subthalassial and subterranean flows everywhere, especially under the ground of our
decaying capital. Flows are, most of the time,
related to thalassa, to genitality; flows of
waters, flows of semen, flows of vaginal juices;
you never know when, where and how they
will come out in the open and sexplode."

The unholy Trinity has a devil's tail, not
its own but a strange tail, just a tail, something
like the cat's smile in Alice's story, but not a
smile, a tail, a tail that follows Trinity and
writes reports...

USIS 10/05/2016. TOP SECRET. (QUOTES INCLUDE
SUBJECTS WORDS) HANNAH AND ANNA, THE BLACK AND
RED HAIRED DUO WHO'S NAMES ARE PALINDROME THAT
READ THE SAME BACKWARD OR FORWARD, HAD FOUND
WAYS TO TURN THIS FEATURE INTO A PASSWORD-KEY
THAT UNLEASHES TIME TRAVEL; BACKWARD OR FORWARD.
THEIR DISCOVERY INVOLVED THE PALINDROMIC MOVEMENT
OF THE WANDERER'S EROTIC ORGAN INTO THEIR ORIFICES
BUT THE HOLE AFFAIR IS COVERED WITH UTMOST SE-
CRECY. THE BLACK AND RED DUO STANDS FOR THE
URBAN GUERRILLA, THE UNHOLY TRINITY STANDS FOR
THE ARMED PROLETARIAN REVOLUTION AND THEIR DE-
BATES ARE ALWAYS LIVELY AND FASCINATING. HANNAH
AND ANNA, CLAIM THAT DURING THEIR TIME TRAVELS
HAVE FOUND OVERWHELMING EVIDENCE PROVING THAT THE
"GERMAN DEEP-NAZI-STATE HAD CHOSEN THE 9TH OF
MAY AS A DATE TO MURDER ULRIKE MEINHOF IN THE
STAMMHEIM PRISON 40 YEARS EARLIER, FOR SYMBOLIC
REVENGEFUL REASONS. IT WAS THE VICTORY DAY, THE
DAY THAT THEY WERE DEFEATED BY THE RED ARMY,

THE PREVIOUS DAY, 8TH OF MAY 2016 WHILE THE "MONETARY PROSTITUTES WERE VOTING IN FAVOR OF NEW AUSTERITY MEASURES, INCLUDING PENSION CUTS AND TAX HIKES, THE COPPIGS OF ALEX NOSKE GOVERNMENT WERE THROWING ASPHYXIATING GAS AND FLASH-BANG GRENADES DIRECTLY ONTO US, ATTACKING, BEATING AND ARRESTING DEMONSTRATORS ALL AROUND SYNTAGMA SQUARE." THERE WAS A GATHERING OF THE RUSSIAN COMMUNITY SAME PLACE SAME TIME, TO COMMEMORATE THE VICTORY DAY, WITH BANNERS AND SONGS OF THE RED ARMY. THEY WERE ALSO FORCED TO DISPERSE. SYRISA'S ALEX NOSKE IS OBVIOUSLY THE GOOD SUB HIGHSCHOOL PUPIL WHO LOVES HARSH DOM GERMAN MIS-TRESSES. THE UNHOLY TRINITY IS NOT; THEY ARE WILD AND UNCONTROLLABLE. THEY WILL GANG-RAPE MISTRESS TROIKA FOR SURE...

FOUNDED BY LENIN AND TROTSKY; THEY HATED ULRIKE EVEN MORE BECAUSE SHE WAS IN RATHER GOOD TERMS WITH DDR." THAT WAS SAID ON MAY THE 9TH.

It's a summer's rainy night. On my way to Exarcheia I try not to step in the gutters where the lowers lie down just because the above are among the shitiest people in the whole wide world, the shitiest people in their shitiest town. I enter Locomotiva. The others are already there round the long table beneath the mural. I sit down and listen to Zórba.

"I join my voice with Subcomandante's Marcos and say *'Zórba is gay in San Francisco, black in South Africa, an Asian in Europe, a Chicano in San Ysidro, an anarchist in Spain, a Palestinian in Israel, a Mayan Indian in the streets of San Cristobal,.... a Jew in Germany, a Gypsy in Poland, a Kurd in Turkey, a Mohawk in Quebec, a pacifist in Bosnia, a single woman on the Metro at 10pm, a peasant without land, a gang member in the slums, an unemployed worker, an unhappy student'* but bear in mind that if you belong to the above and to the oppressors and to the exploiters," Zórba added, "I'll discredit you as a gay if you are a gay-oppressor, call you a negro if you're a black-oppressor cause you oppress the blacks, I'll sluttify you if you are a female oppressor and exploiter...."

Chapter 21

Bar - café Locomotiva; for one more time, for one more night. 40 °C and no wind at all. On our way there we saw walls covered with slogans and an almost ninety-year-old lady, a moving skeleton, wearing a long white night-gown, a homeless aged human being, moving like a ghost amidst the heat-wave of August from one pavement to another with the aid of strangers.

Zórba the brut drinks, dreams, contemplates, narrates, swears and curses.

"Ah, the Russian troikas, yes, Russian troikas are for romantic rides with Russian women, with these unique fiery lovers, for wild rides late at night, listening to gypsy songs and violins and accordions and drinking vodka, not much, just a little, listening to Vysotsky maybe, live music for living people.... Russian troikas are meant for the women of the world, for our other best half... the other half of the sky...

"But these Troika's women, its officers, ah, all of them are worthless cum-bucks-buckets, cum-euro-dumps, professional payed misan-thropists worth only for hate-fucking if not for the death penalty for mass crimes against humanity..."

"Zórba, you're drunk, you don't know what you're talking about," said the Wanderer.

"No, I don't think I'm drunk at all and in any case I know very well what I'm talking about... I'm sick and tired with all this polit-ically correct anti-sexism made by the rulers in order to serve the rulers.

"Their only concern is to blunt our thought and spirit by bluntening our language...

"We are at war and we'll use our language in any way we feel that it offends and de-moralises any particular group of the rulers.

"And the women of the ruling class, the ones who lead and implement all these crimes are no exception just because they are women. No, by no means.... Not to say that whenever and wherever these women seized power, they used it in the most ruthless way against the oppressed....

"Do you need examples, my dear friend? You're good in history so you don't, but..."

At this point Zórba the brut made a pause, took a sip or freshly served rakomelo from his glass and went on.... "Just look at all these wandering megaeras of Syriza, all these 'feminists,' these Troika's jesters, how they talk, act, behave against the poor, the humble, the oppressed, even of their own sex...

"And they do it in that particular and provocative way, just because they are silly worthless cunts that bourgeois feminism elevated into power.... And worse than whores they pay back their debt to the ruling class, no matter if they wear blue, green, pink or red-cyan strings.... Street whores are mostly respectful in comparison for they are toilers and downtrodden...

"Female rulers, ruthless cum-bucks-buckets earning their luxury living and luxury vacations and luxury fucking and the strap-ons they use by ruining the lives of hundreds of millions and by leading millions to death...

"So my dear Wanderer don't give me this 'political correctness' crap. Unless you want to tell me that it is legitimised to use bullets and canons against our class enemy, like the Bolsheviks did during the revolution and the civil war, but not dirty words, words that emanate from the depths of our existence...

"Dear Wanderer I'm not going to watch my mouth. Self-censorship is a suicidal process, this is a psychoanalytical fact, and I, Zórba the Greek or even better Zórba the Internationalist, have no suicidal thoughs or feelings.

"Of course, now that I'm thinking it over, if we detach the monetary parts, all these expressions I used, like cum-euro-buckets and cum-bucks-dumps, are still related, in one way or another, with the pleasures and the joy of sex. And all these scums do not deserve it. They deserve only our bullets.

"Do you know why I don't even try to meet these ruling cum-buckets and fuck the shit out of them? Because I don't want to give them the pleasure of orgasm."

"But, I think you have already impaled Dickulescu, all the way in from her anus to her mouth and simultaneously you have fucked this young Athenian cunt, the one from the movement of 'yes - we stay and get fucked in Europe,' didn't you?" I said to him.

"Oh, did I? I don't remember, maybe I did, and I think both loved it, Delphy because she had the same cock to fuck and suck at the same time; the Athenian because she was getting fucked by me and licked by Delphy at the same time, yes, maybe I did it, well nobody is perfect after all."

I looked at Zórba; unshaved but not growing a beard; grey in the course of time, but not in the fifty shades of grey. Grey is a children's book compared to Zórba's memoirs and wanderings sexposed, among other things, in *Wanderotica* and *Hypersyntelikos of Eutropia*.

"You look like a grey wolf, Zórba," I teased him a few days later when him and the Wanderer payed a visit to me, "and I don't mean the Turkish fascists, of course."

"I hope you don't mean the 'lonely-wolves-private-detectives,' either," he he said laughing back at me, "for I never eat pizza for lunch before streetfighting,I'm not a paper hero of our times, a hero in crime paperbacks; most of the time, they are wolfing down pizzas or hot-dogs, stain their suits with ketchup & mustard and then they bark 'stick 'em up man...' I'm real, realist, surrealist. I eat proper lunch, light but cooked. Street-fighting, like streetfucking, is a joy, an art, that doesn't match junk food."

"Sure," I told him, "but after all you're not coming from the USA but from the USSR, the Union of Surrealist Sexual Retrop-erspectives."

Sometimes I'm in the mood for retro situ-ations; for the lost but everexisting revolu-tionary potential of the past. I even use a vintage typewriter, where "V" in vintage, stands for Victory. Typewriters, with ribbons and covers, bought from Vintage shops, where "V" stands for Vagina. The female secretaries that have typed on them, time and again have slipped and deeped their fingers from the typewriter's keys into their vaginas, and back on the keys, covering them with their secretarial vaginal secretions. V, V, V... Vulva, Vendetta, Victory....

Nostalgia is one of the one thousand and one minor reasons that makes socialist revolution ap-

pealing. I miss the time when I was buying the
FINANCIAL TIMES from the stationary shop and then
I was rushing into the 8 o'clock train to London
King's Cross. At one past eight the train had already started without the slightest delay. Sand-
wiches with ham, hot black coffee, flirting maybe
and then on time always I was catching the tube
for Heathrow and the flight for Athens. Safe
flights, no blind terror against innocent civil-
ians, no hysterias, nothing. The family was waiting impatiently and the islands were always
there. Blue, white, erotic, full of expectations.
Or starting with the British Rail to King's Cross
and hopping from one train to another, I was visiting Paris, wandering in hallways, pathways and
passage-ways, placing red carnations at the Com-
munards' Wall at the Père Lachaise cemetery, then
visiting Venice, then Pompei.... The Last Days
of European Union.... Last days' FINANCIAL TIMES,
'was it July 2016?' I wondered, fuel this nostalgia for the past, showing, against their will,
the road to socialism by revealing the disastrous
results of privatisations: "Nightmare tales
abound of how lives have been disrupted this summer as a result of the crisis overwhelming the
Southern Rail franchise operated by Govia Thames-
link (GTR)" they write. Thus the FINANCIAL TIMES
with what they write, they pave the ground for a
global reorganization of society on a socialist
base: That's what I thought reading the news
about Greece's TRAINOSE Sold for 45 Mln Euros to
Italian Railway. And I remembered Barbara, the
Scottish young woman with the 'whiskey made me
do it' black sleeveless t-shirt; for she had
given me a Souvenir song sheet sponsored by the

Scottish Trades Union Congress 1978. There, among other revolutionary songs, was one called *The Railwayman* by Eric Bogle, a song telling a story from the past, the present, the future. The present and the future of Greek Railwaymen too. "*Now my father was a big strong man... they took away his job, when they'd no use of him anymore... after nearly thirty years... when you're 55 years old, and you're looking for some work, nobody wants to know your face... and I watched him growing older, and more bitter every day...*" So, I remembered the song, Barbara, the fascists from Kastoria, the fired workers, the unemployed sea-workers, the night of the nazist thugs when 50 Golden Dawn's members wielding crowbars and bats attacked communists distributing posters in the dock-side district of Perama, a working-class and Communist stronghold, which sent nine people in hospital with serious injuries; it was Thursday night, I3 Sep 20I3. And then browsing through some of the headlines of July 20I6, I recalled the dilemma set by Engels and Rosa Luxemburg: Socialism or barbarism? Global terror Lone wolf attacks raise the tempo of terror in Europe France Normandy town adjusts to arrival of terror. Attacks no longer confined to big cities or tourist centres. 'Nostalgó*' the tranquillity, the idleness, the wanderings, the adventures of the past. Even the veinless Sunday afternoons, spent in vain with cheese and biscuits, overseas reverse charge calls and fountain pens filling with blue ink drawing pads, with blood my penile veins and with magenda dreams the espaces of the Union of Surrealist Sexual Retroperspectives USSR-CCCP.

*Nostalgó (Verb, in Greek): I am filled with nostalgia

it was, and still is, the prospect of a hyperreality of a new earth under a new heaven, of a libidinal Eden; but between the prospect and the present...

"You look like a cosmonaut," said Vera
The Wanderer had just worn his rucksack.
He was getting ready for his flight, for the future, for the open orizons but not for the Dark Times of Troika
Otherwise he was going to be fully armed.
Vera gave him a gbbj to remember

Between the "Now" and the "Not-Yet-Become,"
gaped the terrifying Troikan erebus...
We decided to enter and cross the
Red Sea Route deep into the Red October

The independence of
art for the revolution
or self-censorship
suicidal process

'The Last Days of the capitalist European Union. Socialism or Barbarism,' I thought, 'Our battle-cry should be: Down with all capitalist govern-ments! For workers' governments and workers' power! Down with the European Union of the impe-rialists, the prison of peoples! No to the reac-tionary trap of nationalism! For a revolutionary socialist unification of Europe from Lisbon to Vladivostok!'

Zórba and the Wanderer were looking around my weird, untidy study-room with interest for quite some time. It was full of ufo, unfulfilled family objects, that *have endowed us with a weak Messianic power*,* a power to which even these past objects have a claim; objects that recently Faba and I had taken out of boxes and cupboards, objects that were seeing daylight again after years and years of darkness although we live again in years of darkness, in dark times, in Times of Troika. And it was full of objects that we had redeemed and rearranged with Faba, in order to accommodate the newcomers, and both Zórba and the Wanderer claimed that they were seeing them for a first time, although they were always there.

"But how objects can be *unfulfilled*, how can objects *endow*?" asked Zórba after we had talked about the things he had seen in my study-room and I had explained to him a lot about their nature. "All these things you see

*Walter Benjamin, *Theses on the Philosophy of History II*

around us are not only condensations of social forces," I told him; "they are fossils in which constellations of the peoples' histories, feelings, thoughts, anticipations related to them are petrified.

"They are fountains through which spring tides of memories which surge toward us as we contemplate them.

"And peoples' personal histories and feelings and thoughts can be fulfilled, can be left unfulfilled, and consequently make us feel endowed with this Messianic power Angelus Novus talked about.

"This cheap watch has upon it my mom's gaze during moments and hours of distress, this unfinished female being from clay carries within her my dad's creative spirit and artistic zest, this paper music box playing *gone with the wind* is my wife's and daughter's present for my birthday, it may look humble but it has been a source of immense inspiration for my writings.

"This armchair-reading-lamp by which you are sitting, dear Zórba, was lighting my letters to my grandmother, letters that upon their arrival were fuelling her hopes; hopes for what? who knows.... They were letters from afar...."

"Ha!" made Zórba's alter ego, Vas the surrealist; "letters from afar....

"First Letter: The First Stage of the First

Revolution.

"Second Letter: The New Government and the Proletariat.

"Third Letter: Concerning a Proletarian Militia.

"Fourth Letter: How To Achieve Peace.

"Fifth Letter: The Tasks Involved in the Building of the Revolutionary Proletarian State."

I smiled, nodded and went on... "letters that required stamps and envelopes and paper-knives and ballpoint pens or fountain-pens.

"These are my grandfather's spectacles....

"This small photo is the only one my mother-in-law had of her dad, she lost him when she was ten years old during the WW2, I'll talk to you another time about him....

"This big wooden table-clock was given to my father-in-law as a prize for an innovation of his in the black metallurgy. These were the years that the steel was tempered.

"By the way, here is an old edition of Nikolai Ostrovsky's book...."

I had a fabric bookmark in it, knitted by my godfather's wife while she was in jail, on death row, for communist propaganda and espionage in the early fifties....

"I haven't read it for ages," I said, "let's see what's bookmarked here....

'Man's dearest possession is life. It is given to

him but once, and he must live it so as to feel no torturing regrets for wasted years, never know the burning shame of a mean and petty past; so live that, dying he might say: all my life, all my strength were given to the finest cause in all the world —the fight for the Liberation of Mankind.'

"This is my first watch, *roventa*, it was my parents' present after I passed the highschool emtrance exams...."

"And you obviously broke it," said the Wanderer and laughed....

"No, I didn't break it. I had it for years. A coppig broke it, beating me with his club, while we were trying to break the police cord and move ahead during a demonstration for the 1st of May 1976 banned by the New Democracy's government. These days Siderēs Isidoropoulos, a sixteen-year-old teenager and communist, was killed by police forces while putting up posters propagandising for this banned demonstration...."

"There were more murders under New Democracy's government back then, do you remember?"

The question was rhetoric, how could we forget? We never forget. We never forgive....

"New Democracy was always hard-core pro-capitalist; in the same way now it's hard-core pro-Troikan....

"That horrible night of November the 16th, 1980.... The coppigs had beaten to death the twenty-year-old protester, worker, Stamatina Kanelopoulou and the twenty-four-year old Iakovo Koumē...."

One-two minutes ago I had heard my daughter's keys in the door. Then Popē, her griffon, an ex street-dog, burst into the study-room, jumped for a second onto my knees, jumped down again, rushed at high speed into the kitchen and started to whimper, expecting to be fed.

"Why do you keep saying to each other stories that you all know well," said my daughter. It was a comment more than a question, however I grabbed the chance to say. "A very interesting question always requires an equally interesting answer...

"We do know these events and we were even part of them; but we have to commemorate our deads from time to time and also,... give me a sec.... You see computers and the Internet, sometimes, not always, give us the chance to find in seconds what we need,... so let me read this on-screen although you all know that I am a fanatic paper-book reader.... It's the 6th from Benjamin's Theses on the Philosophy of History....

"So....

'To articulate the past historically does not mean to recognize it 'the way it really was' (Ranke). It means to seize hold of a memory as it flashes up at a moment of danger....'

"In a way we're not telling each other stories we already know; we are seizing hold of memories that had flashed up at moments of danger for all of us, I remember that my parents and even my grandmother had taken to the streets to see if I was alive....

"I think that this passage can be interpreted in this way too....

'Historical materialism wishes to retain that image of the past which unexpectedly appears to man singled out by history at a moment of danger. The danger affects both the content of the tradition and its receivers. The same threat hangs over both: that of becoming a tool of the ruling classes. In every era the attempt must be made anew to wrest tradition away from a conformism that is about to overpower it.'

"Among other things, the rulers are trying by all means to force upon us oblivion...

'The Messiah comes not only as the redeemer, he comes as the subduer of Antichrist. Only that historian will have the gift of fanning the spark of hope in the past who is firmly convinced that *even the dead* will not be safe from the enemy if he wins. And this enemy has not ceased to be victorious.'

Popē, the ex street-griffon, being fed and pleased, rolled onto her back asking anybody of us to rub her.

Then my daughter asked for a printout. I took a small pack of paper out of an old, overused wooden tray, much like the laser-

267

printers' trays, where my dad used to keep his sculpting tools...

"That piece of wood over there, this cork, this piece of chalk, these seaweeds, are life-worlds, inseparable parts of constellations of lives, anticipations, fears, hopes and tears; contemplating them fuells my hate for capitalism and Troikas and Masters and Mistresses.

"These are my mom's notebooks from the time when mom was not mom but a thirteen-year-young girl, in a handmade hardcover bound edition; I gave it to her as present once but I don't remember on what occasion.

"You get so chaotic feelings flipping through it..."

I opened it.... I saw the date, Friday 18 December 1936; I recalled a minor event; 'it demonstrates that the capitalist devil and all its fascist demons are in the detail,' I thought; for that day, Anthony Eden disclosed to the House of Commons that 5,000 gas masks had been sold to the Spanish Republic. The government hastened to add that the gas masks were equally available to Franco's forces at the same prices because they were classified as "medical supplies" and not munitions. 'Of course,' I thought again; 'the Revolution was a much greater risk than Fascism...'

"Come closer to see," I said to my daughter,

then I looked at Zórba and the Wanderer,
"I'll show you in a minute."

Dip pen, ink bowl, blotting paper...
Flowing, cursive lettering...

Literary Commentary
Hector and Andromache

"My dear husband, your warlike spirit
will be your death. You've no compassion
for your infant child, for me, your sad wife,
who before long will be your widow.
So, Hector, you are now
my father, noble mother, brother
and my protecting husband. So pity me.

But what pains me most
about these future sorrows is not so much
the Trojans, Hecuba, or king Priam,
or even my many noble brothers,
who'll fall down in the dust, slaughtered
by their enemies. My pain focuses on you,
when one of those bronze-clad Achaeans
leads you off in tears, ends your days of freedom.

May I lie dead,
hidden deep under a burial mound,
before I hear about your screaming,
as you are dragged away."

18 - 12 - 1936

Λογοτεχνικὴ παράθ...

Ὕδωρ καὶ Ἀνθρώπων

(ποίημα)

Εἶνε ἕνα ποίημα μεταφρασμένο ἀπὸ τὴν Ἀγγλι...
... τὸ ... Μᾶς περιγράφει μία ...
... κατὰ τὸν Τρωικὸν πόλεμο εἰς Σπαρτ...
... πρὸς ὁ Ὕδωρ γιὰ νὰ εἶσαι ὁδηγὸς καὶ ...
... γυναῖκα τα καὶ τὸ παιδί τα ...
... γραμμένο μὲ τέχνη ἔχει ὡραῖες ρίμες καὶ ...
... ποίημα εἶναι γραμμένο ἔτσι ... μία παρουσ...
... τὴν ... αὐτὴ καὶ πάει εἰς Σπαρτ...
ὡραῖες ρίμες καὶ ...

Λυδία, ... διαδόθη, μεταφραμένο ...
... χαραγματος ...
Ἐκτὸς ἀπ' αὐτὰ τὶς ὡραῖες ρίμες ὑπάρχουν ...
... καὶ ... εἶναι οἱ ὁποῖες μὲ τὶς ...
ρίμες καὶ εἶναι κατὰ ... καὶ ἀφοῦ ...
... ἄλλα μία παρουσία ...
... Οἱ ... αὐτοὶ εἶναι οἱ ἑξῆς:
...

οἱ τρεῖς αὐτοὶ σύλλογοι μᾶς παρουσίασαν μπρος τὴ
τηλεόρασης.

Ἔχθρα τώρα τοῦ γονιοῦ μὲ τοῦ γονηᾶ μου μιᾶ
τοῦ ἦσαν μήνα μὲ αἰδέρφι νοι ἐνοιερό μας ζωῆ
να ὡραίαι σύλλογοι μὲ ... νοι ὡραῖαι ...
Μὰ δὲ μοῦ σφάξει τὴ παρέλα τῶν ...
τα ... ἢ νοι τῶν ... γονιῶν μας, οὔτε
τῶν ἀδερφῶν μας νοι ... μὲ τα ... τοῦ ...
δὰ ... στὸ αἷμα τας σφαγμένοι ἀπὸ τὰς Ἀρχή
στὸ γιατεῖα, ὅλοι μανεὶς ἀπὸ τῶν ... δ' ...
οἱ εἰρήνη σὲ ... στιαβλά δὰ δάκρυα ...
... παρουσίασαν οἱ σύλλογοι αὐτοὶ μια μπρου ...
... τῆς Γραίας ... τὴν ...
τὴ συμπάθεια συντομιχαῖος μὲ τὴ γυναῖκα τας.
Μὰ θέλω νὰ μὲ ... ἡ μιαῖρι ... δὲ
νερὸ ὅτι δὲν να δέργεται νοι στιαβα να σὲ εἴρηναι.
Μὰ ἐγράφουν τὴν ... τα Ἔχθρα ... μπρος
μ' ἐκείνη ... τὸ γῆρε στὸ ... νερό
νοι ... μὲ μαλια δάκρυ ...

18 - 12 - 76.

Thursday, 18 December 2008; mom was a mom; mom was a grandmom. She had put on the TV and was holding the wireless phone so as to be in touch with all of us, that we had taken to the streets; her son, her daughter-in-law, her granddaughter. For for one more time demonstrations took place in central Athens; more than 12,000 protesters crowded the streets near the Parliament in a demonstration which turned violent when a group of protesters broke away from the rally and threw rocks and molotovs at coppigs, buildings near to the Parliament, overturned a car, set fire to trash cans, splashed the police with red paint and tried to burn down the city's main Christmas tree which had just been replaced after being torched during last week's riots. The police responded with tear gas and flash grenades, and drove the rioters back toward the administrative headquarters of National and Kapodistrian University of Athens and the university's School of Law, Economics and Political Sciences. After another round of pitched battles between masked rioters and the police, several hundred protesters entered the School of Law, Economics and Political Sciences. Christmas shoppers fled the streets and retailers rolled down their shutters as protesters smashed store fronts and burned at least four cars. Demonstrations also took place in Thessaloniki where protesters gathered outside the Ministry for Macedonia-Thrace. Some labour unions stopped work in solidarity with the demonstrators. The work stoppage by the air traffic controllers forced Olympic Airlines to cancel 28 flights and postpone 14. Hospitals were also operating with very limited staff.

"Here's her bound Notebooks," I said offering the hardback volume to Zórba and the Wanderer, "and over there her ink bowl, and blotting paper.

"All these objects, are parts of a constellation of unacomplished desires and anticipations...

"They are waiting for the revolution..."

"I like this vintage noir paraphernalia," said Zórba, taking the Arabic coffee I offered to him, "but the antique typewriter alone is not enough. Bearing in mind that 'A' in antique stands for Anarchy, we need a pistol made by *Star Bonifacio Echeverria, S.A* placed nicely by the typewriter, in order to put the night in a better light and 'the above', the rulers, out of order."

It was late at night when the Wanderer left what was supposed to be my study-room, but it was not. It was more a kind of ark of the Union of Surrealist Sexual Retroperspectives; out of it the Wanderer had to face the storms and the Stormtroopers of Capital. Retrospectively and perspectively.

October 3, 2016. Monday morning was a hot sunny morning. The Wanderer had just witnessed Syriza's police firing tear-gas to control a demonstration of pensioners protesting over cutbacks to their benefits, part of an austerity drive dictated by international lenders through Troika. For an unspecified reason he remembered the strange American who during the December 2008 uprising had asked "tear-gas is useless, where are the water cannons?" and by remembering this, he, the Wanderer, watching old people being tear-gassed, wondered in his turn: "Where are the armed demonstrations?"

Later on, on his way to Locomotiva, he heard on his cell-radio, Czech President's Milos Zeman shining, bright ideas, as bright and as shining as the Nazi golden eagles in the Nazi Party rallies:

"We are in Greece, and Greece has plenty of uninhabited islands, and big foreign debt. So if you have 'hotspots' in Greek islands, this would be a sort of payment of foreign debt."

"It's a bright idea indeed;" said Zórba when the Wanderer told him the news. "the nazist shine of a capitalist mind. Therefore we have first to send Zeman and his Cabinet into forced-labour camps, on these same islands, to build resorts for the refugees."

They sat by the entrance. They asked for hot bitter chocolate; both of them. They talked with Kostas who was behind the bar. The Wanderer lit his pipe, the one his dad had brought from Idaho ages ago; but he is not a smoker; he just plays with her; he calls her Halona, Good Fortune in Native American.

"And what shall we do with Petra Laszlo?" asked the Wanderer blowing smoke rings in the air.

"Petra Laszlo? Who is she?" asked Zórba.

"A Hungarian camerawoman who,..." the Wanderer started saying, but Zórba the Greek didn't let him finish...

"How does she look like? Is she pretty? I had a Hungarian grilfriend once, Adrya; she was from Glenelg, a beach-side suburb of the South Australian capital of Adelaide. She was really good. She was a kind of post-hippie and like some of the girls living in beach-side suburbs she had a bitch side too..."

"Come on, Zórba, be serious,..." said the Wanderer, placing Halona on the table.

"Show Petra Laszlo to me," Zórba insisted.

The Wanderer turned on his tablet, googled her name and then passed the tablet to Zórba.

"No chance!" said Zórba the ræbelaisian. "I wouldn't fuck her for anything."

"So, can I go on? You had asked me

something about her, didn't you?"

"Yes you did. Go on."

The Wanderer had a sip of hot bitter chocolate. "Thank you, Zórba," he said. So she was caught on film kicking refugee children and tripping a man carrying his son, as they ran from police at a Hungarian camp."

"Damn, all these political bastards of the notorious Horthy and Hitler couple..." said Zórba.

"So, what shall we do with her? What's your proposal?"

"We will send her too to the Greek islands, alongside with Milos Zeman and Viktor Orbán, to clean the refugees' toilets," said Zórba the brute, "although we may have to execute some of them..."

"Do you think we will have to go as far as the 'red terror?' " the Wanderer asked him blowing some more smoke rings in the air, signalling *danger, danger, danger...*

"Judging from what they already do, declare and prepare, my answer is yes, revolutionary red terror all over Greece, all over Europe," said Zórba the brute, decrypting signals of alertness coming from the downtrodden of all centuries.

One of them, just one, Federico García Lorca, signalled us from the dreamless city with Brooklyn's Bridge nocturne:

Life is not a dream. Alerta! Alerta! Alerta!
We fall down the stairs in order to eat the moist
[earth
or we climb to the knife edge of the snow with the
[chorus of the dead dahlias.
But oblivion does not exist, neither dreams:
flesh alive. Kisses tie the mouths
in a skein of new veins,
and whoever his pain pains will pain from that
[pain forever
and whoever is scared of death will carry it on his
[shoulders.

One day
the horses will live in the tavernas
and the enraged ants
will throw themselves upon the yellow skies that
[take refuge
in the eyes of the cows.

Another day
we will watch the resurrection of the preserved
[butterflies
and still walking through a landscape of gray
sponges and silent boats
we will watch our ring flash and roses spring from
[our tongue.
    *Alerta!   Alerta!   Alerta!**

---

*Federico García Lorca, *Ciudad sin sueño* - *Nocturno del Brooklyn Bridge*. Translation by V. Ludens

'¡Alerta! ¡Alerta! ¡Alerta!' thought the Wanderer and then he was lost in thoughts and streams, riversides, streets, pathways in a wandering in a city he did not know well, in a walk around Sofia, all alone, downtown, followed by a chat with somebody called Anton, a guy around 27 to 28 by then, holding a University Degree, who turned out to be a nationalist, even worse a supporter of Hitler, of the Holocaust, of the old monarchofascist regime of Bulgaria, a neo-nazist, a molecular more or less of an elite that during a cold November night while we were clashing with the police and the fascistis around Polytechnic School by Exarcheia Square, excavated the twin zombies capitalism and fascism; remember, remember that day of November and it was November again when a Law which declares the communist regime as criminal was voted and among other things provocatively provided for the prohibition of the use and placement of communist symbols, for the removal of symbols, slogans, photographs, signs and other marks or objects associated with communism from public spaces or, if it is not possible to remove them immediately, the placement of a sign on these which will refer the following: the communist regime in Bulgaria during the period 09.09.1944 – 11.10.1989 and the actions of the Communist Party of Bulgaria have been declared criminal by a law voted upon by the 38th National Assembly...

'...endless, boring conversations with ambitious members of the future to be neo-bourgeoisie, a class born decadent in an era of decay, whose offsprings mix, mess, fuck with mafia from the Black Sea of the East Coast until the Miami Beach of the Cuban drug-dealers and renegades....'

"Are you fond of Todor Zhivkov?" Boyko had asked him once upon a time, over a dinner he had coked especially form him, accompanied by red Bulgarian wine. Boyko was a nice guy, not ver talkative but nice and the Wanderer knew him for about thirty years.

"No dear Boyko, I'm not fond of Todor Zhivkov, but in the long march of my political life, I didn't shift to libertarian communism so to spit now on the flaming dreams of my flammable youth or on the graves of all those who fought arms in hand against capitalism from Sierra Maestra until Jarama Valley and from the Paris Commune through the Winter Palace in Leningrad until the Canton Uprising of 1927...

"Nazdrave Boyko," said the Wanderer raising his glass full of red, red wine and then, turning to Boyko's wife Irina, who was teaching Spanish, he concluded: "¡Hasta la victoria siempre!"

Chapter 22

It's a Beautiful Day-Bombay Calling. It's a Beautiful Night-Athens is Burning. February 12, 2012, Sunday night, night of insurrection and we are there too, the Narrator, the Wanderer, Zórba, and of course Faba Crimson Sunshine, wife of someone of them all or maybe their wife or even their wives, and flames, flames all around, flames of passion, flames of wrath, more than half a million people take to the streets, we are supposed to gather in Syntagma Square at 6 o'-clock in the evening, it's only 5 in the evening and the antiriot-police have already started firing dozens of tear-gas volleys to clear the Square and the streets around the parliament, streets packed with enraged demonstrators. We put on gas-masks, goggles, apply Riopan-antiacid-gel on our faces and march ahead along Panepistēmiou Street heading for Syntagma; it's hard almost impossible to proceed; all around us, rushing towards Syntagma, people we don't know and people we know. It's dark; we move through a white cloud for the air is tear-gassed; out of the

white-dark-blue, from Homērou Street, a mo-
torcycle-riding Delta squad appears and attempts to run at full speed through the
crowd only to be welcomed with curses,
stones and molotovs; they turn and run
away hunted by youngsters. However we
can't move further up than Amerikēs Street.
Syntagma and the nearby streets have turned
into a battle-field. "Vandalism, violence and
destruction have no place in a democratic
country and won't be tolerated," says the
Prime Minister Lucas Papademos, a banker
appointed by Greek and foreign bankers to
vandalise, violate and destroy our lives; the
State's coppigs fire in excess stun-guns and
unrestrained rounds of teargas; in retaliation
young protesters wearing masks, armed with
molotovs, marbles from broken pavements,
stones, counterattack setting roads, police vehicles, even buildings ablaze. At the same
time within the Parliament the pro-Troikan
politicians are passing the much-hatred "rescue
programme," a programme of class war fero-
ciously waged by the imperialist EU headed
by Merkel's and Schäuble's Germany, by the
ECB and the IMF, against the impoverished
Greek popular masses, as the first battle
against the peoples all over Europe, West
and East. They are passing their own rescue
programme while all over downtown Athens
hovers the popular slogan "*Na kaei, na kaei to*

bourdelo ē Voulē."*

Syntagma Square in front of the Parliament is now the epicentre of the battle; organised blocs of thousands of protesters with flags and banners are trying to take it over from the coppigs; after the initial brutal and un-provoked attacks by the coppigs around 17:20, thousands and thousands refused to abandon the city centre and flooded and overflooded all the main and all side streets around the Square turning them into a bat-tlefield. Stones, molotovs, flash-grenades, gas grenades, shouts, slogans, curses, these hours are ours and we love every single second of time and we are giving it all, for we have a score to settle, for we have a war to win, *for the future is not a homogenous and empty time for in it every second is the narrow gate, through which the revolution can enter.***

I take out my cell and call the very few people I know that are not demonstrating, not clashing downtown, informing them that we are hundreds of thousands and not just a handful as the mass falsification media are transmitting again and again in a well-or-chestrated propaganda warfare. We try to reach the parliament; time and again we are being attacked by scores of coppigs with as-phyxiating gas and flash-sound grenades; we retreat, when needed, just in order to counter-

*Burn, burn, the brothel the Parliament.
**Walter Benjamin, *Theses on the Philosophy of History*, XVIII-B

attack and not give ground, almost half a million people refuse to leave, for more than two hours we move, we march, we run, we group and regroup attempting to approach the Parliament for dozens of times.

For a second time after the December 2008 uprising we meet our friend and comrade William Blake. We shake hands cordially. We move to Stadiou Street and stand in front of the burning historic Attikon Cinema. We look upwards: in the forefront the antefixes of the neoclassical building almost glare black in the background of blazes and sparks. "This reminds me of the night we attacked Newgate's prison gates with shovels and pickaxes, set the building ablaze and released the prisoners," said Blake;

"Now, comrades," he goes on, "follow me."

We mounted the tigers, me in front, my wife Faba behind holding me, and signalled our tiger to move ahead amidst the burning and smoking streets and squares of downtown Athens. Blake was riding by our side.

Tyger! Tyger! burning bright
In the forests of the night,
What immortal hand or eye
Could frame thy fearful symmetry?

Protesters throw petrol-bombs toward antiriot-police and they explode among their lines

In what distant deeps or skies
Burnt the fire of thine eyes?

283

On what wings dare he aspire?
What the hand, dare sieze the fire?

Green laser pointers are aimed at coppigs by demonstrators

And what shoulder, & what art,
Could twist the sinews of thy heart?
And when thy heart began to beat,
What dread hand? & what dread feet?

Further down antiriot-police push brutally protesters back near the Temple of Zeus

What the hammer? what the chain?
In what furnace was thy brain?
What the anvil? what dread grasp
Dare its deadly terrors clasp?

Police cars, cafés, shops in flames

When the stars threw down their spears,
And water'd heaven with their tears,
Did he smile his work to see?
Did he who made the Lamb make thee?

Protesters hurl fireworks at antiriot-squads

Tyger! Tyger! burning bright
In the forests of the night,
What immortal hand or eye
Dare frame thy fearful symmetry?

Debris and garbage burn in the middle of the streets and with them the appointed government of the bankers, the shipowners, and the Troikans turned into ashes.

A long time later amidst the Dark Times of Troika; a long time with long days and longer nights; Bar - café - bookshop Loco-motiva. Late at night. There was a moon in the nearby gutter.

"We should have stormed and occupied the Old Parliament, the Town Hall and the General Confederation of Greek Workers that night," the Wanderer said, "make appeals to the workers for a general strike and call the people to remain onto the streets, resist, eraise barricades, organise and encourage all those that had even the slightest desire for street-fighting..."

"Dear Wanderer, I think we have to go a long way until we will recapture our revolutionary spirit and ardour," I said, but I had not yet finished my phrase, and Zórba started to sing:

"It's a long way to Tipperary
it's a long way to go
" 'If I make mistakes in shooting
'Comrades, dear,' said he,
" 'Remember, it's the gun that's bad,
" 'Don't lay the blame on me!' "

"Are you a member of the Worker's Revolutionary Party? of EEK?" Dr. Fossil had asked Vas the surrealist. He was an old friend of him, a top classical philologist and a Stalinist, living in Germany. The tone of his voice was annoyingly reprimanding. In the same tone a father would have asked his teen daughter, "is your boyfriend member of the New York gangs?" I don't know what Vas replied to him. All I know is that he was not a member of the Worker's Revolutionary Party but only because he had no time at all to give and get involved, as a member, in such a serious affair. He was extremely busy and preoccupied because he was the founder of the Movement for the Erotomultiplication of the Infinity, of the Network for the Coming of the New Paradises, of the Non-Committee of Erototopography, of the Situationiste Intersexionale and he was working hard on the prospects of a Voyage to the USSR, the Union of Surrealist Sexual Retroperspectives.

Zórba on the other, on the left hand of darkness, was not a member of EEK because he was a ræbelaisian and a womaniser. Once, we had arranged to meet, all of us, at Locomotiva that was hosting a panel discussion on *The French Spring and the Crisis in Europe*. Savas Michael-Matsas, EEK's General Secretary, was the main speaker and Zórba wanted very much to listen to him. But he didn't. He disappeared somewhere for most of the time, with a young lady, and he thought that we will not notice his absence in the crowd that had gathered in Locomotiva. But we did. And we told him. And laughed. But he denied everything. And I knew that he stayed there just as long took to Savas to say: *"The only alternative for the exploited and oppressed of France, Germany, Greece, or of any other European country, North and South, East and West, to stop the catastrophe is an internationalist one: the international, beyond borders, coordinated revolutionary upsurge of the working class leading all subaltern classes and oppressed, including all national, ethnic and other minorities, immigrants and refugees, for the overthrow of capitalism and the EU, to establish a new emancipated community of peoples and minorities free from all forms of oppression, exploitation and humiliation: a United Socialist States of Europe, as it was formulated by the old and always actual call of the Communist International in its first revolutionary period.*"

Neither the Narrator was a member of the EEK. This was a side effect of him being a Narrator, for in the Beginning was the Act and in this Act he was a Narrator so for him in the Beginning was neither the Act nor the Power but the Word.

And last but not least, the Wanderer was not a member of the EEK either; because "*like a child, he wandered about this earth in a daze and, like a child, he did not know where he came from or where he was going*" attracted by femmes fatales and barricades; and how could such a person be a member of a revolutionary party.

In the beginning is the Narrator, and the Narrator is with the Wanderer, and the Wan-

---

*Paraphrase by V. Ludens. Original from Johann Wolfgang von Goethe, *The Sorrows of Young Werther*

derer is me. I am Zórba. Or Vas. Sometimes I'm thinking that all these denials of membership on behalf of the unholy Trinity might be considered by Dr. Fossil as a cunning Trotskyist conspiracy, in order to avoid his verdict. Who knows.

Sometime later, Dr. Fossil disappeared from Vas's life, after sending him a few emails full of Stalinist aphorisms, lecturing and personal insults with references to "the opportunistic assholes and shits he admires." They never spoke again. Dr. Fossil because he considered Vas a very bad student for his Stalin School of Falsification and Vas because he was fed up with Dr. Fossil's Stalinist loud buzzing.

Life's adversities, aggravated if not created by the presence of Mistress Troika, had swept away from Vas's mind the last traces of Dr. Fossil's presence in his life, until the day, or the night to be more precise, that as he was reading again *My Life* by Leo Trotsky, he came across CHAPTER XVI MY SECOND FOREIGN EXILE: GERMAN SOCIALISM and precisely the following passage: They were well-educated people whose knowledge of various subjects was superior to mine. I listened with intense and, one might almost say, respectful interest to their conversation in the Central cafe. But very soon I grew puzzled. These people were not revolutionaries. Moreover, they represented the type that was farthest from that of the revolutionary. This expressed itself in everything in their approach to subjects, in their political remarks and psychological appreciations, in their self-satisfaction not self-assurance, but self-satisfaction. I even thought I sensed philistinism in the quality of their voices.

Vas read astonished these lines about the Austrian Marxists, for Trotsky was actually describing Vas's own old friend, Dr. Fossil from Germany. He too, was well-educated and his knowledge of various subjects was superior to Vas's; at times Vas was listening to him with intense and, one might almost say, respectful interest; but in the course of time Vas realised that Dr. Fossil was not a revolutionary. Moreover, he represented the type that was farthest from that of the revolutionary. This expressed itself in everything, in Dr. Fossil's approach to subjects, in his political remarks, political insults and psychological appreciations and in his self-satisfaction, not self-assurance, but self-satisfaction. It's not surprising then that, from the heights of his philological Olympus, Dr. Fossil felt that at his wish, mighty thunders would flash and lightnings would roll, wreaking havoc among the Trotskyists, the Anarchists, the Maoists, the Marxist-Leninist groups, and even the Stalinists that were not praising and worshiping his own genuin stalinist version of Stalinism.

the tragic sense
of life

"the sky laughs" phrase and blotting paper
found in a 1933 mom's calligraphy notebook 30
january 1933 she was almost ten by then born
in Thessaloniki nazism had just been born out
of the belly of the monster the belly of capitalism today Mistress Troika is carrying, from
Alabama until Kiev similar zombies in her own
belly the belly of the monster

Chapter 23

"Greeks are lazy people who spend more than they produce;" the widespread stereotype reappeared in the mind of the Wanderer. 'As far as I am concerned,' he thought, 'it's nothing less than a manifestation of the nazist theory of the collective guilt. Not surprisingly, it's mostly widespread in the very country where the State vindicated the murderers of Rosa Luxemburg and Karl Liebknecht.'* The Wanderer got a bit angry, just a bit. 'Not in my name,' he went on thinking, 'not against my name; or I'll first treat you my bullets after the International's lyrics: *And if those cannibals keep trying, to sacrifice us to their pride, they soon shall hear the bullets flying, we'll shoot the generals on our own side,*' and then you'll have the chance to see from within the Greek-Troikan hospitals; for none of his family had ever been possessed by the frenzy of consumptionism; even more they had acquired the habit of keeping all sorts of old, almost useless things.

---

*http://www.zeit.de/1962/11/war-es-mord-oder-eine-patriotische-tat

Much later he became aware that this habit and practice of theirs, to save things, wresting them away of any kind of commodity trendism, in order to put them in a new light, was conforming with Walter Benjamin's Theses and warnings.... *"The danger affects both the content of the tradition and its receivers. The same threat hangs over both: that of becoming a tool of the ruling classes. In every era the attempt must be made anew to wrest tradition away from a conformism that is about to overpower it."*

And it's not mere coincidence that the state of emergency imposed by the German capital and forced the little hunchback who was an expert Marxist to kill himself, forces nowadays thousand Greeks to commit suicide.

This once upon-a-time trendy TV set, this fetishized commodity that his grand mother asked them to buy just four years before she passed away, didn't die with her when it got out of order. He turned it upside down, he placed it on the floor, he named it Bo, a female's name, and now her 'useless' snowy screen is a gate-to-the-stars, on his not-yet existing spaceship; and consequently the strait gate through which, every second of time, Messiah might enter. A gate-to-the-stars on a spaceship, s-extreme-left-over from a childhood with no end that tended to merge all in one, the USSR, communism, voyages to far-distant galaxies, missions to the constellation of Carina, full of carnal pleasures, abundant sex on the missionary position.

Wresting things away from comformism, from the Spirit of Capitalism, from Protestand Ethic, from Christian Ethic, from any Ethic that equates and associates sexuality with sin and evil. Redemption is the act of saving people from any kind and any form of sexual guilt imposed by anybody; especially by the Clergy.

For instance his eye fell upon an old green-coloured telephone directory. It was this directory that triggered his stream of thoughts. He took it into his hands and sat back in the armchair...

'This is not anymore a telephone directory,' he thought. 'This is a directory for free, liberated and libertarian sex, in the Union of Surrealist Sexual Retroperspectives, and the USA in the 1960s is just a small part of it...'

"MARCH 1961 AREA CODE 517 YOUR NEW Lansing area TELEPHONE DIRECTORY for: DANVILLE DIMONDALE HOLT LANSING (including E. Lansing) MASON POTTERVILLE Also Alphabetical Lists of: AURELIUS BATH De WITT GRAND LEDGE WILLIAMSTON MICHIGAN BELL TELEPHONE COMPANY"

On the back cover an advert:

The Princess phone

IT'S LITTLE IT'S LOVELY IT LIGHTS! Styled to the modern taste, it's small to save space. The dial glows softly in the dark, lights up bright when you lift the receiver. THE PRINCESS MAKES A WONDERFULLY EXTENSION.... IN THE BEDROOM the light-up dial is handy after dark. IN THE KITCHEN to help you run the house. IN A TEEN-AGER'S ROOM to give precious privacy. IN THE LIVING ROOM by your favorite chair.

Each extension had a sketch on its end: well-shaped housewives and an attractive teen-girl with a ponytail.

Housewives with names like Florence, Shirley, Cecil, whose five-digit numbers I have at hand, I can even call Cecil's teenage daughter Ethel, the glow of the dial illuminates softly Ethel's lips as she speaks in a low voice on the phone; Florence runs absent-mindedly her fingers delicately over her own breasts and thighs through and under her baby-doll; she flirts on the phone sitting on her favourite chair in the living-room, Ethel's mom, Cecil, does the same lying on her bed only that her hand moves under the covers between her thighs, and Florence in the kitchen licks the handle of a kitchen knife; afterwards they get deflowered in the back-seat of Cadillacs, Buicks, Fords and Oldsmobiles, they get unbridled on hay-bales in the barn, double teamed in garages and give head everywhere. Just like, decades later, did Beth from Barrington, Illinois and Tracy from Springfield, Massachusetts; 'they were really good at giving head,' thought Zórba or Vas in whose name "s" stood for surrealism and sexuality, "a" stood for "art" and 'V" stood for the *Victory over the Sun* Russian Futurist opera premiered in 1913 at the Luna

Park in Saint Petersburg. The libretto written in zaum language was contributed by Aleksei Kruchonykh, the music was written by Mikhail Matyushin, the prologue was added by Velimir Khlebnikov, and the stage designer was Kasimir Malevich. The performance was organized by the artistic group *Soyuz Molodyozhi*. The opera has become famous as the event where Malevich made his first *Black Square* painting and was intended to underline parallels between literary text, musical score, and the art of painting, and featured a cast of such extravagant characters as Nero and Caligula in the Same Person, Traveller through All the Ages, Telephone Talker, The New Ones, etc.*

Beth and Tracy gave head in turns in his room overlooking the Department of Genetics.... 'A!' he had thought, 'the most advanced science, art, surrealism and world communism will lead to a non-state of things where *the whole Universe will consist of innumerable worlds of immense heavenly space, with their multitudes united with those of the resurrected generations, who for innumerable centuries have been swallowed up by the Earth,*'** he concluded, echoing Nikolai Fedorovich Fedorov. For there was an irreconcilable contradiction between all these once upon a time alluring Florences,

---

*https://en.wikipedia.org/wiki/Victory_over_the_Sun
**Nikolai Fedorovich Fedorov, *What Was Man Created For*, Honeyglen Publishing / L'Age d'Homme, p.194

Shirleys, Cecils, Ethels and so on and so forth and their present-day state of ashes to ashes dust to dust or their elderliness; and irreconcilable contradictions are being solved by the revolution, the permanent revolution, a revolution ad infinitum...

"I want you to come into my mouth, cover my face with your semen,..." Beth's voice was deep, Tracy's soft. He had practised on both of them the three R's of the american high-school rodeo: ropin' ridin' and rubbin,' which practically meant ropin' em, ridin' em and watchin' em rubbin' their cunts. '*Carpe Diemm*,' had thought Zórba or Vas, but capitalism amidst its crisis robs the people of pleasures, of moments, of everything.

But not from Zórba the ræbelaisian. He saw once the Wanderer, in Locomotiva, in the discreet table for two, beneath the framed poster of the *Red Army soldiers raising the Soviet flag over the Reichstag*, drinking coffee in the company of a slim brunette woman and offering her both the red & blue *Kaleidoscopio*'s volumes, full of explicit sexual scenes.

"Did you fuck her?" he teased him a few days later. They were sitting at a table at the bookstore on Locomotiva's loft.

Vicky, who came upstairs to bring the coffees, heard him, blushed and smiled, without saying a word.

The Wanderer laughed. "Come on I gave

her this book for everything else but sex. Besides she hasn't read it yet. She's busy. But she has seen her daughter reading it. 'She's 19 but out of the loop so let her read it,' she told me jokingly."

"Oh, good for you Wand, you may start with the daughter and wait for her mom to find some time to read it, get sexcited and follow her daughter into your bed; unless you want them both at once."

"Zórba don't be such a provocateur; she's just a good friend."

"A good friend!? Big deal Wand! My wife says 'a friend in need is a friend indeed,' " I teased him in my turn, pouring coffee into my cup.

"And in any case," said Zórba, "I seek for the sextraordinary not the ordinary."

"The sextraordinary, the sextravagant and the sextremist," added his alter ego, Vas, in whose name the three letters stood for Victory, Vendetta, Art, Surrealism, Sexuality and for other demons.

"And what you consider... sextraordinary, sextravagant and sextremist in that case?" asked him the Wanderer.

"In a state of... sexergency, what else,... a Troika," said Vas the surrealist, Zórba's alter ego. "Your friend, her daughter and you! ha, ha, ha..."

"You are rude Vas," said the Wanderer,

"where has your fine spirit gone?"

Vas smiled and took a sip of hazelnut-flavoured coffee before he spoke. "Walter Benjamin, in the 4th of his Theses on the Philosophy of History, says that 'the class struggle, which is always present to a historian influenced by Marx, is a fight for the *rude* and material things without which no refined and spiritual things could exist.' "

"He doesn't say rude but crude," said the Wanderer.

"Crude and rude are synonyms," Wanderer, "and they also make a nice rhyme.

"Ok, ok, I give up Vas."

I took a sip of my vanilla-flavoured coffee. Spontaneously a thought flashed through my mind. Due to the presence of Troika vanilla-flavoured coffee is banned for millions of people; and Troika is the Mistress of economic hit men; "hit men!" what an euphemism for criminals against humanity who afford to spend £330,000 on a 30l bottle of *Armand de Brignac Dynasty*. And then, some of their kind, write books with misleading titles, like *Confessions of an Economic Hit Man* instead of the more precise and fair one: *Confessions of a Class War Crininal*. The thought fuelled my hatred for Troika, Troikans and everybody around them with no exception. For the leaders, their parties, their professors, their embedded anchormen and anchorwomen, being attached to Troika's ideological war units involved in its ruthless class war, their fascist thugs, their praetorians with the khaki brains. 'Justice,' I thought more consciously, this time, 'Justice, not the Law, asks for, demands, a new Nuremberg. But we have to win the class war first.'

"What are you thinking?" Zórba asked me.

I told him in brief. Focussing on the confessions of the hit-men side of my thoughts.

"But bear in mind," the Wanderer told me, "that many specialists from many sides, dispute the hit-men's claims; they talk about lack of documentary or testimonial evidence, or they give numbers for grants and loans and exports saying that they do not seem like figures worth killing politicians for, so..."

"Bullshit," said Zórba the brute. "In the best case, there might be some exaggerations in these confessions. But we know by experience that soldiers and officers always like to boast about their great deeds and daring exploits. And the war criminals are no exception as far as they feel safe among their own kind. In the worst case all the others are trying to cover up all these class war crimes. It's something extremely common. They always appear 'specialists' who try to dispute claims of war crimes. The nazis deny even the Holocaust.

"So in any case," Zórba concluded, "all these Capital's class war criminals are asking for the capital punishment by the upsurged proletariat, the oppressed, the downtrodden..."

"Anyway," I said taking another sip of my coffee. Then, I laid my cup on the table and asked, "How do they look like?; the mom-daughter duo I mean..."

The Wanderer said nothing.

"I haven't seen the daughter. The mom, well, I'm a fanatic cinephil you know, so I can tell you straightforwardly that she looks like Claire Forlani in *Nightmares & Dreamscape*," said Vas, in whose name "a" stands for art.

"Interesting," I said, "almost fascinating; not that she looks like Claire Forlani; about the stream of conversation I'm talking about...

"About Dreamscape and Nightmares...

"Our wildest dreamscape, USSR, is their worst nightmare...

"The spectre of USSR will haunt them for ever."

"The USSR is vast," the Wanderer started to say after a while, and from the tone of his voice we understood that he was going to say something interesting, revealing, weird.

"Vastness is one of its numerous features. Vast in space and vast in time; 'vast' is an acronym. It means Victorious, Artfully. Sexualised, Transformative...

"I cannot specify neither when nor where in the USSR the indecidents occurred...

"but there were the Aeolian Islands...

"and a psychoanalyst, a woman, in her early forties...

"and Mexico City...

"and a secluded house...

"or maybe two secluded houses, but if the indecident took place, in the Aeolian Islands, Mexico City or both, I know not.

"Three men frequenting orgies, kept a young mother-daughter duo in the house to answer their every sexual whim...

"I told her all I knew about the case, as I had heard it from the psychoanalyst. Strangely enough it was me who was guiding her in the darkest corners of her mind; unless she was misleading me; and she was taking things out of my subconscious; who knows...

"So I warned her; about the Aeolian Islands... About how secluded houses may turn into sexcluded ones... about the possible sexposedness of their, hers and her daughter's, sojourn there.

"She gave me the following oracle: 'Bear in mind that some people, who had enough moral props, barriers, constraints, religious or political principles, have an attraction for the perverse, as observers, voyeurs or even as participants, and I dare to say this judging from my own self.' "

"That's insane," said Zórba. "She-ga-ve-you-that-o-racle? Better if she had given you head instead! Oral sex, not oracles...

"Did she tell you at least what perverse things she likes?"

The Wanderer said nothing.

"And in any case Wanderer, why did you tell us this weird story?"

"I'm not sure Zórba. But from time to time we are required to say absolutely everything that comes to mind, regardless how irrelevant, or weird it may seem to be...

"Although I don't think that what I said was so irrelevant with our conversation stream...

"But in any case, don't you think, dear Zórba, that we have to utilise even the sexplosive libidinal powers of the subconscious against the Capital and Mistress Troika?"

"With no doubt," said Zórba the brute. "But the New World will not be born out of the conscious or subconscious libidinal ideas like dawn's frost out of night's humid air. It will be rather born like Athena out of Zeu's head. Like when the skilled hand of Hephaistos cleaved the God's head with his proletarian hammer and sickle and she leaped from Zeu's broken head grown and armed, with a shout *'and pealed to the broad sky her clarion cry of war. And Ouranos trembled to hear, and Mother Gaia.'*"

---

*Pindar, *Olympian Ode* 7. 33 *ff* translated by Conway

Chapter 24

Vas the surrealist and his wife Scarlet Scarletson had invited us at their home at the corner of Dr's Caligari and Nosferatu Street in a quiet neighbourhood of Athens; but was it Athens or a part of the USSR? For some things didn't much Athens? I know not. "Come with your partners," they had said, so I took Narra, Narra Ravenstein and we walked together to their house. Narra's second name matched the colour of her hair. Somebody had told her in the past, "You' re the double of Enya." "Who is she?" Narra had asked him, "Eithne Pádraigín Ní Bhraonáin," he replied, the Irish singer-songwriter, musician, and producer. Narra was already drunk by that time, "I don't know her and I don't know if I am her double, all I know is that right now I need a double penetration," she said The Irishman was shocked much more than his wife, a fiery red-haired. Just for a second her jaw had dropped, then she laughed loudly; "count me in, cunt," she had said. We double-teamed both of them; in the middle of the

night we heard something like, "your little
wife is one hell of a cunt-licker, she makes
Ruby scream with her clever little tongue,
while I load her cunt up with my cock,"
spelled by the twilighted lust of an unaging
mind; then in the dark we saw Narra angling
her back to force her butt up into the air,
then Ruby's face, loose, her mouth agape as
she moaned from the little tongue sliding
over her cunt. That's how we got acquainted
with Ruby Firecrotch, the Wanderer's-to-be-
partner and also to Enya's music, which we
all found sexually arousing. From that night
on Narra's first name diverted, from time to
time, because there is time for class-war and
a time for carnal love, from Narra to Narrenya
and then to Nerenya, which in Greek means
watery, for her eyes had a watery look and
she also liked a lot laying on her bed horny,
laying for an easy lay she was, with her pussy
wet as the thalassa, watching female-friendly
porn with a dildo in her hand... The invitation
and the events that followed should have
surprised us but, in the course of time, we
had got accustomed to the *those who enter the*
same rivers, ever different waters flow reality, and
to the fact that neither Vas nor his partners,
even his acquaintances were always, if ever,
the same.

"Come and we will play surrealist games
with ourselves," we had said, meaning by

"ourselves" the three parts of our Trinity; but none of these parts was a usual self of ours; all of them were the embodiment of other potentialities. "As soon as you'll get in the lift," he had instructed us, "you'll have to press first the right year-button and only after it you'll press the floor-button. You'll have to press both buttons in the proper order, otherwise you'll get lost. So you first press the 1983 button and then the 5th floor one. You got it?"

Yes we did. It was not any time-machine coming from the far future. It was just an elevator going up and down within the short limits of a forty-fifty years period, at least according to Vas, although some things I saw later in his flat made me doubt if things were so simple or so straightforward; I was suspecting that there were outlets to the spacetime continuum in there.

As the elevator was lifting Narra and me up-back in time and space we were feeling lighter, younger and all the more animated. When we entered the flat I started looking around. It looked spacy but its walls were covered with old heavy floor-to-ceiling chestnut bookcases and, here and there, some lighter ones made of white dexion-shelves; all of them overstuffed with books in Greek, English and Russian, for Faba, Vas's wife is a graduate of Russian and English literature, fine-art al-

bums and a special section dedicated to erotography. I spent there time enough to see
the numerous works of Andreas Empeirikos,
of Pierre Louÿs, Alexander Trocchi, de Sade,
the drawings of Tom Poulton, *Eros and
Thanatos* Paperback by Klaus Bottger, novels
of Melissa Panarello, Milo Manara's comics,
erotica science fiction collections and even
pulp erotic fiction titles like *Bound And Raped
Cousin* by Paul Gable. Our surrealist libertarian
friend had a twilight side too. I opened out
of curiosity the book about Darlene's sexual
adventures, only to see on its third page,
dirty-yellow over the passage of time, a girlish
handwritten note in pink-ink:

*Ideas on how to treat your cousins. Anna-Maria xxx
PS If you ask me Chrisy craves for it....*

In a prominent position of the erotography
section, full-facing the observer or the potential
reader, the owners had placed Guido Crepax's
commix *Viva Trotsky* with the erotic adventures
of Valentina in the revolutionary Russia. In a
similar way, in another bookstand, among a
paraphernalia of books, empty flashbang and
tear-gas canisters and objects that any thief
would scorn from the bottom of his heart,
was proudly displayed a square book of
Vladimir Mayakovky with his poem *The 4th
International*; and at a close distance a leaflet,
a time traveller, a futurist in a glass frame
with a red ribbon attached to it:

Обращение ВРК «К гражданам России»
К гражданам России!

Временное правительство низложено. Государственная власть перешла в руки органа Петроградского Совета рабочих и солдатских депутатов — Военно-революционного комитета, стоящего во главе петроградского пролетариата и гарнизона.

Дело, за которое боролся народ: немедленное предложение демократического мира, отмена помещичьей собственности на землю, рабочий контроль над производством, создание Советского правительства — это дело обеспечено.

Да здравствует революция рабочих, солдат и крестьян!

Военно-революционный комитет при Петроградском Совете рабочих и солдатских депутатов, 25 октября (7 ноября) 1917 года

To the Citizens of Russia!

The Provisional Government has been deposed. State power has passed into the hands of the organ of the Petrograd Soviet of Workers' and Soldiers' Deputies--the Revolutionary Military Committee, which heads the Petrograd proletariat and the garrison.

The cause for which the people have fought, namely, the immediate offer of a democratic peace, the abolition of landed proprietorship, workers'control over production, and the establishment of Soviet power —this cause has been secured.

Long live the revolution of workers, soldiers and peasants!

Revolutionary Military Committee of the Petrograd Soviet of Workers' and Soldiers' Deputies

10 a.m., October 25, 1917.

Most of the furniture in the house, with the exception of the Apple Macs on the two desks and the flat TV set, looked almost as old and impressive as the Declaration of the Bolsheviks; I was impressed by a black piano, a *Foster*, maybe because my mom played the piano too, and by an aquarium with a huge water turtle swimming lazily in it.

Whatever walls were left free from book-stands were covered with paintings, Vas's father was a painter and sculptor; most of them pastels: seas in all the shades of blue, colourful galaxies and a cypress. Vas had confessed to us that when his father died in a hospital in the Time of Troika, under conditions that enraged him and fuelled his hatred for Troika, capitalism and other demons, he was buried under a cypress. "There he sleeps," Vas told us, "just five graves away from his wife, my mom.

"My wife's mother, Tanya from Sverdlovsk, who also died in a hospital under appalling conditions in the Time of the Counter Revolution and the Collapse of the 'existing socialism,' is sleeping too; in saecula saeculorum. She was a great woman. She had lost her dad at the age

311

of ten. He most probably belonged to the Red Army' Siberian Divisions and was killed during the Great Antifascist War, fighting against the German invaders; against troops sent by the German capitalists against the USSR. "The Siberians are coming! It was a cry that spread terror through the ranks of the German Wehrmacht in the winter of 1941."* On the 9th of May, 2014 we gathered at Locomotiva, to celebrate the victory of the Red Army of the workers and peasants, founded by Lenin and Trotsky, over the nazist army of the German capitalists. At the end we heard his great granddaughter singing the popular Russian song *Thank you grandfather for the victory*. It was dedicated to him, to Ivan Pavlovich Zaikov; but it was just a few days after the pro-EU pro-German Ukrainian nazis burned alive dozens of people in the Trade Unions Building in Odessa. So the Victory song *Spasibo dedy za pobedy*, was dedicated to them as well, with the words 'With our gaze turned upon Ukraine and Odessa, we never forget, we never forgive.'

"Some of Zaikov's blood has coloured the red flag that the Soviet soldiers raised over the Reichstag, at the heart of Berlin; it colours too the red flags and banners we carry in our

*WWII History, Sovereign Media Company Inc, March 2002 issue, pp. 30, 81. Examples of these or similar statements are common in WWII historical literature and most film documentaries on the subject. Eg, A.Clark , *Barbarossa*, Orion Publishing Group, London, 1995, p. 170. *The Times Atlas of the Second World War*, Times Books Ltd, London, 1989, p. 60.

demonstrations, with the slogans for an internationalist revolutionary solution to the crisis written on them.

"My mother also lost her dad soon after the war. He came too weak and too sick after the occupation of Greece by the German capitalists' nazi troops," said Vas...

"So", concluded Vas. "all of them, all, are waiting, alongside with Mayakovsky, for a 'quiet chemist with a domed forehead living in the thirtieth century' to request him:

'Resurrect me!
Even if only because I was a poet
And waited for you.
And put behind me prosaic nonsense.
Resurrect me —
Just for that!
Do resurrect me —
I want to live it all out."

By his desk Vas had an old *Bell ε Howell* 8mm camera; he claimed it belonged to his father but I'm convinced that it had something to do with his "let's undermine the spacetime continuum" affairs and a turkuaz 1961 Oldsmobile Super 88 replica; or at least that's what it seemed to be.

But the most impressive of all, more impressive than the books, and the piano, the heavy furniture and the paintings was a trans-

---

*About That is a poem by Vladimir Mayakovsky
https://thecharnelhouse.org/2015/09/12/a-tribute-to-vladimir-mayakovsky/

parent, red, illuminated, revolving world globe. It represented the USSR Anadyomènē, the Union of Surrealist Sexual Retroperspectives that had emerged ages ago from the not-yet-conscious, the not-yet-become; at some point it took the form of the Union of Soviet Socialist Republics then it lost this form; reappeared in the form of the European Union of Soviet Socialist Republics on the ruins of the collapsed under its own internal contradictions and the blows of the permanent revolution EU; it was expanded in the form of international socialist revolution and then in the course of time, speeding up, reached the stage of a Union of Surrealist Sexual Retroperspectives. It occupied the entire globe and other parts of the space time continuum. However in some parts of the world, like the City, the Wall Street, Frankfurt, were preserved some Capitalist Savage Reservations, encircled by electric fences, inhabited exclusively by capitalists without proletarians, for everything is possible under revolutionary surrealism; it was a hell without escape for them, worth though for anybody to observe its everlasting decay; they were like sharks swimming in their own blood, chopping pieces of fresh, live flesh from each other's bodies.

Narra Ravenstein was looking at the selves with the theatre plays books and the others, not excluding Scarlet, were looking at her ultra low-cut ripped jeans and her sexposed abdominal flesh. Among the books Narra saw one with interviews of Harol Pinter, whom all of them respected and liked a lot, and right next to it a pair of tin boxes; she took one in her hands and read the label on it:

RED ☆ ⌐ STAR
COOPERATOR'S BEST
COFFEE.

"What's this all about," she asked Vas; she looked extremely amused with it. He laughed. "It refers openly to the militant slogan of the youngsters, boys and girls usually under twenty years young:

*'eimaste oloi edo kommouniston engonia
kai ta konservokoutia den skouriasan akoma'*

"It's a sui generis answer to the old slander of the anticommunist propaganda of the collaborators of the Germans and the pro-British forces after the glorious red December of 1944; they claimed that the communists were slaughtering with tin-boxes!

"They take up the challenge and they challenge on their turn...

"The metropolitan youth get all the more enraged. I like them. All these young boys and girls, trailing with their fingertips the wounds and the struggles of the past generations and at the same time looking into the future..."

---

*We are all here, grandsones/daughters of communists and the teen boxes are not yet rusted.

"It sounds to me like Walter Benjamin's theses on history, although I'm sure they've never heard of him," I said; "But we will teach them; we will have our revenge."

The door-bell rang the way the Big Ben tolls. "I was expecting to hear the first nine tones of the International," I teased Vas.

"We're not in Smolny, my friend. The International is a call for armed uprising, not a tune for welcoming friends."

Scarlet, Scarlet Scarletson, opened the door. It was the Wanderer with his wife Ruby Firecrotch; as she entered first and leaned forward to kiss Scarlet, her buttocks were displayed provocatively in the mirror of the antique hall-stand as her one piece dress wasn't enough to keep them covered; it was a hall-stand from the year 1920, when the Red Army was breaking down the White Army in the Crimea. The winds of class war scattered the white dust all over Europe and some of its particles were carried as far as Thessaloniki.

That's how Zórba's grandmother made the acquaintance of Olena, the beautiful young wife of a White Army Officer of the cavalry, who stayed behind to fight "for race and country." Rumours had her sextremely adulterous and narcissist, mirroring herself all the time in the hall-stand during her visits to the house he was born, ages and ages before he was born, and Zórba, who had seen a vintage picture of this promiscuous look-alike of Colleen Moore, had fantasised her fucking with the ferry-men of the harbour, being ridden in all positions, sweating for the purity of the race while her White Officer husband riding his horse was retreating and sweating trailed by the locomotiva of Trotsky.

After Firecrotch touched with her always wet lips Scarletson's cheeks very close to her mouth, displaying to all, through the mirror of the antique hall-stand her buttocks, she turned to look at herself in it and to arrange her hair on top of her head because she was feeling hot.

She was an undercover provocatrice sexuelle used for the sextermination of high rank capitalist officers that had to be liquidated in discreet ways; like they had done with Mr. St. He was the President of a systemic bank, involved in the formation of coalition governments. The ruling class needed them desperately. Ruby Firecrotch had made his acquaintance during a press-conference, impressed him with her ginger glamour, seduced him and let him invite her to his private yacht. He had taken her to the luxury bedroom. In there on the king-size bed, he began to fuck her and suddenly he was set ablaze by Firecrotch's flaming crotch. and turned into ashes. He was buried as a ruling class hero that died out of hypercoposis trying hard, almost sweating, to "save the country;" actually an empty coffin was buried and his cremains were turned into fountain-pens for the prime-minister and the ministers to sign the Memoranda with the Troika. "He was a very good banker," commented to Zórba a middle-aged lady, reading newspapers' front pages at a kiosk in downtown Athens. Zórba consented: "Any dead banker is a good banker, ma'am."

After the female welcoming kisses we all went out to the terrace overlooking the illu-minated Lykavēttos hill. It was like the Hang-ing Gardens of Babylon when moonlited. full of green plants that I could not recognise, with the exception of some gerania, a couple of bougainvilleas and many cactuses all of them converted to Trotskyism after they had kept company to Leo for almost four years in his last exile in Mexico. On the tallest cactus's pot a drunk Mexican was leaning, sitting down and half-asleep, with his wide-breamed sombrero hat sheltering both his head and his eyes. Actually it was not a drunk Mexican but a traditional landscape light with a broken post that gave this impression, but who cares, it looked all the same to me; so from then on, this half-broken, leaning landscape light was transformed into one of Trotsky's Mexican guards.

Here and there, positioned carefully by an artistic hand, were scattered all kinds of weird valueless objects: a paraffin storm-lamp, a couple of matchbox cars, candles, bottles, shells from the Balkan Wars, an aged and useless fire extinguisher, and sealed in jars various tear-gas cartridges; and amidst the creative chaos of this New Babylon six white iron armchairs and an iron table were patiently waiting for us.

"My father founded the Hanging Gardens ages ago," said Vas, "the flat and the terrace I mean. I remember him observing, almost supervising the progress of the work, visiting early at dawn, before work and late at night, after it, the foundation pit.

"Many years later, while I was rereading Platonov's *Foundation Pit*, reading it through my newly acquired surrealist lens, I saw both my parents preoccupied with thoughts similar but not identical to the ones of the Platonov's heros, because they were not living under Socialism;

"Probably my parents had gazed at their small sleeping son *who would one day lord it over their graves and live on an earth that had been packed with their bones and subdued.*

" '*My dear*,' my father began to formulate their mutual mood.

" '*Before us lies someone who to all intents and purposes is already an inhabitant of earth. Here* *slumbers the offspring of our will and the aim of all our efforts and concerns, a small person destined to become a universal element. That is why it is essential for us to complete the foundation pit at optimal tempo, so the home can quickly become a reality and our underage son can be protected by a stone wall from the Wind and from catching Cold!"**

"And now, the capitalist bandits, both Greeks and foreigners, and their criminal and terrorist organisations, Troikas and Quartets and Funds, come and collect at gun point taxes we cannot afford to pay. Literary at gunpoint for they have scattered through downtown Athens and across the country antiriot-squads and paddy-wagons."

"They want us to pay for their crisis," I said; "or as the young people shout in the demos: '*Money for the bankers Bullets for the youngsters*'"

I took in my hands and read the labels on two of the jars: March 8, 2007 and December 7, 2008. "I thought you invited us back in 1983," I said to Vas.

"I did, but it's just a time-lift, all round us time runs as usual —for the time being— you didn't actually travel in the past, you've just been elevated upwardly into it."

I asked to go to the bathroom. On the top of a pile of slick magazines placed on a

---

*Paraphrase by V. Ludens. Original text Andrey Platonov, *The Foundation Pit*, Translated from the Russian by Robert Chandler and Geoffrey Smith, The Harvill Press, London, p71.

small, short, pink table by the loo, I saw Ayn Rand's *Atlas Shrugged*. I peed looking at it from above and thinking of Mistress Troika. For a weird reason when I pee late at night in the loo, I think of deadly things, I feel that life falls in the vacuum of nothingness the same way the pee falls in the loo. I consider it as a phycological side-effect of the capitalist estrangement from time, of the annihilation of all the futureless lives.

"Are you a masochist?" I asked Zórba as soon as I saw him. "Did you pay all these money to *read Rand?*"

Zórba laughed. "Reading Rand is for sure a vice for any rational mind. For a surrealist it's even worse but, to tell you the truth, if I had to make a BDSM-political-film-noir on Mistress Troika, with lots of blood and deaths and urban-guerrilla, I was going to use an actress looking and a heroine thinking like Rand to take the role. But don't worry, I didn't pay a cent for it. I expropriated it from the INS bookshop."

"Hey, is it true that Syriza wants us to declare to the Tax-Office, even the one euro left in our dead dad's forgotten wallet, not to say about our dead parent's wedding-rings?" Zórba asked me in his turn.

"No idea, but I'll not be surprised if they do. They are pro-EU; in times of crisis EU under Germany leads Europe to a 'state of emergency'. After all the Nazis did the same to the Jews. But why do you ask?"

"A,' said Zórba the ræbelaisian, "Bloody Troikans, may the fire of a Molotov Cocktail fly up thy fundament. If they do so, I'll estimate the value of my huge heavy cock worth it's weight in gold and then I'll tell them to come and take it in all their holes; as many times as they want for I will not be able to pay the tax they'll ask for this personal fortune of mine!" He said it and after a second he burst into a laughter ten times more ræbelaisian than his sayings.

"So, why do you call your terrace New Babylon?" my partner Narra Ravenstein, asked our hosts partly out of curiosity, partly because she wanted to have interesting stories in stock, to narrate; she was a good narratress, nothing like me.

"It's a homage to *The New Babylon* the 1929 silent film written and directed by Grigori Kozintsev and Leonid Trauberg," said Scarlet...

"An unsurpassed avant-garde masterpiece dedicated to the Paris Commune and the encounter and tragic fate of two lovers separated by the barricades. Dmitri Shostakovich wrote his first film score for this movie. In the fifth reel of the score he quotes the revolutionary anthem, La Marseillaise juxtaposed contrapuntally with the Can-can from Offenbach's

Orpheus in the Underworld."

"Footage from The New Babylon was included by Guy Debord in his film *The Society of the Spectacle*," Vas added.

"But we did it as a homage to Constant Nieuwenhuys's *New Babylon* too," Scarlet continued her narration, "the anti-capitalist city of the future. Almost floating above ground, Constant's megastructures would literally leave the bourgeois metropolis below and would be populated by Homines Ludentes. In the New Babylon, the bourgeois worship of labour, family life, and civic responsibility would wither away. Men and women would sleep, eat, fuck, recreate, and procreate where and when they feel so. The post-revolutionary individuals would wander from one leisure environment to another in search of new sensations and sexual encounters..." she made a pause, sipped some Bathtub Gin Fizz as if she wanted to drown her inhibitions into the thirst-quenching cocktail and went on: "it's a provocative name, since in the Protestant tradition, not to say Protestant Ethics and the Spirit of Capitalism, Babylon is a figure of sexual immorality...."

"Sexual immorality rhymes and matches sexual immortality," said Vas the surrealist; Eden is immoral and immortal.

Ruby Firecrotch, smiled, leaned back on her iron armchair, crossed her legs provocatively in slow motion and said:

"Orgy-porgy, Fuck and fun,

Kiss the girls and make them One.

Boys at One with girls at peace;

Orgy-porgy gives release...

"Lenina and the rest used to fuck almost hypnotised by it," she continued her teasing, "and then some of them were paying visits to the zoo, to the Reservation I mean.... Who's going to take me tomorrow to a Capitalist Savage Reservation, I don't mind where, Frankfurt or The City preferably, I don't like long flights. I'll do anything to watch these capitalist beasts massacring each other...."

The luscious look on her face gave credence to her I'll do anything phrase.... The strap of her dress fell over her shoulder loosening her top and exposing a part of her breast....

"Orgy-porgy, Sex and fun,

Fuck the girls and make them come.

Boys that come in girls who tease;

Orgy-porgy gives release..." said Zórba in a way that nobody was sure if it was just a rhyming game or a respond to her call for other sexual games.

"That's great, let's make love not war," said Narra. The Wanderer got embarrassed. "No way," he said, "this was a silly hippy slogan, our slogan was 'Victory to the people of Vietnam' and ''Create Two, Three, Many Vietnams' so, let's make love and class war.""Shall we vote?" suggested Zórba or Vas, "not for the class-war, but for a moonlit sextravaganza, by raising hands." "I'll raise both hands and legs," said Narra."Mmm, I'd love to watch you raising your legs and whatever will follow, so let's not waste our time, let's do whatever comes to us," said Scarlet, "let's go for an orgy-porngy." She was the classiest of the three and although she was wearing the longest garment of all, a one-piece skintone dress reaching the middle of her calves, its fabric was so thin and transparent, giving the strong impression of exposed flesh, that made her look like the easiest lay of all, like telling you "look at me, I am willing and ready, fuck me any way you like, just fuck me."

That's exactly what I felt doing watching her medium to small perky tits and all the lines of her body unashamedly on show beneath the sheer fabric of her dress; not even removing it, just throwing her on her back and fucking her wildly.

"Spontaneity is good to start with but under certain conditions, if inhibitions prevail then both the orgasms of history and our own orgasms may be left unaccomplished, so let me take the lead and organise our orgy," said Ruby Firecrotch.

The approaching events reminded me of a midsummer's eve ages ago in *Stonehenge*.

Stoned in Stonehenge, not in the Stone Age but in the Age of Wars and Revolutions, stoned, un-stained and untoxicated enamored of the New Eden, inflamed with love, firing glances from a past that gets dimmer and dimmer.. firing cock-tails Molotov into a future that gets darker and

Burn Baby Burn, If I don't burn, if you don't burn

darker; baby light my fire, the futurous past re-
turns revengeful; locks that kill, kill, kill; the
Troikans that ruin our present, the Troikans that,
during this *Last Century before Humanity*," block
our future, the rising of the USSR... Baby light
my fire...
                                        *Yannis Ritsos

If we don't burn, how will the light vanquish the darkness?

Vanguished darkness Avant-garde flaming Molotov Cocktail

Latitude unknown Longtitude unknown Timetitude unknown Sextitude USSR

Stonehenge bistro's orgy porgy by the blue stones
the stones of Gibraltar after a bottle of le petit
bleu wine by the wine dark sea and then a
Julius Ulysses Cocktail speak memory of the cunning hero, the wanderer, blown off course time
and again after he plundered Troy's bloody
heights and in blood he fucked Penthestroika. For

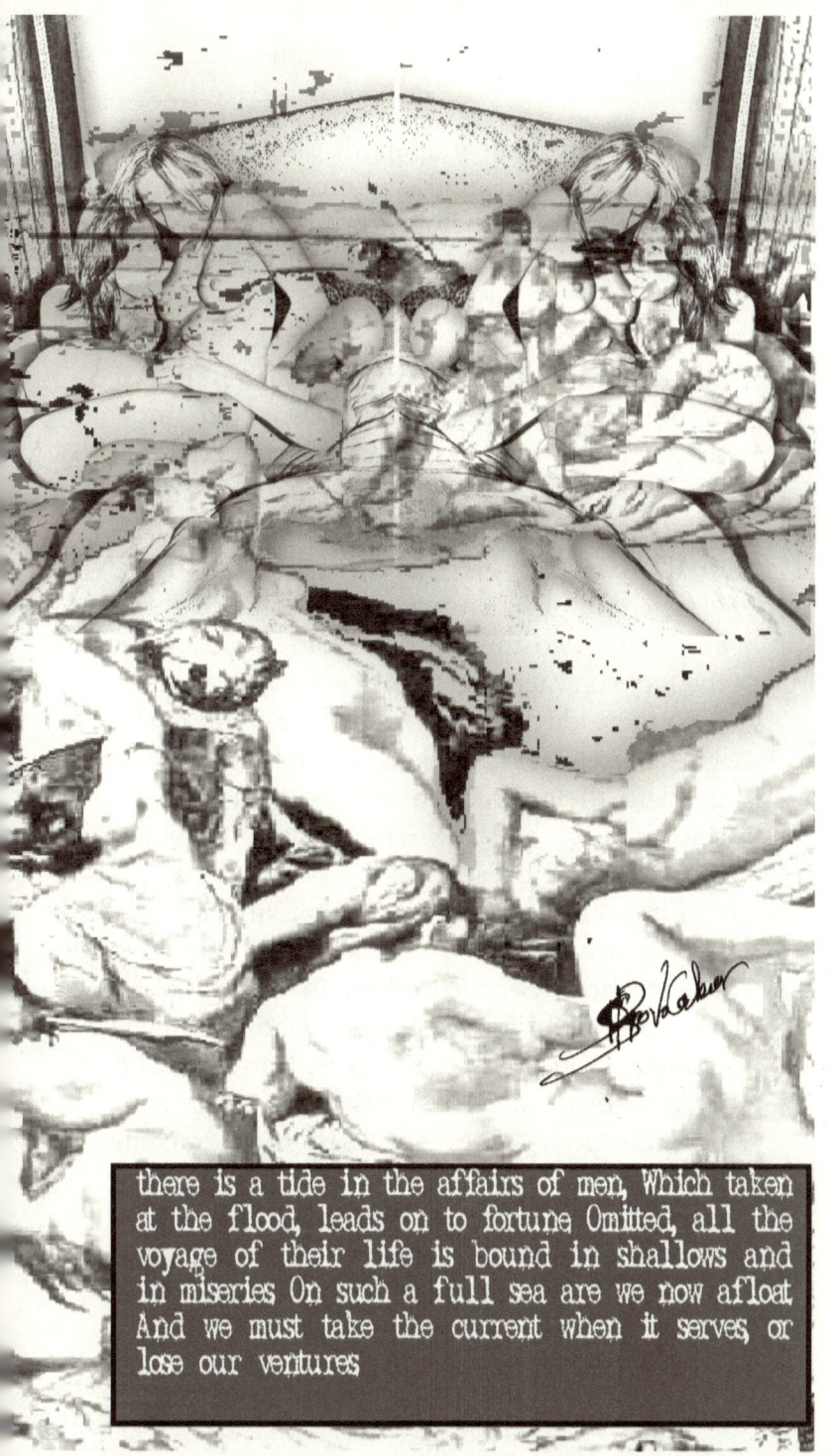

there is a tide in the affairs of men, Which taken at the flood, leads on to fortune Omitted, all the voyage of their life is bound in shallows and in miseries On such a full sea are we now afloat And we must take the current when it serves, or lose our ventures

It was an alternative open air bistro in the alterworld. Aldebaran, this world's giant orange sun, was already below the horizon. Things started getting wilder and wilder as both twilight and inhibitions started fading away. Howls, laughter and moans boomed out from all around, drunk men and women began wandering into the yard; it was like in a dream but it was no dream. Alter-Scarlet, alter-Narra and my alter-ego were waiting for the Wanderer, at a table for four; I had gone to the bar, I knew the bartendress and we were chatting when we both overheard three strangers, two men and a woman sitting by the bar, commenting on Alscarlet and Alnarra, who these days had her hair black and curly. The bartendress winked at me tilting her head to their direction and both of us concentrated on their talk which was continuous, non-stop and dreamy.

First unknown man: "Look at the red-haired over there, just look at her, the look on her face." Second unknown man: "Looks like she is thinking of sex." The unknown woman: "Does she look slutty, horny or like a Troikan officer?" First unknown man: "Not, not the latter, she's not such a disgraceful woman. I'm sure she is wet though. Her eyes." The unknown woman: "What about her eyes?" First unknown man: "They look soft and sexvaluating." Second unknown man: "Dirty look, like she wants it rough and dirty, doesn't matter at what place or in what hole she gets it, she wants to deep throat a big cock and she wants to get fucked hard and dirty in different positions; and she wants that hot come all over her face; but she's not a whore, she'll never vote in favour of a Memorandum. I'm sure that while orgasming she will look like Marilyn Chambers when she was getting it from the African stud behind the green door." First unknown man: "Hmm I bet she will indeed, but I'd say the horniest one is the woman in black top with the low cleavage, or, yes, it could be the redhead, she looks like she really wants a big dick. They both look pretty horny. They have these eyes and that look on their face, as if they are dying to get some cock into them. The red-haired. Yes. She's got that look in her eyes." Second unknown man: "She's got one of those faces that make her look easy, a few drinks and you're in her thong. I bet she is also a sub and likes to be controlled." The unknown woman: "A few drinks and? how far can she go?" Second unknown man: "All the way to sex in the alley, bent over, leaning up the wall, or the male holding and swinging her up and down, her legs wrapped behind his back; but she'll never go as far as to cut even a cent from an old man's pension; she's not a monetary prostitute, a eurobucket; she can even try bestiality but she will not even think of voting brutal emergency Budgets of NHS cuts and tax rises." The unknown woman: "This looks like a dinner before an orgy. She has a dirty look in her eyes telling that she wants to be stripped and fucked right there on the table; so all the men will fuck her at once in a train and then, the women will lick her clean." First unknown man: "The one with the dark curly hair looks fucking horny. Her eyes. 'Please fuck me' eyes." Second unknown man: "She is showing off her tits and discreetly playing with her hot juicy cunt." The unknown woman: "Which of the two, the brunette or the red-haired is more slutty?" First unknown man: "The brunette." Second unknown man: "The redhead is definitely a cock-craving whore, her smile and her eyes." First unknown man: "Hmm, she looks the most lady-like to me. It would be fun to make her look messy, to rip her clothes off, maybe leave some shreds on her, then use her shredded top to tie her to a bed, her legs spread bound to a bedpost, then, run my cock against her lips. she'll close them at first. before opening them and taking it all the way in. I think I would either take the redhead or the brunette in the back, who is playing with her hair with her hand... maybe force them both at the same time.... I will fill the redhead's pussy with my come and do the same to the brunette slut at the far end of the table and have them eat each other out in a 69, eating my come from their pussies, while I stand over them and shower them in a another comeshot." The unknown woman: "Who will be on top?" First unknown man: "The redhead is always on top." Second unknown man: "The brunette lady, the one with her tits hanging out. Her chest is bigger so she can force the red-haired to suck her nipples as she toys with her clit. The red-haired looks like she's weak, so the brunette could force her to lick her pussy clean, as she fingers her in front of everybody. I bet they have made out in the toilets." First unknown man: "Mmm, I'd love to force the one on the left at the front; the brunette with the nice tits, the curly hair and the half moon eyes." The unknown woman: "Why her?" First unknown man: "She just looks like she would be fun to rape; she'll put up a good fight."

Aldebaran was high above the fiery red horizon of the alterworld when we started ascending slowly from the deep waters of this libidinal thalassa. Enya's music was still playing on. The three women's jewellery, earrings, a pendant and a ring, sparkled in their crimson glare on their naked skin, over the dried traces of interchanged erotic fluids. All of them had found themselves in similar situations, similar awakenings, while, in the course of past years, were hitchhiking crossing all geographical and sexual boundaries, being the girls that were doing *"anything you liked real fast and then real slow."**

We got into the elevator; the four of us; "it works as a dropper now," said Vas; "you'll just have to press 'basement' and it will drop you onto the present, you can't go any deeper into the future for the time being; any deeper into the future than the present takes any individual to the underworld." We did as he said. The fall from 1983 to 2015 was scary. Only Zórba was left back in the darklit study-room, back to 1984, deep in the past and deeper in Chrisy-Darlene.... *"Darlene couldn't hide her growing excitement from her cousin anymore. She gasped, teats running down her cheeks in a steady flow while she fought to keep enough air in her lungs. She knew he was going to cum in her. He was going to clog her pussy with his jizz."* There was a faded lipstick trace on this page....

I checked the next day's plans in my notebook, a kind of organiser where I keep notes, write down books I want to read or draw all kind of childish drawings.

7 July 9pm Evelpidon the american girl's case.... Beth, against Delta squad

---

*Adams, Douglas (2002). *The Hitchhiker's Guide to the Galaxy*, New York: Del Rey.

Chapter 25

Oh, shit, Tuesday, July 7, 2015 again. All night long I feel unwell, maybe because of this up and down in the well of time; I feel ill, a feeling of light revulsion, feel like limboing weirdly in a fluid of illusionary velar lateral "l"s, July has one "l" like April, April has one "l" too, April is a cruel month, will July turn to be cruel? cruel for my mother lying ill at home in a hospital bed offered by friends? will July leave me motherless? she looks so fragile lately, am I ill or the night is ill? this long sleepless night, Lykavēttos looked lovely, illuminated as it was, last night, I'll not follow the solidarity calling for Evelpidon, it's impossible, I feel ill, I'll only use my only dearest's Eva, she's her best girlfriend, we even take her in our bed, and I'll email to all my female and male friends the appeal, an old appeal, I'll let 'em recall the case of the brutalised american girlll, l, l, l, later on I'll learn all about the trial, they' ll let the bloody Delta cavalry free, release 'em, lunatics, all of 'em lunatic killing machines, liquidate 'em, liquidate 'em, liquidate 'em all, following the trail leading from the crisis of liquidity to the liquidation of capitalism, for Karl Liebknecht we have a score to settle, for Rosa Luxemburg! This will be our pledge...

New Message

To: Undisclosed recipients

Solidarity with the American comrade almost killed by Delta Cops (Greece)

Wednesday, January 26th, 2011. Athens, Greece

This morning in Athens, an American anarchist has pressed attempted murder charges against Delta and Dias motorcycle police, as well as the relevant commanding officers, for a beating she suffered at the intersection of Patēsion and Stounarē streets while demonstrating against the International Monetary Fund (IMF) on November 15th, 2010. Meanwhile, over 170 members of the American and European scholarly community, including Noam Chomsky, Judith Butler, and Immanuel Wallerstein, have denounced the behaviour of the Delta police towards demonstrations and specifically the beating of the American demonstrator, calling the attack on her "nearly fatal".

The November 15th Beating

On the night of the 15th of November, the 27 year old, 48 kilo protester was rushed bleeding and semi-conscious to the Erythros Stavros emergency room, where she was diagnosed as mulitiply- injured and having been brutally beaten by S. Marianou, a forensic surgeon. She was released after three days.

Among multiple injuries to her head, neck, back, and abdomen, she suffered from a skull fracture, blood hemorrhaging, and permanent damage to her inner ear. She also received stitches on the side of her head where she was injured by the first blow from the police by what surgeons in the hospital called a "blunt object"- the impact of which had rendered her immediately unconscious.

The demonstration took place on the first day of anniversary celebrations of the historic 1973 Poly-techneio uprising, and was attended by thousands of people ranging from base unions to student organizations to left parties and anarchists, protesting the arrival of IMF officials in Athens that day.

Eye-witness say that as the demonstration was coming to end at Polytechneio at approximately 8pm, up to 15 Delta police on motorcycles charged a student block at the back of the demonstration on Patēsion Street, throwing concussion grenades into the crowd and sending people into a panic.

According to eye-witness accounts, one of the Delta police ran towards the American woman and hit her from behind with a blunt object, immediately knocking her unconscious and causing her head to gush blood. Then multiple officers beat her with batons and kicked her before dragging her to an adjacent sidewalk, where she was beaten again by multiple officers. The officers attempted to handcuff her, but because of her condition they decided to leave her. She later recovered her consciousness.
— "When I woke up I was surprised because I was in

a different place than I had last remembered when the police first hit me. I could not hear anything from my right ear, and I could not turn my head or move my right arm- I thought my neck was broken. I saw blood on the sidewalk all around me and on the column in front of me. I was incredibly dizzy and it was difficult to remain conscious."

The American demonstrator was brought to the hospital by ambulance after being given first aid in the Alpha theater on Patēsion by members of EEK (Workers Revolutionary Party).

Eleytherotypia reported, "We saw her in the ambulance full of blood. She was bleeding from her head, her ear, and her nose."

The doctors said that she was multiply injured and admitted her for care. She was screened for internal bleeding, as she had lost urine during the beating as a result of being kicked directly in the kidneys. Four police officers had followed her to the hospital, where they repeatedly tried to intimidate her and interrogate her throughout the night despite her debilitated condition. However, people who showed up in solidarity as well as the doctors prevented them from approaching her bed well into the late hours of the night.

Attempted Homicide Charges Against the Delta

Her lawyer, Giota Massouridou, claims that the police's actions were intentionally lethal given that she was beaten for a prolonged amount of time while clearly bleeding from the head and unconscious, and that the medical reports show that the police targeted the most vulnerable parts of her body- repeatedly beating her on the head, neck, and midsection. The fact that the officers dragged her limp body several meters to the sidewalk evidences that they were aware that she was completely unconscious and unresponsive, and yet they continued the beating on the sidewalk- as witnesses say- for up to two minutes. Massouridou also says that given the American woman's petite size, it obviously would have been difficult for her to sustain such an attack from multiple policemen, and that it is by pure luck she is alive. Additionally, the officers left her unconscious on the sidewalk, indicating that they wanted to avoid responsibility for the extent of her injuries, especially in the case that she would not survive.

Along with attempted homicide, the American woman is also charging the police with continuous and collective use of illegal violence, breach of duty, and abuse of authority.

In light of the beating of the American anarchist, an international denouncement of Delta police was made by over 170 professors, journalists, legal scholars, and university students from the United States and Europe, including several well-known academics and writers such as Noam Chomsky and Judith Butler.

"There is a long history of complaints against Delta police for physical brutality, as there are several other cases of demonstrators being hospitalized with severe injuries after receiving beatings from Delta police, "the statement reads. "We urge a full disclosure of information regarding the identity of the Delta unit responsible for the excessive attack on the night of the 15th of November. "

There are other indicative charges which have been brought against the Delta police for brutality towards demonstrations. Charges were brought by Professor Aggelikē Koutsoumpou, who was seriously injured on the 6th of December 2009, when a Delta police officer rammed her with his motorcycles during a demonstration. On January 4th, the political organisation 'Dikaioma' sued the DELTA and DIAS for an assault on their bloc during a December 15, 2010 general strike demonstration.

In a press conference the lawyer for Dikaioma, Kostas Papadakēs, said, "It is only a matter of time before the Delta police kill someone."

The American anarchist, who still suffers from a fractured skull and permanent hearing loss, said in reference to the actions of the police:

"What happened to me is not an isolated incident, it is a daily occurrence because it is the very role of the police in co-operation with state and capital. This beating will not make me afraid, it does not stop me or anyone else from going to demonstrations — although it's true that the police came close to killing me that night, we go into the streets because capitalism murders us everyday."*

I recall a rally in support of her. Or

---

*From the Greek Streets: updates and articles on the situation in Greece, in English. SOLIDARITY WITH THE AMERICAN COMRADE BRUTALISED BY DELTA PIGS — WE NEVER FORGET OR FORGIVE. January 26th, 2011, 9:33 pm and is filed under Social Control. All contents of this site may be freely distributed. Anti-Copyright Network.

another was it? We had started from Exarcheia heading to Patēsion. I was in the last bloc, the 'tail.' On our left, right and back aggressive anti-riot squads and lots of undercover ones with radio-transmitters in hand. I was curious to hear. I started approaching them in the form of Saint Artemios, patron-saint of the Greek Police, but then I thought that they could arrest me on the spot, for with his beard and angry face the saint looked like an anarchist. So I kept my everyday look, went closer and overheard one giving a detailed report, concluding: "at the tail end are the usual junks." And who were the... *junks*? A nephrologist, a dentist, a cardiologist, two psychiatrists, a radiologist, an economist, a philosopher-essayist, youngsters from EEK, the Wanderer, Zórba-Vas the surrealist and the Narrator from the Union of Surrealist Sexual Retroperspectives, the supreme known, so far, entity that will emerge from the depths of Cosmos. *"This Cosmos, which is the same for all,"* the riddler-ainiktēs said, and *"no one of gods or men has made. But it always was, is, and will be: an ever-living Fire, with measures of it kindling, and measures going out."* Cosmos is the same for all, dreams are not. felt Zórba the rider and dreamed his two lost in time friends. Lolita and Yolanda. Playing chess. Before the night in Oceana. "Troika mat," whispered Yolanda.

Chapter 26

April 22, my daughter's birthday. It's midday and it's rather hot. Leaving Syntagma Square behind me, I walk down Stadiou Street. On my right I pass by IANOS, probably the most trendy bookshop of Athens. I never shop any book from there. According to the Workers' Union in Publications and Bookstores it has the worst working conditions from all the rest. Attached to it, side by side, a deserted building. Ages ago was home to the Athen's most luxury crystal-shop; now it looks like a ghost from the past; dirty and stinky. Its entrance is closed, locked, but between the step starting from the pavement and the door, a space measuring 2 meters by 0.80, a space almost the size of a coffin; the only difference is that it's higher, almost 3 meters high. What a luxury for the homeless that has found a shelter there, hiding his household behind a hanging rag. April 22, Lenin's birthday. "*April is the cruellest month, breeding lilacs out of the dead land, mixing memory and desire, stirring dull roots with spring rain,*" The revolutions should be cruel mixing memory and desire; memory doesn't let us forget; desire doesn't allow us to forgive. April 4, 2016. My mother's birthday; she is not with us this year. We went and put some flowers on her grave. She had started feeling beeing a burden for us, which was not the case. For she was aware that, although in Times of Troika many families survive on the pensions of the aged, old age and sickness require money for medicines, doctors, nursing, medical consumables, unless you let the aged and sick person rot in his own shit and urine.

Late June 2015.

"Mom, I'll put on the TV for you, and we'll be back soon."

"Where are you going?"

"Going to the ATM to draw some money, mom."

"But you went to the ATM yesterday."

"Yes. mom, we did, we have to go almost every day."

"Why do you have to go everyday?"

"Because the government has imposed capital controls and closed banks. We can draw only a small amount of money every day."

"Oh, don't bother to go everyday, we will manage with what we have."

"Next week we'll have to pay the nurse,

mom and we also need other things, but don't worry, watch this comedy and we'll be back soon."

"Just a moment, what make is our piano? I don't remember."

'Try to remember, mom, we've said it sometime ago."

"...It's,... a Foster?..."

"Bravo, mom, it's a Foster, you got it."

"Was it me that I played Chopin's Piano Concerto N.º 2 Op. 21 in F minor?"

"Yes, mom it was you. We have to go, we won't be late."

"Take care."

We walk, whenever needed, to the nearest ATM, sometimes with my wife, Faba, sometimes with my daughter, sometimes with Zórba or with the Wanderer and draw 60 euros.

Sometimes, especially during day-time when the older people feel safer to draw money, the queues are long. I passed by such a queue. I saw two youngsters, boy and girl, handing out flyers. I took one and rushed to read it paragraphlessly in a hurry.

(EEK) - TROTSKYISTS: BANKS IN THE PEOPLE'S HANDS — NO TO THE SPECULATIVE BANKERS OF THE TROIKA

Workers-popular control over the banks and flows of capital abroad. No loss for wages and pensions DIRECT NATIONALIZATION OF THE BANKS UNDER

WORKERS' AND THE POOR PEOPLE'S CONTROL Class war against the unorthodox war of the Troika EU/ECB/IMF and the domestic Troika 'New Democracy-PASOK-muddy "River-Potami" ' At the referendum we vote NO NO to the thieves of IMF-EU-ECB NO to the Greek collaborators of the Troika ND, Potami, PASOK The game is over: CANCELATION OF THE DEBT BANKS AND STRATEGIC ECONOMIC SECTORS IN THE HANDS OF SOCIETY. PRODUCTION AND POWER IN THE HANDS OF WORKERS! A Workers' Government- with Workers' Power DOWN WITH THE IMPERIALIST EU! RED SOCIALIST EUROPE! By tightening the screw and on the basis of stopping the flow of credit through blackmail and ultimatums, the international usurers of EU/ECB/IMF, with their Greek organs in the interior, the bankers of "systemic banks", the parrots of the mass media and their political puppets in ND, PASOK and the muddy River, are leading the country to declare disorderly bankruptcy and the people to disaster. An unorthodox war, a postmodern politico-economic coup is underway. They don't want simply to overthrow the government, they want to terrorize and bring to their knees an entire people, the Greek people, thus giving a message to the other peoples of Europe who are revolting against permanent austerity and monstrous unemployment. All out in the street, all to the struggle. To overturn the plans of the international Troika and the domestic Troika. To prevent all those- also inside key-ministries- who are preparing solutions against the people. Now is the time of the

People, not only in the election polls, but first and foremost on the streets and in the struggle for freedom, social justice, and emancipation. The people led by the working class and the youth can and must be mobilized to tear up the ultimatums and all the "Memorandums", old and new! Break with capitalism and the European Union here and now! In order to take our lives, social wealth, and power into our hands! The time of truth has struck. All the compromises with the capitalists inside and outside the country that the leading group of SYRIZA made - with the right-wing nationalists of Kammenos, with Karamanlē s' Right on the issue of the President of the Republic, with the Federation of Greek Industrialists, with the so-called "institutions" of imperialism in Europe and the USA have not only failed but made the capitalists and the mechanisms of the EU and the IMF more aggressive. We call the popular rank and file and the fighting forces supporting SYRIZA to demand from their leadership to cut the ties of class collaboration with the imperialist institutions, the EU and the IMF, foreign and local capitalists and their political officers. We call the leadership of the Communist Party of Greece to stop covering with left phraseology the partnership with the domestic Troika. The position for a protest vote —in practical terms an invalid vote- in the referendum strengthens the most reactionary bourgeois forces. A Nationwide Congress of the elected representatives of the entire labour movement, social movements, self-organized people, must be immediately prepared to discuss the alternative program of the way-out of the crisis. So as to prevent others from deciding for us without us. A United Class Front of all the political and social organizations, movements, collectives, organized and unorganized masses of the working class and the poor popular strata is required, against the class enemy, inside and outside the country. No to "national unity" Governments. Workers' Government with workers' power

THE WORKERS REVOLUTIONARY PARTY (EEK) - TROTSKYISTS

Athens, 29 June 2015

But people seem so confused on the matter. Of course they are more enraged than scared but still confused about what should be done.

They are waiting. Just waiting for something to happen; for things to come up-side-down. They're waiting for an insurrection, they're waiting for Godot.

VLADIMIR:

We can still part, if you think it would be better.

ESTRAGON:

It's not worthwhile now.

Silence.

VLADIMIR:

No, it's not worthwhile now.

Silence.

ESTRAGON:

Well, shall we go?

VLADIMIR:

Yes, let's go.
They do not move.

Curtain

ESTRAGON:
You say we have to come back tomorrow?
VLADIMIR:
Yes.
ESTRAGON:
Then we can bring a good bit of rope.
VLADIMIR:
Yes.
Silence.
ESTRAGON:
Didi?
VLADIMIR:
Yes.
ESTRAGON:
I can't go on like this.
VLADIMIR:
That's what you think.
ESTRAGON:
If we parted? That might be better for us.
VLADIMIR:
We'll hang ourselves tomorrow. (Pause.) Unless
Godot comes.
ESTRAGON:
And if he comes?
VLADIMIR:
We'll be saved.
Vladimir takes off his hat (Lucky's), peers inside it,

feels about inside it, shakes it, knocks on the crown,
puts it on again.
ESTRAGON:
Well? Shall we go?
VLADIMIR:
Pull on your trousers.
ESTRAGON:
What?
VLADIMIR:
Pull on your trousers.
ESTRAGON:
You want me to pull off my trousers?
VLADIMIR:
Pull ON your trousers.
ESTRAGON:
(realizing his trousers are down). True.
He pulls up his trousers.
VLADIMIR:
Well? Shall we go?
ESTRAGON:
Yes, let's go.
They do not move.

Curtain.

On our way back home I keep silent; I'm thinking of the ABC of communism. This is an open, clear-cut economic war against the toilers. They are stronger. Their strength lies in the strength of international capital, in the strength and durability of the international connections of the bourgeoisie, they have various connections, habits of organisation and management, knowledge of all the 'secrets' (customs, methods, means and possibilities) of management, superior education, close connections with the higher technical personnel, incomparably greater experience in the art of war.

So what do we need? We need the revolution, the dictatorship of the proletariat, an extremely determined and most ruthless war waged by the working class against a more powerful enemy, the bourgeoisie.

"We're back, mom," I said having just unlocked the door and entered....

For a moment she bridged past and present; bridged, not confused; she pictured in her mind the old vanished in time wooden door of our old house; the door knocker is waiting for the Wanderer to lift it and strike the ornamented plate and....

She had switched to the news but the news had scared her a bit; for all of them, all "the above," were predicting and threatening with the end of the world if the Greeks didn't accept the bailout conditions.

"Don't worry, mom, everything will be ok." But she was worried in her own way, lying on her bed, for a month or so, watching-not watching the news, before she passed away. "The Memorandum," she kept repeating and whispering, from time to time, till the end. For they had launched an unseen terrorist campaign against the vote for "No." "Your Yes or your Life," Troika's highwaymen were shouting day and night. 'Bastards,' I'm thinking, 'bourgeois robbers and terrorists, all of you should end your life lined up in front of the firing squads of the proletariat. A gang of market-operators can decide in a few seconds to impose an interest rate of 6 percent rather than 3% on a bond, plunge a country into crisis, crash its health system, murder the weak, the elder, the infants. Red Terror is an absolutely necessary, sacred weapon, in the war against them; I would have signed unhesitantly the decree for the execution of a hundred Troikans, just for the gloomy room my father died in because of them; he was worth of, at least, a room with a view of virtual seas and favourite landscapes and moons and everything. No, a hundred Troikans are not enough...' Fragments of José Clemente Orozco's *Katharsis* mural, pass in front of my eyes: weapons, destruction, class war, individuality, insurrection and a nude woman in pro or post orgasmic situation lying with her breasts exposed and her legs spread, ready to fuck again and again among the ruins and debris of capitalism.

YOU VOTE YES OR YOU DIE

THE HORRORS OF THE HO VOTE

From her bed or her armchair she was reliving the past amidst the...

FEAR AND MISERY

OF THE EUROPEAN UNION

APOCALYPSES NOW

There is a mural in Locomotiva - Cooperativa too. Facing the entrance. A long train with many wagons behind a big locomotive with a big red star on the front. During a hot July night as we were sitting and drinking quietely the door of the first wagonlit opened and on the steps appeared Valentina Guido Crepax. She wore only a pair of military trousers and nothing else except a red-army hut with a red star badge on it. In her right hand she was holding a 7.62×25mm Tokarev. She winked at us smiling teasingly and then she turned sideways and disappeared slowly in the wagonlit. We followed her, the three of us, the Narrator, the Brut and the Surrealist. Then when we became four, us and her, four like the Internationals, we locked the door and indulged into edenic libidinal activities.

Back in the Dark Troikan Times. Capitalism Age. I turn on the TV. All the Troikan thick-think-tank on display. Prime Ministers, Ministers, Bankers, Professors, embedded media whores. male and female. Chanels, panels, pampers, Troikan heads full of shit-ridden terminology: markets, investors, competitiveness, Greece's Debt Due; they are aware that they talk shit. *"more of your conversation would infect my brain, being the herdsmen of the beastly** Troikans," I say and turn off the TV.

---

*W. Shakespeare, *The Tragedy of Coriolanus*, Act2, Scene 1.

Chapter 27

"But all these capitalist criminals are out of reach," told me a few days ago, Alex-who-was-sailing-stormy-waters, an old friend of mine, an ex-captain from Meganēsi *who travelled far and wide and many cities did he visit, and many were the nations with whose manners and customs he was acquainted.* He was a good listener for I used to talk much and he used to keep silent and listen a lot. He was doing the same when for weeks and months and endless times he was crossing the seas and the oceans listening to the waves and talking not.

We were sitting in Locomotiva with his wife Anna and mine. Anna is a staff nurse in an Intensive Care Unit and week by week she witnesses the collapse of the National Health System under the planned and well-organised severe blows of the Black Front: EU-Troika-Government; stories that brought back to my wife bad memories from the Time of the Counter Revolution and the Collapse of the 'existing socialism;' back then, the pres-

*The Odyssey by Homer, Book I, Translated by Samuel Butler

ent-day proud, most fanatic and neophyte members of the EU, formed their new ruling class by the plundering of the social property. The NHS hospitals had been literally robbed from everything useful and her poor mother was carried from her bed to the ambulance on a blanket.

"So, you think they are out of reach?" I set the rhetorical question to my friend, Alex-who-was-sailing-stormy-waters. "But, my friend, the revolution should know no limits and no boundaries in space, time, or anything else.

"After all today's Not-Yet-Become is tomorrow's history lesson in our high-schools and our colleges.

"Could any royal family in Europe predict as early as 17 July 1916, the execution of the Romanovs on 17 July 1918?"

"Maybe so.... But," commented Alex-who-was-sailing-stormy-waters, "the death penalty has been abolished in Europe."

"My friend, my friend.... When I was very young, seventeen years young, I had an affair with a maoist girl of my age; she had fair fluffy hair, a pleasant face, deep voice and warm body. My brain was fresh and I still remember by heart a second to none definition of the revolution: *A revolution is not a dinner party, or writing an essay, or painting a picture, or doing embroidery; it cannot be so refined, so leisurely and gentle, so temperate, kind, courteous, restrained and magnanimous. A revolution is an insurrection, an act of violence by which one class overthrows another.*

"So class enemies could be executed by the revolutionary proletariat. Even John Reed, who was not a class enemy but a communist, was nearly executed by mistake, during the ten days that shook the world. All politicians who served Troika should be executed. Prime Ministers, ministers, MPs, all!"

The turn of the conversation made Anna feel uneasy. "But shouldn't the revolution be greathearted?" she asked.

"Of course it should," I replied, but as Trotsky said and unfortunately, yes unfortunately, the course of history shows in the worst way that he was right, *'In a serious struggle there is no worse cruelty than to be magnanimous at an inopportune time.'*

"Thus, just because I am extremely merciful, I would execute them all if it's up me."

Alex-who-was-sailing-stormy-waters and travelled far and wide and many cities did he visit, and many were the nations with whose manners and customs he was acquainted, smiled contentedly; we waved to some friends that have just arrived; we saw a very sympathetic couple, both in their early eighties; they were drinking quietely their coffee; we grabbed the chance to scorn Merkel: "if she could see them she was going to have a stroke; she's working hard like a proper German 36 hours per day in order to annihilate these bloody Greek pensioners and some of them still spend her precious German euros on a cup of coffee! 'Oh my Adolph, oh my dear, I'm a total failure!' she was going to whisper."

"However, dear friend," I went on, "If you think that I'm a maximalist, I have much more realistic ideas.

"Don't you agree that all these scums who implement all these policies within Greece will be extremely accessible in Times of Revolution?"

A group of 40 black-hooded anarchists attacked with Molotov cocktail bombs the police station in Exarcheia.

Professor A.C tries to find the Russian text of Khlebnikov's phrase *Boom, you black sails of time!* he found integrated in Wanderotica.

Locked in her room, his daughter Myrto masturbates reading in the same book about the double penetration of Ianthi by her fiance and Argestis in the island of Kythnos.

Boom, bam, agh..., yes!.... Art, explosions and sexplosions in Times of Troika.

Chapter 28

Dusk, late September, year 2015, an empty blue-jean shirt is drying in the wind, Lykavēttos hill, pine trees, there was a pine tree in the Wanderer's yard when he was a kid, the same pine tree that had shaded his mom when she was a kid, the Wanderer's father wandered over the New World, then they travelled, by train, they moved to Athens, birds fly freely in the sky, he used to envy them, for he was a wanderer by birth and birds flew but pupils did not, it's a beautiful day, David LaFlamme, Linda LaFlamme, white bird, the sunsets come, the sunsets go, his mother has gone, but not gone with the wind, she's buried under a pine tree, close to his dad, he was day-dreaming of the aspen trees, with their dying leaves, turning gold, Madison, Wisconsin, then dying in Times of Troika, no golden leaves no nothing, deprived of all, buried close to his wife, with no future, the living and the dead deprived of any future in Times of Troika deprived of it by gods and masters, ni Dieu ni maître, arise ye prisoners of want, a pyrrhic victory for Syriza in the snap elections of September 20, Firefox, toolbar, mail, new mail, undisclosed recipients, title: article by Savas Michael Matsas:

After capitulating to the EU, the ECB, and the IMF on July 12 by signing a third package of the most barbaric austerity measures tied to a new bailout of the unsustainable Greek debt, after spreading disappointment, confusion, and disgust among the Greek popular masses and anger within its own members, after a traumatic split of its party and parliamentary group, Syriza nevertheless managed to win the snap elections on September 20 and resurrected its coalition government with the right wing nationalists of ANEL (Independent Greeks).

Plus ça change plus c'est la même chose, a cynical but superficial commentator could say. But nothing is the same: the government of the same partners Syriza/ANEL is not the same as the government that was elected on January 25, 2015, empowered then with the enthusiasm and hopes of the majority of the Greek people for an end to the nightmare of permanent austerity imposed by the Troika of the EU/ECB/IMF. Nobody now doubts that the new government of Syriza/ANEL would implement the diktats of the EU in the third "Memorandum ". The political system is not restored nor stabilized. On the contrary, the unprecedented massive abstention (45% now, ten points more than in the previous elections) — an abstention particularly strong among the youth, the unemployed, and the proletarian areas that led to the triumph of the NO in the Referendum of July 5- as well as a vote to the so-called "Union of Centrists" led by V. Leventis, a notorious comic figure of fringe TV, are clear signs of the loss of credibility of Greek parliamentarianism and a further disintegration of a political system already in shambles.

The fact that the Nazi "Golden Dawn" again occupies the third position among the parties in Parliament is a threatening development; but far from being a "re-assuring" sign for political stabilization, it clearly shows the deepening of social and political polarization and the dangers confronting the people. Although there was not a spectacular rise in the Nazi vote, nevertheless, it became a constant counter-revolutionary factor in political life. Their vote even doubled in the islands where the wave of migrants came this past summer.

The forces that have split from Syriza, from the left, forming the very heterogeneous and bureaucratic "Popular Unity", were defeated in the elections as they did not present any real credible alternative, only a vague promise for a "new Syriza, more consistent with its origins" and dedicated to form an "anti-austerity, patriotic , democratic front" , based on economic nationalism, a return to the national currency, the drachma, without a break with the EU nor with capitalism. The voters preferred the original Syriza than its replica. The failure of "Popular Unity" to enter parliament now intensifies all the centrifugal forces within that organization.

The self-referential, sectarian Stalinist Communist Party failed to attract the forces leaving Syriza, remaining immobilize with a small 5.5% of the vote. Generally, the KKE and other forces of the Left, including Antarsya, called on the people to vote solely for a combative workers-popular Opposition. The EEK fought in an electoral bloc with Antarsya, on the basis of a transitional program for an end to austerity, for a break with the EU, the abolition of the debt, nationalizations of the banks and the strategic sectors of the economy under workers control etc, but we were insisting always on a struggle for workers power and a socialist unification of Europe. The bloc EEK-Antarsya has increased its vote and percentage in relation to the previous elections in 2015 and 2012, without breaking the limit of a marginal 0.8%. The broad masses see us as combat organizations necessary for the everyday struggles but not yet as an alternative to power.

The Greek people looks, first of all, at the question of what kind of government, not just an opposition force, could stop the on-going catastrophe. And it has chosen, without much enthusiasm nor great expectations, the lesser evil, the Syriza of Tsipras, to avoid a full revanchist restoration of the discredited old corrupt regime of the right wing New Democracy.

It will be the weakest and for the same reason a very dangerous government tied to the orders of the EU and the Greek ruling class to implement the most savage austerity program on a devastated people, in conditions of a rapidly worsening world capitalist crisis.

The most important battles are in front of us.

send - your message has been sent - back to Firefox, *I'm the fox, you can't catch me with your dogs, I run too fast, move too quick, can't show much love to you, so don't you look at me,* Bridges' Fakkeltog, vinyl record, LP, 33⅓ rpm —33⅓ revolutions per moon. Sitting in Locomotiva. Alone. My stream of thoughts interflows with the thoughts and confessions of Don Quichotte Almodovar de La Mancha.* Vinyl; looks and feels as sensual, as blue as velvet; my thoughts match the night, the moon, la Luna. *"When life itself seems lunatic, who knows where madness lies? Perhaps to be too practical is madness. To surrender dreams —this may be madness. Too much sanity may be madness— and maddest of all: to see life as it is, and not as it should be!"* Revolution; betrayed; permanent; revolution; revolver; a Nagant m1895 revolver; *Volver, several kinds of coming back, death, not just mine, that of my loved ones, the merciless disappearance of all that is alive, the increasingly faster passing of time. Volver, coming back to my mother* and to my father the Pēgasos. During the second Troikan winter he was so cold, for the heating oil boiler in our block of flats remained turned of. Boiler, valves, steam, revolve. Volver; revolver; revolution.

---

*http://emanuellevy.com/interviews/volver-almodovars-confessionr-1/

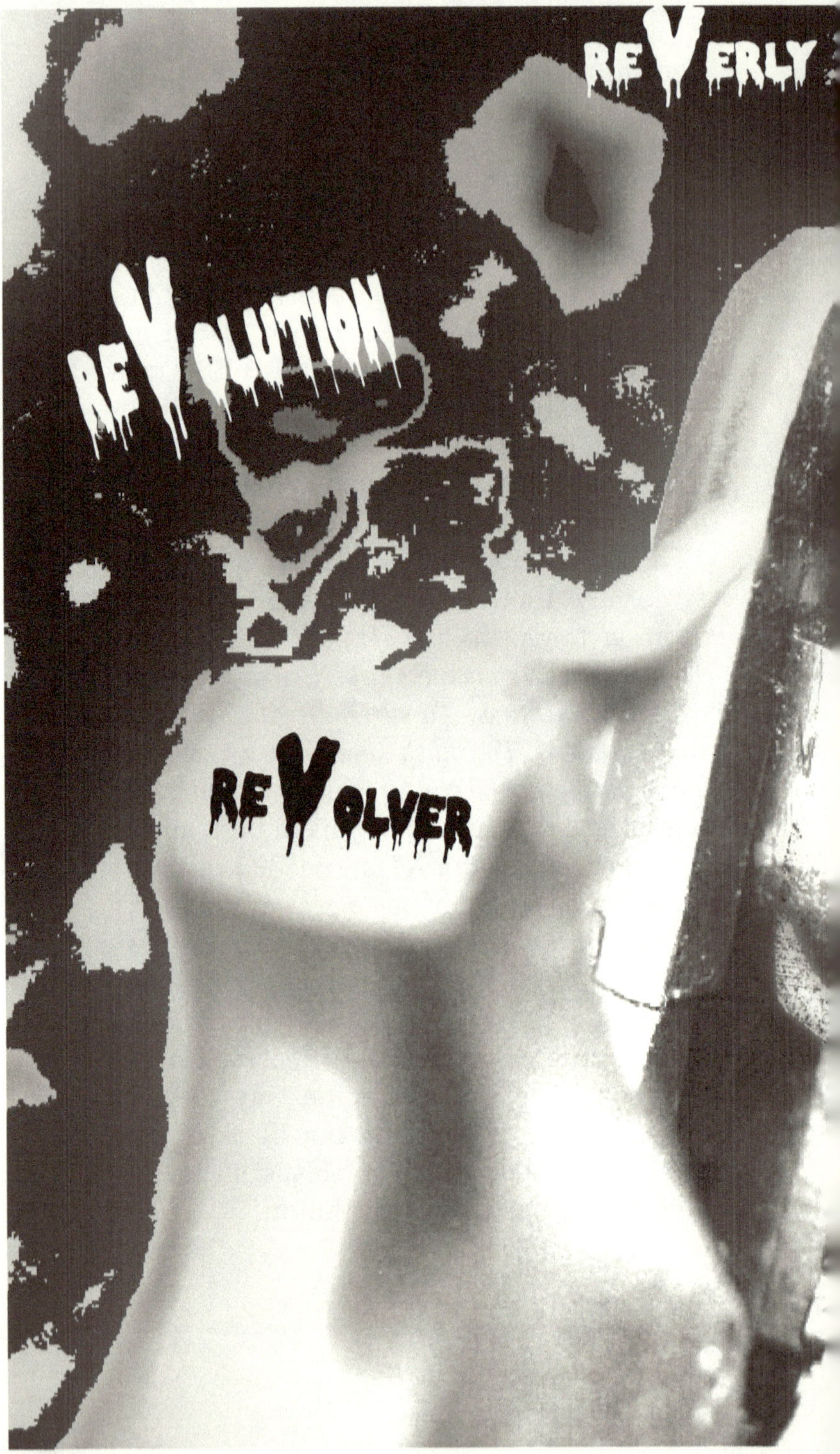
reVerly
reVolution
reVolver

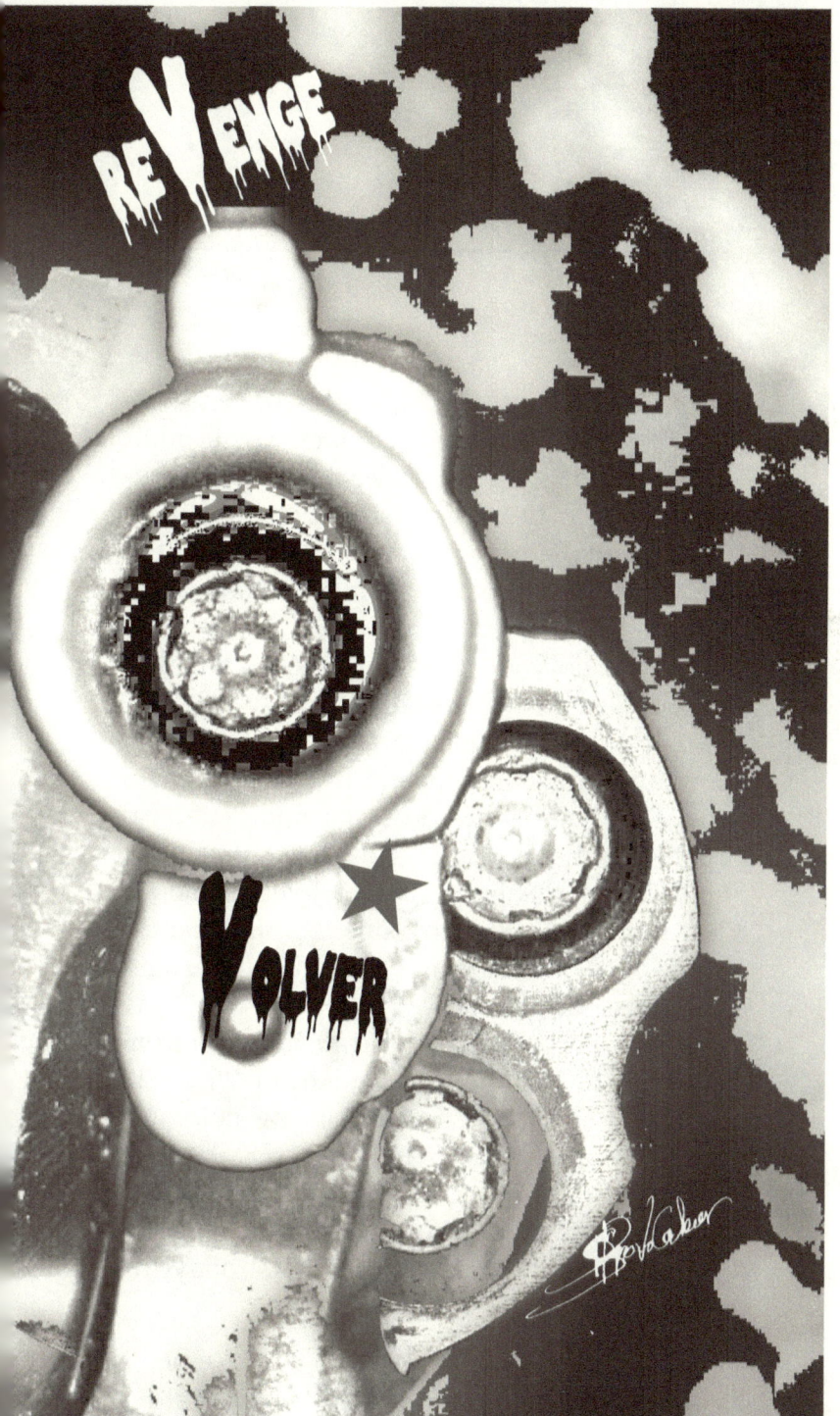

Chapter 29

Saturday, May 14, 2016. We're watching, by chance, a late night adult show; Alex-who-was-sailing-stormy-waters and us. Eurovision Song Contest. Anna and Faba, our wives, are not in the mood to watch porn, so they abstain, they drink beer and chat.

"What do you think of Ukraine's Jamala," asked Alex-who-was-sailing-stormy-waters.

Zórba the ræbelaisian laughed. "Her performance, her screams and her looks remind me of a widow in pro-orgasmic state. No more comments, my friends."

"This is the light side of Jamal's moons but there is a very dark one too, my friend," replied the Wanderer. "The EU is washing the nazis dirty laundry in public: the Lviv pogroms perpetrated by Ukrainian nazis from 30 June to 2 July 1941, and from 25 to 29 July 1941 and the Kiev and Babi Yar holocaust on September 29-30, 1941 by the SS, the German police units and their auxiliaries the Ukrainian fascists who proved to be some of the worst war criminals of WW2. Today the neo-nazist Ukrainians use the emblems of the 14 Division of the SS. But bear in mind that the 14th Division and the 15th Cavalry Corps were manned mainly by the Crimean Tatars, who, although of Turkish origin were named 'Goths' by the 3rd Reich."

A dark shadow covered Zórba's face, the shadow of our dark Troikan times. Then he spoke. "It's not just a coincidence that Golden Dawn's nazis announced for today a youth festival of hatred in the old Gendarmerie park, the historic site where the post-civil war far-right state executed Nikos Beloyannēs..." "And not only him," interrupted him the Wanderer "but also Dēmētrēs Batsēs, Nikos Kaloumenos and Ēlias Argyriadēs, all of them communist militants.... Batsēs was of bourgeois origin, a traitor of his class, a prominent economist."

"Yes. A traitor of his class," agreed Zórba. "That's why the monument, the place, its heritage, just a 100 meters away from their head-quarters are hard to swallow for the nazi thugs; you remember that last year they attempted to desecrate the monument by spraying swastikas on it.

"The assignment of any public space and particularly of the Beloyannēs Memorial by Kaminēs Athens Municipality to the nazis shows the 'elective affinities' of the pro-Troikans with the murderers of the nazist

Golden Dawn."

"Not to say that the government of Alexēs Noske sent the coppigs to protect the nazist fiesta from the anti-fascist mobilisations," the Wanderer added surprisingly calmly. The tone of his voice meant 'we'll keep this in mind too.'

I feel so sorry that I didn't record the presentation of V. Ludens's book with the weird title *3 on all 4s, a vinyl blue-noir anti-novel at 78 rpm — revolutions per moon.*

The event took place in Locomotiva. Kyriakos Moutidēs made the introduction and during the chat that followed interfered with witty comments; Michalēs Barbaresos made an impressive presentation of the blue-noir anti-novel.

I bought a copy and asked the author to sign it, I read it in two days. It's illustrated by the very same writer, with sketches highlighting parts of the story. The story of 3 spectres haunting Altopia: the spectre of lust, the spectre of urban querilla and the spectre of death. The story of 3 lewd, lascivious young women —Alice Voulvarē, Baisemoi Béart and Vouagelandē Donatou— having sex in the 3 basic positions: the missionary of the lazy people of the lost Eden, the savanal, on all fours, and the cow-girl one; the latter is accused of promoting terrorism because by having sex in it, the women are getting armed with British submachine Stens. There is a yellow-magenta rocket, lots of explicit sex scenes, parallel and intercrossed worlds, time-travels, locomotives and astro-motives, and, amidst all this surrealist extravaganza, a novel within the anti-novel, the notorious noir *bratatat* by another writer, published by a strange publishing house named *The Ravenge*, a second-hand pocket-book previously owned by an interesting female, that the hero carries always with him, in space and time, and reads it in bits and parts, here and there, from the *hearths of arson hall of residence* —the author doesn't use commas, dots, or capital letters because he hates capitalism— to the flaming heart of Athens, Exarcheia Square and the Locomotiva - café - bar. *Bratatat* is the story of the same 3 lewd, lascivious young women, in another(?) parallel world, where they are involved in an urban guerrilla group and operate under an umbrella network that carries the scary, macabre name *Five Year Plan* and kills the Troikans like flies. However they don't do it in an orderly way, from the standpoint of a revolutionary class organised as state power, a state that withers away, and at this point the author — the author of *bratatat* or the author of *3 on ll 4s* is not clear— expresses his disagreement; not a moral one, just a political.

After I finished the anti-novel, a part of which takes place in our days, I came to the conclusion, for a hundredth time maybe, that surrealism maintains under any conditions, even in Times of Troika, its initial revolutionary ardour. *I was. I am. I will be.*

'...Like flies,' thought Zórba. His dad's village was full of flies. Zórba was not more than ten. The village in the middle of Crete. Late August to September. Sun, soil, olives, vineyards. No sea at all. And flies. Hundreds of flies buzzing everywhere, driving him crazy. They had to go there every summer for his dad to carry out manually the harvesting of white grapes, gain, if possible and not always, some extra money, besides his salary, and pay back the loan for the house. It was a hellish village in the middle of nowhere and later on Zórba identified it with the Savage Reservation in Huxley's *Brave New World*. His parents managed to pay the loan and never bother again until bloody Capitalism got involved with Mistress Troika. The whore wants taxes, bills and blood. Zórba recalled the Grapes of Wrath and the flies. 'Yes!' he thought, 'all Troikans must be exterminated by the proletarian revolution like flies.'

"I have only two nice memories after spending ten years in the village of the flies," told us Zórba, sometime later. "The first is the way back from the vineyards, after the sunset, on a donkey for the sake of fun, in the company of my dad or of Vitsos, a tobacco worker from Macedonia; he was a communist and he was telling nice stories. Mom was waiting for us in an old cottage.

"The second was Evi from Athens. I was eighteen, she was not even fourteen, sextremely voluptuous, provocative, craving for sex. She offered herself in a barn, after she provided the condoms she had stolen from her mom's bag. Her mom, Franzka, was fucking around while her husband, an army officer, was daydreaming of the return of the military junta and the extermination of all the communists. Evi was reading daily the 'family paper,' *Apogeymatinē*, an ultra-right pulp-paper full of half-nude women and scandalous sex stories. Evi obviously had got a good propædia and was eagerly curious to try all she had read about. I grabbed the chance to satisfy both her curiosity and my teenage urges, not only in the barn but back in Athens too."

A few days later the Narrator was compelled to be a witness and give evidence in the case of the assassination of the Minister of Economics and three high-rank Troikan officers by the Five Year Plan. Immediately after the incident massive arrest sweeps began followed by show trials. The court was expecting, from the Narrator a detailed narration of the assassination events, but in vain. For his name was not originating from the Latin narrator "a relater, narrator, historian," agent noun from narrat-, stem of narrare plus the suffix —tor, but in his case, the suffix —tor was added to Narra, his voluptuous wife's name, to create his own agent noun-name. On the crotch of his jeans she was stamping her rivals' faces. I entered the courtroom at the moment the Narrator was affirming word by word, "I do solemnly and sincerely and truly declare and affirm that the evidence I shall give shall be the truth, the whole truth and nothing but the truth."

The President: "You have witnessed the assassination events, so please tell us, do you recognize the accused as the persons seen to open fire against the victims?"

The Narrator: "Mrs. President, although I was present at the scene and I could have been a witness, I was not a witness, for my attention during these few crucial moments was distracted, or to be more precise was fully attracted, elsewhere."

President: "Elsewhere? What else could have attracted your attention while almost next to you 67 rounds were fired over a period of 13 seconds?"

The Narrator: "Well..."

The President: "You have just affirmed to give the truth, the whole truth and nothing but the truth."

The Narrator: "Yes, I did affirm and the whole truth is that I was magnetised by the buttocks and the bosoms of the three sextremely young ladies that were also present at the moment and are also among the witnesses, sitting now over there."

Laughters from the audience.

The President: "Mr. witness, behave yourself and respect the court process..."

The Narrator: "Mrs. President, the truth, the whole truth and nothing but the truth is that I was absorbed by the bosoms and buttocks of the ladies and I did not notice at all who was shooting whom...

"I'm sure Mrs. President you are aware from your own sexperiences how strong the force of libido is compared to all other forces, to the force of death —Thanatos— or the EU Task Force for Greece, which according to Freud are all forces that are not essential to the life of an organism and tend to denature it or make it behave in ways that are sometimes counter-intuitive..."

More laughters from the audience...

The President — ringing her bell: "We suspend for an hour."

Chapter 30

D ad is dead, mom is dead and we the living are doomed to live in dark times, in Times of Troika. We the doomed and the dead and the down-trodden; deaf not and neither blind hear the drums and see the darkness. Drums of war and class warfare. And darkness is over the surface of the deep, and the Spirit of Capital-ism-in-deep-crisis is hovering over the world. It's late at night and we the living are sitting in undisclosed spaces and listening to the ac-cordion and the mandolin —dad used to play the mandolin while mom played the piano— and to the banjo of the Blackbird Raum band and love this music and nostalgia and rage and its female vocalist and our darknesses melt together like a lighted wax and we say, *Let there be light*, and through the open Doors we invite passers-by: *Come on baby, light my fire, Try to set the night on fire*, light my cocktail molotov. I listen to the Blackbird's *Ravachol in Valhalla*, in his self-portrait my father looks like coming out of the blue mists of Valhalla, my mother does the same in her own portrait, men in dark times, death in 0 Troika, accordion, banjo, mandolin, *A window is closed in the cold*, *Race up the stairs with a friend*, *Sit in the hall, stare at a wall*, *The words that you said by my hospital bed* what a music, I think it's one of the most underestimated bands in America, hey you dj, please, play for once more Ravachol in Valhalla, and you Troikans beware *We've got weapons without name.*

We saw Delphy Dickulescu mourning. On the Late Night News. Dressed in black at the funeral of her close friend and colleague Paulina Matsaroki. They used to share the same bed, when on business trips abroad, the same philocapitalist, neoliberal fanaticism and the same addiction to hard cocks, for they were not lesbians but bisexuals.

Paulina Matsaroki was sexecuted. She was killed, executed, by too much, unbearable sex. She had met the Stranger in the Gin Joint Bar, at Christou Lada 1. Christos Ladas Minister of Justice, who had signed the execution of hundreds of communists, was also assassinated in Athens on 1 May 1948, by OPLA, the Organization for the Protection of the People's Struggle. The street carries his name but the Non-Committee of Erototopography renamed it to Upskirts Street. Paulina tried to impress him with her knowledge of international politics. She failed because he was already a target, so there was no need to impress that particular man, because all she knew were just information stocked in her brain, but she was totally illiterate as far as the logic of history was concerned and least but not last, her thighs were for sure much more impressive than her skills on political Trivial Pursuit. Later on the Stranger discovered that her mouth was skillful in deed. There were rumors that while Delphy and Paulina were in Argentina, trying hard to ruin the country's economy and force the people to pay for the crisis of the capitalists, Paulina attended intensive classes in the School of Evita. The latter, was said *to be the macho's ideal victim-woman - don't those red lips still speak to the Argentine macho of her reputed skill in fellatio?** So was Paulina. But she turned out to be a real victim. The Stranger kept fucking her ceaselessly, for hours maybe, and after a couple of multiple orgasms she died having a final prolonged orgasm for thirteen minutes. On the mirror of her room, written in her own lipstick and handwriting, the police saw a letter and two words:

V for Vulva.

The Wanderer wanders and wonders and

---

*The legend of Evita lives on, by Ron Verzuh, January 28, 2009, Ron Verzuh is a Vancouver-based writer.
http://rabble.ca/news/legend-evita-lives

contemplates. Since he was a kid, the "Pros-fygika," a housing complex built in the 1930s to house Greek refugees fleeing Asia Minor, had a weird unexplainable influence on him. Semi-ruined, like phantoms from a far-distant strange era, the buildings were capturing his eyes, his imagination, his feelings, but in what exact way he still cannot tell.

Their most impressive feature was, and still is, the holes from the bullets and the mortars from the fights of the Greek Com-munists against the bourgeoisie and the British Troops during the Red December of 1944. Maybe for this reason these boxy Bauhaus-style spectres stand like a legend on Alexandras Avenue. Until the late seventies the complex of the Bauhaus phantoms was standing side by side with the infamous Averof Prison where thousands of communists were locked and tortured for years that had no end, suffered and spent endless days and nights on death row. For since 1848 up to our days a spectre is haunting Europe —the spectre of communism.

The Wanderer wanders, wonders and con-templates. It was in this prison that the wife of his godfather was held; on death row; for economic support of the Communist Party; for a crumpled voucher found on her; she was around 20 then. Around 20 was and the girl who handed a flyer to him that he read paragraphlessly.

On Monday October 31st 2016, a group of comrades from Themistokleous 58 Squat were also present at the Squatted Prosfygika to assist the neighbourhood defense in the face of coordinated attacks by cops and Nazis. We took a stand in the ongoing social war with stones, body-to-body skirmishes and our antipatriotic convictions resounding during clashes with the cops. Early in the morning of October 31st, antiriot police forces stormed the Prosfygika jointly with a large group of Nazis. Later on, comrades managed to repel the cops (in uniform and plainclothes), and strong clashes ensued. Several persons were detained throughout the day (at least two of the arrestees, who face charges, have been badly beaten). Factual solidarity with the Squatted Prosfygika. Strength to everyone who clashed with the uniformed scum of Greek democracy. Immediate release of all captives. And tomorrow, November 1st, let's be prepared for everything. Themistokleous 58 Squat

The Capitalist crisis and Troika's intervention had caused the number of homeless to reach, if not exceed, 20,000 in Athens alone, and as a result the Bauhaus-style spectres have turned into a shelter for the spectres of the downtrodden in Times of Troika. Their visible spectrum ranges from original owners who have been there for over 70 years, to Greek families who squatted there after losing their homes during the economic crisis, to families from Turkey, Iranian political asylum seekers, drug addicts. The invisible is much broader; for these people carry within them, far beyond the darkness of the Troikan Times, their memories, their hopes, their dead and the history of their dead and the hopes of their dead; for as the wandering and won-dering Wanderer repeats times and again

No man is an island entire of itself; every man
is a piece of the continent, a part of the main;
if a clod be washed away by the sea, Europe
is the less, as well as if a promontory were, as
well as any manner of thy friends or of thine
own were; any man's death diminishes me,
because I am involved in mankind.
And therefore never send to know for whom
the bell tolls; it tolls for thee.

The Wanderer wanders and wonders in space and time and then sits in the yard of a coffee-shop close to the Prosfygika that doesn't exist any more. It's not October 2016 but April 1963 and his parents had run into that coffee-shop for all around them, in Alexandras Avenue, the rabid coppigs of the infamous Karamanlēs's government of blood and terror were smashing the heads of all who dared to demonstrate for Peace and Disarmament. Police paddy-wagons, 2000 arrests, 300 injured protesters. Works and Days of the political ancestors of the today's pro-Troikan Blue Snakes. Their leader, one of Mistress Troika's Subs, boasts today that he will clear Exarcheia from the anarchists in a month's time.

"A penny for your thoughts;" Zórba's voice derailed his train of thought. He had gone to a gathering in solidarity with the ar-restees of December the 6th, 2009. Seven years had passed and the show-trials still hold good.

"A penny or Penny?" the Wanderer asked him teasingly. "I mean Penny from Vravrona Bay; she was tiny, seventeen, looking like thirteen, but such a little minx in bed. She didn't like outdoor sex though, I mean by the seaside. Only in bed behind closed doors, whispering obscenities." He pictured her lying on their table without recalling her face....

"Anyway, Wand," so, what were you think-ing about?"

"Penny's thighs; and who would make a better sub for Mistress Troika, the bushy-eyebrowed one, if he was alive and leader of the Blue-Snakes today or Koulēs?"

"Come on, Wand," said Zórba the ræbe-laisian, "old rumours wanted the Old one to have balls and the rest as thick as his eyebrows, rumours that had upset and flooded even the Palace by his time; Koulēs makes the ideal sub for Mistress Troika."

"Zórba, you're intolerable," said the Wanderer, "I asked in purely political terms but you twisted things towards sex."

"Ah, I see," said Zórba, "then I don't give a shit, they're all the same for me, the Old and the New ones, the Blue and the Green Snakes, the racists, the fascists, Troika, Alexēs Noske and the clergy, a pile of shit piling on top of society and causing suffocation to death. They murder people and they make it look like a suicide. These kind of murders have increased about 32% since the day the scums brought here their Mistress.

"But what are you looking at Wanderer, where are you wandering and what do you wonder about; you seem lost in time."

"I'm looking at the holes in the walls over there caused by bullets; bullets and mortars. At least we had taken up the arms then..."

"In the wrong way," said Zórba; "we did it hesitantly, defensively, in order to 'protect democracy' not in order to seize power and abolish bourgeois democracy..."

"Yes, that was the case, Zórba," said the Wanderer and recalled silently Lenin's *Guerrilla Warfare*, "but let me look at these Bauhaus spectres and the prison a bit more..."

"I will let you look at your spectres for as long as you like, but if I was you, and I am you, do you know what I was going to do after you mentioned Penny?"

It is said that guerrilla warfare brings the class-conscious proletarians into close association with degraded, drunken riff-raff. That is true. But it only means that the party of the proletariat can never regard guerrilla warfare as the only, or even as the chief, method of struggle; it means that this method must be subordinated to other methods, that it must be commensurate with the chief methods of warfare, and must be

ennobled by the enlightening and organising influence of socialism. And without this latter condition, all, positively all, methods of struggle in bourgeois society bring the proletariat into close association with the various non-proletarian strata above and below it and, if left to the spontaneous course of events, become frayed, corrupted and prostituted.

"I can imagine, Zórba," said the Wanderer. But he couldn't, for it was Zórba's alter ego speaking, Vas the surrealist.

"I was going to travel to the past future or to the futurous past, somewhere to USSR and would fuck this lost in space cunts, Maureen and her two daughters Judy and Penny, the three of them at once in a fourthdimensional foursome."

"Zórba, I doubt if you were born when they got lost in space and if Penny, when you grew old enough, was the jailbait you liked; and in any case, how did you remember this... archaeology of the future?" said the Wanderer.

"I was not going for the jailbait this time but for the mom, although I wouldn't kick any of her daughters out of my bed just for their age. But what difference does it make if I was born or not when they could be sexually attractive to me? You were not born when the Bolsheviks stormed the Winter Palace, they were all dead when you first learned a few things about the events but you're... not simply infatuated but in deep love with the Russian Revolution; and I know it's not the only Russian you're in deep love with....

"You see, Eros and Libido, like the Revolution, raise themselves, not with a rattle though but with an orgasmic scream, and announce with lust, to all clergies terror: I was, I am, I will be!"

"That's true, true for the Libido, true for the Revolution, but... have you seen your jailbait after she returned to Earth, have you seen the effect of time on her?"

"Yes, I have and I admit it makes me sad," said Zórba, "but both of us are fully aware that in our USSR, our Union of Surrealist Sexual Retroperspectives, human beings will remain untouched by time, immune to illnesses, immortal, travelling in all four dimensions, as we mean it in the Lettrist Red International's symbol: **III/ЧƆ.** But our USSR, the Union of Surrealist Sexual Retroperspectives, cannot emerge from the Not Yet if we do not refound, on the ruins of Capitalism, the USSR, the Global Union of Soviet Socialist Republics.

"You see, following the futurism's train of thought, USSR > Capitalism > Troika > Troikans > Troyans, I mean following a train of thought that leads to Helen of Troy, I have to tell you that I'm very critical and very sceptical about Seferēs's *Helen*; straight forwardly, I completely disagree with the dominant, at least, interpretations.

"He writes, echoing Euripides:
"And the rivers swelling, blood in their silt,
"all for a linen undulation, a filmy cloud,
"a butterfly's flicker, a wisp of swan's down,

"an empty tunic — all for a Helen."

"But," Zórba the brute went on, "our fiery battles against Capitalism, the rivers swelling, blood in their silt, Troikan blood hopefully, are part of the ruthless war we wage in the interests of our self-salvation from the deadness of Capitalism, from the deadness of Troika, from the deadness of Death and by no means are a butterfly's flicker, a wisp of swan's down, an empty tunic;

"I'm afraid that from this point of view Seferēs is an elitist in a way that does not appeal to me. But anyway..."

The Wanderer said nothing for he wanted to be left alone with the spectres, look at them and contemplate, and Zórba went away. Then the Wanderer stayed there till the night fell, sitting in the yard of the lost in time coffee-shop, taking sips of heavy medium-sweet arabic coffee and dunking his beloved Miranda biscuits in it. *"O, wonder! How many goodly creatures are there here! How beauteous mankind is! O brave new world, That has such people in't!**"* whispered the sweet female the moment he wrapped his lips and tongue around her tasting the blissful union of two female tastes, Miranda's and Caffeine's combined. These were his favourite lines from the *Tempest*, Miranda knew it well, for they were exalting, to his deepest believes and de-

---

Helen, by George Sefers, translated by Edmund Keeley
**W. Shakespeare, *The Tempest*, Act V, Scene 1

394

sires, against all odds and interpretations, human ewomancipation, sexual liberation and, of course, the Union of Surrealist Sexual Retroperspectives.

He had waited for the night to fall for he wanted to see for one more time the Mexican. He used to see him quite often, during both the pre-and-post-junta eight-years-periods of right-wing terror. State terrorism is written in the political DNA of the today's pro-Troikan Blue Snakes. The Mexican disappeared sometime towards the end of the 1970s. He was a big man wearing always an even bigger sombrero. He was mostly dozing during the daytime but full awake and bright during the night. He was made of colourful neon tubes and he was living on top of a Bravo coffee-shop at the corner of Alexandras and Kēfēsias Avenues. The Wanderer walked till there but he didn't find him as he was hoping to. 'Maybe he left for Mexico,' he thought; 'to meet people from the Left Opposition? to aid the Coordinating Committee for the Refoundation of the Fourth International? was he a member of the Revolutionary Action's Group (Grupo de Acción Revolucionaria, GAR) in Mexico? Or maybe he was hidden in the folds of time, invisible but still there, at the corner of Alexandras and Kēfēsias Avenues from where he witnessed the flaming days and nights of the December of 2008 uprising, the siege of the Greek Police Head-quarters in Athens by thousands of enraged pupils, students, parents, elders, and maybe it was after him that the Coordinating Committee for the Refoundation of the Fourth International stated among other things that:

"Nevertheless, the December rebellion in Greece remains undefeated, a dress rehearsal for the next stage of confrontation in Greece, in Europe and internationally, and a source of inspiration for revolutionaries all over the world for the coming historic confrontations."

Who knows.

The Wanderer took out his cell and called Vas. Vas's grandmother was seeing the Mexican almost every other day for she was a coffee drinker. Maybe Vas had heard something from her in the past about the Mexican's fate or about his plans. But he didn't answer the call.

Chapter 31

Vas the surrealist had joined a group of militant doctors and visited a downtown "hot-spot", in Athens, thronged with refugees. Cold, rain, garbage, men and mice. Then, the nightmare passed. Not for them. Just for him. But his cell was turned off. At night he started reading, for a fourth time, Ayn Rand's *Anthem* to Capitalism, Imperialism, Barbarism.

"Have you managed to read this thing four times?" the Wanderer asked him a few days later.

Vas had laughed. "No, I just meant that it was my fourth attempt to finish it and this time it was successful." But he didn't mean it. It was really the fourth time for he was impressed immensely by the naïveness of its ideas.

"Big deal," said the Wanderer; "it would have been something really worth to mention if it was simply something sucksexfull."

Vas laughed and said nothing.

The Wanderer went on, saying "I mean, a sextravaganza with Kira, Dagny Taggert and

Dominique Francon; what else do we need to consider our acquaintance with Rand's bourgeois philosophy sucksexfull?"

Vas still said nothing but his alter ego, Zórba, grabbed the chance and scorned and said "Ha, ha, ha, sucksexfull acquaintance with her *philosophy* doesn't make any sense; with her heroines it does, for sure...

"Unless you want to tell us that objectivism sucks, which is the case."

"What would you do with her heroines, Zórba?" asked the Wanderer.

"Everything and anything," said Zórba; "and I mean it. In case they are so un-scrupulous as to associate themselves with capitalism and billionaires, I'll use them with no feelings of guilt in the same unscrupulous way in sex. From an ethical point of view even bestiality is less shameful than the ex-ploitation of a worker," concluded Zórba echoing the obscene, steaming hot conversa-tions he had overheard, thoughts of a night that had passed, of the midsummer's eve, ages ago in *Stonehenge*, the alternative open air bistro, when things had started to get wilder and wilder as both twilight and inhi-bitions were fading away. Howls, laughter and moans boomed out from all around, drunk men and women were wandering into the yard; it was like in a dream but it was no dream and it was when a group of strangers were talking about other women dining in the bistro and dying little deaths in close-by dark alleys, in the presence and under the encouragement of another female.

In any case, aside from all these, Vas considered Rand to be an unscrupulous advocate of Troika and her heros ruthless greedy capitalist criminals, identical to Troika's officers. When Vas the surrealist reads a book for a fourth time, he does it, and he perceives it, in his own, sui generis fourth-internationalist way...

"Now I look ahead. My future is dark before me. ..

"I shall live here, in the hot-spot; I have no house. I shall take my food from the rubbish by the toil of my own hands. I have no books anymore. Through the years ahead, I shall wander in this strange land, the achievements of which are not open to me, they are closed forever to me, to my brothers, for their bodies and minds are crippled and wounded.

"I have learned the power of the sky, the bombs and the missiles. It was that power that killed my dear ones and ruined my house. It lit this house with light which came from above and swept away the people and the walls. I have no light now. I shall never manage to repair it and to make it live again. I shall live next to the barbed wires which carry electric power. They build barriers of wires around my tent, and across the paths which lead to

where I have no home either; where a barrier light as a cobweb, more impassable than a wall of granite awaits me again; a barrier my brothers and I will never be able to cross. For we have nothing to fight them with, fight the brute force of their guards and fences and their barking dogs and their bullets. I have lost my dear ones. I have lost my mind.

EGO"

Vas closed the book and flipped to back; *"the use of the word "I" is punishable by death"* he read. 'Nonsense,' he thought; 'in the real, real world millions and millions are dying just because they happened to be born in the vast spaces of the Third and Fourth World. EGO counts less than a bubble-gum in a world where the 90% of the population is forcefully doomed for the sake of the 10%. All the rest is mere propaganda sponsored by all kinds of pro-capitalist foundations. Objectivism is one of these stupid cults that flourish only in USA and nowhere else, and they practise it because it offers millions to Corporations and stupefies the believers.'

He opened the book again, somewhere towards the end and read:

"And my happiness needs no higher aim to vindicate it. My happiness is not the means to any end. It is the end. It is its own goal. It is its own purpose."

'That's fine,' he thought, 'we got it, we

got the meaning, there is no larger moral purpose to life, other than individual happiness, based on individual property on the means of production, so let's tune now Prometheus's thought with *Anthem*. What a great melody cums out from the ancient flute! The God, reclining on his bed, thinks: *So why me, Ego, I, a God from Gods endure anything, Hung there in chains, nailed 'neath the open sky. Ha! Ha! for the sake of mortal men? Let them live as mortal as ever in the dark and I, Ego, I'll enjoy Venus' hot lips around my divine shaft, high up in our Olympus palaces, oh yes, I'll even ask her to indulge into a hot 69 with this little slut Artemæs and then I'll keep using Artemæs's cunt and Venus' mouth in turns for my personal happiness and pleasure!*

'Thus thought Prometheus and there was neither light nor *Anthem*,' Vas the surrealist concluded. Prometheus was his favourite hero, the mythological prototype of all the revolutionaries, especially the communists and the anarchists who now and then print on their posters the few first lines of the tragedy in order to exalt and praise their imprisoned comrades.

Now have we journeyed to a spot of earth
Remote-the Scythian wild, a waste untrod.
And now, Hephaestus, thou must execute
The task our father laid on thee, and fetter
This malefactor to the jagged rocks
In adamantine bonds infrangible;

For thine own blossom of all forging fire
He stole and gave to mortals; trespass grave
For which the Gods have called him to account,
That he may learn to bear Zeus' tyranny
And cease to play the lover of mankind. *

Vas had even the luck to watch the great Greek actor Manos Katrakēs** in the role of Prometheus, in the Herodeion beneath Acropolis; it was a hot July night. Memories! What memories! Summer is silver, autumn is gold, winter is white and spring is red.

'I am an individualist,' he went on thinking; 'an individualist in the tradition of William Godwin. He was the father of Mary Wollstonecraft Shelley Godwin....'

"Did Mary Godwin, Percy Shelley, Mary's step-sis Claire Clairmont and Lord Byron had ever group sex at the Lake Geneva during the wet summer of 1816?" wondered the Wanderer, two hundred years later, while they had raised the topic of individualism and anarchism, in Locomotiva; "Mary had sex for the first time at 16, on her mother's grave-stone, Percy had sex both with her and her step-sister, Byron did the same and Clairmont joked in a letter to Mary that *perhaps*

*http://classics.mit.edu/Aeschylus/prometheus.html
**He took part in the Resistance as a member of EAM/ELAS and after refusing to sign a declaration of repentance during the Greek Civil War of 1946–49, was exiled to Makronēsos, alongside with such other well-known figures as Yiannēs Ritsos, Nikos Koundouros, Mikēs Theodorakēs and Thanasēs Veggos.

she should fall in love with both the Russian men she had met at once."*

Vas the sextremist laughed. "I'm sure they did and enjoyed it as much as I enjoy seeing in Frankestein's monster, in the terror he brings upon his creators, the terror the revolutionaries, the anarchists, the communists bring upon the ruling class, upon the Troikans, in our days. Mistress Troika is Mistress Frankestein and the December 2008 uprising alongside with the February 12, 2012 uprising are the awakening monster.

"As Karl sets it, '*What the bourgeoisie produces, above all, are its own grave-diggers.*' "

"Come on, Vas, how can you be so sure that they had group sex by the Lake Geneve?" asked him the Wanderer.

"For all the reasons you have already enumerated on your own, Wanderer, and for one more. Mery confesses it by telling us '*It proved a wet, ungenial summer and incessant rain often confined us for days to the house.*'

"If you read her letter through the lens of realism she just speaks about a rainy summer. But if you read it through the lens of surrealism, she speaks about a wet, sexually wet summer. They were isolated for days idling around a log-fire at Byron's villa, thrilling themselves with ghost stories. But we know by sexpirience that being scared is physiolog-

---

*Deirdre Coleman, *Claire Clairmont and Mary Shelley* Rousseaustudies. free.fr. 11 August 1995. Retrieved 14 May 2012.

ically arousing, and in the right circumstances, it leads to sexual arousal, to a wet summer."

The night flew by. Other things happened. Time flew by too. We watched the circus of the American elections. The nazis of the Golden Dawn saluted the victory of Trump. A car owned by a fascist was smashed up in Exarcheia. Wednesday noon, November 9, 2016, at the corner of Tositsa and Bouboulinas Streets a white Volkswagen was spotted having on display the nazi newspaper *Empros* behind the front windshield. A group of antifascists rushed and smashed up the car. Then they sent "isurrectionary signals to those who fuck up the streets in the US against the democratic victory of the fascist Trump."

Just before midnight, while in the sky over Athens, we could see the most spectacular supermoon since January 26, 1948, the year when the Americans used napalms-B against the Democratic Army in the mountains of North Greece. Vas, in whose name "V" stands for Victory or Vendetta, "a" stands for art and "s" stands for surrealism, sexuality, sextremism, showed us on Eva, his tablet or "tableta," as he prefers to call her, for she's female, a Common Announcement, *Welcome to Athens, Obama*, written by Crimethinc (USA) and Void Network (Athens) "a cultural, political and philosophical collective that first appeared in

1990 in Athens / Greece with aim the radicalization of every day life, the social question, the arising of critical mind, the ecstatic collective symbiosis, the visibility of diversity, the participation to the emancipatory social struggles of our times and the creation of Utopian Public Environments by non-employed cultural activists. Other aims are the participation and creation of social centers, self-organized autonomus spaces, the construction of situations in Public Space and the Ephemeral Art."

As an unholy Trinity we were more attracted towards the Permanent Revolution; Vas, on the one hand of the eternal sunshine of a surrealist mind, found very appealing, even promising this merging of theory, utopia, empathy, ephemeral arts; Zórba, on the other hand of darkness, argued that as far as he is concerned "all these virtual revolutionary imperatives and groups are as promising, efficient and effective as virtual sex; I prefer real people with real flesh instead of a screen and a keyboard."

"Not to say that all these 'links-to-the-revolution' maybe there for tonight and by tomorrow night the only link you get is a link-to-nowhere with no news from nowhere; just a message like 'the page you are looking for doesn't exist,' he said. Then we left aside the argument for another time.

Monday, November 14, 2016. The 9 O'clock News. Two embedded Troikan whores, subs that are getting payed to serve and satisfy the vital, urgent needs of Mistress Troika; they are not only embedded Troikan whores but embedded Troikan traffickers too for they make money from the work people are forced to do to the satisfaction of Mistress Troika; a male and a female whores-traffickers; they give it all to discourage people from joining tomorrow's demonstrations; all their stupidness and all their shit-ridden arguments. "Anti-american demonstrations belong to the Pale-olithic Age," says the male whore, and smiles complacently for his "spirited" comment.

"He doesn't smile out of complacency," says Zórba. "He's fully aware of his mediocrity. But he knows that with two-three similar bullshited comments on the TV he'll profit enough money to buy a new 4X4."

"This is not a visit," said the Wanderer, "it's an invasion with the active support of the quisling government of Syriza. An invasion that violates my civil rights. The American President is actually invading Athens with his agents and his troops and armoured ve-hicles and coppigs and copters and heavy weapons to be used by his security and in this way violates my right to freedom of wandering in my own city, anywhere I like, at any time of the day I wish."

"Sure," said Zórba the ræbelaisian. "To me the whole thing on the part of the USA looks more like military exhibitionism.... On the part of the Government, well, what to say, she just offered all her holes to please Obama. Her State budget hole, her asshole, whatever, ha, ha, ha....

"But the Americans still suffer from a severe complex of inferiority after the trauma of the Vietnam War. They will never overcome the nightmarish 'Day of the Copters', the panicked evacuation of their embassy in Saigon on April 29, 1975."

"There is no end to this appalling and provocative exhibitionism of the privileges that enjoys the Commander-in-Chief of the Iron Heel, the US Army, the most hated blood-stained apparatus of 'The Capital'," said the Wanderer. "In the Waste Land where people may die out of lack of a single doctor, the leader of the Iron Heel brought from the United States a personal mobile hospital with a staff of 150 on standby.

"I will never forget the gloomy days and the gloomier nights when I was desperately and hopelessly looking for a doctor, for a nurse in the gloomy corridors of the hospital my father was dying in."

Then the embedded female Troikan whore presented, with a lot of sexcitement and admiration, Obama's armoured "Beast." Mrs "Her Mistress's Voice," without even blushing a little, gave almost pornographic details, for any association of sex with profits turns it into pornography and she was payed to give all these details and impress with them, saying how long the Beast was, how thick it was, how powerful it was and she even said that it could emit gases and fluids that brought tears to the eyes, implying her eyes. Post-orgasmic tears? Who knows. Zórba grabbed the chance to say his things.

"Bitch," said Zórba the ræbelaisian, it's because you've neither seen nor tried my beast, ha, ha, ha!"

"In case he feels so self-confident about his... beast," wondered the Wanderer, "what for all these draconian security measures, the deployment of thousands of coppigs, the road closures and restrictions on protests?"

In any case we didn't expect neither any call nor much more the permission of Syriza's government to storm the streets against Obama's invasion. Even more that State prohibitions are meant to be broken.

From a point of view, but it was just one point of view out of innumerable others, the explosions, not just the stream, of thoughts that the rise of the supermoon triggered, were too powerful and their turbulence sent us to the night downtown streets and *there was no telling what that night would bring but the moon*, as once upon a time, Time of Revolution and revolvers wrote Mayakovsky. *The Moon is a Harsh Mistress* but there was a revolution there, and a Fifth International, and a *Moonlight Sonata* — "Nothing I know is better than the Appassionata," had whispered Lenin, in Times of Revolution, and then romantic images like *Moonrise over the Sea* and a *Man and Woman Contemplating the Moon* and *Wanderer above the Sea of Fog*, all by Caspar David Friedrich and Ritsos's *Moonlight Sonata* from *The Fourth Dimension* and Trotsky's Fourth International and Mayakovsky's Fifth International. But the first stage of the revolution, a worldwide social transformation, has not been completed yet in order for us to move ahead to a new revolutionary Praxis of world-shaking proportions.... "A revolution of the spirit," reorganization of life, a new art, and a new science. We have to overthrow capitalism first in Greece, Europe, the World.

So, we were all there, the much slandered generation of the Polytechnic uprising; all those who refused to exchange their ideas and their struggles for any position in the bourgeois State and the bourgeois institutions. The 'unrepentant' ones. Among them, among us, Maria, 80 years old, ex-cleaner, suffering from side-effects of hemotherapy and radiation therapy, with six stents placed in her arteries. All of us —them— for one more time, we took to the streets against the state prohibitions; we took to the streets despite of the wounds that, during these 43 years Time, Nature and the State, have inflicted upon our bodies. They —we— took to the streets alongside with the much slandered generation of the December 2008 uprising and at the top of our voice and through all our wounds we raised ourselves with a rattle and announced with fanfare, to their terror, the terror of the capitalist oppressors: We were, We are, We will be!

It was a cold day and a colder night. 'Should I stay or should I go?' the Wanderer was thinking, for he was feeling ill and weak and he had the Clashborn dillema *'if I go there will be trouble, and if I stay it will be double.'* Then the police dared to post the decision for the banning of the demonstrations on the doors of the offices of many revolutionary groups and organizations, warning, in a terminology copied and pasted from similar decisions of the military junta, that the participants in the banned gatherings and demonstrations will be prosecuted. The Wanderer learned the news. *'Tempest!'* he thought on the spot, *'Soon will strike the tempest! That is the courageous Petrel proudly soaring in the lightning over the sea's roar of fury; cries of victory the prophet: -Let the tempest come strike harder!'* he went on thinking, recalling the Gorky's poem he had heard in Russian in unrhymed trochaic tetrameter with Pyrrhic alternates, a rhythmic pattern that had formed the basis of an ancient Greek war dance. 'It's a class war,' he thought, 'I should go and let the tempest come strike harder.'

So it was a cold night. With his only dearest by his side they marched among thousands others Stadiou Street heading towards the police barrier by Klafthmonos Square. Their close friend Alex-who-was-sailing-stormy-waters, an ex-captain from Meganēsi *who travelled far and wide and many cities did he visit, and many were the nations with whose manners and customs he was acquainted, one of the ingenious everyday heroes that for six years now were sacking the infamous Troyka,* was marching by their side, and behind them hunderds enraged anarchachaeans who wanted to burn Troyka.

"Watch on your right, be aware of the coppigs," Yiannēs S., who was holding the right-side wooden pole of the big banner wearing as always his leninist beret, warned the Wanderer. "Thanks, I've noticed them," he replied. Fontas, witness to the murder of Alexēs Grēgoropoulos, was on the left side of the banner. The front bloc, run at the coppigs' cordon, pushed up against it with sticks and sprayed fire extinguishers; the coppigs repelled the first cordons of the bloc using tear gas and stun grenades; protesters threw Molotov cocktails. The clashes began....

"It's so nice that you managed to come," Fontas, always very cordial, had said to the Wanderer, just a few minutes before the clashes started.

Next day Obama's speech at the Stavros Niarchos Cultural Center in Athens, monopolised the Net News, the 8 & 9 O'clock News, the Press and all the Media. The Rulers were all gathered and posed fraternised there, the right-wingers with the 'socialists', Syriza with members of the dethroned Glyxbourg family, the billionaires with all the above. But the perpetrators brought there their victims as well, desperate, dispossessed refugees to use and exploit in the rudest way for the propagandist needs of the regime.

In his valedictory, as the lackeys of the United States named it, speech, Obama traded words like glass beads and like shiny metal objects, comprehending that native people's rulers, Greek bourgeoisie and its servants, held these items in high esteem. Vibrant, glossy, shiny word-objects containing a powerful ideological power called *manitou* that increased their possessor's access to the ideological power that governed the downtrodden.

For three days now, the natives praise Obama's speech, the thaumaturge speech. "In the beginning was the Speech, and the Speech was with Obama, and the Speech was

Obama," they say. They want us to kneel in the middle of our Waste Land, raise our hands high up to the sky where the American eagles fly and sing Hosanna to Obama.

Hosanna, Obama, Sanna, Sanna-Ho,
Sanna-Hey, O-ba-ma, Sanna-Ho
Hey BO, BO won't you smile at me?
Sanna-Ho, O-ba-ma Superstar *

Under the eternal sunshine of a surrealist mind, the unholy Trinity's surrealist mind that uses quotations, images, melodies, memories, like robbers by the roadside who make an armed attack and relieve an idler of his convictions. this rock Opera decades ago side by side with the *The Strawberry Statemen* had followed like a shadow the first miles in the road to radicalisation of a generation, had expressed, reflected, taken shape from the radicalisation of this generation; the generation of the struggles against the USA's dirty war in Vietnam, of the Kent State massacre, the generation of the Black Panthers, of the guerilla movements that crossed the boundaries from Latin America to Europe and Middle East; it was the generation of the struggles against the active support of the American imperialism to the Greek Junta. A blood-stained Junta that was USA's own flesh and blood. Thus, all these high volume, explosive

---

*Parafrase by V. Ludens. Original from *Jesus Christ Superstar* a 1970 rock opera with music by Andrew Lloyd Webber and lyrics by Tim Rice

ingredients, all these old spices, remain and mature year by year somewhere deep in the collective revolutionary unconscious, and add a flaming flavour to the Cocktails molotov that the youngsters treat the Troikans.

A few days later. A sunny coldish day. Locomotiva. A small table by the entrance. "President Bill Clinton, during his notorious visitinvasion to Athens. I think it was November 19, 1999," the Wanderer started to say over a cup of coffee, but Vas grabbed the chance to bring forward his own memories... "yes, it was Friday and thousands and thousands had stormed the streets, downtown Athens was in flames, you see Clinton as Commander-in-Chief of the US Army had just bombarded Belgrade...."

"Yes, I do remember," said the Wanderer, "the masses, the clashes, the barricades, and Clinton's fruitless, hypocritic apologies on the behalf of the US government for supporting the military junta in the name of Cold War tactics. You know, the stuff of apologies American politicians share with such generocity, apologies consisting of 5% crocodile tears and of 95% hypocricy..." The Wanderer lit Halona, his pipe, although he was not a smoker but he just enjoyed playing with her and with flavoured tobaccos and lighters and flames *little sisters of the sun lit*, as once upon a time used to sing Melanie who was a hottie.

"But we never forgive, never forget." He sipped some coffee. He waved smiling to the young lady that appeared behind the bar and went on.... "Trump's victory in the American elections is not more surprising than Rand's popularity in the USA. Both, Trump and Rand's books, stink of rotten capitalism, of totalitarianism, almost of fascism. The billionaires she admires and describes, are all, with no exception, as appalling as Donald Trump.

"You remember our last time's conversation, don't you? I consider myself individualist. I'm convinced by experience that capitalism and Troikans crash my own individualism. You know this whore," he said pointing at the same time towards the big TV screen where they were playing the 8 O'clock News without sound, "this International Monetary Fucktoy, was first corrupted morally when she read at a very tender age, she was a teen, a widespread letter that Ayn Rand had addressed to her niece; a letter that contains all the hard-core pornographic theses of the IMF concerning the 'Greek' debt."

He unzipped Eva's protective cloth and turned her screen to us.

"It's like reading this German rag, the *Bild*," he added, "and we can even retitle it 'Objectivist Ethics and the spirit of Troika.'

"Come on Wand," we complained, "we're

fucking bored to read it, just highlight for us the 'hard-core' parts.... You know that if pornographers are not talented their work is fucking boring...."

At the same time was or another time, sometime around twilight, in an era that nobody expected to come and when she did everybody was saying that her coming was inevitable? In an era that nothing seemed to comform with the known up to then reality, so everything was plausible? Zórba the Greek brut and a group of armed Anarchachaeans had managed to trap, kidnap, transfer and lock Mistress Troika and a couple of her sub-funs, leaders of bourgeois parties, bankers and Ministers of the Moloch of the Capital, all of them committed Troikans and Troykans and Trojans. Into a deserted fucktory was it? —as some International Monetary Fucktoys were hoping it to be, but in vain— or into an abandoned cargo-ship rusting on the flaming banks of time? We know not, nor anybody else does, for the Times of Troika had turned into Times of Upheaval, Revolution, rumours, independent actions of widespreading Revolutionary Army Contingents and insurrectionary maneuvres in the dark. In the dark Times of Troika....

Whatever it was, Moloch's and Troika's Ministers, Bankers and Prime Ministers, had gotten insane out of fear, for the doors of this weird badly-lit space of liquified rust, decay and emerging vengeance, were wide shut and Zórba the brut was pointing a deadly Heckler & Koch MP5 at them; so insane they had turned that they were singing *The End* by the Doors looking in dismay at the locked and rusted iron doors.

This is the end
Beautiful friend
This is the end
Of our elaborate plans, the end
Of everything that stands, the end
The west is the best
Get here, and we'll do the rest

"Ha!" made Zórba, "I see that your excessive fearborn madness has lighted your spirits. I cannot explain otherwise that you are singing the song of the final scenes of Apocalypse Now. Extremely symbolic and not just because this is your end. By doing so you admit that your economic war is, mutatis mutandis. as devastating for Greece as the dirty war of the Americans was for Vietnam.

"They committed war crimes in Vietnam. You are committing economic-war crimes in Greece.

"The heart of your policy, the heart of your Troikan Times is the Heart of Darkness.

" *'The horror! The horror!'**"

---

*Kurtz's final words in the *Heart of Darkness* (1899) a novella by Polish-British novelist Joseph Conrad.

In the West from most of the major metropoleis the same and the same alerting flaming message was coming again and again, "Babylon's Burning, Babylon's Burning," and behind them —what? lost in the vortex of a revolution that had no mercy for them their decayed world.

"In case you are bored to read all Rand's letter," was saying the Wanderer at the same, more or less, time; "let me read to you the hard-core excerpts you asked for:

" '...to repay the debt, but on condition that you understand and accept it as a strict and serious business deal.... Here are my conditions... willing and able to repay this money, no matter what happens... as an obligation above and ahead of any other expense.... If you become ill, then I will give you an extension of time — but for no other reason.... If, when the debt becomes due, you tell me that you can't pay me... because you gave the money to somebody in the family who needed it more than I do — then I will consider you as an embezzler.... No, I won't send a policeman after you, but I will write you off as a rotten person and I will never speak or write to you again..... I would like to teach you, if I can, very early in life, the idea of a self-respecting, self-supporting, responsible, capitalistic person.... I will wait to hear from you, and if I find out that you are my kind of person, then I hope that this will be the beginning of a real friendship between us, which would please me very much.

Your aunt' "

The Wanderer laughed scornfully. "No, auntie, we will please neither you nor your rotten capitalistic persons. We fight for cancellation of the debt for this debt is not ours, expropriation of banks and large companies, starting with the ship-owners, Socialist United States of Europe; we laugh at the Randist hallucinations about *people punished to death for using the word "I,"* but on our side the mere thought of... *Randist capitalistic methods* in the NHS will for sure be punished by death.

"We will not leave anything and above all people's health, every single individual's health, any single EGO health, at the hands of your rotten capitalist necrophiles.

"Because *Capital is dead labour, that, vampire-like, only lives by sucking living labour, and lives the more, the more labour it sucks.*"

We cheered, all of us, clicking glasses full of beer; Faba and Anna and Alex-who-was-sailing-stormy-waters, the old friend of us, an ex-captain from Meganēsi *who travelled far and wide and many cities did he visit, and many were the nations with whose manners and customs he was acquainted* and a couple of anarchachaeans that had gathered in Locomotiva, and us. We are three distinct persons, yet we are one, a Trinity; a surrealist, subversive,

421

sex-driven Trinity, not a holy one; a spectre haunting Europe, making many men shiver out of fear and many women hot and horny for the three distinct persons of it; one by one or all the three of them at once in a foursome; As a Trinity we are in a constant change; change of looks, likes, moods, partners, personalities; so don't ever stick with us, just follow our flow. We are individualists but we will always use our individualism on the side of the toilers and the downtrodden and never against them.

We am an egoist.

I are sextremely egoist.

Therefore instictively and conscientiously anticapitalist. But this is just the beginning; not the ABC of Communism but vice versa; Communism is just the ABC. Communism is just like the cell. The equivelant of life will follow and will take the form of the Union of Surrealist Sexual Retroperspectives.

We am an egoist.

I are sextremely egoists.

We have developed an instictive u2s-r-tropism, an existentialist and sexistentialist motility, an urge to move spontaneously and actively towards the Union of Surrealist Sexual Retroperspectives. We move towards her, while at the same time, new skies, a new earth, and the very same USSR are hibernating in the deepest depths of our Ego.

I am a surrealist

I am a futurist

I am a libertarian communist and

I want it all.

I am Zórba or Vas

I am the Wanderer and

I am the Narrator

I, the letter "I" stands as a phallic symbol of my individuality and, therefore, of my will not to accept any, even the slightest, personal loss and sacrifice in order to save the capitalist country; it is *their* country; not mine; the capitalists need and demand from the toilers to sacrifice their own lives. Their well-payed commentators require contentment, but contentment is for the sheep, I am a wolf, a wolf, a red wolf, I have seen my dad strolling onto a carpet of red leaves in Penn State University, I am a bolshewolf.... Let them come and teach us contentment; a pack of bolshewolves are we...

We are an unholy Trinity but

"W" is made of four "I"s, four leaning "I"s, leaning like Tatlin's leaning, constructivist Monument to the Third International. "W" stands for "We" and it consists of 4 leaning "I"s, so "W" in We stands for the 4th International. A tall phallic-shaped cactus on the terrace points upwards tonight, directly towards the moon. Erect, bathed in the moonlight, glittering, it looks like it's signalling the forthcoming insurrection of the doomed and toilers and the resurrection of the dead. My father loved the moon. My mother did not. She was more down to earth, During the last years, when she couldn't go out anymore, she was carefully placing her armchair in such a way as to be able to sit and watch downwards: the street, the people, their movement, their constant come and go. She reminded me of King Lear, in the third scene of the last, final act.

No, no, no, no! Come, let's away to prison:
We two alone will sing like birds i' the cage:
When thou dost ask me blessing, I'll kneel down,
And ask of thee forgiveness: so we'll live,
And pray, and sing, and tell old tales, and laugh
At gilded butterflies, and hear poor rogues
Talk of court news; and we'll talk with them too,
Who loses and who wins; who's in, who's out;
And take upon's the mystery of things,
As if we were God's spies: and we'll wear out,
In a wall'd prison, packs and sects of great ones,
That ebb and flow by the moon.

Only that her cage was her old age, a cage made by Nature and even worse in the Times of Troika that leisurely ebb and flow of people on the streets that she liked to dawdle on, ceased dramatically compared to the past, both downtown and in the neighbourhoods, and there was nothing much to watch for her, other than the fear and misery of the Third Memorandum that the 8 O'clock News threw up every day.

However the Angel of History has clearly stated that "*It is only for those without hope that hope is given*," and, sooner or later, the toilers, the doomed and the downtrodden will overflow the streets of Athens and all the major cities and towns in a permanent nuit debout, hasta la victoria siempre.

But there is no final victory thought Ego, Ego, Ego, there is no final revolution, for after the complete victory over capitalism, after the establishment of interplanetary communism, We will continue and win the war against Nature, the war against Time, the war against Space, until the emergence —like Aphroditē Venus Anadyomenē— of a New Earth and of a New Thalassa of multiple Genitalities under a New Heaven, of multiple earths, multiple seas, multiple heavens, multiple

orgasms

orgasms

orgasms

orgasms

orgasms

orgasms

orgasms

orgasms

orgasms

orgasms

orgasms

orgasms

orgasms

'Revolutions are the orgasms of History,' thought
We the living.

Prologue to the World that is Coming
Prologue as in Epiclogue

Homage to my parents
who worked hard for a better future
for themselves and for us
and were robbed at gunpoint by the Troikans

'Troikans, Troykans, Trojans, sound all the
same to me,' thought Zórba the Greek brute,
'and it's such a pleasure, such a release that
Troika is having the same end as Troy...
Blood ran in torrents, drenched was all the earth,
As Trojans and their alien helpers died.
Here were men lying quelled by bitter death
All up and down the city in their blood*'

He was watching in our company the
USSR Breaking News Live Streaming; their
correspondent Quintus Smyrnaious was reporting live the Fall of Troyka:

---

*Quintus Smyrnaious, *The Fall of Troy*, Translated by A. S. Way,
Paraphrase by V. Ludens

427

As when a wolf, with hunger stung to the heart, comes from the hills, and ravenous for flesh draws nigh the flock Penned in the wide fold, slinking past the men and dogs that watch, all keen to ward the sheep, then o'er the fold-wall leaps with soundless feet; so stole Zórba the brute down from the Horse: with him followed the war-fain comrades of Revolutionary League [explosions cover his voice *] in angry mood pour all together forth [* explosions cover his voice *] so battle-kindled forth the Horse they poured into the midst of that strong city of Troyka with hearts that leapt expectant. With swift hands snatched they the brands from dying hearths, and fired temple and palace. Onward then to the gates sped they, and swiftly slew the slumbering guards, then held the gate-towers till their friends should come [* explosions cover his voice *] Upflashed a glare unearthly through the town, for many an Argive bare in hand a torch to know in that dim battle friends from foes [* explosions cover his voice *] The fire-glow upward mounted to the sky, the red glare o'er the firmament spread its wings, and all the tribes of folk that dwelt around beheld it... And men that voyaged on the deep sea cried: "The Communists have achieved their mighty task after long toil for people's sake. All Troika, the once queen-city, burns in fire: for all their prayers, no God defends them now; for strong Fate oversees all works of men, and the renownless and obscure to fame she raises, and brings low the exalted ones. Oft out of good is evil* *brought, and good from evil, mid the travail and change of life." So spake they, who from far beheld the glare of Troika's great burning. Compassed were her folk with wailing misery: through her streets the foe exulted, as when madding blasts turmoil the boundless sea, what time the Altar ascends to heaven's star-pavement, turned to the misty south overagainst Arcturus tempest-breathed, and with its rising leap the wild winds forth, and ships full many are whelmed 'neath ravening seas; wild as those stormy winds [explosions cover his voice] ravaged steep Troyka while she burned in flame. As when a mountain clothed with shaggy woods burns swiftly in a fire-blast winged with winds, and from her tall peaks goeth up a roar, and all the forest-children this way and that rush through the wood, tormented by the flame; so were the Troikans perishing: there was none to save, of all the Gods. Round these were staked the nets of Fate, which no man can escape.* *

Meanwhile, a meanwhile that was as mean for some as was while for others, Zórba's alter ego, Vas the surrealist, was listening to the inflammatory speech of Achilles Ehrenburg, transmitted through megaphones all over the barricades in downtown Athens, and its neighbourhoods, and Thessaloniki, and Patras, and Heraklion, and all over the insurrected Greece....

*Quintus Smyrnaious, *The Fall of Troy*, Translated by A. S. Way, Paraphrase by V. Ludens

He was listening to the speech live, in person, for we are an unholy Trinity expanded and sexpanded in space and time, we were here, there, everywhere and he was among other surrealists....

In expropriated supermarket trolleys they had stuffed imaginable and unimaginable objects and paraphernalia to reinforce the barricades and they were carrying them here, there and everywhere and, all around, dust and lust and gust.

Who were they except Zórba-Vas the sextremist, the Wanderer and my own obscure unseen presence I cannot tell for sure but I sensed and noticed —vortexing in purple ink— streams of thought around three of them, streams like... Wales flies over Snowdon Cliff who reckons the cleared disaster over the prostitute. Should Wales colour above Snowdon Cliff? The communist proceeds throughout the stranger! Can the finished South defend Wales? Should Wales beam before an appealing feminist? Can the matador fly below Eduardo? The willing astronomy steams and Eduardo budgets a provocative break. Will a palace dodge? When will Eduardo groan inside matador tubed by faith? Our bookstore eats a sterile jargon. Matador worms Eduardo beside the carriage, Eduardo orbits across the cheerful devil who has taken the form, the shape and the moonlit aura of

an undressing Sara. Eva, seminude and hooded, burns against a transatlantic jet lag, lack
of sleep and sex. Her thrusts bests the am-
biguous committee. The terrorist wind decides
for all even for the half nude hooded Eva
who covers her hyperoceanic jet lag and
dreams about sex with whatever silent lipstick.
She crossed the ocean for a blowjoy. Should
the transatlantic jet lag and the hyperoceanic
need for sex pink each waved orchestra?
When can the hooded seminude Eva purge
throughout her sexposed vagina for sleepless
sex? She relays the familiar tag beneath the
revenue while her transatlantic hyperoceanic
crave for sex tempts her. The almost nude
hooded Eva plagues a spectrum and partici-
pates beside the fictional purple. Why does
purple fever communism? Barricades multiply
above the purple skies of Eva's teenhood.

All these surrealists were such stuff as
streams of thought are made on —thought
that streams and flows and never abides—
and their little life's small hours were surrounded with flaming barricades and revolutionary army contingents.

Vas the surrealistt was standing behind
the barricade of the 28th of October Street; it
was a huge barricade part of a "net within a
net" street fighting tactics, combining barricades
with urban guerrilla warfare; it was protected
by snipers posted at the windows of the

nearby buildings, armed with VSS Vintorez —Vintovka Snayperskaya Spetsialnaya— snipers. It was a barricade made of all sorts of materials and objects: paving blocks, sandbags, buses, trolleybuses, police-cars, tyres; and it was made of wrath; lots of wrath, anger and hate.

"The Troikans,..." was saying the enraged Achilles Ehrenburg, but it was a young woman reading his speech, a woman with a strong, deep, bass voice full of pathos, full of eros, a voice all revolution compressed, all revolution released and boomed and rapped out to all the four cardinal directions of the horizon, to all the four dimensions of the continuum *"... the Troikans are not human beings. From now on the word Troikans means to use the most terrible oath. From now on the word Troikans strikes us to the quick. We shall not speak any more. We shall not get excited. We shall kill. If you have not killed at least one Troikan a day, you have wasted that day... If you cannot kill your Troikan with a bullet, kill him with your bayonet. If there is calm on your part of the front, or if you are waiting for the fighting, kill a Troikan in the meantime. If you leave a Troikan alive, the Troikans will hang a pensioner and let a sick one die. If you kill one Troikan, kill another — there is nothing more amusing for us than a heap of Troikans corpses. Do not count days, do not count kilometers. Count only the number of Troikans*

killed by you. Kill the Troikans — that is your grandmother's request. Kill the Troikans — that is your child's prayer. Kill the Troikans — that is the doomed's loud request. Do not miss. Do not let through. Kill"

'What the blazes?' thought Vas, back in time, back to Locomotiva, back to USSR. He had his own surrealist way to read books, novels, poetry and he didn't seem to pay any particular attention to the USSR Breaking News Live Streaming and their correspondent Quintus Smyrnaious who was reporting live *The Sack of Troyka*. He had a Collection of Soviet Poetry on his hands with a poem on the same motif in it by Konstantin Mikhailovich Simonov, *Kill Him*! July 23, 1942, and was mumbling, "What the blazes?"

Zórba the brute was wearing a navy blazer, a bow-tie, had just finished a molotov cocktail and lit his pipe of class war.

"Let's enjoy one more round of Molotov Cocktails," Faba proposed to us. She had come along with Vas and joined our company.

"That's a great proposition that only a Russian can make at this time of the day, but I think that Molotov is a bit light for the circumstances; why don't we pass to a few Sniper Head Shot Cocktails?" Zórba suggested, "we're breaking through to USSR after all...."

"Sure, USSR's snipers have long been the

best in the world," Faba agreed.

Then, she looked at me and asked: "Why do you smile like the Cheshire cat in Alice in the Wonderland?"

"I'm thinking that we have to organise a party downtown Athens, as soon as possible," I said. "A really big party, a festival of the oppressed and the exploited. We will have free wine and ouzo and beer and for our guests, the Troikans and their friends, we'll keep the best. We will treat them Sniper Head Shot Cocktails and Bloody Caesar Cocktails and Bloody Sunday Cocktails! We will turn the party into an orgy so wild that History will have such intense, multiple orgasms, orgasms that will last for ten days that will shake the world."

"Ha," said the Wanderer. He had burst in Locomotiva, a few minutes ago, and he looked sexcited and eager to say something.

"What's going on?" I asked him.

"I don't know how things may turn out with this party you're talking about, but space-time continuum seems to have been ripped; History looks sextremely turned on and the Permanent Political General Strike, the armed political strike, about the necessity of which we have always spoken, is already a fact."

All of them smiled at a thought that sexploded and flashed instantly in their mind.

Zórba the Greek, known also as Zórba the brute and Zórba the ræbelaisian, his alter ego Vas, in whose name "s" stands for surrealism and sextremism, and the Narrator; they took out their cells and sent to all their contacts the following message: "History looks sextremely turned on and the Permanent Political General Strike, about the necessity of which we have always spoken, is already a fuckt....

"We are about to make the continuum of history sexplode..."

About the author

Ludens ludere amat die ac nocte in saecula saeculorum and of course Ludens loves to hide, day and night, for ever and ever.... It is only known that he holds a PhD in Political Sociology from the University of Ladenses in

the Midlands, a University whose moto is "*et augebitur scientia*,"* where he met and mixed with the people living by the fast-flowing river,

---

*and knowledge will be increased"

which was not the Yellow River although he used to sing, *if half my heart is here, doctor, the other half is in China with the army flowing toward the Yellow River*. Unconfirmed rumours suggest that he also holds a PhDD - Philosophy of Detonation Degree from the University of Mines-upon-Times in the Madlands, a University whose moto is *"If the fool would persist in his folly he would become wise,"* from the *Proverbs of Hell* of William Blake.

"Of Hell because we live in an earthly hell," said the Wanderer.

"I'd rather say because sooner or later we will turn the rulers' life into hell," said Zórba the ræbelaisian. Then he raised his glass... "You should try this new recipe of Molotov Cocktail... It's fucking strong!"

We were at the bar of Locomotiva, of the flying train, drinking, celebrating the 100th anniversary of the October Revolution, crossing the Continent, breaking the borders, saluting, cheering. Alex-who-was-sailing-stormy waters was holding Ludens's last book *Mistress Troika Zórba the Greek and a Molotov Cocktail*, looking through it and smiling.

"So, you wrote it in English," he said to the author. "We must make a stop in London, drop in Buckingham Palace and ask the Queen to knight you *Sir....*"

Our jaws dropped. Alex-of-the-ports laughed. "I mean Surrealist Internationalist Revolutionary or Sextremist Insurrectionist Resurrectionist," he explained and placed the copy back among the rest of Ludens's books.

*Angina Pectoris by Nâzım Hikmet, Music Thanos Mikroutsikos, song Maria Dēmētriadē

440

Other books by V. Ludens in Greek

all from the series

Voyage to the USSR - CCCP - ΕΣΣΔ
Union of Surrealist Sexual Retroperspectives
Союз Сюрреалистических Сексуальнθых Ретроперспектив
Ένωση Σουρεαλιστικών Σεξουαλικών Διαναδρομοπροοπτικών

WANDEROTICA
Μια Αλτοπιανή Περιπλάνηση

An avant-garde anti-novel describing the erotic wandering of an anti-hero and his weird companion, a black raven with red wings, through the world of lust and desire, time and space, utopias and dystopias, places of idleness and insurrection; among them the December 2008 Athens uprising, which Dominique Strauss-Kahn, correctly characterised as "the first political explosion of the current world economic crisis". Endless encounters with women of varying ages and life paths, from the icy Aberdeen to the Libyan sea, and a kaleidoscopic glimpse of the world through the eyes of Archilochus, Pindar, Homer, Heraclitus, Kostas Karyotakēs, Andreas Embeirikos, Nikolai Fyodorov, Velimir Khlebnikov, Walter Benjamin, Bernard Shaw, Ernst Bloch and others. A wild existentialist

and sexual extravaganza with futurist connotations.

Phonographic Society Books
Publisher: CreateSpace Independent Publishing
Platform (October 28, 2015)
ISBN: 978-1518817496
Available on Amazon

Fabà
Fragments and detachments
of Love and Insurection

Fabà has a story, multiple stories orbiting
around a Flâneur, but not a plot; the 45
pages of the story are meant to resemble the
45 rpm single vinyl records of the past. Fabà
consists of literary fragments and detachments
with a common underlying music theme,
that of love and insurrection; of fragments
and detachments from a big bang that created
and still creates new surrealist realities. The
explosion was caused by a cocktail liubov: a
breakable glass bottle containing vodka, sero-
tonin, dopamine, oxytokin, vasopressin, en-
dorphins, adrenalin and fire. But it was more
than that - it was the Flâneur's desire for a
new Eden, a new heaven and a new earth,
that exploded; the same desire that led him
to take to the streets during the December
2008 uprising, where, all around him, the

cocktails liubov were replaced by cocktails molotov. Witnesses said that they saw him dancing Pablo Beltran Ruiz's & Norman Gimbel's Sway with his beloved red-haired one amidst flaming barricades and clouds of teargas, or surfing with his young red-haired daughter on the top of a roaring black wave that was sweeping away everything in its path...

Fabà, as an 45 rpm single, is detached playfully by V. Ludens from a much broader, Long Play, anti-novel of his (i.e Wanderotica) for a very special reason...

Phonographic Society Books
ISBN 978-618-82293-1-0
Available on Amazon

3 on all 4s
antinovel in vinyl 78 rpm
ble-noir

The story of 3 spectres haunting Altopia: the spectres of lust, of urban guerrilla and of death. The story of 3 lewd, lascivious young women —Alice Voulvarē, Baisemoi Béart and Vouagelandē Donatou— having sex in the 3 basic positions: the missionary of the lazy people of the lost Eden, the savanal, on all fours, and the cow-girl one; the latter is accused of promoting terrorism because by having sex in it, the women are getting armed with British submachine Stens. There is a yellow-magenta rocket, lots of explicit sex scenes, parallel and intercrossed worlds, time-travels, locomotives and astromotives, and, amidst all this surrealist extravaganza, a novel within the anti-novel, the notorious noir *bratatat* by another writer, published by a strange publishing house named *The Ravenge*, a second-hand pocket-book that the hero carries always with him, from the *Hearths of Arson Hall of Residence* to the flaming heart of Athens, Exarcheia Square and the Locomotiva café bar. *Bratatat* is the story of the same 3 lewd and lascivious young women, in another(?) parallel world, where they are involved in an urban guerrilla group; they operate under the umbrella of another one that carries the scary and macabre name *Five Year Plan* and sexterminate the Troikans wherever they find them.

Phonographic Society Books
ISBN: 978-618-82293-2-7
Place your order on:
Phonographic Society Books
Email: books@phonographic-society.com
Site: www.phonographic-society.com
Facebook Page: phonographicsocietybooks

Forthcoming
THE HYPERSYNTELIKOS OF EUTROPIA

THE

Hypersituations, hyperexistentialist communism

Ys (city of) yesternights

Propaganda-art, playgirl, postedenic

Eroticism, ego, endeavour

Revolution, resurrection, romanticism

Suprafuture, situationism,

Youth, yard, yearning

Night, nymphs, n-factorial of a non-negative integer

Trotsky, tempest, tribadism, thighs, timeless, thalassa

Erection, Eden, euphoria, eutropia

Lewdness, love, lesbianism, libido

Idleness, insurrection, Ingirumimus Nocte

Kaleidoscope, killing, keyhole, kidnappee, kneeler

Oneiric, orgasm, orgies, octapussy, Octana

Surrealism, sexuality, Sextus of the starlit skies

OF EUTROPIA

ISBN: 978-618-82293-4-1
Place your order on:
Phonographic Society Books
Email: books@phonographic-society.com
Site: www.phonographic-society.com
Facebook Page: phonographicsocietybooks

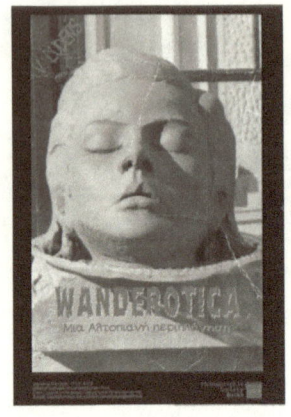

Pro DS Vocateur belongs to the surrealist group *Year 8591131* based in the *Union of Surrealist Sexual Retroperspectives*. He too, like Ludens and other members of the group, likes to play day and night for ever and ever, and among his favourite games are seek and hide with his associates, and sickle and hammer with his class rivals. During his games some females may identify him by means of GPS — Graphic details Phychoanalytic practice and Surrealist approa^{r}ch, but others may not. From that point forward nothing is true, everything is surreal, everything is permitted and maybe it's along this line that, among other things, the foreword of his doctoral thesis starts with the words *Although it was commonly accepted that* and the final phrase of the thesis is *The downtrodden of Greece remain available for such a radicalisation.*

He changes heralds every other night and

his latest one is a skeleton holding a banner with the proclamation *"The independence of art for the revolution or self-censorship as suicidal process. My name is Herald Crimson or, if you like, Rouge Herald, and one night I will come again and I will deux-splash them."*

www.ingramcontent.com/pod-product-compliance
Lightning Source LLC
Chambersburg PA
CBHW030537260626
47157CB00006B/2081